Praise for Widdershins

'A dark and wonderful novel, rich in historical details, herbal lore, traditions and superstitions. Steadman's clear-eyed storytelling and colourful period voice give life to a vibrant cast of characters drawn against the backdrop of tragic historical events. A compelling and memorable tale!'

— Louisa Morgan, *A Secret History of Witches*

'A compelling tale of two young people whose destinies are intertwined, a witch-hunter and a witch. But is she really a witch? This meticulously researched account of a bigoted man's inhumanity to women in the seventeenth century will make the modern reader grateful to have been born in an enlightened age.'

— Mari Griffith, *The Witch of Eye*

'Made my feminist blood boil. Powerfully challenges our lingering, stereotypical views of witchcraft.'

— Lisa Botwright, *Optima Magazine*

'Infused as it is with aromas of rosemary, fennel and lavender, even the healers' herbs do not mask the reek of the injustice that sits at the heart of *Widdershins*. Powerful and shocking.'

— Wyl Menmuir, *The Many*

'A compelling and nuanced account of the clash of cultures that claimed so many lives. Steadman's carefully interwoven narrative conjures a world of herbal lore, folk practice and belief and convincingly portrays the psychological and ideological forces that form a perpetrator, and the social structures that sustain him.'

— Helen Lynch, *Tea for the Rent Boy*

Praise for Sunwise

'Sometimes charming, sometimes disturbing, and very firmly set in its time and place – don't expect an easy ride, though!'

— Lexie Conyngham, *The Tender Herb*

'The novel is rich in fascinating details: Jane's remedies and the village customs, partly Christian, partly pagan. Ancient names for plants and festivities, both seasonal and Christian, add colour to the narrative.'

— Lynn Guest, Historical Novel Society

'A great read, not to be missed. Steadman's skillful and resplendent prose leads the reader easily into villages, manses and cottages, festivities and day-to-day lives, with amazing detail and descriptions of a past age that jump off the page of the novel. The historical research is rich; scenes and spaces, deliciously visual, and the language employed by the protagonists and throughout the narrative is authentic and consistent, transporting us back in time just by virtue of its ancient tonality.'

— Susana Aikin, *The Weight of the Heart*

Praise for The Running Wolf

'The meticulous research that has gone into writing this book about the Solingen swordmakers of Germany set at the turn of the 18th century just shines through. We see their lives unfold in northeast England with their struggles resonant of the experiences of so many immigrants today. I learned so much in a totally immersive and captivating read with characters that are brought to life through Helen Steadman's powerful writing. Highly recommended to all lovers of historical fiction!'

— Rosalind Russell, *The End of Where We Begin*

'Steadman obviously carried out a lot of meticulous research for her book. An unusual novel that brings a little-known area of history and its craftsmen to life.'

— Kate Pettigrew, Historical Novel Society

'Steadman has an easy approachable writing style that leads you into a historical past and immerses you in the time so that you feel you are there with these almost tangible characters.'

— Fin Gray, *Duplicity*

'The author gives a fascinating insight into the difficult decisions that people must make during times of community suspicion and political intrigue.'

— Mark Whitley, *Countryman Magazine*

God of Fire

Helen Steadman

First published by Bell Jar Books, London, 2022

British Library Cataloguing in Publication Data.
A catalogue record for this book is available from the British Library

ISBN
978-1-73-97762-0-6 (e-pub)
978-1-73-97762-1-3 (paperback)
978-1-73-97762-2-0 (hardback)
978-1-73-97762-3-7 (large print paperback)
978-1-73-97762-6-8 (large print hardback)

Developmental Editor: Julian Webb
Cover designer: Heike Schüssler, Judge By My Covers
Chapter illustrations: AVS-Images

For Oliver and Leon

Contents

Part I

1. The Fall 3
2. Sibling Rivalry I 8
3. The Prodigal Son 15
4. A Gift for Mother 25
5. Sibling Rivalry II 33
6. Baby Steps 41
7. Owl Eyes 50
8. Stealing Fire 56
9. The Summons 62
10. The Sentence 67

Part II

11. A Vision 75
12. A Beautiful Evil 82
13. All the Gifts 88
14. The Priapic Horde 95
15. The Legion of Sisters 103
16. The Prankster 108
17. A Cull 117
18. A Pithos for Pandora 123
19. Lifting the Lid 129

Part III

20. The Good Father 137
21. The Secret 145
22. The Morning After 153
23. The Marital Aid 161
24. Friendly Fire I 167
25. The Bad Father 173
26. The All Seeing Eye 180
27. One Hundred Eyes 187
28. One Hundred Knots 193

29. One Hundred Virgins 198
30. One Hundred Hands 205
31. The Herald of Winter 210

Part IV

32. The Monstrous Flock 219
33. The Staff of Life 227
34. The Return of Spring 235
35. A Test 244
36. The Dry Patch 248
37. Sibling Rivalry III 255
38. A Marriage of Convenience 261
39. A Sting in the Tail 267
40. The Golden Apple 274
41. Friendly Fire II 280
42. Troy 287
43. Resurrection 294
44. Friendly Fire III 301
45. A Period of Mourning 307

Also by Helen Steadman 313
Acknowledgements 315

“There is geometry in the humming of the strings. There is music in the spacing of the spheres.”

— Attributed to Pythagoras

Part I

The Fall

Less than an hour old, fatherless and despised by his mother, the squalling infant fell from the heavens. Fell all day and fell all night through vast starry skies, on through the firmament, down to the humble blue and green orb below, until he landed on the sea with a sickly crack of breaking baby bones. The fallen god let out a scream that shook the world. Yet no one came.

Finally, the briny maw engulfed the child and he sank through the indigo depths, the cold threatening to extinguish his inner flame and leave him in permanent darkness. As the night entered his soul, two hands grabbed him.

Deep in an undersea grotto, an icy teat was forced between his lips. Immediately, he ceased squalling. The milk yielded was brackish, but freely given, and more than he'd received from his mother.

Surf-like, a voice pounded in his mind. 'Your saviour is Thetis the seawitch. I have healed all your wounds, except one. You are Hephaestus: he who shines by day. Quite a mouthful for such an insignificant wretch so I will call you Heph. You are god of fire.'

In spite of her stony embrace, he clung on and the tide of

milk flowed into his belly, making him one with the ocean. The pain in his leg ebbed a little, if not the pain in his heart, but the shattered ankle wasn't worth worrying about. He was a god – which is to say, perfect – so lameness was not an option. The bone would heal soon enough, although nothing could erase the wound of maternal rejection, of being tossed from the celestial mountain as if he were no more precious than a pomegranate skeleton. But what of his other parent? Hephaestus searched inside himself, seeking the waymarkings of a father, somebody he'd been moulded on and formed by, but found no answers.

In the meantime, at least the seawitch had saved him from the murky fathoms and taken him as her own. Greedily, he suckled on her left teat, his free hand possessing her right as if to stop another infant latching on. There, he drew comfort and imagined he was at his mother's breast, warming himself as he sheltered beneath the skin of the sea. Thetis was not known for kindness but cared for him as if he were a fallen nestling. On he drank and on, endless his hunger, until a bony finger forced itself into the corner of his mouth and he was deprived once more.

'That's enough, Heph. Leave a drop for someone else.' She held him at arm's length. 'Go to Eurynome and let's have a look at you.'

Prised from his source of comfort, he prepared to yowl, instead inhaling a large quantity of ocean as he was thrust onto a soft belly. A round, translucent face loomed over him, smiling.

'Eurynome,' said the surf-like voice, 'creatrix of the universe, exalted dove, wide wanderer and consort of Thetis.'

The seawitch appeared beside the creatrix, frowning. Silenced, Hephaestus looked at his saviour. Beautiful, yes, but also terrifying. Black of eye. Fingers tipped with jet. Blue-green tresses clinking with bruised pearls. Clad in a couple of scallop shells and a few fronds of seaweed. A goddess as dark and cold as the ocean itself.

'Ugly little scrap of divinity, aren't you?' said Thetis as she tugged his plump bottom lip between thumb and forefinger. 'No wonder they didn't want you up there, and being noisy with it can't have helped your cause.'

The seawitch's words cut him like a thousand shards of coral, but despite her sharp tone, she patted his backside and tucked him under her arm as she went about her chores. Gradually, he settled, watching her spinning sea moss into spools of yarn and knitting them into miniature cloaks and baby blankets, which she stowed in a wooden chest inlaid with gold. Fascinated, he watched her nimble fingers working the needles.

Little did the god of fire know, but these clothes would never cover *his* back. They were for another child. A true son of Thetis. Achilles is his name. But no more of him just now for his time has not yet come.

Thetis woke Hephaestus from a sound sleep, swaddled him in sealskin and tied him to her before swimming into the ocean where tendrils of kelp ensnared them, impeding their progress. As they travelled, it was hard to tell where they were going, but the severe drop in temperature suggested the colder, deeper water that lay in trenches. The godling snivelled, salt tears lost in the sea. It was happening again. First, his birth-mother had rejected him and now his foster-mother was casting him out. Where would he turn next in this precarious life?

Suddenly, he was borne upwards. The night air on his wet face scared him and he pressed himself to Thetis. All he could see were dim outlines, and all he could hear was water hurling itself at the rocks. Why had they left the grotto? Thetis shushed him and whispered that Poseidon was hunting her so they had to be quiet.

Walls of water rose, sucking the seabed dry and exposing twitching sea creatures, but just before they drowned in air, the water collapsed and surged inland. The sky blackened as Selene hid her bright face behind a passing cloud and Thetis sent up a prayer. Hephaestus hoped his father would hear it and protect them from this terrible Poseidon, but when the plea was answered by thunderbolts raining down, he flinched.

'Almighty Zeus is here to save me from Poseidon and not to harm you.'

His guardian petted him while he got used to the sight and sound. The intermittent light revealed the sea god in silhouette, locks trailing down his back like knotted ropes. Ignoring his brother's aerial onslaught, Poseidon continued striding through his domain, waist-deep and holding his trident, comfortably absorbing the bombardment.

In a new tactic, Zeus spread purple sheet lightning, and when Poseidon turned, his locks eddied around him, destroying the foolish whimbrels who flew too near. Water funneled from the sea to the sky, taking birds and fish with it. So many sent to their doom. How many must die when gods collide?

The sea god pushed on, half in his world and half in that of his brother. Why did Zeus not venture down to the sea? Was the thunder god weakened by water? Up to his shoulders and haloed in lightning bolts, Poseidon moved to the deeper sea, storms following him until the funnel receded and the water swirled shut.

'The god of the sea has been vanquished and Zeus has spared my chastity so we should give thanks.'

Kneeling, she raised the child overhead and sang her siren song. The offering must have gratified the almighty as the luminous god descended to earth and waved a benediction. Scraping his head on the night sky and shoving clouds out of the way, Zeus ranged over his lands, platinum mane flowing behind him.

Thetis lowered Hephaestus and clasped him to her breast. 'The sea has hidden Poseidon but you can tell where he is by the whirlpool above him. It would pull you under in an instant, so be extra cautious when Poseidon is on a stalking mission. He'll wade through his realm to his palace, which is said to be magnificent, but I'll never go there and neither should you. Be ever wary of him and his brothers. The three of them are cut from the same cloth. Zeus, Hades and Poseidon, always wanting what they haven't got and taking it, regardless.' She pinched his cheek. 'But no need for you to fret.'

He snuggled into her shoulder, bracing his sore leg against the crook of her arm as he nursed. Since Poseidon had gone below and Zeus was beyond thc horizon, the rain of thunderbolts faded. Encouraged by the newly calm night, Selene returned, her soft light spilling in a silver river across the placid sea.

'Come on, it's safe to go home.'

But home no longer felt safe for Hephaestus, and even though Thetis hadn't cast him out this time, there was a risk she might. It would be easy to earn her wrath so he'd make himself small and silent to avoid drawing the fury that must nestle in the heart of every mother.

Sibling Rivalry I

The fire god's fears proved unfounded and for years he lived contentedly in and on the sea. Daily, the family breakfasted at the beach and while they picked lobster meat from their teeth with sparrow bones, a bevy of blue-haired nymphs cleared up, singing and laughing as they toiled. Hephaestus marvelled at their lively movements and the light work they made of their labours.

Life with the two goddesses was good and he had the run of the grotto, apart from a locked grate that he was warned off. He also had the run of the surrounding waters, spending blissful days teasing octopuses and chasing swordfish through underwater caverns. With Eurynome looking on, Thetis and their foster-son raced around the islands on dolphins, and he was happy. Or at least, he *was* happy, until one day, the seawitch vanished into the surf, abandoning him on the shore. Valiantly, he clutched his staff of cornel wood and hobbled after her.

'Mother, wait!' he called, thinking he was alone until he heard sniggering.

'Fool!' said a voice from a cave. '*She's* not your mother.'

'Are you sure?' asked Hephaestus, peering around.

'I'm sure,' said the voice. 'As if your mother would be seen half-dressed in seaweed and seashells.' The owner of the voice revealed himself: an enormous boy with blood-red eyes and a shock of black hair. 'The greatest goddess, Hera, is your mother, and mine.'

'And mine,' announced a petite girl with the same colouring. She had a downturned mouth and a plait poised over her head like a scorpion's tail. 'We're twins. I'm Eris, goddess of strife, and he's Ares, god of war.'

Admittedly, his siblings didn't resemble Hephaestus since he had brown curls and amber eyes and this Ares was easily four times his size. Still, family was family.

'If we share a mother,' he ventured, 'then you must be my brother and sister.'

'*Half*-brother and sister,' clarified the girl. '*Our* father is Zeus but you don't have one. That's why you're so short and ugly.'

This couldn't be right. Surely everyone had a father. 'I don't need one,' he lied. 'I have three mothers instead. One who gave birth to me and two who take care of me and love me.'

'Just as well, because Hera certainly doesn't love you,' said Eris. 'She hates your withered leg and so do we!'

'I hate you too,' said Hephaestus. 'You're both horrible!'

Incensed, Eris kicked away the lame god's staff and he stumbled. Ares seized him in a headlock and punched him so hard that ichor gushed from his nose. Daisies bloomed from the drops of golden blood, and when his captor released him, he sank onto the bed of flowers, only for Eris to kick him in the belly. He curled into a ball to protect his tender parts but the blows to his pride hurt more than those to his body.

Momentarily tired of physical violence, his tormentors started running rings around him, chanting 'cuckoo' as they went. All he knew of cuckoos was that such a bird graced Hera's sceptre. Was that what they meant? If they shared the same mother, and he was a cuckoo, then so were they.

Hephaestus dared to echo the insult and Ares leapt on him, his immense weight crushing the breath from his hapless victim.

'You're the cuckoo, not me,' said Ares, twisting his smaller brother's arm until it was on the verge of snapping.

'Understand?' asked Eris, pinching his nose.

'Yes! Yes!' promised Hephaestus, chin quivering, not understanding at all, but afraid to disagree.

'Hey, stop that! Get off him! Pack it in!' yelled a chorus of voices. In the distance, three young gods sprinted towards them.

On realising they had company, the two bullies stopped torturing their half-brother and ran off, hotly pursued by the new arrivals. Hephaestus watched them go, wondering who his rescuers were, before limping home, determined to shun his half-siblings in future.

When he reached the grotto, he charged at his foster-mothers, scattering yarn and needles, babbling his snot-filled report.

'Cuckoo?' asked Thetis as she disentangled him from a knot of knitting and settled him on Eurynome's lap. 'It simply means you were toppled out of Hera's nest and into ours.'

Toppled out? Shoved out, more like, but he let it go.

'Am I definitely related to them?'

'Yes, unfortunately for you,' said Thetis, restoring her ball of seaweed. 'Steer clear of them.'

That should be easy as he had no intention of going anywhere near them ever again. 'What about the three who saved me?'

'Persephone, Dionysus and Prometheus? They're alright and Prom especially will treat you kindly.'

Prometheus lived up to his reputation for kindness. Unfortunately, the god of foresight came with a brother, Epimetheus, who shared his beauty, but not his gentle nature.

Instead, he was always boasting about how he'd made all the animals out of clay, how he was the most gorgeous god going and how he was the fastest runner.

Often, he would goad Prometheus and his friend into racing but every step was costly to Hephaestus and his heavy-footedness translated itself into a heaviness of the heart. Trudging along the shore after the competitive brothers, his spirits dragged as much as his foot, and he was pleased when Thetis stepped out of the water.

'Let them run,' she said. 'Don't hark after what you haven't got and can't have or it'll make you weaker. Grow strong in other ways and follow your own path.' She fossicked in her bodice and pulled out a fragment of dolphin leather. 'Here, wear this to keep one eye intact and I'll summon three old friends to set you on the right road. They need quite a bit of space so get back. Further back than that. You might want to hold onto a tree.'

Obediently, he edged into a nearby grove and hugged a young oak.

'Cyclopes, the day has come.' She stood facing away from the sea, locks blowing in the rising wind, and raised her sceptre. 'Brontes, Steropes, Arges, I summon you from the earth.'

Gaia heaved and three gigantic men sat up, shaking sand from their massive bald heads. Each had a solitary eye, surrounded by tattooed concentric rings. When they clambered to their feet, they cast the whole beach into shade. Without troubling their mouths, the giants spoke, and their words reverberated in the god of fire's head without troubling his ears.

'Quake, little one, quake,' they said. 'We are risen. Ready to create, destroy, renew.'

Their order was impossible to disobey and the child feared he'd never stop quaking.

Thetis whacked the nearest giant's kneecap with her sceptre. 'If anyone is ordering anyone to quake, I will be doing the ordering and you will be doing the quaking. Understood?'

All three giants rubbed their knees and nodded.

'Good,' she bristled. 'Heph, don't be afraid. The biggest Cyclops is Brontes, in charge of thunder. The smallest is Steropes, in charge of lightning. And the one reckless enough to stand within striking distance of me is Arges, reputedly in charge of brightness. They are the mighty smiths who created Zeus' thunderbolt, Poseidon's trident and Hades' helmet of invisibility. They have guarded your legacy. Come and get it.'

He didn't trust these colossal smiths but he trusted Thetis so he shuffled over to them. The Cyclops called Arges handed him a curiously hot oyster shell.

Again, the strange voices resonated. 'Here is your sacred fire, which we have kept safe for this fateful day.'

Hephaestus opened the shell and warmth radiated through him, evaporating his aches and exhaustion. Inside, was a mound of smouldering ash. Some legacy. The first Cyclops formed a ring of large stones, the second placed the shell in the middle, while the third emptied sacks of charred wood onto it. Together, they breathed on the heap, kindling a fire.

Thetis observed for a while before ushering away the Cyclopes, leaving her ward alone to find his future in the flames. The orange tongues wavered in the breeze and white smoke billowed until his eyes watered and the haze filled with visions of machines that would do his bidding. But where to begin?

The giants returned and hurled rocks into the fire, then blew on the flames until they became an inferno and the sky burst with explosions. The boy's mind span in circles as a river the colour of Helios flowed along the ripples sculpted in the sand by the waves. All day, he listened to rocks exploding and followed molten metal wending its way to the shore. When the noise finally stopped and the river stopped running, the weary god curled up and fell asleep.

Shivering, he awoke to the sound of his gargantuan

friends snoring next to a pile of glowing embers. The yellow river was now cold and dull grey, weakly reflecting the sun. He tested the river with a toe, discovered it was firm and walked across it, wondering what magic had taken place while he slept. As Helios climbed higher, the surface warmed beneath Hephaestus' feet but remained solid. Did this mean fire was hotter than the sun? Perplexed, he roused the Cyclopes, who explained that Helios was more intense but also more distant, while iron needed heat that was both fierce and immediate to regain its beautiful colour. They proved it by rebuilding the pyre to make the rivers of gold flow again.

Crouching carefully, he carved animal shapes in the sand with his staff, casting creatures from land, sea and air. If only he could give them life – that would show Epimetheus!

'Start small,' said the giants. 'A mouse, perhaps, but first you need something for that leg of yours.'

They moulded a gold cage with their calloused hands, cooling it in the water before fitting it. The support was rigid and grazed his skin but it did help him to stand up straight. Next, he was given some long tongs and a hammer, and taught how to use them. While working, he forgot his pain, absorbing every word and memorising every action. Bending low, the Cyclopes showed him how to cast his mouse and when Brontes touched the rodent, it sprang to life, snuffling and scurrying, feinting left and right, making it hard to catch. Absorbed in chasing his pet, Hephaestus only noticed someone was watching when he heard a discreet cough and turned to see his foster-mothers.

'Fine work, Heph,' said Thetis. 'It would impress the pantheon.'

This unexpected praise made him blush and he was even more delighted when she picked up the mouse by its tail and dropped it into his hand. It landed on its back and scrabbled at the air until he righted it. Once on its feet, the mouse ran up one arm, across the nape of his neck, and down the other arm before he caught it and placed it on his shoulder. The little inventor couldn't stop grinning.

'You know who would love that mouse,' Thetis continued. 'The sun god, Apollo. His pet mice last less than a year and he's perpetually upset. The other gods complain when he sings sad songs. Hermes can drop it off.' She looked thoughtful for a moment. 'Even Hera might be impressed. You should return to Olympus and show her your skills.'

His heart lurched at these words but Eurynome stilled him with her gentle smile.

'You're always welcome here,' said Thetis, 'and the Cyclopes will continue to teach you, but as god of fire, it does you no good to dwell beneath the waves.' She glanced up at heaven. 'I'll wangle us an invite. Your mother will learn to love you. She just needs time.'

He sighed. Time was all he had, and plenty of it.

The Prodigal Son

In a shimmer of gold, Hermes arrived at the smithy, shoved the Cyclopes aside with his caduceus and presented a palm-sized stone tablet.

'Thetis and Eurynome are invited to a ball on the mountain in one moon's time.'

'Why don't you tell them yourself?' asked the giants.

Hermes admired his winged sandals and tapped his helmet. 'I'm keeping my wings dry so the saltwater doesn't ruin them.'

'The boy cast those wings from gold pure enough to withstand most insults, so they'll be safe,' intoned the Cyclopes. 'You're welcome, by the way.'

The dismissive messenger tutted. 'I'm here now, so do you want this or what?'

The young smith flipped up his eye-patch and took the tablet. The front was inscribed with a gibbous moon over the Olympian palace. The reverse featured a graphic caricature of his foster-mothers, which he quickly covered up. When he shyly asked where his invitation was, the messenger brushed him off, suggesting the palace had forgotten about him.

'Pay no attention to that gadfly,' said the Cyclopes. 'Half

the time, he doesn't know where he's going, and more often than not he's flying backwards, so your invitation must be lost in transit. Isn't that right, messenger boy?'

Hermes smiled, and from his pitying glance Hephaestus understood he still wasn't wanted on Olympus. His mother had hated him at birth and nothing had changed.

'You know me,' laughed the messenger nervously. 'Careless to a fault. Anyway, it's a masked ball so I'll swing by to ensure everyone's disguises pass muster.' He fluttered his wings. 'Must get on. Messages to deliver. Gossip to spread. Love to the mothers.' And with an air kiss, he was gone.

Hermes scrutinised the goddesses. 'Really? Was this worth getting my wings wet?'

'Eurynome isn't going to the ball because it's after sunset, so she'll be out wandering, and *I'm* fine as I am,' replied Thetis through thin lips.

The messenger flapped a hand at her. 'Those lobster-feeler necklaces may be acceptable down here, but they'll laugh you off the mountain if you turn up looking like an old seawitch.'

'An old seawitch is exactly what I am.'

'I don't know why I bother sometimes. You can't go as yourself.' The messenger seized the lad's shoulders, newly broad from hammering. 'You, on the other hand, can go as you are, or at least you could if you were invited.'

Before Hephaestus could respond, the mercurial god had vanished.

'Never mind him. Eurynome says you can have her place.'

He hugged the creatrix gratefully and she glowed.

'What do you think?' asked Thetis. 'Be honest.'

Her hip-length locks clinked with more pearls than usual, her robes were woven from red seaweed and her fish-scale slippers sparkled. She was lovely to Hephaestus but he couldn't bear the thought of the Olympians treating her with contempt.

'Try not to worry,' he said. 'I'll make sure you impress them.'

'Who said I was worried?' She examined her slippers, which were showing the first signs of decay. 'Still, the whole idea is to impress your mother so do your best, lad.'

He had something in mind but would need to search for treasures to adorn his gift. Wondering how to traverse the world in time, he recalled the revelations he'd had on the day he received his fire. Grinning, he swam to the shore and summoned the Cyclopes to the smithy.

As soon as the iron chariot was complete, Hephaestus trained herds of seahorses to pull it. He collected his foster-mothers and set off, yelling with excitement, his anxious passengers clinging to each other. The seahorses flashed in various shades of cerise, aquamarine and violet, and he laughed so hard he forgot his pain. Now that he had wheels, who needed feet?

Unleashing the seahorses, he raced up sea mountains, hurtled down dark trenches and blazed through the rib cages of ancient whales. Shoals of rainbow fish parted in fright and startled jellyfish quivered on the surface. From the blue waters of home, he moved into the grey north, forcing his way through forests of icebergs until he circled home to warmer climes. Exhausted, he reined in the teeming seahorses outside the grotto and tucked his shaken guardians into bed.

'Beware,' said Thetis, voice muffled by a quilt of sea urchins, 'Poseidon is a jealous god and when he gets wind of your chariot, he'll steal it, and although we never left the water, I bet Helios had his hot eye on us.'

Hephaestus shrugged off her warning. 'I'll make them one each but not before I've created your gift.'

He arranged his loot at the foot of his bed and in his

dreams he smelted, hammered and filed, making the best present any goddess had ever seen, praying it would impress his so-called mother.

~

When the day of the ball arrived, Thetis twirled in her finery. 'What do you reckon? Not bad, eh?'

The audience of two pondered her disguise in silence.

'What? Say something!' She shook her heads at them. 'Fifty heads too many?'

Hephaestus bit his lip while Eurynome's eyes watered with the effort of holding in her laugh.

'Maybe a few too many,' he spluttered.

She pretended to strike him with her sceptre.

'*A few*, he says. If you're so clever, Heph, tell me what to wear.'

He chewed his thumbnail. 'Actually, I have an idea.'

She listened, nodding all fifty heads, before waving her sceptre and throwing up a vortex. Behind it, the surplus heads dissolved, leaving one, which promptly grew into a point. When the water cleared, a giant cuttlefish hovered before them, magnificent beak shining blackly, eight arms and two tentacles bobbing gently.

'Perfect,' he said. 'You can change colour to blend in or stand out as you choose.' More importantly, a solo head would show off his gift without forty-nine additional heads vying for attention. 'Are you ready for your present?'

After receiving a solemn nod, he produced a circlet. Sea snakes coiled beneath a silver band, and above that, glittering fish swam through fronds of waving seaweed. He crowned her, gently arranging her tentacles while the snakes slithered loose before tightening to achieve a perfect fit. He tapped the band and nine eyelids blinked open, each displaying a precious stone: amethyst, carnelian, diamond, emerald, jet, pearl, ruby, sapphire, topaz. At his command, they closed again.

'Thank you, Heph. We'd better disguise you before we go but what can you wear?'

Eurynome solved the problem by producing the sealskin they'd used as a sling to carry the rescued infant. The cuttlefish pecked three holes into it and Hephaestus yanked it over his head, adjusting the fur so he could see where he was going. The creatrix kissed them goodnight and left until morning.

When the cuttlefish and her driver arrived on Mount Olympus, fashionably late and unfashionably damp, their path was marked with flickering torches that lit the marble palace in swirls of purple and teal. Above its open sky dome, a pair of owls patrolled. Unfortunately, the sea-dwellers were detained by a giant, the cowherd, Panoptes, who was doing double duty as gatekeeper. His entire hide was speckled with turquoise eyes, and when he confiscated the chariot there was a brief, but tense, staring contest between the giant's one-hundred eyes and the nine in the crown. While Panoptes was busy examining the reverse of the invitation, rather more thoroughly than strictly necessary, two guests swept in, faces hidden by serpent headdresses.

'See those dark-haired goddesses?' whispered the cuttlefish. 'The one in umber is your aunt Demeter, goddess of the harvest, and the one in black with the poppy coronet is your cousin Persephone, who you'll remember from that day at the beach. From your mother's side, of course.'

The *only* side, if Ares and Eris were telling the truth. Perhaps his aunt and cousin might shed some light on his origins.

Inside, the palace was awash with deities disguised as glorious beasts and monsters. Naiads draped themselves across reflecting pools and fountains, while Dryads stood erect in every available corner. Golden-haired Apollo strolled among the multitudes, wearing a gilded mask and strumming a lyre. Hephaestus was ridiculously pleased to see his metal mouse perched on one shoulder. Sitting on the ledge of a circular hole in the floor – the window on the world, by all accounts – he spotted the terrible twins, both wearing eagle masks. They were too busy swinging their legs and hurling meteorites at earth to notice their little brother, but he was glad of his mask.

He enjoyed the spectacle of Centaurs galloping noisily from one end of the palace to the other, falling to their knees and skidding across the ballroom floor, to the annoyance of several hundred dancing goddesses, who demanded that Chiron compel his charges to behave. On a tiered stage reclined the Muses, whose voices soared up to the dizzying heights of the sky dome, their songs carried in the throats of a myriad birds, plumage brighter than anything Iris could conjure in her rainbows.

When he saw the vision that was his mother, he wished he were back at the forge. Too much to absorb in one eyeful, she was barely dressed in a silver chiton, dark hair cascading in long ringlets, with bracelets at bicep, wrist and ankle. So, he'd inherited his mother's colouring but not her height, stature or beauty. Beside her, Zeus exhibited his thunderbolt to full advantage in a platinum chiton that matched his eyes, hair and beard. The king and queen of heaven looked exactly like their images on the olive oil jar at home, and it was obvious they'd made no effort to disguise themselves. Hephaestus was in sparrow brown, and as his mother's attention was fixed on the cuttlefish, she failed to notice him, let alone realise he was her son. He reminded himself that while he had one birth-mother, she had three children and he shouldn't expect her attention, especially when she had no idea of his identity. He hid from himself the certain knowledge that she'd not thrown away any of her other children.

The queen of heaven stalked towards his foster-mother, careful to avoid any tentacles.

'Pray, which guest dares to wear such a remarkable crown in *my* palace?' Before its owner could reply, Hera reached out to snatch the treasure. 'Give it to me. It's far too good for the likes of you, whoever you are. Show yourself at once.'

Faced with a mute cephalopod, the hostess positioned her

fingers on her rival's head and heaved. The cuttlefish's eyes flared, black pupils zigzagging in fury as clouds of ink seeped from her. If his mother didn't get out of tentacle's reach, she'd spend her party in a state of paralysis. The worst half of him hoped it would happen. Despite the queen of heaven's best efforts, the crown stayed put, but as she persisted, the nine eyes winked and the cuttlefish lurched so hard, the glamour erased itself, revealing Thetis wearing her homely outfit, along with the astonishing crown.

'Well, well, well.' Hera smirked, but took a step backwards all the same. 'How did a common seawitch come by such a marvel?'

When there was no reply, she huffed, adjusted her bangles, spread her feet wide for leverage and gripped the coveted headwear with renewed vigour. Although the circlet did not budge, the strain stretched Thetis' neck until it spooled on the floor. Not to be defeated, Hera raised a sandalled foot and pressed it over a loop of neck.

'Take it off,' she said, 'before I do something you will greatly regret.'

Knowing what his mother was capable of, this was no idle threat. With an apologetic smile at his foster-mother, Hephaestus commanded the snakes to uncoil and the crown fell off. When his mother lifted her foot, Thetis' neck retracted. Hera jammed the now-slack crown on her own head, promenading triumphantly until the snakes began coiling and she clutched her increasingly purple head, rocking it from side to side and screeching. The crown was designed to be worn only by its rightful owner, and its creator relished the scene for a moment before releasing his mother, who rubbed her temples and summoned her husband.

'What is it, dearest?' The god of gods continued to languish on his couch, attended by several nymphs and an affronted cupbearer, who held a brimming pitcher out of his thirsty master's reach.

Hera breathed heavily through her nose. 'If you care to

come here, Husband, you'll see for yourself.' She clicked her fingers at the nymphs, who scattered. This cheered the cupbearer so much that he rewarded his master by topping up his drink.

Zeus groaned, got up and rearranged his chiton, sloshing nectar from the overfilled goblet in his wake.

Hera pointed at the silver circlet. 'I want one of those.'

'So? Take that one.' Zeus smiled as he noticed his replenished goblet and quaffed for a while before wiping his mouth on a passing Dryad. 'It's pointless being married to me if you can't help yourself to an occasional trinket.'

'I've already tried,' she wailed. 'But it squeezed my head tighter than you squeezed your *friend* the day you brought him here.' She glared at the cupbearer. 'I need *that* crown but made to measure.'

'Easily done,' said Zeus, pausing to ogle the seawitch before addressing her. 'I suppose this is the Cyclopes' handiwork?'

'Not the Cyclopes,' she replied, 'but a mighty smith who learnt at their knee.'

'Who is this smith?' Hera asked. 'Have him brought to me this instant.'

'My humble driver is the smith,' said Thetis.

The humble driver removed his hood and inclined his head slightly, thrilled that Zeus had likened his work to that of the Cyclopes.

'This is your son, who I suckled and raised as my own.'

On recognising her unwanted offspring, Hera drew in a jagged breath and pink-breasted robins fell around her as softly and wetly as dew-covered roses. A tremor ran through the mountain and golden platters fell from divine laps.

'How dare you defy me by reappearing, boy?'

Thetis patted the trembling child and spoke for him.

'Your temper put your son in my hands but he can be yours again. He'll make an artefact better than my crown for no more than a drop of love.'

The sight of his mother's countenance softening only at the promise of a superior gift did nothing to warm the boy to her.

'Return to me, your true mother, and I will create a majestic forge where you will work night and day to further my glory.'

Should he leave two mothers who loved him for one who'd rejected him? He'd have to earn Hera's love with endless gifts, each more fantastic than the last. Was it worth giving up Eurynome's soft embrace to be held by his mother? New feelings surged through him but they weren't enough to drown out the old ones and he remained by his foster-mother's side.

'This is not a choice, Hephaestus. Come home at once. I am your mother and those two had no right to steal you.'

'Th…they didn't steal me,' he stammered. 'They rescued me.'

'Don't be so gullible. I tossed you out of heaven to test your mettle but you were snatched before I had a chance to retrieve you. I'm prepared to overlook this offence as anyone stealing *you* had to be desperate, but mark my words, when one of them has a child from their own womb, they'll get rid of you.'

It had never occurred to him that his foster-mothers might desire a child. They looked too young, but who could tell with goddesses, and what if his mother was right? He mopped his brow, conscious the music and dancing had stopped and thousands of deities were waiting for an answer. Was he some sort of surrogate until his foster-mothers had a child of their own? It explained why Thetis was so keen to fetch him to the palace – she planned to offload him. Head down, he handed the sealskin to her. Seeing this, Hera plucked a tail feather from a passing peacock and pointed it towards the far reaches of the palace, where appeared a forge with twenty anvils.

'The child only has two hands,' said Thetis.

'Yes, but he'll have dozens of slaves.'

'What? So they can steal his secrets?'

'My dear seawitch, imagining problems where none exist.

I'll simply tear out their tongues or turn them into rocks after each shift. We're not short of disposable divinities around here.'

Her shrill laughter shrivelled Hephaestus' little nutsack and he clutched his loin cloth. Under a veneer of beauty, his birth-mother was beyond vicious, but he had nowhere else to go, and at least it was an opportunity to find out who his father was. If Zeus saw more of his work he might acknowledge him, and Hephaestus would have his longed-for father at last. He did not notice his foster-mother, whose anguish was only given away by her hands gently wringing the sealskin.

A Gift for Mother

After Hephaestus declined the Cyclopes' latest offer to tattoo concentric rings around his eyes, they released him and helped create two golden girls and twenty golden tripods. The gilded mannequins did the fine work and the three-legged tables dashed up and down Olympus, fetching and carrying at the speed of Hermes, but without the lip. Once the heavenly forge was fully staffed, it worked night and day.

When she wasn't busy bathing in goat's milk, Hera passed by to check her son was working diligently, but it was difficult for him to invent between her constant presence and the other gods popping in to issue orders. A pair of silver lions for Zeus. A chariot apiece for Helios and Poseidon. A shiny shield for Hades. A herd of bronze hares for Epimetheus. A bow and arrows for Artemis. Not to mention the endless amounts of sharp metal thieved by competitive Ares, who was hellbent on becoming a smith. Only Prometheus never asked for anything other than his company.

So far, the blacksmith had fobbed off his acquisitive mother with some jewellery, promising that he was testing various prototypes, but on her latest visit, she'd issued a deadline, demanding delivery of the special gift on her birthday.

Desperate for inspiration, he escaped to earth, lay in a meadow and watched the starlings darting above the wheat in search of insects. In the distance, cousin Persephone and aunt Demeter harvested armfuls of wheat, their sleeves and tresses grazing the crops. They waved before following his example and resting.

Demeter tucked Persephone between her knees while she braided the girl's midnight locks and fashioned a coronet of scarlet poppies. Labour of love complete, the mother kissed her daughter, and a flame flickered in his heart at the memory of his grotto family, but these feelings for Thetis and Eurynome didn't stop him wishing Hera were more like her sister. Still, he supposed, while he'd drawn the short straw on the mother front, at least he knew who she was.

Living on the mountain had not aided the quest to out Zeus as his father since the king of heaven spent more time with his favourite heifer than he did at home. If his mother were left to her own devices, Hephaestus would never determine his father's identity, so a new strategy was needed to force Hera to confess his paternity. But first he owed her a gift. If only there was a way of killing two birds with a single stone…

Thetis and Eurynome arrived at the earthly smithy and peered up at the monolith stationed outside.

'A present the birthday girl wanted,' Hephaestus grinned, 'and a present she will get!'

'Impressive work,' commented Thetis, 'but since it's nearly the same size as Olympus, you'll never drag it up the mountain by yourself.'

'The Cyclopes are coming with me to help.'

He woke Brontes, Steropes and Arges, who lumbered out

of the forge and greeted the goddesses before shouldering their burden.

'Wait,' said Thetis. 'It's missing something. You should wrap it up.'

The Cyclopes looked askance at her, hands braced against colossal thighs while they waited.

'It'll take too long,' said Hephaestus, 'and I can't be late.'

'Allow me.' Thetis gyrated her sceptre, gathering speed until a purplish-green cloud shrouded the gift, its stinking vapour giving Eurynome a coughing fit. 'Perfect. A surprise is always best.'

'Yes,' Hephaestus said, eyes watering as he patted Eurynome's back, 'my mother will be surprised alright.'

Thetis sized up the sea fret. 'Perhaps a dab of decaying sea turtle and a dash of—'

'No,' he gasped, 'that's quite enough *fragrance*, thank you.'

'I'll come along to keep a weather eye on this.' The seawitch sniffed then clicked her fingers and the puce taint faded from the cloud, and with it, the stench of rotting squid.

As the daylight faded, Eurynome went wandering and the others left for the palace. After their moonlit ascent, the quintet arrived to find the Olympians scattered about the rose garden.

The guest of honour was pinned against the central fountain, fighting off Poseidon, who was noticeably smaller out of his own element. The revolting god's mouth was actually watering. Unfortunately for Hera, and fortunately for Poseidon, her husband was too fascinated by a goddess in a gossamer gown to notice or care what his brother was up to.

'Who is that?' breathed Hephaestus.

'Aphrodite,' replied his foster-mother primly. 'Goddess of love. Fresh from renewing her maidenhood, and if you believe that, you'll believe anything.'

The boy stared at the divine deity's cascading red tresses, her wide green eyes and her sun-kissed skin. No matter how hard he stared, he could find no straight line on her.

Thetis leant close, placed a finger beneath his jaw and shut it. 'Good looks mean nothing. It's what's underneath that counts.'

'I know,' he whispered, blushing. 'I've already seen what's underneath her robe.'

Thetis gave him a long look. 'She's almost as old as the hills, boy, and even if she was prepared to entertain you, there's quite a queue.'

'I can wait.'

The new arrivals crossed the garden and the other guests fell quiet. Although Hera must have spotted them – after all, it would be impossible for anyone to miss the Cyclopes – she affected not to see them, and started giggling at Poseidon's attentions, this unseemly coquettishness making her son cringe.

As the curious procession neared the queen of heaven, she began to choke. The enveloping mist had regained its vile puce taint and accompanying stench, but the seawitch was all innocence, pretending to admire a nearby statue of Apollo.

Hand over nose, but still locked in a clinch with her admirer, Hera was forced to acknowledge her son's presence. 'Hephaestus, did you have to bring the sea with you? The damp's making me cough, which is ruining my party. As for you, Thetis, you're most definitely not welcome, so begone, and take those horrible giants with you.'

Thetis raised her chin in greeting while waving her sceptre.

'Don't mind me. I'm only here to assist with the unveiling.'

When the fog cleared, Hera unclamped the slimy sea god's hand from her buttock and examined the gift, fondling a filigree leg.

'Better late than never,' she said, 'but what is it?' She took several strides backwards, straining her neck. 'A throne?'

A floating, silver throne whose backrest was a fan of peacock feathers, with each armrest ending in a pomegranate. Roses climbed the legs, which rested on four mechanical cuckoos, fluttering furiously to avoid touching the floor.

In spite of himself, Hephaestus flushed as his mother

plumped herself down on the spider-silk cushion, the throne pitching so violently that a cuckoo screeched as it was crushed. He limped over and adjusted the birds so they'd flap their wings faster and avoid any further incidents. There was some smoke but nothing too troubling.

'Are you comfortable?' he asked.

'Very.' The birthday girl smiled, hands resting on the carved pomegranates, sandalled feet swinging in mid-air.

'Excellent. Then we'll begin.'

'Begin what?'

On his command, a secret door opened in the backrest. A pair of metal hands slid out and gripped his mother's waist.

'How lovely!' She wriggled with pleasure. 'What else does it do?'

In response, five silver snakes emerged and wound around her head, wrists and ankles. The queen of heaven found this rather less lovely and bared her teeth.

'Get me out of this contraption, immediately!'

'Patience, Mother, patience.'

But this was a quality Hera lacked and she howled to her husband for help.

'Save your breath. No god can undo another's spell.'

'We'll see about that. Zeus, leave your trollop alone and force this repulsive little brute to liberate me.'

'Unfortunately, my dear, he is correct,' said Zeus, tearing himself away from Aphrodite. 'Ugly, but correct. Nevertheless, I take a dim view of this, Heph, and could punish you in innumerable ways.'

The blacksmith faced the king of heaven.

'You could, but then your wife will be trapped for eternity. Alternatively, she can free herself by answering one question.'

'Is that all?' she said. 'Then fire away.'

'I hadn't finished. You must answer honestly, because if you lie…'

'I won't lie.' At the sound of a click to the left of his

mother's throat, her eyes slid sideways. 'Ask me your damned question.'

It was hard for the boy to disguise his excitement. Soon, he would uncover his origins and be embraced by his father. He took a steadying breath.

'Who is my father?'

'Is that it? A wasted opportunity, when I possess the power of prophecy. Instead of your ridiculous question, ask me what lies in your path – *who* lies in your path – or ask me to grant you the power of prophecy and see for yourself.'

Unimpressed, the young smith repeated his question.

'Who is my father?'

'Oh, Hephaestus.' She smiled at him and it was almost a motherly smile. 'You have no father.'

He swallowed, tears pricking. 'Do you swear on the River Styx?'

Everyone understood the outcome of lying under a stygian oath: a fate worse than death.

She didn't hesitate. 'I swear on the Styx that I spawned you myself.'

'Sorry,' said Zeus, 'but it is the truth. Heph, I am not your father. My wife's bloodline was thinned by nothing and no one, and Ouranos knows it's thick enough to start with.'

Shoulders heaving, the boy hobbled to the window he'd been tossed through on the day of his birth and swung his legs over the sill.

'Stop,' shouted the queen of heaven, 'I answered your question so you must let me go. Hephaestus,' she wailed. 'Let me go! It's my birthday, and I *am* your mother!'

He watched as she battled against her restraints.

'I have no mother,' he said and leapt from the window.

He landed in a heap of smashed bones. Racing by, Dionysus stopped so suddenly that fifty Maenads crashed into him and collapsed into a squirming mass.

'Heph? You look in a bad way,' said the god of the vine, freeing himself from his drunken disciples. 'Woman trouble, is it?'

'Sort of. Not just any woman, though. Hera.'

'Ah, the woman to end all women. What you need is some of this.' Dionysus hefted a bulging wineskin out of his ardent followers' reach. 'Seriously, try some. Cures any ill and – hey, stop that!' A Maenad, who had slithered over to lick Hephaestus' neck, now revealed her fangs and was poised to bite, but when her master quelled her with a look, she hissed and her fangs receded. 'That lot will sleep for days,' said Dionysus, 'so tell me what's up.'

Hephaestus wasn't convinced the Maenads *were* sleeping and eyed them uneasily while explaining his predicament. Dionysus' solution, as it was for most problems he encountered, was to pour nectar down his patient's throat until his bones set.

Gagging, Hephaestus swallowed the musty fluid and kept swallowing. The horizons span and he was nauseous yet strangely euphoric. His laughter bounced off the surrounding hills, exploding into cyan and vermilion while Selene and Helios passed overhead, changing places, again and again and again.

When all but one of his bones had knitted together, strength surged through him once more. He grasped the scrubby grass to haul himself to a sitting position and rainbows of joy circled his head.

Dionysus shook him. 'Alright, my son, up you get. We need to make tracks.' But the happy drunk was having too much fun to go anywhere. 'First-timers,' moaned Dionysus. 'Ouranus, spare me.'

A short while later, the inebriated smith found himself lashed across the backs of six donkeys. Dionysus slapped the nearest creature's arse and they trotted uphill. Their undulations were very funny and Hephaestus laughed all the way up Olympus.

He laughed as they ambled through the palace gate. He laughed as they entered the hall of the gods. He stopped laughing when he saw his mother. Etched on her face was the pain of millennia, and no longer was she the terrifying greatest goddess, but someone pathetic, someone he could perhaps love.

Dionysus unfastened his captive from the donkeys, then picked him up off the floor and dusted him down.

'Go on, Heph, you won't regret it, I promise.' He turned to the king of heaven. 'My friend *won't* regret it, will he?'

Zeus nodded once. 'You have my word, Heph.'

Accepting the almighty's promise, Hephaestus knelt at his mother's feet.

'I don't want your submission, fool,' she barked. 'I want you to set me free.'

Sighing, and against his better judgement, he flicked a switch to retract the manacles. Some people would never change.

Sibling Rivalry II

After a morning of diving from white cliffs into turquoise water, some of the young gods basked beneath Helios, catching their breath while the salt dried on their brown bellies, and amused themselves with humorous cloud shapes.

Epimetheus and Dionysus spotted crude images, Persephone pointed out corpses, severed limbs, skulls and monsters, while Prometheus claimed he could see only blue sky. To Hephaestus, clouds were clouds.

Dionysus swigged from his bulging wineskin. 'Heph, get some of this down your neck.'

'What for?' asked the god of fire.

'For fun,' yawned Persephone, brushing salt from her skin and replacing her coronet of poppies. 'Remember fun?'

'He doesn't want any nectar,' the god of foresight said, shoving the wineskin out of the way. 'Remember your mother's birthday, Heph? An afternoon of hilarity isn't worth the suffering tomorrow.' Self-consciously, he took out a bag of marbles.

Epimetheus snickered. 'Toys, Prom? At your age? Come with us and suffer in a good cause. Leave your crab-footed friend here if he can't keep up.'

Prometheus scowled at his brother. 'I'm staying for a game. Heph's got a stone I've had my eye on for ages – the red one that makes cold water hot and vice versa.'

Taking the hint, the god of afterthought shrugged. 'Suit yourself,' he said, and swaggered off down the cliff, guzzling nectar.

Hephaestus shifted awkwardly. Maybe they were too old for playing but Epimetheus was bad enough when sober and he wished the annoying god wouldn't hang around. Dionysus donned his serpent headdress, swung Persephone onto his shoulders, staggered slightly and followed the god of afterthought.

'Be on time for the banquet, Prom,' warned the goddess, 'Or Zeus will start auditioning for a new favourite.'

It was a relief that the other three had gone and left them to it. Epimetheus liked to think he was best at everything and delighted in goading the others, Dionysus was generally drunk and Persephone was like a dark cloud, come rain or shine.

Hephaestus followed the footprints on the beach below, and when the three gods had vanished out of sight, Prometheus turned to him.

'Ignore my brother. Just because he produced the animals, he thinks he's better than me.'

'It's alright.' The god of fire felt some creatures left a great deal to be desired, particularly the mosquito, but thought it wiser to keep his own counsel. 'So, marbles?'

Agreed on playing, they crawled under the shade of an olive tree and started flicking small spheres to and fro. There was nothing wrong with a restful game on a warm day and the monotonous click of stone on bone was quite soothing. Or it was until the peace and quiet was broken with a cheer when Prometheus captured the coveted red stone and tossed it up and down.

'I'm bored,' announced the victor, stowing the spoils in his marble bag before tying it with a careful knot and hanging it on the leather thong around his neck. 'Epi was right, after all. Playing marbles *is* dull.'

Typical. Now he'd never win that marble back and it was his top scorer as well. 'What would you rather do then?'

'Put on your chiton and follow me.' The god of foresight picked up his sack. 'I've got a plan.'

'Where are we going? Is it far?'

'Not too far, and if your leg hurts, I'll ask Hermes for a lift.'

'But what about the feast at the palace?'

'Trust me, I won't let you starve.'

Their destination was still a way off when Hermes appeared, hovering at shoulder height, arms folded and lips pursed.

'It may have escaped your attention, godlings, but I'm not at your beck and call.'

Before agreeing to drop them off, the messenger extracted a promise from Hephaestus to service his winged boots, complaining they were sluggish, all the while sucking in his gut. The blacksmith accepted the deal but privately considered it would do Hermes no harm to take an occasional walk.

When the messenger was informed of the destination, he arched a brow, but didn't demur and deposited them at the clay pits before departing in his usual shimmer of gold.

As soon as they were alone, Prometheus jumped into a quarry, scraped up some mud and rolled it into a large oval, a wonky ball, and five tubes of varying length. Was he making his own marbles? If so, they were on the large side and not remotely spherical.

'Prom, why do you keep looking at me? Is Zeus not adequate for you these days?'

'Shut up and stand straight.' The god of foresight melded the five rolls to the oval and perched the wonky ball on top of the shortest roll. 'Ta-dah!'

The god of fire scrutinised the resulting monstrosity and it dawned on him that this collection of poorly assembled misshapes was meant to be him, in miniature.

'You may be many things, Prom,' said the offended source of inspiration, 'but dextrous you are not.'

'Agreed. So why not lend a hand? Do me if you're up to the task.'

Up to the task? What a nerve. Hephaestus lowered himself into the quarry and clawed up a fistful of clay. By holding an imprint of his friend in his mind's eye, he didn't once refer to the original while he laboured, his fingers as nimble as his gait was clumsy.

'Heph! Your little fellow is the absolute double of me.'

'It could be better.' He closed his fist, ready to scrunch up his prototype.

'Unwise to destroy something made in a god's image,' said Prometheus, 'in case it tempts the Fates and gives them ideas.'

'As if the Fates don't have enough ideas of their own.'

'True, but rather than expecting perfection straight away, just do your best. Make a second version of me and I guarantee it'll be an improvement on this one.'

Hephaestus allowed himself to be persuaded and agreed to continue working. The gods quarried and were soon beyond the reach of the sun, their clothes filthy and their flesh chilled in the damp pit. Once they'd completed the final batch, they clambered out, stretched and rubbed their aching limbs under the bemused eye of Helios.

'We should have made them when Helios was high,' said Hephaestus, 'because they'll never dry at this rate.'

'They'll dry,' said the nonchalant creator, dismissing his concern with a lofty wave, 'and with less chance of cracking.'

The population of clay men covered the surrounding slopes. They were not at all uniform and the early tries were far from perfect, but Prometheus was right – of course – and as the gods' hands had grown accustomed to the clay, their constructions grew taller, straighter and more finely honed.

Hephaestus had to admit that his own efforts were pleasing to the eye whereas his friend's attempts looked like the work of a bear: bulbous blobs that were heavy of brow and jaw, thick of torso and stumpy of limb. He should scrub his playmate's face in the dirt for implying these thwarted failures were modelled on him. Where were his broad shoulders and powerful arms? His muscular neck and chiselled jaw? As for hair, the blacksmith despaired. Where he had tumbling locks, these poor relations wore a scraggled thatch, and in place of his wide eyes, they had dots of dirt. If only Prometheus would stop patrolling and go to sleep, he could skulk down and tweak them here and there before they dried.

Idly, he tossed a figure in the air. It landed with a splat. So they'd never fly. Swimming might also be out of the question. Would they sink or disintegrate? He dropped one in a nearby stream. Sink. Wood might have been a more suitable material because it floated.

'What shall we do with them, Prom?' he called out. 'Stand them up to make armies – Olympians versus Titans – or use them for catapult practice?' With that, he aimed a rock at a group, flattening them with a satisfying squelch.

'What did you do?' Prometheus raced over, consternation on his face as the drying fragments crumbled to dust. 'They're ruined. Honestly, you're worse than Ares.'

While Hephaestus detested his half-brother, this insult hurt less than it should have, and he secretly enjoyed the comparison.

'Settle down, Prom. Plenty more clay where they came from.'

'That's not the point, is it? Stay out of the way while they dry, and don't get any more bright ideas with that catapult.'

~

Belly-down on a hill, the two gods scrutinised thousands of slowly baking bodies, the moisture leaving them under the dying rays of the warm evening sun.

'It's time for the next step,' said Prometheus, jumping up.

'And it's also time we were at the palace so why not leave the next step, whatever it is, for another day?'

'No, it has to be tonight.'

Hephaestus pointed to the newly risen moon. 'But Selene is at her fattest and there are to be revels.' The famished blacksmith's mouth watered just thinking about tender lamb roasting on skewers. 'You promised we'd be back for the feast.'

'I said you wouldn't starve, and you won't, but I need as much light as possible while Helios is away feasting, sleeping or whatever it is he does in the dark.' Prometheus held the first replica god of fire to his lips and breathed into it. 'But you go, Heph, because I can hear your stomach rumbling from here.'

At the sight of this act, all thoughts of food fled from Hephaestus' mind. 'What are you thinking? Zeus will have a paroxysm of some sort at the very least!'

As if to agree, Selene, that soul of discretion, blinked and plunged the sky into darkness, leaving only the winking stars. By the time she'd recovered, Prometheus was cradling his first creation in his palm.

'He's breathing by himself,' he whispered. 'I've created life.'

Indeed, the clay man was pushing out the god's breath and drawing in his own. No longer a lump of mud, but a living being. So that's what this was all about: one-upping Epimetheus.

Hephaestus jabbed a finger towards its abdomen. 'We forgot to give them belly buttons.'

'Is that all you have to say on such a momentous occasion?'

'Hardly momentous,' he said, diplomatically not pointing out that Epimetheus had beaten his brother to it, as this was obviously a bone of contention between them. 'I've already created life with my walking tripods and forge assistants, not forgetting Apollo's mouse.'

'Firstly, the Cyclopes helped you, and secondly, your creations are machines. This isn't a machine.' He laid it down reverently. 'It's a small god.'

As he watched the smooth belly rise and fall, Hephaestus worried about what they'd done. Making animals was child's play but these beings would surely draw the almighty's wrath.

'Prom, you can't do this.' He gripped his arm. 'Think of Zeus! What will he say?'

'Nothing.' The creator shook him off. 'He was thrilled with Epi's endeavours, especially the woodpeckers. Besides, the almighty loves me more than the other gods put together.'

Apart from anything, Hera had better not get wind of this claim. There were distinctly worrying rumours circulating about what his mother was capable of when her jealousy was roused.

'I know you're his pet, Prom, but Zeus lives in terror of being overthrown.' He recalled the stormy battle with Poseidon. 'The almighty is bound to punish anyone he suspects of trying to encroach on his realm.'

'Always so dramatic,' said the god of foresight as he examined the second little form, gave it life and set it on the ground. 'Zeus will be too busy feasting to mind and in the morning he'll be amused, you'll see. The almighty has to have something to do when he's not shape-shifting and impregnating everything in sight.' He paused to animate a third man and then a fourth. 'Plus, there's a limit to how much dancing anyone can tolerate,' he said breathlessly. 'Are you going to stand there arguing or are you going to help?'

'No way am I breathing into anything.'

'Fine.' Prometheus exhaled loudly. 'Pass them to me and I'll breathe into them. It'll speed things up. Zeus won't mind, I promise.'

This was highly unlikely and surely this confidence in

Zeus' good nature was misplaced. Even so, the blacksmith stooped to pick up the next figure.

~

Perched on an escarpment, brooding over the clay men, Hephaestus swung his left foot, making a crater in the chalk sill with his leg guard. Famished after missing out on the big spread, he idly wondered how the beings tasted but kept this to himself since Prometheus was a tad over-sensitive when it came to his charges. Probably tasted like clay, anyway.

'Cut it out, Heph, or you'll have the entire edifice down and they'll all be crushed.'

'Not a huge loss since they don't exactly do a lot, do they?'

'Maybe not now but wait for the sun to come up,' said Prometheus, mysteriously.

'I thought you wanted to stop Helios seeing what we were up to?'

'Only to stop him blabbing and interrupting our labours but now we're done it doesn't matter and we can have our own feast.' From his sack, he removed a flask of wine, a ball of cheese, handfuls of olives and a hunk of bread. 'It's not roasted lamb, but it'll do.'

'Hmm, I suppose it'll have to, won't it, and what will your men eat?'

'They'll suck milk from she-goats, eat the wild honey dripping from trees and fill up on an acorn or two. Epi can always make more animals.'

'So long as there's plenty to go around.' Hephaestus helped himself to bread, hoping that he'd never be reduced to dining on acorns.

Baby Steps

Helios glowered at the life forms and his warmth roused a creature, which stretched and wriggled. Slowly, its eyes fluttered open, squinting in the bright rays, then grew wide as it beheld its creators.

'We should stay out of sight,' suggested Prometheus, so the gods retreated to a large rock and peered over the edge. 'He'll recover, but at least the first one is up and the rest will be sure to follow.'

As predicted, several figures awoke, while the early riser rolled onto all fours and scuttled off. His brothers copied him and soon the land was alive with scurrying masses. An adventurous type adopted a more crouched position and straightened his spine before pulling himself up so he was erect. He put out a hesitant foot and promptly lost his balance.

'Come on, you can do it,' sighed the god of foresight as the man got up again and took a tentative step and then a second. 'You beautiful boy!'

Each man observed and imitated, until they were all tottering along, holding out their hands, unsure what they were for. Once used to walking about, they bumped into each other, which led to wrestling and capering in the sunlight. A group found a waterfall and lapped, delighted to discover they could create waterfalls of their own, drenching themselves and their friends.

When the fun wore off, they started grabbing fish, snatching and taking bites. Judging by the fighting that had broken out, mankind lacked their benefactor's leanings towards goodness.

'Not very patient, are they?' said Hephaestus.

'It's because they're young,' retorted the indulgent parent, 'and time passes more slowly for them. Patience comes with age.'

'Let's hope they live that long.' He watched two big specimens haul a smaller one up a crag. 'Perhaps we can stop them. Too late, there he goes. Do you think they're a bit on the violent side?'

'They're just clumsy.' But even Prometheus gaped as his creation was impaled on a shard of rock, twitching as red ichor bled out and a diaphanous shadow ascended, pierced in the middle.

'Prom, what's that hanging over the body?'

'His shade.'

'Shade? He has a soul?'

'They all do.'

'It's scaring the others. Can't you resurrect him and shove the soul back in?'

'*Shove the soul back in?* Have you heard yourself, Heph? I don't want them to rise from the dead. That's the whole point.'

'So, if they're not immortal, they must be *mortal*. Not a bad name...' When these words fell on fallow ground, he hurried on. 'Maybe you should intervene and prevent this sort of thing.'

'Why intervene when I've given them free will?'

'Is that wise?' Hephaestus tossed some ripe olives into his mouth. 'You know how the Fates feel about being in charge.'

'They won't mind. They're too interested in the divines to worry about anyone else.'

Prometheus was innocent to a fault. The three goddesses of destiny were renowned control freaks, who'd mind a great deal, and they'd never allow someone made in a god's image to wend his sweet way through life, exercising something as casual-sounding as free will. Once they got wind of this, Clotho, Lachesis and Atropos would no doubt appear on earth – spinning, measuring, cutting – and the latest species would be fortunate to see out the week.

After a few hours, Helios tired of the novelty and washed the sky red as he voyaged west and sank behind a hill, leaving a twilight filled with despondent cries. Once they'd enjoyed his warming brilliance, the beings refused to be deprived and chased after him, screaming.

When the source of light and heat failed to return, they collapsed, shivering and calling out with pitiful, guttural sounds, and not even the appearance of Selene and her gentle beams soothed them. Prometheus gazed at their moonlit forms with such tenderness that Hephaestus' fatherless heart ached. If only they could explain that the two luminaries changed places faithfully, no matter how often they threatened not to.

In the west, some shadowy figures got to their feet. What were they up to? After a significant amount of pushing, shoving and muttering, the pack selected the smallest of their number and carried him, aloft and squalling, to the top of the hill the sun had vanished behind. When there was no sign of the big ball of fire, they clobbered their bellowing brother with stones, and a particularly well-built man held up the twitching torso until it twitched no more, and a crumpled shade rose in Selene's waning radiance.

Helios emerged from the east, his rays revealing the horde, and very passable they appeared in the morning light. Bathed in gold, they were silenced by their own powers and circled their leader, genuflecting as he turned slowly, bearing the corpse of their littlest member. Was it Hephaestus' imagination, or did the golden god glow at this blood sacrifice, however accidental? As the others woke up, they roared and raced eastwards.

'If they imagine they control Helios with that rite, they'll make a habit of it. You should have a word with them.'

'No need. Free will, remember?' Prometheus yawned. 'I must get some sleep. All this creation has worn me out…'

'Wake up, Prom. How committed to this notion of free will are you?' He pointed to a stream where a few individuals were busy drowning their weaker neighbours, and scores of small shades fluttered overhead. 'What have you breathed into them to turn them so vicious?'

'They aren't vicious as such but they have no comprehension of fatality. To them, death is no worse than falling asleep. I'd rather they were kinder but they're only children with much to learn.'

With a loud cheer, some 'children' stampeded downhill, crushing their slower fellows underfoot. The flock of souls darkened the sky and the aggressors howled. The men were completely out of control and would die out before they'd developed a conscience. Further away, a gang was stoning a bull to death, although it was impossible to tell whether it was to appease the gods, fill their bellies or amuse themselves.

'So much for milk, honey and acorns,' said Hephaestus, pointing at the revellers, 'but they'll have a job hacking it into pieces.'

The proud parent's face lit up. 'Not necessarily. See how they're dropping stones from the cliff onto the rocks to create sharp tools? Ingenious, eh?'

'If you consider mimicking crows ingenious. What if they use these sharp tools on their compatriots?'

'Always a risk until they learn right from wrong, but as they've learnt how to slaughter animals, how about giving them some of your fire to—'

He was interrupted by a thunderbolt shooting out of the pale blue sky. It struck the westernmost hill, obliterating the sacrificial throng, resulting in squeals from those who'd borne witness to this worrying development, and they fled, falling over their own feet in their panic.

'Gods of foresight and fire,' boomed a celestial voice, 'what in the world were you thinking? Oh, try not to look so surprised. I *am* omniscient, and despite what Hermes may say, I know what goes on around here.'

His words crashed off the hills and rumbled through the valleys. Helios, who was never fond of these storms, faded away, leaving mankind quaking in abject terror.

'Horrible little barbarians, charging about all over Gaia, doing unspeakable things to her. She is not pleased in the slightest, let me tell you that for nothing, and she's started swallowing the miscreants. Now, where to begin with the pair of you? Such an act of hubris I've yet to witness. It was one thing your brother creating animals, Prom, but this is quite another.' Zeus shook his head, scattering clouds. 'What are the revolting organisms meant to be, anyway?'

'Mortals,' replied Prometheus, aiming a wink at Hephaestus.

'Bit of a weird name, if you ask me. What do they taste of?'

'They're not for eating so they taste of nothing.'

'Then what is their purpose?' asked the puzzled ruler.

'They have no purpose and exist purely for the sheer joy of living.'

The greatest god bestowed a beatific smile before remembering himself.

'While I can't pretend to be happy at being out-godded by my favourite young companion, once I get over my bruised pride, I suppose your creations might be amusing, although that lot over there are hideous,' he said, squinting disapprovingly. 'But this personage paying tribute to me is rather handsome.' A brave volunteer bowed before the almighty, proffering a chunk of the dead bull. 'Yet, he dares insult me with a paltry portion.' With that, Zeus raised an enormous sandalled foot.

Foreseeing an unhappy ending, Prometheus was swift to arbitrate, flexing his muscles and showing off his shoulders and thighs as he took the full carcass and passed it to the king of heaven, who appeared temporarily mollified by the morsel and lowered his foot without incident.

'Ugh, raw meat,' he said, spitting out the bull.

'Perhaps,' said Prometheus, fluttering his eyelashes shamelessly, 'they could have fire to cook the flesh. It would be tastier for you and safer for them. They could stay warm at night…'

'Out of the question,' said Zeus, picking bits of skeleton from his teeth, 'or they'll get ideas above their station. The divine flame is forbidden to mortals. They will eat their meat raw. Do you understand me, Prom?'

Solemn faced, he yielded. 'Understood, mightiest of mighties.'

'You too, Heph. Under no circumstances hand over a single spark, because Prom can be most persuasive.'

'I won't share my fire,' promised Hephaestus stoutly. While he had some sympathy for the mortals, especially the shivering and the sickly, he wasn't willing to risk any aggravation to give them a leg up.

'Count yourself lucky I hold you in such high esteem, Prom, or you'd be dangling in Tartarus right now.'

Not relishing banishment to the abyss of torment, the minor god remained silent, but when Zeus helped himself to a shrieking handful of mortals, Hephaestus had to restrain his friend to prevent him attacking his patron.

'Naturally, I won't complain at the prospect of thousands of slaves and perhaps the odd bedmate or two.'

He dangled a potential candidate before his eyes, harumphed and threw down the reject, who landed with an unfortunate crack of the neck. Prometheus stiffened but Hephaestus maintained his grip – he was sorry for the pointless death, but if provoked, the almighty wouldn't hesitate to wipe out the entire population.

'But they are killing themselves at an alarming rate,' Zeus went on, 'which does concern me. Someone must cleanse them of their blood guilt, and to be frank, the pantheon has neither the time nor the inclination. You, blacksmith, create some kings to maintain order.'

He snapped his fingers and in response, Hermes materialised. 'As for you, messenger, since you didn't bother to report this misadventure to me earlier, I charge you with taking these shades to Hades.'

'As if I have nothing better to do,' said Hermes, bridling at the injustice, 'and why is nobody else being punished?'

Zeus shrugged. 'An additional job title should cover the inconvenience. How about psychopomp?'

'*Chief* psychopomp?' came the sullen reply.

'As you wish but start now. We can't have these souls hanging about, making Gaia untidy. Besides, it makes the survivors gloomy and I've no desire to listen to weeping for months on end. Straighten your face, Hermes, and next time you spot godlings up to high jinks, I will hear about it immediately.'

Prometheus drew in a breath, ready to speak, but Zeus spoke over him.

'Not one more peep out of you. I've had a bellyful of this *free will* of yours. I fancy myself as more of an interventionist god, so I'll compose some commandments.' He smoothed his beard while he contemplated. 'Nine should suffice but it'll be a lot of work and I do my best work lying down. Prom, come with me. You look in need of a nap yourself.'

~

Following his lengthy 'nap' Prometheus collected Hephaestus and they returned to the clay pits, mercifully without Epimetheus who had tried to muscle in.

'What on Mother Earth is that?' said Hephaestus, prodding a grotesque figure.

'Isn't it obvious?' asked its wounded-looking creator. 'He's a king. Guess who I've modelled him on.'

'Surely not the almighty?' Who would go berserk if he realised this hefty lump of clay was how his pet godling viewed him. 'It's definitely massive enough.' He examined it closely. 'But the thunderbolt is so minute it's almost invisible. If the Olympians see this king, they'll ridicule Zeus and he'll have you slung out of heaven, or worse. Why does it have three eyes?'

'Two are his normal ones and the third represents his omniscience, obviously. I should have let Epimetheus tag along and you could work together since you're both so clever at everything.'

'Hardly, but if you insist on making Zeus-like figures, try to ensure they're halfway decent.'

At length, Prometheus unclenched his fists and the high colour left his cheeks. 'It *is* fairly monstrous.' He flicked the tiny thunderbolt with his pinkie and it fell off. The deities grinned at each other. 'How about one king per thousand men? It won't take me long to knock them up.'

'Maybe, Prom, but the rocks on the shore are more apt to resemble the king of heaven than anything made by you.'

'You do them, then. My ideas aren't bad but there's often a slip between my head and my hand.'

Slip was putting it mildly. 'Leave it to me and save your breath until I've finished.'

While Hephaestus laboured, his colleague lazed under an ancient olive tree, actually snoring. It galled the blacksmith, being lumbered with the work, but in all honesty, he enjoyed seeing things take shape, and the size and majesty of these beings would hopefully stop their smaller brethren from slaughtering themselves into extinction.

When Prometheus awoke slightly before dawn, he sprang up to inspect the twelve kings.

'Perfect. I'll give them life so they can purify their more impulsive citizens.'

'Impulsive? That's an interesting way of describing the murderous mob. And remember, the kings have to impose order as well as cleanse blood guilt.'

Nodding, the god of foresight breathed into the future sovereigns and laid them out to dry. When the dawn sunshine woke the original mortals, they clustered around the new creations. The gods kept a close watch in case anyone took advantage of the sleepers' unconscious state and massacred them, but their concern was unfounded as the originals occupied themselves by braiding grasses with flowers and placing the woven circlets on their leaders' heads.

'The men have coronated their kings and paid tribute. Are you going to demand tributes from them?' asked Hephaestus.

'Absolutely not. They'll make their own luck without having to depend on divine goodwill.'

'You saw the almighty's face at the measly portion of bull he received. There are too few minor deities to placate the pantheon, so rest assured, mankind won't be excused from sacrificing to them.'

'You're probably right and Zeus will want all the adulation available since he's not getting any from Hera of late, if Hermes is to be believed. Sorry, I keep forgetting she's your mother.'

'Don't worry, so does she, but it's best not to believe every word that comes out of the messenger's mouth, Prom. I generally dismiss half of whatever he says.'

'Me too. Look, the first king is on his feet!'

Indeed, he was on his feet. One after the other, the remaining eleven kings arose, and their subordinates bowed, danced and twirled before them as they paced their territory, testing out their limbs.

'Heph, the tallest monarch has his subjects grovelling and insists on being carried about as if he's an actual god, and now the others are copying. It's as if there are a dozen Zeuses down on earth.'

'Just what the world needs,' groaned Hephaestus.

Owl Eyes

Hephaestus, Prometheus and Persephone stood side-on to the incoming sea, while the wind blew behind them, sending spirals of sand eddying across the beach. Although the three gods were stationary, the sand appeared to shift beneath them and the god of fire enjoyed the illusion of speeding along with no pain or discomfort in his leg. This enjoyment increased manyfold when the goddess of love emerged on the far side of the shore, shadowed by a bevy of comparatively ugly nymphs.

'See that lot?' said Persephone. 'Aph hates competition so she won't have any pretty attendants.'

The god of fire ignored his jealous cousin, who failed to see how compassionate Aphrodite was for patronising the unfortunate-looking nymphs. They should consider themselves blessed to be in her company. Look at the breeze lifting her tresses and her robe, and the lucky sun kissing her skin. What he would give to be Helios. With every step Aphrodite took, anemones blossomed, creating a luxurious carpet of white flowers to hide her unattractive disciples' ungainly feet. Such kindness. Naturally, the most divine of all deities was too busy admiring the butterflies surrounding her to be aware of anyone, let alone a humble blacksmith. This was his chance, but he'd have to do something impressive to win her attention. As the goddess and her acolytes passed by, he raised his hands in front of him, gradually lifting them overhead, impersonating Zeus conjuring the North Wind. He felt majestic and was certain Aphrodite had spared him a glance but his big moment was ruined by Persephone digging him in the ribs.

'Heph, stop showing off! Why are you pretending to be Artemis? You've got no chance. Aph isn't aware of your existence, and even if she was, she wouldn't be interested in you.'

He peeled his eyes away from the object of his desire and glared at his cousin. 'You have no idea what you're talking about! She *was* looking.'

The mischievous goddess smirked. 'So, you want her to take notice of you, eh? Easily done.' With that, she hooked his bad ankle with her foot, knocking him off balance so he fell headlong.

When the ugly nymphs tittered, Aphrodite turned to see what had attracted their attention and sweetened the air with her own laughter. Hephaestus' cheeks burnt with shame as Prometheus hauled him up.

Dusting himself down, he scowled. 'Are you tired of living, Seph?'

'Actually,' said Persephone, sounding distant, 'I've always wondered what death would be like…'

'Show me up again and you could find out.'

In response, Prometheus gave him a dead arm, but before Hephaestus could return the favour, Helios vanished without warning, leaving a pewter sky, marbled with lightning. The atmosphere filled with a horrible roar, whose force made their hair and clothes ripple. Rain pelted from the heavens and Aphrodite and her nymphs scampered off in search of shelter. What did this strange weather presage? He soon found out when Hermes arrived, winged cap askew. 'Blacksmith, you're wanted,' he yelled over the racket, snatching Hephaestus and transporting him to the forge, where the messenger edged past heaps of charwood towards the fire, trying to dry his livery. 'You delivered yourself, by all accounts?'

'If I hadn't, I'd still be inside Hera's belly.'

'Come on then, and bring something sharper than your wit.'

'Why?'

'Because,' said Hermes with infinite patience, 'Zeus is about to give birth and he's suffering terribly so you must help him.'

'Again?' Had he heard properly?

'Seeing those little mortals running about has made him broody. Hurry up and don't forget your birthing paraphernalia.'

'Can't you do it? Didn't you deliver Dion from the almighty's thigh?'

'Yes, but trust me, I didn't exactly cover myself in glory, which is why I've been ordered to stick to the day job and fetch you instead.'

'What about Artemis? Isn't she in charge of childbirth?'

'Gone fishing, so it has to be you. Get a move on. Providing it's a girl, you have nothing to worry about.'

'And if it's a boy?'

The messenger sucked his teeth and ahemmed. 'Every time the greatest god has a son, he lives in fear of being overthrown. You know how it is. Zeus ousted Cronus, who dethroned Ouranos prior to that. It was touch and go for Ares and Dion when they were born. Fortunately for them, they're none too clever, and fortunately for you, Zeus is not your fa… Anyway, gather whatever equipment you need and pray for a female child. Are you coming?'

As if he had any choice in the matter. Half-heartedly, he placed a few tools in a sack and once he was finished, Hermes spirited him through the lashing rain. If the birth went well, he would be in the king of heaven's good graces. It was best not to visualise what would happen if the birth went badly.

The greatest god lay on the riverbank, clutching his head and roaring fit to burst. He hammered his temples with the heels of his hands, sending sparks flying, inadvertently scorching an airborne flock of his wife's peacocks so the sooty corpses landed with soft thumps. Just as well Hera was not in the vicinity.

Hephaestus planted himself firmly, braced foursquare against the storm, and took out his wooden wedge and long-handled beetle mallet. 'Zeus wants me to crack his skull?'

'Yes,' Hermes bellowed over the commotion, hanging onto his hat. 'Damned if you do. Damned if you don't…'

'What's keeping you?' the expectant father moaned, rolling from side to side. Get it out of me for Ouranus' sake!'

Gingerly, Hephaestus gripped the patient in a headlock, positioned the wedge behind his left ear, prayed to all the ancient gods and whacked the wood with his beetle. A small crack opened in the almighty's skull, which was followed by the wet sound of flesh ripping and a powerful blast threw the midwife backwards.

When he could see straight, he sat up to find a goddess shouting so loudly that his eardrums were in danger of rupture. The latest addition to the pantheon was beautiful, with white ringlets and a trim figure. Here she was, fully fledged and fighting fit. Her skin was bronzed and her limbs long-boned and muscular. She was already wearing a plumed helmet and carrying a spear and shield, which she smashed against one another, adding to the din.

He'd secretly hoped the newborn might be flawed like him, but she was perfect, requiring no nurture, and there was no likelihood of *her* being thrown out of heaven. Unless, of course, jealous Hera got wind of her… Horrified at himself, he shook off the notion. What had he become? Sometimes, he hated himself for his ingrained bitterness and envy.

Once the pandemonium ended, the messenger stepped

forwards, applauding.

'Welcome, Athena, birthed from the head of Zeus! My congratulations!'

The recovering father remained recumbent, golden ichor haemorrhaging from the wound at an alarming rate, oak saplings sprouting from his sacred lifeblood. The greatest god groaned, rolled over and clambered to his feet. Apart from the dripping cranial dent, he seemed otherwise hale.

'Daughter of mine. My very own creation!'

Hephaestus wondered how Hera would take this. Had her husband finally run out of beings to impregnate?

Athena raised her chin but didn't bow or avert her gaze.

'Greetings, honourable Father, I express gratitude to you for my birth.' She looked around her. 'Where is my mother?'

Zeus massaged his temple. 'You have no other parent, my dear. I'm *it* on the parental front, and you'll thank me for it, believe you me.'

The goddess paced awhile, thinking. 'I *do* have another parent: Metis the Wise. You swallowed her whole but she still lives within you. I can sense her. Metis has become pure thought and will know everything that crosses your mind before you know it yourself, and by extension, so will I.'

Was that a blush marring her father's otherwise flawless complexion?

The almighty coughed and waved a hand. 'Details, dearest daughter, mere details, but there's no need to repeat the M word in my presence, and definitely don't mention it within earshot of my wife. I expect *she'll* make herself known to you in due course.' Zeus tapped his jaw and held his ear to the side as if draining sea water after a swim. Already, the cut had knitted together.

'Father, we shall discuss my mother later.' Athena levelled her owl-grey eyes at his platinum ones. 'In the meantime, I express further gratitude to you for making me god of war.'

'Ah, *goddess* of war,' said Zeus, rubbing his wound.

'We shall discuss that later, too,' she said. 'Until then, I have priests to audition.'

'You mean *priestesses*, surely?'

'I mean what I say. After that, I will introduce myself to the other god of war.'

'Perhaps we should have a chat ahead of you meeting your brother.'

But she wasn't listening, and in a single fantastic leap, was gone.

The messenger whistled. 'There goes trouble.'

'They grow up so fast,' remarked Zeus.

Hephaestus decided this was as good a time as any to depart. 'If you're finished with me, I'll be going.'

'Wait,' said Zeus. 'I must reward you for delivering my daughter.' The king of heaven tugged on his beard. 'I'll give you a third forge. It's pleasantly situated under the mountain at Aetna.'

'Your gift is greatly appreciated, mighty one,' said the reluctant recipient, not seeing the point of such a lengthy commute when he could work from home easily and efficiently. 'But I was happy to help and don't expect anything in return.'

'Nonsense, you've earned it. Besides, all the banging and clanging on Olympus gives your mother dreadful headaches and she's a martyr to them as it is. Consider it a boon to me.'

'As you wish, almighty.'

This gift of the forge at Aetna felt worse than Hera's earlier present of the Olympian forge. Zeus' reward was effectively a second banishment from heaven, and to add insult to injury, the blacksmith would either have to work out a shortcut to Aetna or spend his life sailing.

Typically, the messenger was nowhere to be seen, so Hephaestus set off on the long trudge to tell his friends about the new arrival. Hopefully, she'd be nothing like Ares, who loved slaughter for its own sake. Prometheus would be distressed by a second war deity, although Persephone would warm to anyone with the remotest tendency towards death and destruction.

Stealing Fire

Hephaestus was wondering why the forge smelt of aniseed when a clatter made him look up to see a bar of gold roll across the floor. He removed his eye-patch, retrieved the gold and spotted two feet beneath the bellows. He'd recognise those toes anywhere.

'I know you're not here for knick-knacks and trinkets, Prom, so why are you lurking? What are you after?'

He waited while the intruder eased himself from behind the bellows, holding a gigantic stalk of fennel.

'I'm after a light,' he said, the forge flames reflecting on his face, so his features flickered in the darkened smithy.

'Is that all? No need to skulk.' The smith swept a magnanimous hand past a smouldering heap of charwood. 'Help yourself.'

The would-be thief shuffled his feet. 'It's not for me.'

'Then who… oh, wait a minute, not for your mortals? You must be joking. You promised. *I* promised. Zeus will do hideous things to you, and me, and I mean *truly* hideous.'

The two gods looked at each other and considered some of the punishments the greatest god had meted out in the past.

Prometheus broke the spell. 'I want my men to stay warm

at night and eat cooked food. Who wants to subsist on raw flesh? They need a helping hand as they're worse off than animals in many respects. Not as fast or strong and no horns or fangs.'

'Has Epi been mocking our efforts again?'

'My brother has a point.' He indicated an anvil. 'Give my men a flame and they may gain some of your wisdom with it so then you could teach them to fabricate rudimentary tools.'

This couldn't end well. 'The damage that lot could do if they got their hands on metal.' Armed with sticks and stones, they fed themselves adequately, but every mouthful they took was a mouthful less for the gods. Armed with fire and metal, they might spend their days wolfing down roasted meat and empty the world of beasts. 'During their short existence, they've killed and maimed many of their own number and who knows what they'll get up to with sharp implements.'

'In that case, I'll command them to reserve fire only for cooking.'

So, the grand concept of free will could be dispensed with when convenient.

'Zeus will still be incensed.'

'Why?'

'Why do you think? Imagine him going to lie with his cattle, only to find your little fellows spit-roasting his favourite heifer. Do you fancy spending eternity propping up the heavens alongside Atlas?'

'You worry too much. This is a risk I must take. If you don't want to be party to my plans, flip your eye-patch down and turn a blind eye. That way, the almighty need never know you were involved.'

'That's not what I'm worried about. Stop being so foolhardy and relying on your good looks. It's unlikely Zeus would pardon such a deliberate rebellion and even your fine physique won't save you.'

'A lifetime existing on raw food? Would you wish that on anyone? Please support me in this. If you can't force yourself to rebel against the almighty, go for a swim and I'll do the dark deed while you're gone.'

Hephaestus glanced outside, where the sun was shining brightly. Night was best for committing crimes as Selene was renowned for keeping secrets.

'Supposing I agree, how do you plan to carry off your ill-gotten gains with that old blabbermouth, Helios, watching your every move?'

Prometheus raised his stalk. 'In this.'

'You won't get far with that but on your head be it.'

Hephaestus proffered his long tongs and stood aside while his friend harvested a charwood ember and tucked it into the stalk. Surprisingly, he didn't carry away the fennel and instead aimed what was now a flaming arrow over the sea to the mainland.

The mortals quailed at the fiery projectile and ran screaming in all directions. The missile landed in dry brush, devoured the parched wood and caused a conflagration unlike anything Hephaestus had ever witnessed. As the blaze roared across the land, it trapped those men and beasts too slow to escape. Their death throes were appalling and not even the tears of Prometheus were enough to quench the inferno.

When the ferocious flames and suffocating smoke gave way to a warm red glow, the survivors returned, drawn by the mouth-watering smell, their initial terror overcome by the craving for roasted flesh. They alternated between feasting and playing with fire, quickly discovering they had the built-in ability to extinguish it. Once sated, the remaining kings feared the flames were in danger of going out and ordered their minions to conserve some for future use.

Initially, there were burnt fingers galore until mankind learnt to manipulate flat stones to pick up cinders. They were quick learners and preserved glowing embers under a mound of ash, conducting them from one place to another, trailed by worshippers who did everything in their power to protect the precious commodity.

Following a fair number of life-changing injuries, the men worked out how to control the sacred element. As well as bringing terror when wild, it could bring delight when tame. The mortals loved fire and what it did to food, so they were careful to hold up burnt offerings to their benefactor, who was unconcerned whether they remembered to give him his portion or not, for Prometheus was easily the least capricious god.

As Helios sank, the men built pyres and sat in a circle to share stories, cheering when they realised the fanged animals feared this gift from the gods. When Selene took flight and silvered the sky, mortal bellies were filled with meat and their hearts with cheer, and they sang songs while circling the flames, shaking their heads, shoulders and limbs as they went.

The divine spark breathed into the mortals by Prometheus had kindled something in their minds. Watched over by their creator, the species grew bigger, stronger and cleverer. No longer were they merely concerned with praying the sun would rise and clubbing animals to the verge of extinction. Now, they sharpened stones to fashion spear heads so they could hunt more effectively, until their patron warned them to live more lightly on the land, ever fearful of his brother's wrath. Paying no heed to the kind god, as the herds followed the pastures, so mankind followed the herds. Always roaming, they designated some creatures beasts of burden, harnessing them with the hides of their predecessors.

One day, in a bout of boredom, a gang tossed rocks into the flames and the reputedly non-interventionist god fanned them higher with his breath until the rocks cracked and liquid the colour of Helios setting in winter flowed over the sand, as it had for Hephaestus in times past. Some of the mortals died sizzling deaths, while others lay howling, begging for mercy, but most of them navigated the bright river without incident.

In the morning, Hephaestus awoke to a gargantuan bronze mirror bouncing Helios' rays back at him. The neophyte metalworkers danced around their fantastic invention, gingerly touching it with toes and fingers before walking on it, spreadeagling their bodies on it, pulling faces and moving their hands slowly to and fro in amazement. Prometheus supervised them like a mother hen, wincing at the occasional oaf who was so fascinated by his own reflection, he clubbed himself unconscious. Still, the men had never appeared so festive nor his friend so pleased.

When Helios didn't leave after his allotted interval, blocking out the livid moon goddess, Zeus arrived to investigate and found the vain sun god admiring himself in the shiny surface covering the sand while a few mortals amused themselves on the warm bronze. To say the greatest god was cross was a massive understatement. On seeing the almighty's furious face reflected in the mirror beside him, Helios immediately made himself scarce. The suddenly dark sky was lit by a flash of light and thunderbolts rained down in tremendous storms.

'If you want your creations to have fire, Prom, then fire they shall have,' decreed the king of heaven, sending lightning bolts to ignite forests, his platinum eyes glinting as the air thickened with acrid smoke and the screams of the dying.

Time passed with no sign of Helios, so earth turned colder and darker. Since they'd learnt the sun rose and set on a fairly regular basis, this abrupt departure distressed the hardy survivors, who huddled together, demanding celestial intervention.

'This is a catastrophe,' said Hephaestus, 'so I'd better have my flame back.'

'Not possible, short of destroying Gaia, so Zeus will have

no choice but to bear it. You'll see. I am the god of foresight, after all—'

Before he could finish boasting, a thunderbolt fractured the rock he was sitting on and the resulting splinters killed those nearby mortals who'd not already been scorched to death. The god of fire put a comforting arm around his friend's shoulders, but he threw it off, his mouth twisting with the effort of not crying.

'I don't think Zeus *will* bear it,' said Hephaestus. 'Come on, let's get it over with.'

The Summons

The evening air was so heavy that a hush had fallen over everything and everyone on earth. Exhausted by the heat, Hephaestus sat near a mountain stream and removed his leg support, rubbing his chafed flesh. He slid into the cold water and floated on his back, wishing he could stay there.

'If you get a move on,' said Prometheus, waving a sack, 'we'll manage a bite to eat.'

'What have you got?'

'Ripe figs, curds, comb of honey, drop of wine. A last supper before our destiny is revealed to us.'

Hephaestus hauled himself from the stream and sat in the shade of a crag where he gladly accepted the warm, sweet food. 'What do you think will happen?' he asked, pausing between mouthfuls of fig.

'I have no idea, but we're both immortal,' said Prometheus, full of bravado, 'so how bad can it be?'

Not wanting to envisage how bad it could be, Hephaestus stood up and brushed the crumbs from himself. 'Come on, we'd better face the music.'

~

The pair trooped into the palace, glancing at the crescent of empty thrones as they crossed the great hall to kneel before the almighty, whose head was swathed in purple clouds. On their journey up the mountain, the god of foresight had agonised, not about himself, but his charges. How would they cope without the sacred flame if it were taken away? How would they cope with any divine punishment? How would they cope if their creator were sent to Tartarus?

Hephaestus, on the other hand, was heartily sick of hearing about them and was more concerned about himself and his fellow god. He had no desire to spend eternity dangling from a long chain. Either way, they'd soon find out.

The greatest god addressed them in thunderous tones.

'Is this your doing, blacksmith, letting the mortals have your magic after I forbade it?'

Wary of lying, but reluctant to cause further trouble for his friend, the smith concentrated on the mosaic floor.

Prometheus spoke up. 'This is solely my doing. When I gave man my breath, I gave him something of me, but…' He faltered before going on. 'I wanted him to have more, so I stole fire against your wishes. It was wrong, I agree, but the divine flame has lit his imagination. That has to be a good thing. Why should such a wondrous element be reserved for the gods?'

The almighty flushed to match the clouds overhead. Would he wipe out the mortals in a jealous rage? Hopefully not, but the god of foresight was pushing his luck and shouldn't rely on his status as favourite.

'Heph,' continued Zeus, as if no one had spoken, 'when you created these fellows, did you give them something of yourself? The higher-quality ones have thrived while most of Prom's efforts have died. Fair enough, he breathed souls into them, but you've given them your skills. See…' he urged them to go and look.

Cautiously, they surveyed the world, whose inhabitants had progressed to fashioning rudimentary bowls, tools and weapons. In the short time since the rebel gods had left, mankind had evolved from bashing each other with stone clubs to bashing each other with bronze hammers. Some had harnessed an odd-looking implement to a horse and were scratching furrows in a field.

The greatest god harrumphed. 'Granted, when they were innocent, they were stupid but amusing and quite lovable, particularly those made in Prom's image.' On that note, he squeezed his protégé, who reddened. 'I've grown somewhat fond of them myself, but they've learnt a considerable amount already, and who knows where it will end? Not me, and I'm in charge around here!'

Indeed, men did excel at learning and striving. They were far busier than any god, including the industrious ones. What was their hurry? Being mortal was the hurry. Not living for thousands of years meant cramming in as much as possible during their allotted span and not knowing the length of that span must lend speed to their hands and minds.

Zeus thought for a while and the young gods stepped back to avoid the fizzing thunderbolts that always accompanied such thinking, watching them plummet to earth instead. Helios soon departed and the sky darkened as lightning forked down, scorching forests and sending men fleeing for caves and warrens. Now the earthlings possessed fire, the king of heaven appeared relieved he could let himself go properly.

When the almighty's period of contemplation ended, he returned to his throne, Helios came out of hiding and the men emerged from their shelters, bowing and pouring libations. Zeus regarded the wayward gods, all the while drumming his fingers.

'You're very dear to me,' he said, beaming at his pet, 'but I can't allow this transgression to pass unpunished. Sit down, Heph. Prom, remain standing. Three times you've betrayed my trust: first by giving life to clay, second by giving fire to mortals in spite of my express orders and third by sharing the secret of metalwork. However much it pains me, I have to make an example of you.'

Zeus whistled for his owls. On command, the sky dome opened and they flew out to deliver his summons. When the other Olympians arrived, they stationed themselves on their thrones. Once the entire pantheon was set to bear witness, the lesser divinities coursed in until the hall was filled with giants, nymphs and monsters. The hall of the gods was both fuller and quieter than ever before. Epimetheus turned up late, mimed an apology and wedged himself in between Hera and Aphrodite.

After hearing a summary of the charges, the assembled deities were unusually solemn, and even the Satyrs, Centaurs and Maenads were subdued. Only after the judgment was there any sound. The accused remained silent, but many of those present wept, including Epimetheus. The sentence was more than anyone could abide, even a god, and so pitiless that it raised eyebrows amongst the Furies. Hephaestus approached the almighty, knelt and seized his knees.

'Please, this is too extreme…' he looked at his friend, who stared straight ahead. Why would the king of heaven punish his favourite so badly? It made no sense. No god could withstand such torment but the wounded god could. He'd been in agony from his birth day onwards and was used to it. 'Mightiest of mighties, I realise someone has to be punished, so will you permit me to be proxy?'

The greatest god brightened visibly. 'A proxy, you say? Hmm, it might work.' His eyes glittered as he considered this offer. 'I'll consent to it. Swap over at once!'

Prometheus shook his head. 'You will not take my place, Heph. This is my doing and I accept my penance. All the pain in the universe is worth it, and I would do it again,' he said, marching towards the door.

When would the god of foresight learn to keep his trap shut? Shoulders drooping, Hephaestus took a final look at the pantheon then went to the forge to pick up a few bits and pieces, dawdling while he pretended to search for his beetle and wedges. Outside, Prometheus was gnawing on a cuticle, no doubt fretting over the mortals' fate more than his own. Most gods would have taken the chance to run away, but not this one, who seemed to crave martyrdom.

Why would a deity sacrifice himself to save a few measly men? Perhaps these creations were not just playthings to his friend. Hephaestus doted on his gilded girls and tripods, especially the tripod that slept at the foot of his bed, but they were only animated machinery, whereas these little scraps of clay had souls as well as their own belief systems, hopes and dreams. Unlike most of the other animals, they lifted their eyes to the heavens, gazing at the stars, observing the celestial siblings changing place at the open and close of each day, maybe imagining themselves reflections of the gods in their firmament.

'Are you ready?' he asked Prometheus.

The god of foresight nodded. Side by side, in silence, the two friends trudged down Mount Olympus.

The Sentence

The two gods journeyed to the Caucasus Mountains by land and by sea. Not once did monster, god or giant stand in their path. Zeus must want his favourite punished so badly that he'd prevented any interruption in the voyage towards the dreadful fate. The route was lined by mortals, and to a man, they fell on one knee to worship their saviour. The modest deity walked on, head bowed, hand covering his heart, acknowledging his creations. Hephaestus could not bring himself to look at them, knowing what he must shortly do to their guardian.

They arrived on the far shore of the Black Sea, crossed the scorching sands before reaching a welcome canopy of shady pines, and headed for the foothills.

Their ascent of Mount Caucasus was prolonged by the lame god dragging his foot more than usual. Halfway up, the pain became excruciating but he kept going. It was nothing, considering what his friend was about to endure. To overcome his suffering, he slowed his breathing, which slowed his pulse until he was moving and thinking at the speed of the mountain. His bare feet felt the force of Gaia straining to push ever higher.

The god of foresight beckoned him. 'There's no point putting it off, unless your ankle troubles you?'

'I'm fine,' he lied, forcing a smile. 'Come on, we're nearly on the last leg.'

The stark terrain of Caucasus was entirely different to that of homely and comforting Olympus, although Helios shone dutifully, offering warmth and solace. When they'd dragged themselves to the summit, the blacksmith scouted about until he found a suitable ledge. Jutting out above a jagged range, it overlooked the water, which sparkled like a dark sapphire. A pleasing aspect might provide a useful distraction so he paced it out and waved to Prometheus, who was leaning against the crag.

'How about here, Prom, so you can see the sea?' As if a view could take anyone's mind off what was coming.

'Thank you, brother.'

Evidently, he didn't care either way and no doubt if chained facing the bare rock, the victim would consent without a murmur.

'I wish you wouldn't submit to this. Why not appeal against the ruling or ask for a clumsier executioner, who might fail?'

'No appeal. No clumsy executioner. You'll do a clean job. That's why you were chosen – well, that and to torture you too – but there will be no reprieve for either of us, so let's get it over and done with.'

For someone blessed with foresight, Prometheus had some strange notions. Eternity meant this punishment would never be over and done with. In a futile attempt to delay the inevitable, Hephaestus tarried with his work, taking an age to hammer chains to the rock while the prisoner flicked moss off the ridge beside him.

The bloodthirsty king of heaven had stipulated not only shackles but also wedges through hands, feet and torso to reduce the risk of escape. This was unnecessary brutality as the captive had no intention of absconding and had accepted his sentence passively. Doubtless, he'd stay put and shoulder whatever came without attempting to move, but the almighty had insisted. Hephaestus offered his wineskin for a drink but this was politely declined.

'I'm ready, Heph. Do it now.'

Bracing himself, the smith hefted his beetle to hammer the first wedge through Prometheus' palm and into the stone. In unskilled hands, this job would have been gory, but he drove it in with a single blow, so not a drop of ichor was shed. When the second wedge pierced Prometheus' right hand and the third went through his crossed feet, there was no scream, no cry.

What more hateful task could there be, but what more loving? As he thrust the fourth and final wedge into his left flank, the light left the martyr's eyes. Relieved, Hephaestus drew the chains crosswise and secured them, hoping that deep slumber would obviate the coming terror. That hope was destroyed when the captive spoke.

'Leave me, Heph, please. There's no need for you to bear witness.'

'There's every need for me to bear witness.'

He could have stopped him – should have stopped him – but hadn't foreseen such a hideous penance. Belatedly, it occurred to him that as god of foresight, his friend must have known this would be the outcome, yet he'd proceeded regardless and given fire to man. Defiant to the last, the prisoner turned his face to Olympus. Good. If Zeus wanted to hand down such a cruel penalty, then he would be forced to behold what he had ordained.

'I refuse to abandon you,' Hephaestus said, bedding himself in for the night as the sun sank over the sea.

When setting Helios brushed against rising Selene, monstrous wingbeats gathered in the air and twin eagles ascended, finger-like feathers silhouetted in black against the red sky. They landed lightly and their claws clicked across the ledge.

When their curved beaks rended tender belly flesh, screams flooded the valleys, echoing and magnifying until the peaks echoed with a million shrieking gods. Oblivious, the pitiless birds continued tearing into their carrion, and ichor ran freely, soaking their white ruffs.

Drops of golden blood pooled on the barren crags and small flowers bloomed: saffron crocuses springing up on double stems, petals as orange as fire but veined with the scarlet sap of mortal blood.

Wishing whole-heartedly that he could have swapped places, Hephaestus turned away from his friend, instead watching hundreds of the curious blossoms budding in the moonlight.

Unrelenting, the voracious raptors persisted in their sanguine duty throughout the night, their victim's cries fading gradually until they were no more than the moans of an ailing child.

Mercifully, the first finger of sunlight appeared from the eastern horizon, and sated on divine flesh, the eagles unfurled their wings, flapping slowly as they took flight, wheeling high above the mountains.

The strengthening sun revealed the gaping wound. Prometheus' head lolled to the side, chin against shoulder. No longer was he moaning and his breaths were less laboured. Merciful Hypnos at work but only his brother, Thanatos, could bestow real respite from this torment. Hephaestus snorted at his own naivety. Death was a luxury denied the gods.

Finally, the wound was dry, and under the soothing beams of Selene, Prometheus raised his head. Pale and wretched, the boy had gone, and in his stead was a man with terrible wisdom in his eyes.

Warmth. Knowledge. Inspiration. Why deprive mankind of these qualities? Why shouldn't mortals be equal to immortals? Why *did* the almighty begrudge them divine fire?

It didn't cost Zeus anything, so he must be driven by resentment and fear of being outshone. There weren't enough hours in eternity to catalogue the Olympians' faults, but jealousy and vanity must top the list.

'Don't despair, Prom, as Zeus may forgive you eventually. After all, you did hold back from giving mankind eternal life.'

'I'm not despairing, and I *did* give them eternal life, after a fashion.' He paused, contorted with pain. 'Fire in the soul makes the mortals fast, brave and clever, so their noble deeds and works will live on after them, making them immortal that way.'

A pleasant enough fancy, but there was little benefit to be gained from immortality if you weren't alive to enjoy it. Still, Prometheus' heart was in the right place, Hephaestus supposed. In fact, he could almost *see* his heart, but at least his liver was regrowing, helping to restore some of his friend's former passion.

'Not the same, though, is it?' asked the god of fire, gently.

'No,' conceded Prometheus, 'it's not the same.'

Hephaestus maintained the vigil as his fellow god's umbles vanished beneath a newly forming membrane. Slowly, a layer of skin grew over the new liver, thickening a little with every heartbeat. When the sun set for the third time, there was no sign of any injury.

'Leave me, Heph, I can tolerate it. The second devouring won't be so bad. Return home and care for my men. I suppose they'll die out soon…'

'I can keep an eye on them for you but a solution will suggest itself. You *do* have the gift of foresight.'

'For all the good it's done me.' The weary deity smiled grimly. 'Ouranus knows, I'll have plenty of opportunity to think. Go, Heph. Please.'

The god of fire cupped his friend's face. 'I'm sorry, but I won't desert you.'

'Don't waste your life grieving. My mortals have the whisper of knowledge, along with light and warmth. It was worth it.'

The sun bade a silent farewell as the god of foresight's eyes closed and Hephaestus wondered at the damage to his soul, never mind his body.

'Nothing is worth this, Prom. I shouldn't have let you do it.'

'You couldn't have done anything to prevent me from stealing fire. I'd have found another means to achieve my ends. Now, go home.'

Hephaestus preferred to stay but the choice was taken from him when his friend called upon the almighty to summon Hermes, who arrived to the sound of beating wings.

As the messenger and his reluctant passenger departed, the heinous birds flew towards their prey and the night filled with screams once more.

Hephaestus looked backwards. Under Selene's leaden light hanged a wounded giant, chained to a desolate mountain peak at the far reaches of the world for all time.

The god of foresight was wrong. Each devouring would not be easier. Each devouring would be harder. Each devouring would be weighted with the memory of all those that had gone before it.

Part II

A Vision

In the middle of the night, a clamouring awoke the mortals, who went outside to find Zeus trying to couple with Selene until the modest goddess cloaked herself in shadow and the almighty gave up. Listening to the men's wails, Hephaestus thought of Prometheus on the barren mountain and realised guiltily he was overdue a visit. It was upsetting thinking of the diabolical punishment but seeing it was unbearable. Part of him didn't want to go, but he couldn't let his fellow deity suffer alone, and he summoned Hermes to take him to Mount Caucasus.

At the summit, the first thing he saw was ichor flowing and the peculiar twin-stemmed crocuses blossoming thickly. He crossed the crag and examined the martyr's five wounds. His condition defied description. Of all the Olympians, only the blacksmith had withstood pain from infancy, but it was nothing compared to this. The god of foresight was wise in so many ways but lacked the guile needed to spare himself, or the desire. This self-sacrifice on behalf of mortals made no sense. For his part, Prometheus seemed oblivious to his visitor's presence and stared across the bleak miles, eyes flickering as though watching flames. Hephaestus touched his upper arm and gently dripped nectar into his mouth, dabbing at the spillage.

'What do you see, Prom? What is it?'

'A vision…' he replied in a hoarse voice.

'Continue, if you can.'

'Zeus searching for Thetis. Intent on…' This short speech exhausted him.

It was obvious what the king of heaven was intent on, and despite being the prospective victim of a serial offender, the seawitch stood to lose a great deal at the hands of jealous Hera but also from Eurynome. The creatrix had banished her vexatious husband to the underworld, but only after kicking him so hard he'd parted company with his teeth. It was awful to think of any harm coming to Thetis and this conundrum needed careful consideration. Deep in contemplation, he perched on the ledge and gazed out to sea. Slowly, a plan took shape. It had several flaws but would have to do.

'Prom,' he said. 'I've worked out how to protect my foster-mother from being raped *and* have you released from this misery. It means bringing Zeus here, but you mustn't address him. Instead, agree with everything I say. Can you do that?' To prevent any objections to being rescued, he hurried on. 'If not for your sake, for Thetis?'

As the god of foresight's last reserve drained from him, he was too weary to disagree, and in this case, silence was taken to mean assent.

Just before Helios rose, in the coldest, darkest portion of the night when everything that drew breath was at its weakest – whether mortal, beast, monster or god – Hephaestus returned to Caucasus, accompanied by a credulous king of heaven. It had required days and nights of bargaining, but here they were on the high ledge, conveyed by Zephyr. The eagles had almost finished their bloody work, which was fortuitous timing. With his wound so fresh, Prometheus wouldn't be able to speak or, more importantly, contradict. The birds took flight as the dawn sun limned the peak, revealing the prisoner sagging so the wooden stakes tore into him more than was strictly necessary. His right flank lay open to the world. How could anyone bear such cruelty? Even Zeus had the decency to recoil when brought face to face with his emaciated victim. Hopefully, that would make the forthcoming duplicity easier to get away with.

'I have heard your revelation,' said the almighty. Is it true?'

Prometheus was as close to death as any immortal might ever come. He remained motionless, unable to utter a word, which suited the plotting blacksmith's ulterior motive. Unfortunately, the greatest god was not content with this state of affairs.

'Give him succour to loosen his tongue.'

Obediently, Hephaestus soaked a sponge with sour wine and raised it to the visionary's mouth. He sucked feebly, lips cracked and throat constricted.

'Tell me if this is true,' said Zeus. 'Talk to me, boy.'

Only a croak emerged, then Prometheus nodded once and lost consciousness.

'There you have it,' said Hephaestus. 'He may be many things, but Prom's no liar.'

Zeus considered the evidence. 'Thief of fire. Disobedient servant. Betrayer of benefactor. But you're right, Heph. Liar, he is not.'

At this, the almighty peered deep into Hephaestus, who slowed his heartbeat, knowing that he wasn't much of a liar either, especially under such soul-searching scrutiny. Bringing all his might to bear, he played out the vision in his mind's eye, but included an epilogue: Zeus succeeding in his quest to rape Thetis, who grew large with child and birthed the pretender to the Olympian throne. The greatest god was ever conscious of how he'd overthrown Cronus, who'd overthrown Ouranos prior to that. Antiquity was littered with tales of sons eclipsing fathers, dethroning them and ending the existing order, as regular as the waves of the sea.

The king of heaven had innumerable sons born of divine

mothers but did not fear these offspring. Nevertheless, Zeus' history was also his destiny so he was subject to fate in the same way as his ancestors. Even for the immortals, dominion was not forever, and the current king must one day surrender his crown. This fear was a weakness and therefore easy to exploit. Hephaestus forged the son of Thetis in his mind, as solid an artefact as if cast in bronze. Powerful. Beautiful. Colossal. Mightier than Zeus, this ultimate deity would rule over all. The strain of the deceit made the false prophet shake and it was a blessing when his interrogator's eyes closed against the image of the blasphemous son who would depose him.

The almighty dismissed the vision with a blink. 'Never mention this again.' He patted the wounded captive. 'I forgive your crime, Prom, and give thanks for your prescience. You are free to go but remain under sentence and will report to me every seven days. In addition, you will wear a ring to remind you that you are my prisoner. Put it on the finger that contains the vein to the heart. Heph can make it.' He sighed deeply. 'Enough. I have to visit Thetis.'

This was distressing news. Had all his effort been in vain and was his foster-mother to be raped after all?

Zeus held up a hand for silence. 'I go to the seawitch with compassion and pure intentions, but she has to hear it from me that she will never lie with a male god. I refuse to be unseated by a divine son of hers. On a final note, ensure you leave before my eagles reappear. They are fated to return in perpetuity and I am powerless to call them off. Zephyr, take me to the grotto.'

Shortly after dawn, sunlight warmed the air and pinked the sky. Prometheus' liver had regenerated, and with good fortune, his innards would never again see the light of day. Soon, it should be possible to extract the wedges and escape.

When some colour was restored to Prometheus' gaunt face,

Hephaestus eased out a wedge but panicked at the amount of ichor and the thousands of new crocuses suddenly blooming. He pushed the wedge back in and decided to wait until the wound to his flank was fully healed. In theory, immortals could not die, but no god had endured such prolonged torture, so it was not a risk he was prepared to take.

In the late afternoon of the third day, Hephaestus successfully removed the wedges, relieved that there was only a thin trickle of golden lifeblood and not too many new flowers. At least these would be the last of their kind to grow here. Once his labour was over, he laid the unconscious deity amidst the blossoms, framing him in their curious petals, hopeful that they had some curative properties. Prometheus was quite beautiful, if somewhat frail. No wonder Zeus favoured him so.

It would be wise to let him rest ahead of summoning Hermes. While waiting, he considered picking the strange flowers, in case they did have some medicinal benefit, but as these crocuses had sprung from suffering, they were best left behind.

When he regained consciousness, Prometheus marvelled at his immaculate hands, but his expression soon changed.

'Heph, what have you done? You can't liberate me. What one Olympian commands, another may not undo. You grasp that better than most.'

'The king of heaven himself made a pact and pronounced your freedom. Think back.'

'Yes, he was here, he… Zeus forgave me?'

'Indeed,' said Hephaestus.

'But why?'

'All you need to know is that Thetis is safe from rape, and you're free from eternal torment, except for a bit of nonsense about some jewellery.'

'I don't understand.'

The god of fire laughed, but kindly. 'You don't have to understand. The pact means you can never discuss your vision. Not with Zeus. Not with Thetis. Not with me. Not with anyone.'

'But—'

'Ah-ah.' Hephaestus held a stubby forefinger to his lips. 'Say no more.' He checked the sky, which Helios had stained crimson, but it was darkening with every second that passed. 'We should get going before those hellish birds turn up.'

When the sun took his leave, wingbeats echoed through the warm night. The convalescent was too fragile for a journey with Hermes but Zeus must have taken pity as Zephyr soon arrived and Hephaestus carried his friend to the West Wind's chariot, cradling him in his arms as they were wafted homewards, whisked within a whisper of the eagles flying blindly towards Caucasus.

Upon discovering their prey gone, the raptors' frightful screech circled the mountains and Prometheus shuddered at the sight of his old station. Surely to Ouranus the god of foresight had suffered enough. Nobody could have sacrificed more. Did the mortals know or even care about the debt they owed their altruistic creator? Of course, Prometheus was not concerned about mankind's opinion of him. Alone amongst the immortals, he didn't demand prayers or tributes. Not for him the burnt offerings and entrails of slaughter, the poured libations of milk and honey, the tithes of fruit and grain. With no hope of reward, he'd laid down his life simply so men could be warmed by the divine flame.

As they flew low over the sea, a waterspout rose and cut through the surf, racing along the shore, churning up shipwrecks, rocks and skeletons in its wake. So, the verdict had been served on Thetis. For reasons she must never know, the seawitch could not marry a male deity or conceive his child. Hephaestus felt a pang of remorse that his foster-mother had to pay the price for his friend's freedom, but how bad could it be?

She'd shown no interest in men thus far and appeared settled with Eurynome, so it seemed a small price and one she would be happy to pay. In the unlikely event she did want a man, she could have a mortal husband and children, and although she would lose them, after loss would come more love. Her life might be filled with a million men and their offspring. In time, her initial sorrow would fade and the joyful mother would give birth to multitudes down the ages.

A Beautiful Evil

After rescuing the two gods from Mount Caucasus, the West Wind took his passengers straight to the palace. The god of foresight rubbed his flank ruefully before alighting from the chariot and entering the great hall. The Olympians were ensconced on their thrones, apart from Athena, who was busy working a loom. Hephaestus was careful to keep his left leg on the side facing away from Aphrodite.

'Ah, Prom,' said the king of heaven, looking up from a groaning platter, 'you're back, so let's say no more about that unfortunate incident, eh?'

As pardons went, it fell a little short on majesty, but Prometheus was never known to stand on ceremony. 'Thank you, gracious Zeus,' he replied blithely, as if his time on Caucasus had never happened.

The greatest god accepted these thanks with a nod. 'It seems to me that your mortals are having far too much fun. It's impractical to retrieve fire from them so I'm inclined to punish them in some other way instead.' He shook his head to silence Prometheus, who was about to protest. 'I know what they're missing,' he said, indicating the vacant throne next to him. 'In the unlikely event you're wondering where your mother is,

Heph, she's having one of her "heads". I've been married scarcely a minute, but already it feels as though a whole epoch has passed.' He waved at the window on the world. 'See that lot down there. Nothing better to do than wine, dine and frolic.'

Below, was a swarm of naked mortals, who were indeed frolicking, their burnished skins sweating under the blazing sun.

The queen of heaven sauntered into the hall, perched on her throne and slipped her feet into her husband's lap.

'Isn't it typical,' she remarked, 'you are the supreme being, yet who do the blessed creatures worship? Helios, because he's easier on the eye and makes them feel so happy.'

'They won't be happy for much longer,' said Zeus, spitefully. 'Why should they have all the fun? If they wish to live like deities, they should enjoy all aspects of the divine experience. They have fire, so let them try marriage next. Let's see how frolicsome they are once they have wives and children to contend with.' He studied his own wife before continuing, rather grandly. 'An evil gift is what they need. A veritable plague on men! A female foil should give them plenty to complain about. Heph, you are to create her.'

Marriage and family were everything the lonely blacksmith wanted so this sounded more of a reward than a punishment to him. It was a good idea, though. While the kings had imposed some order and deterred a few murders, misadventure still caused many deaths, and this new mortal should save the bother of replenishing the population.

'What's up, Prom?' asked Zeus.

'You'll ruin their lives,' Prometheus objected. 'They're perfectly content gambolling about.'

The king of heaven beamed. 'Of course they are, and who wouldn't be content gambolling with creatures modelled on you? But unless you and your friend plan to spend eternity fashioning new pets, they'll die out before too long. Alternatively, it might be kinder to put them out of their misery now.' He extricated himself from his wife and joined his favourite at the window. 'Say the word, Prom. What'll it be, eh? Flood? Lava? Drought? You name it.' Ignoring his favourite's horrified expression, he ruffled his hair and went on. 'Better than letting them dwindle to death. The poor things grow old and feeble so quickly.' He wagged a finger. 'Heph, it isn't like you to build something with a fatal flaw.'

Hephaestus didn't quite know how to reply but he was spared by the god of foresight.

'It's not a flaw! They die by design so they make the most of life. It's the nature of loss. Their short lives have value.' He gestured at the pantheon, slumped on their thrones, moving occasionally to drop a carcass into their jaws or pour a pitcher of nectar down their gullets. 'I didn't want them to be as lazy and unmotivated as the gods.' In response to rumblings from the Olympians, he held up a hand to staunch their complaints. 'I meant no offence. We're indolent because we have all the time in the world.' His shoulders sagged. 'But you're right, we should mitigate against either Heph or I becoming… incapacitated.'

'Excellent. I'm so glad you agree.' Zeus flopped onto his throne. 'Heph, your handiwork will guarantee the survival of mortalkind. Here's what I—' He broke off as Hera returned her feet to his lap.

Since the greatest god hadn't been involved in creating the original mortals, he appeared determined to atone for this omission. His wife tapped her toes while he reeled off his long list of requirements.

'Milk bags,' he said, cupping his hands before him then holding them out further until he noticed Athena's glare. 'Breasts, I mean. These should be functional but also beautiful so both father and child are equally keen to sup. She must fulfil every need. Clavicle: delicate. Throat: soft. Neck: able to hold up her head but unable to withstand the clasp of man.'

The goddess of war rose from her loom, veins throbbing at her temples, but the almighty hurried on.

'This individual will possess wiles aplenty to outwit men so she doesn't require his physical strength or size.' He stalled his daughter. 'If she's too big and strong, the entire race risks fighting itself into extinction so this mortal *has* to be weaker.' As Hera's toes found a tender spot, Zeus swallowed and dabbed his watering eyes. 'Yes, weaker, and therefore co-operative, and in return, she'll gain the protection of her superiors.'

He stood up, pacing the room while he declaimed. 'Her skull can be small since she won't serve in the civic sphere. Mankind is to have dominion over her as he has dominion over the beasts.' After a scowl from Athena he conceded that the woman could have higher status than the beasts.

'But she will have a brain, yes?' demanded the goddess of war. 'Or is she to be no more than a gormless automaton?'

'Rest assured, she will be capable of accomplishing simple tasks, such as reproduction, but she won't be as clever as you, my industrious child.' He leaned towards Hephaestus and lowered his voice, 'We can't afford to have a female warrior roaming the earth, but a tiny brain should do no harm.'

'What size shall it be?' The blacksmith held out his left hand as if holding a walnut and his right a cantaloupe.

The king of heaven opted for the walnut. 'This piece of clay shouldn't be entirely empty headed and she'll be amused by trifles. Her interests should be restricted to serving her betters, so her hands must have sufficient dexterity to oblige her master and raise his progeny, but not enough for metalwork. That magic is reserved for the male population, and it irks me that *they* have metal, without letting a woman loose on it.' He patted his bottom lip while deliberating over his list. 'In fairness, she should have another quality, but what?' He turned his back on the queen of heaven. 'How about the allure of Aphrodite: impossible to resist and as dangerous as sweet poison?' Both gods looked at the goddess of love, who was busy picking apart a lamb. 'What else?'

'A tongue?' suggested Aphrodite, with a mouthful of meat.

'Hmm. Best avoided in light of the mischief caused by gossip, but then, there are compensations.' He glanced hopefully at his wife, who laughed nastily. 'Yes, Heph, furnish her with a tongue, a nimble one at that. It would be wrong to deny mortal men that pleasure.'

Down on earth, several fortunate mortals were currently receiving that very same pleasure from their fellows, and a particularly fortunate mortal was managing it all by himself.

'But try to stop her from talking,' said the almighty.

Tying a tongue was fairly easy, but Hephaestus considered silent Eurynome and Selene, who heard everyone's secrets but never spoke. 'Perhaps her children might enjoy hearing stories from her?'

'Very well, but she doesn't need oratory powers for storytelling. Grant her a modicum of speech so she can entertain infants and please man, but not so much she irritates him. There again, she's intended to be an irritant, so give her plenty of tongue. Why should I suffer alone?'

'Do you think I was born yesterday?' exclaimed Hera. 'This creature isn't designed to punish anyone. You've just discovered a way to extend the herd for your personal satisfaction. Well, two can play at that game.'

'Speaking of suffering,' said Zeus, ignoring her. 'You are excused from this venture, Prom. Go home and rest.' When Prometheus tried to argue, the greatest god raised his voice. 'That is an order! Heph, stay there. I have a few more instructions before you get to work.'

After listening to the king of heaven's instructions, which went into extensive – and, it had to be said, prurient – detail, Hephaestus was at the claypit, modelling a figure based on the goddesses. While intended as retribution against mankind, this woman would ultimately ensure the perpetuation of the species. He wondered why this idea hadn't occurred to his friend at the outset. Possibly because he was the only god immune to Aphrodite's substantial charms.

The brain still worried him because, if the female was to

be slighter than her male counterpart, her skull would have less volume. For a while, he experimented with the clay, pressing and rolling it until, with clever coiling, he could pack the same amount of matter into the smaller skull. How would he face Athena or Thetis if his creation were no more than a humble helpmeet without two brain cells to rub together?

Aesthetic appeal was easy and he made the doll in the image of Aphrodite, running wet fingers over the clay, shaping and refining. His blood warmed at the thought of her naked form and he had to concentrate hard on her other features, scattering flecks of flame in her green eyes, the rising hue of Helios in her tumbling locks, and the shade of his setting in her lips.

For a final flourish, he brushed her hide with gold dust. She was somewhat bare. Beard or chest hair were hardly essential when staying warm at home, creating babies, but something was missing. It would be difficult to entice men away from each other, so he thatched her here and there, under her arms and between her legs, to carry her musk. Satisfied, he smoothed her belly, unmarked by a navel. The first mortal woman.

'Not bad. Not bad, at all,' he said, 'if I do say so myself.'

All the Gifts

The god of fire returned to the palace, followed by twenty tripods, their leader draped in a sheet. The Olympians were all present, sitting up straight for a change. Hephaestus commanded the tripods to stop before the crescent of thrones. As the procession halted, the king of heaven stood up and jabbed a finger at the leading tripod.

'Done already, Heph? She must be rough around the edges.'

There was nothing rough about Hephaestus' work, and nothing that could fairly be described as an edge, but there was no point arguing when his masterpiece would speak for itself, so he whipped away the sheet.

Zeus leaned low, greedy eyes swooping up and down the curves of the latest creation. 'She is the model of Aphrodite, is she not?' he leered.

'She is,' said Hephaestus, hating the fact that the almighty knew this.

After inspecting her thoroughly, inside and out, the greatest god declared himself pleased. 'But why isn't she breathing?' he asked. 'Where are the Four Winds? Oh, forget them. Prom, you do the honours, with my blessing this time.'

Zeus watched fondly as his favourite approached the tripod. Prometheus sucked in his breath and picked up the figure with his left hand so his patron could admire his ring. Slowly, he breathed into the clay woman. The gods congregated to watch her chest rise and fall, and there was an appreciative silence until the goddess of love broke it.

'I admit she looks good but that's no surprise when you take into account the inspiration.' She side-eyed Hephaestus. 'Although I dread to think how you know my proportions so intimately. But when you get down to it, she's no more than a useless lump of clay.'

To avoid Aphrodite's gaze, the blushing blacksmith peered intently through the window on the world. Below, men romped in water, rutted in forests and reclined under Helios, pleasuring themselves in ones, twos, threes and dozens.

'They do seem very keen on each other,' he noted, wondering if he should have thatched the female mortal more thoroughly.

The king of heaven eyed the nubile form. 'Hmm, you may have a point. We must bait the hook. What else can we give her?'

'Wisdom. Personality. Fire.' Athena circled the tripod, counting off traits. 'Judgement. Cunning. Bravery.'

The greatest goddess rose from her throne and added to the list. 'Fidelity. Sagacity. Curiosity. The latter is essential, because in my experience, a questioning nature seldom went amiss in a marriage.'

'That's not quite what I meant,' said Zeus, 'and besides, it's rather a burden to load onto such a delicate creature. Plus, it might put the men off.'

'Trust me, nothing's going to put them off, so she needs clothes.' Athena flicked an appraising eye over Hera. 'You can't toss her down there as if she's a morsel of meat. Have you seen that priapic horde? I'll get weaving while I decide what other traits to bestow. A keen intelligence for a start.'

'She won't need it,' said Hephaestus, continuing her

thread. 'I've already installed a small brain to help her raise children and so on.'

'A small brain?' jeered the goddess of war. 'Lucky, lucky girl. Well, she's definitely going to have intelligence, and plenty of it.'

The greatest god pulled a face. 'Is that wise? Somewhat wasteful for a toy.'

'A toy?' She fixed her father with a hard look. 'Do you consider *me* a mere plaything?' She snorted. 'If your plan is to make men's lives as miserable as your own…' She paused to stare down Hera. 'Then you have to give them someone to sharpen their wits on.'

Abashed, the almighty capitulated. 'Daughter, you are endlessly wise. Beauty isn't enough on its own and she does require other qualities.' He gesticulated at the pantheon. 'Each of you must provide a birth day present. Heph and Prom, consider yourselves excused as we don't want her to have foresight or metalworking skills.' He snapped his fingers. 'Awake!'

At the sound, the newborn opened her eyes, saw the deities and bawled, flailing her arms and legs, revealing some of Hephaestus' more intricate workmanship.

'Hungry, little one?' said Athena, dripping nectar into her mouth, which soothed her and stilled her limbs, much to the chagrin of several of the more lascivious gods. 'What were you thinking, Heph?' she asked, shielding the naked mortal with her own body. 'You should have animated her earlier so she was prepared before inflicting the entire pantheon on her.' Of course, the poor soul had no control over her bodily functions, and with surprising gentleness, Athena cleansed her before pressing a fingertip to her forehead. 'I grant you intellect, wisdom, needle skills, and war in your heart.' Because she'd been granted knowledge, the mortal looked up, bright with intelligence. The goddess tucked her into her tunic, stalked to the loom and threaded it with silks. 'Watch carefully,' she said, 'and someday you'll be a fine weaver, too.'

Before long, Athena had woven a square of silver fabric and stitched it into a miniature gown, which glittered as it moulded to its dainty owner's form. The garment looked suspiciously similar to the type favoured by the queen of heaven, who huffed at the sight of it.

Hera's wasn't the only nose put out of joint, and Aphrodite glared at Hephaestus, but what did she expect him to do, ignore the almighty's instructions? It was beyond him how she could be jealous of a clay figure, albeit an exquisite one. Best to keep an eye out in case she got any ideas about causing her diminutive rival's untimely demise. With a jolt, he realised how sad he'd feel if anything happened to his creation, and not only because she resembled his beloved.

'Try to walk,' said Athena, placing the mortal on the floor and encouraging her to take a first clumsy step. After witnessing the ensuing spectacle, she called from her loom for help. 'Aph, come and show her how to move more elegantly.'

'What, and make her even more alluring?' sniped the goddess of love. 'I think not!'

'Suit yourself,' said Athena, still deftly weaving. 'Just so long as you don't object to someone who resembles you stumbling along like a bear interrupted from hibernation—'

'Oh, for Ouranus' sake!' Aphrodite succumbed to the jibe and crooked a finger. 'Come here.' Obediently, the woman plodded over to the beckoning goddess, who ran her fingers the length of the petite body, adjusting her posture and inclining her towards loveliness. 'Copy me,' she said, and the novice obeyed until her movements mirrored those of her lithe teacher. 'Good. Good. Better. Now, listen to this...' She murmured into the minute being's ear, until she flushed. Her tiny nipples hardened and her eyes filled with longing as secrets poured into her.

Once the ministrations of love and passion were complete, Hermes knelt down. 'Here's my gift,' he said, touching the woman's mouth.

She rubbed her lips together before opening them and uttered her first words. 'Thank you, kind god,' she squeaked.

'You're most welcome, and here are some ideas to talk about.' As Aphrodite had whispered in her right ear, so the messenger whispered in her left and a number of expressions crossed her lovely countenance, leaving it twisted in an unkind smile.

Beautiful Apollo strummed a chord on his lyre and stretched, gaining everyone's full attention before crossing the hall to grant music, dance, poetry, healing and a conscience. Afterwards, he turned slowly before the open-mouthed woman before tossing his golden mane and padding back to his throne.

Poseidon tied a pearl necklace around her throat. 'Keep this necklet intact, my pretty, and you'll never drown,' he said, running a talon down her chest and making her cry.

'The god of the sea is very free with his hands,' remarked Athena, snipping threads. She snatched up her latest handiwork, marched across the room, shoved Poseidon out of the way and smoothed a cobweb veil over the woman's head.

Hephaestus crowned her with a diadem writhing with miniscule monsters and beasts: octopuses crowding for prominence against winged horses and horned rams. Newly coronated and robed, she moved before her audience, graceful and lovely. What *had* he wrought? Before them was a creature of infinite complexity, endowed with talents from the pantheon. The men were no more than clay, whereas the future mother of their children was imbued with qualities from the best and worst of the gods. Was it fair to inflict her on the innocents below?

'Listen carefully, because *I* have two gifts for you.' Zeus ogled his commission. 'First is your name, Pandora, because I've granted you all the gifts.' He raised her up. 'You go to earth as a beautiful evil, who will destroy mankind's enjoyment of life. You are a clever deception whose beauty will blind men to your wickedness, but if they want to reproduce, they will be forced to accept you.' Ignoring his livid wife and daughter, he ploughed on. 'You will be mother to the race of man, faithful in times of plenty, but treacherous in times of paucity. While your husbands work their fingers to the bone, you will laze about, feeding your face, and—'

'Father,' shouted Athena, 'this is too much, even for you!' She cradled the terrified mortal. 'You've already tasked Pandora with populating the whole earth. Since you've given birth twice yourself, you should realise that it hardly counts as lazing about. Your problem is that you're angry at all females – goddesses and cattle alike – as they won't do your bidding. Just because you can't tame your own lust doesn't mean you get to blame your victims. A bit unreasonable of you to be cross with Pandora before she's barely had a chance to draw breath, let alone eat!' Hera gave a slow handclap and Aphrodite winked. 'To be fair,' she went on, 'if anyone's guilty of lying about stuffing himself, it's you!' For emphasis, she prodded him in the gut and he buckled slightly.

'Anyway,' said Zeus, clearing his throat. 'I haven't told Pandora about her second gift yet.'

'You'll have to wait,' said Hera. Either sufficiently infuriated by her spouse's high-handed rhetoric, or inspired by his daughter's tirade, the queen of heaven joined the fray. 'And as for not being able to resist Pandora, mankind isn't always a slave to his loins, unlike some.' Here, a scornful glance at her husband. 'These men may prosper during their short time in the sun, but without offspring, they are fated to wither and die, so we need to make sure they're happy with the mother of their children, and more importantly, that *she's* happy with them.'

With a bored air, the king of heaven tossed a few thunderbolts in Hera's direction, which she nimbly sidestepped. 'They may prefer to wither and die,' he said, 'than end up married, condemned to a life of misery and abuse—'

'You do me a grave disservice,' said the greatest goddess.

'When it comes to misery and abuse, *I* have suffered at *your* hands, and not the other way around.' She picked up Pandora and adopted a softer tone. 'You are not evil, my dear, and you will not be abusive. Rather, it will be your lot to suffer. Your progeny will grow big in your belly and cleave you at birth. You are stronger than man can ever know. You have great forbearance. You can endure immense pain. You can sacrifice yourself for the good of your children. In this, you will take after Prometheus, who sacrificed himself for the salvation of mortals.'

The Priapic Horde

Together, the pantheon escorted the first woman from Olympus, the goddesses filling her ears with sage advice. As they descended, the deities cast gargantuan shadows on earth and the inhabitants cowered.

'I bring mankind a gift,' proclaimed the king of heaven. He studied the ranks of prone mortals on the beach, who were afraid to raise their heads. 'A gift who carries within her gifts from each of the gods. Show yourself, Pandora.'

With a nudge from the almighty, she slipped from the pantheon's shadow and walked slowly into the light. Thousands of men looked up to admire the new mortal, who stood before them, petrified at the attentions of her prospective partners.

'I command you to arise,' said Zeus.

The worshippers got to their feet, quaking, and as one, inched towards their female counterpart, but before they reached their target, Athena snatched her up.

'Father, call an about turn. Have you seen them? They'll tear poor Pandora limb from limb as soon as our backs are turned.'

When he didn't reply, she stormed up the mountain, swiftly

followed by the other goddesses. With a grunt of annoyance that sent lightning forking through the air, Zeus snapped at Hermes.

'Take us back to heaven so we can learn what has upset my headstrong daughter.'

The gods arrived in the palace to find the goddesses surrounding the pale and quavering mortal.

'Athena,' panted the greatest god, 'I hope you have an explanation, unless you have an ambition to be eagle bait on Mount Caucasus?'

The goddess of war squared up to her father.

'Rescuing someone from being raped to death is reason enough, I'd say.'

At this, Zeus could only bluster.

For once, the queen of heaven stood shoulder to shoulder with her step-child. 'Quite apart from sparing an innocent from a dreadful end, your daughter has a point. You've not thought this through, have you? A mortal woman can probably birth a baby a year.' She flicked her chin towards the earth. 'That lot will be dead or past it before Pandora's birthed a dozen children. What she needs is an army.'

'Whatever do you mean?' asked Zeus, mystified.

'An army of female mortals is what I mean. Go on, Hephaestus, start work.' Hera silenced her husband with a look. 'Be sure to create plenty of them but don't take all day about it this time. Make them less like Aphrodite and more like Athena.'

'But I haven't announced my second gift,' protested the king of heaven, 'and I've yet to commission the god of fire to invent it for me.'

'As he is my son and not yours,' she replied, 'you can wait your turn.' Meanwhile, I'm going to choose a divine mate for Pandora because my son's craftsmanship is far too sophisticated to waste on mere mortals.

On hearing his mother's compliment about his work, a charge shot through Hephaestus, and to top it off, she was about to reward him with a wife! He smoothed his apron, preparing his proposal, when Epimetheus strolled in, drenched with sweat and munching on a limb from one of his animals.

'What have I missed?' he asked, looking about the great hall, leg of mutton halfway to his mouth.

Prometheus obliged by pointing. 'The greatest god's gift to mankind is what you've missed, Epi.'

When the god of afterthought finally spotted the woman, he flushed. 'I wouldn't mind some of that,' he said. 'Which lucky tyke gets her?'

Hera cupped a hand over her husband's ear, and as she whispered, a smile crept over his face. This was it, his mother had made the case, and he was to have a bride!

'As a matter of fact, Epi,' said Zeus, '*you're* the lucky tyke.'

It was hard to say who was more shocked, Pandora's future lover or her creator.

'For real?' said the astonished Epimetheus, wiping his greasy mouth on his bicep.

'For real,' said Zeus. 'Off you both go, before the blacksmith implodes and does us all a serious mischief. Speaking of which, Epi, shrink yourself before you do Pandora a serious mischief.'

'Wait.' The queen of heaven held up her hand. 'There's something we must do first. The girl has to be married to set an example to her sisters.'

This compulsory monogamy proved too much for Aphrodite and she spoke up. 'You're forcing Pandora to marry? Little point when she won't live more than a few decades. Let her couple with whoever she wants.'

Ignoring this petition for free love, Hera wondered aloud who was best placed to wed the pair.

'Who better than the blacksmith to meld two beings together against their will?' said Zeus. 'If they *must* suffer a lifetime of bondage, then they should wear rings the same as Prometheus to show they're under sentence. Heph can do the honours.'

Talk about adding insult to injury. Not only was Hephaestus' second-most hated god marrying his beloved creation but he also had to forge the rings and conduct the ceremony. To think of the wedding night Epimetheus would enjoy at his expense. With any luck, in his shrunken state, the god of afterthought would be eaten by one of his own creations.

Once the rings were cool, the happy couple held hands over the smallest anvil in the forge. Ever stoic, the reluctant celebrant tried to ignore Aphrodite's glare and proceeded with the rites.

'Feel the blood pulsing in your partner's body. Hear their heartbeat.' He thought of his own matrimonial yearnings. 'Be loyal always, and kind. Do you both agree to these terms?'

The couple agreed, gazing at each other. The ungrateful woman hadn't so much as looked at her creator since opening her eyes, which made her even more like her prototype. He bound their fingers with gold, which was good enough for these two, and pronounced them married. They'd have to consummate the marriage, but with so many onlookers it could end unpleasantly, what with gods always wanting what they couldn't have.

'Felicitations,' said Zeus, gracing the bride with a leer. 'As my wedding present, you will stay in heaven for a moon and sup on mead as guests at the palace.'

Hephaestus frowned, as the ceremony wasn't finished.

'Er, in the meantime, you may kiss.'

As the married couple joined lips, Zeus and Apollo cheered, spurring Epimetheus on to greater heights. Their libidinous encouragement was soon interrupted when Athena barged past.

'That'll do, you two.' She appealed to Hera. 'Get the newlyweds out of here, can't you?'

The greatest goddess gathered Pandora to her bosom.

'They'll remain in my private quarters, under a silk pavilion, away from prying eyes. But first, I want a word with this young lady on managing wayward husbands.'

Hephaestus took his mind off the honeymooners frisking under their pavilion by busying himself at the claypits, accompanied by the god of foresight and the goddess of war, who'd insisted on coming to help. Unfortunately, Athena was a sterner taskmaster than her father, and her idea of helping meant overseeing, fault-finding and hindering his work.

'Steady on, Heph. As your mother said, make them less curvaceous, or you'll be out of clay within minutes.'

Before replying, he reminded himself that the meddlesome goddess was the king of heaven's daughter.

'If you want to be useful, fetch me some more clay.'

'I'm not here to run your errands. If material is scarce, you'll have to cut some corners, and by corners, I mean curves. Serves you right for going mad with that batch.'

He bristled under this criticism as he appraised the batch in question. They were by far his preferred shape and he wished they were all so lovely. 'Fine. The next consignment can be shorter, which should leave some clay for spares.'

'Spares?' Athena's head whipped round so quickly it was a wonder she hadn't snapped her neck.

'You've seen how they carry on down there. The species teetered on the brink of extinction again last year. Even when they're not fractious, they're remarkably clumsy, and some of their so-called japes are positively dangerous. So we'll need a woman for every man, plus a few extra.'

Prometheus took a breather and joined the discussion.

'*Every* man? Are you certain? They seem content as they are.'

'They *were* content,' said Athena, 'but once they saw a

female, it was as plain as the… nose on your face what they wanted.'

'The novelty will soon wear off,' grumbled the god of foresight as he returned to breathing into the dolls.

'They should be much thinner,' said the goddess, brandishing a plump figurine. 'Pinch some off here and there.'

'Leave her alone,' said Hephaestus. 'She's perfect as she is.'

Athena tutted but gave way for once and handed back the figure. 'They don't all have to resemble Aphrodite. Women aren't there for men's pleasure, irrespective of what you and my father think. They're beings in their own right and should take after me, as per your mother's suggestion.' She watched him readjusting the model. 'Now, you're being ridiculous. How will she stand without pitching forwards?'

'Maybe she won't need to stand…'

'That's very unkind, Heph. How would you feel, being stuck on your back your whole life?' She held up a hand, palm forwards. 'Don't answer that.'

'I could pad her backside.' He smothered a grin, added more clay and presented the doll for inspection. 'That should balance her nicely.'

'Look, you could make two figures out of her, maybe three. Thin her out.'

The god of fire grunted. In his considered opinion, this version was lovelier than the original but Athena's eyes bored into him so he relented. He'd remove some bulk but from where it mattered less. Between breast and hip there wasn't much that was essential, so he planed her middle, creating a narrow waist. The thighs he left as they were but he slimmed down the calves and arms and made the hands and feet smaller.

'How will that poor mite hold up her head,' demanded the goddess, 'let alone carry anything?'

'She'll hold up her head because she has strength as well as grace, and her hands are deft, her fingers nimble.'

'What about childbearing? Have you left room for an infant to grow?'

'No need.' Gods, Athena was really getting on his nerves. 'Her belly will swell when she's with child and recede after birth.'

Watched over by Helios and Selene, the three deities worked side by side, bickering as they compared models and set them out to dry, visited by various goddesses who endowed those who most resembled them with favours. This worried Prometheus, who was resolute that all endowments should be shared equally, scurrying after each visiting goddess, taking what they'd given and distributing it amongst the growing population.

'Wasted effort, Prom,' said Athena. 'Thanks to you, they might have the same number of favours at the beginning, but they won't end up that way.'

'Free will means that's down to them but at least they'll have a fair start.'

The goddess of war tossed her hair. 'Or as fair a start as anyone can have when they're shorter, lighter and weaker than the other half of the population. I'll grant them additional wisdom, which should help, along with a touch of the warrior spirit.'

'But not to that group there.' Hephaestus pointed at a row who'd been visited by Artemis earlier. 'Unwise to combine hunting *and* war.'

'Why ever not?' she asked. 'What's your problem?'

'I haven't got a problem but it's a wide load for such narrow shoulders.'

'They're tall so they'll carry it off,' she said. 'Get cracking. You're taking ages.'

'Of course I am. It took me ten times as long to create Pandora as it did each male mortal. It isn't easy, making a reproductive system.'

'Tell you what, skip the wombs and so forth from now on.

Beyond me why anyone would want to have sex anyway, never mind giving birth.'

'But giving birth is the whole reason for their exis…' Seeing Athena's furious glare, he didn't finish the sentence.

'Do as I say and hurry up. You can't afford to waste so much time.'

'What for?' It was almost as if his mother were here, handing out orders. 'It isn't as though we're short of time.'

'*We're* not, but Pandora is, and I'm worried about her safety the longer she spends on Olympus. My father is fascinated with her and won't be able to control his lust and then jealous Hera will kill her.'

Prometheus breathed into the last figure before setting her with her sisters. Thousands upon thousands of women slept in the warm night under Selene's soothing moonbeams.

When Helios appeared in the morning, the new beings awoke, blinking in the sunlight. Once they'd been fed and cleansed, they rose and danced about in their excitement – chattering, giggling and caressing their neighbours.

'You were right but for the wrong reason,' Athena said. 'We should have made some spares, after all. I hadn't factored in that some female mortals might prefer each other.'

That *we* again. 'Well,' said Hephaestus, 'they're each delightful in their own way so you can't blame them.' He eyed his creations. 'Some men will want men. Some women will want women. Some will want everybody. Some will want nobody…' He smirked at the celibate goddess, who refused to see the funny side, so he gave up. Really, she had no sense of humour. Still, the mortals would work everything out somehow. After all, what could be more straightforward than sex, love and marriage?

The Legion of Sisters

When the honeymoon was over, the Olympians gathered to see off the married couple. Pandora stood apart from her husband, her forehead wrinkled and mouth sulky, while he clenched his fists.

'Ah, good,' said Zeus. 'Why should I be alone in my suffering, eh?' He laughed and the mortal covered her ears. 'Ahead of you is a task that is tiring, but by no means unpleasurable. You will repopulate the world with sons of Epimetheus and daughters of Pandora. You will mother a new race, who will be born and not made. You will know them by their navels, something formerly reserved for deities, monsters and some beasts.'

When she tilted her head, ready to speak, the miniature god of afterthought gave his wife a warning look but she ignored him and spoke in her fluting voice.

'You want me to be like a deity and create life?'

This brought the king of heaven up short. 'More beast than deity. You'll carry a divine child within you, but subsequent generations will move further from the divine, so they're coarser and, um, less godlike.'

Judging by the almighty stumbling his way through this

explanation, being less godlike should be a blessing. When Hephaestus created something, the newer version was always an improvement on the old because he learnt from his mistakes. Perhaps mortals might inherit some of that quality, with each generation becoming more refined than its predecessor. It was a lot to hope for. Down on earth, several men were stoning their brother to death. He worried about sending the weaker sex amongst them and wished he hadn't made their necks so slender.

'Never fear, Pandora' said the greatest god, 'you'll have help. Fortunately for you, we've exhausted the claypits to produce a legion of sisters. Together, you'll go forth and multiply.'

With that, the doors to the great hall opened, and thousands of female mortals entered, gazing about them in wonder. At her loom, Athena had tailored numerous small silver robes, many of them a little too small. While Hephaestus had been generous with his clay, the goddess had been miserly with her cloth, and each robe was uniform in length and girth, regardless of the size of the intended wearer. The effect was amusing, but not displeasing, as the taller women's robes skimmed their thighs, showing off their legs, the more curvaceous spilled out of their garments, and the smaller, thinner women fitted into theirs perfectly. So they were all appealing, which was surely the plan, and most of the male deities were very pleased.

'Wonderful work, wonderful. So much beauty. So much evil.' Zeus grinned while Hera's lips all but disappeared. 'Ladies, go to earth and populate it with children. Epimetheus, hurry ahead to prepare your brothers. Pandora, lead your legion. At his command, she followed her husband out of the hall, her army bringing up the rear. They walked down the mountain, out of time, not in any particular formation, some circling back to chatter, while others lolled about, giggling over nothing.

'What's going on here?' The almighty scowled. 'These

creatures are very different to men. Why can't they march efficiently? None of them has any urge to race the other. Why aren't they more competitive? Hermes, get down there. Your services are required.'

The wing-heeled messenger swooped and whispered in a few ears. He didn't reach everyone but covered an impressive number. Before long, there was scratching, biting and hair-pulling, the siblings bent on destroying what was best in the others.

'That's better,' enthused the greatest god. 'Much better.'

Despite the army of sisters, there weren't enough to go around. As foreseen by Prometheus, not every man wanted a woman, and as foreseen by Athena, not every woman wanted a man, so the population was evenly matched. The aggravating factor was the gods, and once they got their eyes on the women, they would not stay in the heavens. Poseidon and Hades refused to remain in their respective realms, and Zeus had discovered the art of disguising himself to elude the queen of heaven's watchful eye. Most problematic was Helios, who found it hard to stay at his station, continually dashing down and plunging the world into darkness, forcing Selene to rise well before her time to provide some light.

This became confusing for all concerned. Whenever the sun set prematurely, the mortals flew into a panic, burning and sacrificing everything in sight, hoping to make the big yellow god return. The beasts slept where they stood in the fields, and the birds fell from the sky with sickening cracks and splashes as they landed. Someone would have to remonstrate with Helios, but who? Zeus was never anywhere to be seen and took advantage of the impromptu spells of darkness to impregnate as many women as possible.

These visitations caused widespread confusion when the sisters found their bellies full of divine children, and the brothers spilled their seed on Gaia instead, incurring her wrath.

The world was filled with mortals and deities alike, which occasioned no end of unhappiness, especially for Mother Earth. Hera had taken to shadowing her husband and sparing his victims by turning them into laurel trees for their own safety. This further depleted the female populace, and the god of fire was forced to visit the clay pits again and again.

When the greatest goddess proclaimed it was time to choose husbands, there'd been frenzied fighting and more than a few deaths as partners were chosen and rejected. This was definitely a design flaw but one the gods were fated to suffer as well. A man would fix on a woman, who'd be fixed on a different man, or woman, and then the fur would fly. Had Hephaestus unwittingly worked into the clay the juices of his own unrequited love and jealousy? Was there any pain greater than loving someone who did not, could not and would not reciprocate that feeling? Too late, he realised his error in using Aphrodite as a template, which had resulted in a ubiquitous reminder that his beloved would never spare him a glance.

In a futile attempt at matchmaking, Hera lined up the mortals in pairs. With some rare exceptions, who liked their prospective partner as much as they were liked in return, there was considerable dissent. A major stumbling block being that nearly everyone deemed themselves worthy of a superior spouse. None were able to accept their own shortcomings. Hephaestus laughed bitterly. They were more like the pantheon than he'd ever credited, with their pettiness, jealousy, vanity and the inevitable consequent skirmishes.

Eventually, Hera wearied of trying to matchmake. As fast as she paired up a couple, the goddess of love would appear and point out more attractive alternatives. It was sad to witness Aphrodite causing as much misery and strife as Ares and Eris, and the three of them revelled in the ensuing mayhem. Already, the number of bodies piling up was most upsetting, which enraged Hermes, who had to keep taking their souls to

Hades. Prometheus was distressed by the behaviour of his creations, although it was perhaps unfair to expect them to behave reasonably when the Olympians hardly set an example.

Reluctantly, the god of foresight agreed to leave them to it and walked up the mountain with Hephaestus. Occasionally, they peered at the world, where tiny women in flimsy robes wrestled with men, each other, and on occasion, various animals. Here a lion, there a serpent, next a swan and finally a shower of gold.

The two gods grimaced at one another. 'Zeus!'

The Prankster

The god of fire was leaving the grotto when the sea parted and several unwary fish landed on the seabed. Above him, the sky was red as the sun set, and to either side of him towered walls of glittering water, alive with colourful creatures. He didn't fancy his chances if this lot collapsed on him. The floor shook and the reason for it soon became clear when an ocean-sized Poseidon came striding towards him, vast in his own domain.

'Have no fear, Heph,' he roared, revealing teeth the size of palace doors, encrusted with incandescent shells. 'I bear you no ill will. Instead, I bring glad tidings. At least, *I'd* consider them glad were I in your sandals.' He picked up Hephaestus in one hand and the fish in the other, setting the creatures free on top of the waves. 'By Ouranus, you've not grown much, have you?' His guffaw made the walls of water wobble worryingly. 'Your short stature makes what I'm about to say even more surprising, but it's the gods' honest truth. Listen…'

Poseidon's whisper felt as though Boreas were blowing through his mind. The news *was* surprising, but he had no axe to grind with Hephaestus, so there was no reason to disbelieve him. The enormous deity raised an arm overhead, groped about blindly, and dropped the blacksmith near his earthly forge. He landed with a thump, wishing fervently that the other members of the pantheon would stop dropping him from tremendous heights. Still, no bones broken for a change.

~

Hephaestus positioned himself outside the smithy in the shade of a flowering olive tree, his second-favourite anvil resting on a stump. Dressed in his best eye-patch, bearskin apron and loincloth, he observed a peahen fleeing from a stalking cat. The hen was an admirable runner, but the cat managed to snatch a brown feather. Why didn't the stupid bird fly away from its predator? His idle speculation was interrupted when, true to the sea god's word, Athena turned up.

'You're in,' she said. 'Just as well. I'm after some new armour and—'

Before she could finish, he embraced her. Gods, she was straight up and down, and nothing like his beloved Aphrodite, but she had a powerful effect on him. To his consternation, he lost control of himself and aeons of pent-up desire fountained from him. Purple in the face, the goddess of war shoved him so hard he fell against his anvil and dislocated his shoulder. While he forced his arm into its socket, she hiked up her chiton and examined her thigh.

'Ugh, you vile beast.' Desperate, she spotted a pile of wool he kept for polishing blades, grabbed a handful, wiped her thigh and tossed the soiled tuft into the air, where it was snatched by the East Wind.

'Heph! What in Ouranus' name were you thinking, lunging at me?'

'Sorry.' Appalled, he lowered his head. 'But...' It sounded unbelievable to his own ears. 'Poseidon, you see. He reckoned you needed some armour, and...' He petered out, too ashamed to go on.

'What did he say to you?' she asked. 'Look at me when you answer while I decide whether you're telling the truth.'

'He told me the armour was a ruse.' He groaned. 'That you were secretly in love with me but too shy to speak up, so I should make the first move and embrace you.' It came out in a rush.

'Did he, indeed?' She tapped her foot. 'You shouldn't trust a word that crosses the old liar's lips.' She squinted at the sun. 'Yes, you heard me, Helios. I called your friend a liar. So run along and tell on me.' The affronted god vanished behind a cloud, casting earth into shadow. 'Oh, get over yourself,' she snapped, glaring at the sky until the big yellow ball showed himself again. Seemingly, no male could stand up to the goddess of war. 'Heph, you have to wise up. When someone tells you something, don't take it at face value. In future, ask people if they want to be embraced, and until you learn to control your…' Here, she pointed at his loincloth. 'Don't lay so much as a finger – not to mention any other appendage – on anyone else, or even think of embracing them. Understood?'

'Understood.' What a complete donkey he was. He was so much in thrall to the other Olympians that he took them at their word. He should have realised no goddess would want him touching her. The mere thought of her thigh made his face burn. 'As for your… leg, I don't know what came over me.'

'If only I could make the same claim.' Athena eyed him and he clamped his lips together, determined not to worsen an already terrible situation. 'Hmm. I believe you,' she said, 'against my better judgement. You were gullible to swallow Poseidon's tall tale, though. Didn't you take into account that I'm not remotely shy, or interested in men, or women, come to that? Ask in future – not me, never me – but anyone else.' Her tone softened. 'Heph, you're a naive idiot, but I doubt you're a rapist, so I won't castrate you. This time. But no more of this behaviour. There's far too much of it from the pantheon without your help. Do you hear?'

'Yes,' he said, aghast that he'd not considered any of this.

'It did sound too good to be true. You have my word, but what does the sea god stand to gain from setting me up. Why do it?'

'Easy. He wants me to go to my father, outraged, so he'll pick a fight. Anything to trigger a civil war so Poseidon can get his webbed hands on the heavens. The best thing to do is keep quiet and start on my armour.'

'Of course, and I won't charge you.'

'You will charge me full price,' she said. 'I pay my way. Here's what I… Wait, what's that tearing sound?'

Beneath them, the ground juddered and the flat water reared up, slammed against the shore and threw both gods off balance.

'It's coming from the south, whatever it is.' She righted herself and gazed out to sea. 'From Athens. I'd better go and—'

Without warning, Hermes materialised, holding a swaddled bundle at arm's length, while nipping his nose.

'Something of yours, I believe?' the celestial courier asked the goddess.

'Mine? I doubt something so foul smelling is any of my business. What is it? The heart of an enemy? Ares? Wait, that's too big to be his heart.'

With that, the delivery bawled and Athena crossed her eyes. 'A child? How on earth can it be mine when I've sworn a vow of chastity?' Here, a sideways glance at Hephaestus.

The sheepish god took the noisy bundle and loosened its swaddling. Inside was a newborn. He continued unwrapping to see whether it was male or female, but paused when he saw a serpent's tail in place of legs. When the tail flicked, it was all he could do not to shudder.

'That is a seriously ugly baby, courtesy of Gaia,' said Hermes. 'Apparently, a nasty wad of wool landed on her. Bang! Next thing, she's pregnant. You know how fertile she is. Just have to look at her the wrong way and—'

'Stop!' said the goddess. 'This is nothing to do with me. If it belongs to either of us, it's…'

The messenger held out his delivery to the dismayed blacksmith. 'So, *you're* the father. Unlucky. Gaia is having none of it. Says she's repulsed by it. No offence, Heph, I'm only the go-between. Anyway, one of you will have to accept it because I'm not taking it back.'

'Give it here,' said the goddess, relenting. 'Since I intend to remain chaste, this may be my only chance of being a mother, but you're not to mention this to anybody, and I mean *anybody.*'

The envoy shrugged and examined his cuticles. 'Far be it from me to gossip.'

She took a step towards him. 'I mean it. Swear on the River Styx.'

He tutted. 'Absolutely no fun at all.'

Her nostrils flared.

'Alright, alright, keep your helmet on, but if I have stay quiet, first I get to hear the whole story.'

'Once you've sworn. Properly.'

'Fine,' said the messenger with a roll of his eyes, 'I swear on the Styx not to breathe a word. So, tell all.'

To the smith's mortification, the goddess did tell all, sparing no detail.

The messenger could scarcely contain himself. 'What on Mother Earth possessed me to swear to silence? The *mischief* I could cause with this snippet! What a wag that Poseidon is, eh?'

Athena narrowed her eyes at him. 'And he's the very god who mustn't find out about this. If he learns his prank produced progeny, especially this revolting, who knows what stunt he'll pull next. He's trying to provoke me to run crying to my father, in the hope of triggering another war and taking over heaven, but I'm determined to maintain peace at any cost.'

'Novel approach for a war deity but suit yourself. Anyhow, you two can argue over whose business this is,' trilled Hermes before vanishing.

What an awful day. Hephaestus had manhandled his

friend, impregnated his great-grandmother, despite being nowhere near her, and to crown it all, he'd fathered a hideous child.

'What are we going to do with this bundle of joy?' asked Athena, holding out the bawling newborn.

'As he's my responsibility, I should take him home to the grotto. Thetis and Eurynome won't mind.'

'Unwise.' She shook her head. 'We need to hush up this little episode. If you take him anywhere near his realm, Poseidon will realise the outcome of his prank and work it to his advantage. It'll spur him on to worse things. Make a basket. I've had an idea.'

While the smith started work, the goddess examined the infant.

'I suppose you need a name so what shall we call you? Perhaps not after your father. How about a combination of wool, strife and earth? Erichthonius? It has a certain ring to it.'

'A lot of name for such a scrap,' said the new parent, belatedly realising his opinion wasn't welcome. So this was his firstborn. Erichthonius, son of Hephaestus and Gaia, however unintentional. He handed over the finished basket, which would protect the baby and muffle his screams. 'What's your idea then?'

'Gaia has another son who's also half-man, half-serpent – a king, who'll shelter Erich from the sea god's machinations. Trust me on this. When he's older, I'll grant him oracular powers to compensate for his difficult beginning, and Father will catasterise him into a constellation when his time comes. As for you, keep your distance. The boy has plenty to contend with as it is.'

Before he could disagree, Athena summoned Hermes, who reluctantly agreed to deliver the basket to the serpent-tailed king.

When his son was gone, he turned to her. 'Why are the creations from my hands perfect and those from my lower body repulsive?'

Athena gave him a long look. 'Maybe spare the pity for your child.'

She was right, but he couldn't help thinking about it. Something inside had made him repellent to his mother, and now he'd passed it on to his progeny.

The goddess of war nudged him in the ribs, none too gently. 'Are you making this armour, or what?'

The god of fire wasn't entirely surprised to be summoned to Olympus and dragged his foot more than usual, dreading his immediate future. Of course, the king of heaven had got wind of the outrage. Hermes might have sworn to silence on the Styx, but Helios had borne witness, and the big tattle-tale couldn't resist snitching to the almighty. Hephaestus' trepidation increased when he found the Olympians, minus Poseidon, already enthroned. What horrible punishment was to be meted out? It would be no good blaming the devious sea god because Athena knew her father well. It risked triggering war. He'd have to resign himself and accept his fate, which would no doubt be worse than having his liver devoured by eagles. He approached Zeus' throne, knelt and grasped his knees.

'Oh, get up,' said the aggrieved father. 'A little bird told me everything – well, a big yellow bird – but naturally, such a gross act can't go unpunished, especially when the victim is my daughter. The punishment will fit the crime, so I sentence you to a lifetime of…' Here, he leant away from Hera before continuing. 'Marriage, which is the worst penalty to my mind. No. That's not true. *Now*, I've thought of the worst penalty. Marriage to my aunt.'

Hephaestus scratched his head. This sounded like the opposite of punishment. It would be heavenly to have his own wife, and perhaps children, ideally without serpent tails. But if the nephew was older than the ages, how old was this aunt, and would she still be fertile? When Dionysus whispered the identity of the aunt, he wasn't sure he'd heard properly.

'It's decided. In fact, I'll swear to it.' Zeus glanced at his aunt, who was busy admiring the decorative chain encircling her left ankle. 'I hereby swear on the River Styx that I will wife my aunt to you. Now, what shall the bride price be? Oh, I've got it! A golden mastiff.'

'Gold?' asked the smith. 'Wouldn't you prefer silver? It's harder to refine, which makes it more valuable.'

'Your honesty is commendable, but it must be identical to the mastiff who guarded me in my crib. Make sure it always catches its prey, and give it flashing red eyes. Now we're agreed on the price, you may claim your spouse.' He raised his voice. 'Auntie, come and meet your new husband.'

At this pronouncement, the distracted aunt looked up.

'What? You're forcing me to marry? How am I expected to love freely if shackled? You have no right to promise me to any deity, and especially not *him*. I belong to nobody, and I'm not yours to give, *Nephew*.'

The greatest god laughed aloud and created cataclysms.

'You may not be mine to give, Aph, but you are mine to sell, so a bride price has been agreed.' He shrugged. 'I've sworn on the Styx so there's no going back.'

Undeterred, she continued arguing until the almighty stood up and stamped his sceptre so the palace shook, and every deity, including the furious Aphrodite, fell silent.

'God of fire and goddess of love, from this day forwards, you are bound to each other. Congratulations. You'll have to encourage her, Heph. She won't come quietly.'

'Yes,' added Hera. 'Take your wife. She doesn't want you either, I note. Poor Hephaestus, destined to be rejected by everyone he loves.' She flicked her chin at his lower left leg. 'When Aph has finished with you, the wound I inflicted will seem no more than a scratch.'

The god of fire dismissed his mother's heckling. He needed to remember that he was an immortal, and not just any immortal, but an Olympian. Hopefully, he'd grow into the role and stop feeling like an imposter, but it was difficult when the other gods had limbs as straight as they were long, and they were all so beautiful.

'Chop chop.' Zeus clapped his hands. 'Pick her up and carry her home, Heph, unless you prefer to stake her out on Caucasus.'

'That would certainly be preferable,' remarked Aphrodite, 'to spending eternity in bondage to a blacksmith, an ugly one at that.'

'Believe me,' said Hephaestus, 'you wouldn't prefer it. Are you coming?' When his bride refused to budge, he picked her up and slung her over his shoulder, avoiding Athena's eye as he left the hall, Aphrodite hammering on his back with both fists.

'I hate you,' she yelled. 'The eagles can eat my liver! Who wants a wife who doesn't want to be wifed, let alone to someone so short? I'll never love you!'

'My mother has never loved me, so why should you be any different?' He sighed and adjusted his burden. 'Either way, I swear on the Styx that I will love you for the rest of my life.'

A Cull

After their impromptu honeymoon, the not-so-happy couple sat on the slopes of Mount Aetna, overlooking the vineyards as mortals laboured under Helios. The goddess of love was still outraged about her enforced wedding and it was nothing short of a miracle that the marriage had been consummated. The god of fire had planned a romantic picnic for two, but his plans were thwarted by a pair of gooseberries in the shape of his friend and his cousin.

The foursome lazily passed back and forth a pithos of nectar. Below, men, women and children were bringing in the harvest and provided excellent entertainment as they couldn't get along with each other for more than a few hours. Persephone stopped twirling a poppy under Prometheus' chin to indicate a brawling mass, intent on pummelling themselves to death.

'They're at it again,' she said. 'Your people have a certain charm, but they must cause you an awful lot of trouble.'

The god of foresight sat up. 'Not at all because I leave them alone in the main.'

'Oh, spare us another lecture on the merits of free will,' yawned Aphrodite.

The hurt god ignored her and hunched forwards to watch his creations.

They had decent lives, Hephaestus supposed, spending their days frolicking and fighting, occasionally meeting a terrible end after being pushed off a cliff, or having their brains dashed out by a rival. More often than not, most of them died quietly in their sleep. It was a pity they didn't last long and although they were mewling babes one minute and had white whiskers and bent backs the next, his friend showed no urge towards improving their lot. Not even for Epimetheus, whose wife looked set to pre-decease him by a few millennia.

'I have to admit,' said Persephone, propped on her elbows and chewing her poppy stalk, 'that I enjoy watching them once their hearts stop beating and their flesh is pecked away so their skeletons are revealed, the same as the beasts, birds and fish.'

'Ugh! Please can we not talk about bones,' said Aphrodite. 'It's so depressing.'

'But it's fascinating,' said the morbid maiden. 'Death is interesting to think about because we can't have it.' She opened her small hand, which was filled with black specks. 'Poppy seeds, anyone?' There was a unanimous chorus of refusals. 'Don't you reckon there are too many mortals?' she asked, waving at a landscape scattered with skeletons. 'They're merrily munching their way through everything on earth. Mother says Zeus is cross because soon there won't be enough animals to feed the pantheon.' She leant over and twirled the red flower under Prometheus' chin again.

'What are you doing?' he asked.

'Seeing if you like opium,' she said. 'Maybe you should consider a cull, Prom?'

'What a ghoulish suggestion,' he replied, shoving her away. 'And get that blessed thing off me, Seph. Opium's awful stuff and I haven't got over my last run-in with you.'

'Stop changing the subject, Prom. I bet you have no idea of the world population to the nearest thousand.'

He shrugged and scraped a pattern on a dusty boulder

with his finger: a tree with an endless number of branches. He kept rubbing out and adding.

'Not a clue, have you?' said Persephone, pointing at the odd sketch. 'We're overrun since they started breeding. At first, they were constantly killing each other so it balanced out but some of them grow more peaceable as they age and the murder rate's gone right down, which is a shame.'

She wasn't wrong. It wasn't so bad when men were on their own, but once the women arrived, they'd put the rabbits to shame. As a result, mortals outnumbered immortals, so it was problematic keeping track of them. While each generation was more refined than the one before, they still carried the twin impediments inflicted on them at creation. Small stature and frailty. On the whole, though, the pantheon was amused by the short-lived people, especially since some had dedicated themselves to their favourite deities by building temples, burning beasts and children as offerings, pouring libations and leaving fruit, flowers and honey as tributes.

These days, every other mortal was a priest or priestess, presiding over orgies and other revels, in the vain hope that the gods would smile upon them. In return, the gods took a close interest in their lives, which was not always a good thing, particularly when Aphrodite meddled in mortal marriages, often with devastating results. In addition, many of the most beautiful women had mysteriously vanished, and his wife had been equally mysterious about their whereabouts.

'The child argues a fair case,' said the goddess of love. 'Do you want to witness Zeus deprived of his hourly ration of a dozen spitted lambs? Imagine his temper. Someone should do something.'

This was rich. As if Aphrodite cared a jot about anyone else's hunger. It was pure self-interest, cutting down the competition. But if Persephone was right about the perils of over-population, there had to be a kinder way, instead of resorting to destruction.

'Maybe we could slow down the birth rate,' suggested

Hephaestus. 'They do multiply alarmingly fast. Perhaps if they spent more time growing crops and less time copulating.'

'Life with less copulation wouldn't be worth living,' said Aphrodite. 'I've got a solution.' With that, she walked towards a rock, flexed her pretty foot and pushed the stone off the mountain. It tumbled down, gathering momentum, bouncing and clattering, freeing other rocks as it went, until the rumbling mass spread across the cornfield below, flattening all in its path.

Prometheus leapt up and stared at the massacre. Several craters had appeared where the boulder had bounced along the valley before coming to rest, and in them lay broken and bloody mortal remains. Aphrodite smiled, pleased with her efforts until the god of foresight grabbed her arm, spinning her around to face him.

'What did you do that for?' he demanded, looming over her, teardrops sparkling on his lashes.

The goddess prised his fingers free. 'I was helping us to avoid the wrath of a hungry Zeus. There are so many now, you won't miss a few.'

White-lipped, the anguished god paced. 'A few? Dozens crushed to death as if they were no more than insects.'

'Oh, don't fuss,' she said, reclining gracefully once more. 'More of them die from free will.'

'That's different. They need to learn to look after each other without gods interfering, for good or ill.'

'Heph could easily knock up some more if you're that concerned,' Aphrodite went on. 'He could make them more akin to those golden mannequins of his – harder to crush.'

Hephaestus looked from his stricken friend to his wife, wondering how someone so beautiful could be so cruel. He tried not to compare her with his mother.

'Look! There go the little shades,' she said, airily waving in the general direction of the dead.

'*There go the little shades?*' Prometheus whipped around so violently, his hair swung about his ears. 'You don't get it, do you? Their hearts beat. They love. They have fine feelings. They're brave. They're the same as us, only better.'

The atmosphere darkened with shades blocking out Helios so the afternoon cooled. Beneath the rocks, the survivors were now conscious and screaming.

'Of course they aren't better,' she insisted. You crush me with a rock and I stand up, which is more than can be said for your mortals.'

'How can you say that, Aph?' he asked. 'You above everyone? Of all the pantheon, you should show compassion for your fellow beings.'

'Compassion?' The goddess laughed, the silvery peal at odds with her callous heart. '*Erotic* love is what I'm interested in, but this concern for fellow beings as you call them, is very much outwith my divine remit.'

Persephone rolled onto her back. 'Pack it in, Prom. Stop being so mean to Aph.'

'Why should I, after what she did?'

The raven-haired goddess frowned. 'She was trying to help. The world can't continue as it is, with that lot scoffing everything in sight and cluttering up Mother Earth with their primitive shacks. Gaia is devastated. Tough decisions have to be taken. You've made your argument so let it go. Have some poppy seeds. Ideal for dulling pain.'

What that girl saw in poppies, Hephaestus failed to comprehend. She spent half her day sleeping in fields and the remainder picking more flowers. It was no life. He stood beside his friend and placed a sympathetic arm around his shoulders.

'You know,' he said gently, 'Aph might have a point.' When Prometheus threw off his embrace, Hephaestus chose his words carefully. 'I mean, about making the mortals sturdier. I could work out how to prevent them dying and create a new batch.'

'That would worsen matters,' said Persephone, 'the world would overflow and then we'd be in a real dilemma. Soon, there'll be nine billion of them. It'll be too much weight and Gaia will simply let herself fall from the sky.'

'Always so dramatic, Seph,' drawled Aphrodite. 'Gaia would smite the horrible creatures long before doing anything that drastic. I'm just saving her the bother.'

Slowly, Prometheus turned to the other gods, his eyes dark with sorrow. 'None of you understand. This mortality was a deliberate choice, and it's not a flaw, but a privilege.'

Some privilege, to be alive on such a glorious day when, without warning, a stone could plummet from heaven and bring eternal darkness.

A Pithos for Pandora

The god of fire rode the golden mastiff to the palace, dismounting unexpectedly when it lunged at the silver lions guarding the gate. It took a hasty intervention with his hammer to break up the consequent fight. Because the guard-lions were the first layer of palace security, and the mastiff only a glorified lapdog, he toned down its aggression. After patching up the various injuries, he entered the great hall, restraining his new creation by its collar. Zeus' eyes lit up, and in one powerful leap, the hound landed on its master's knee and licked his face.

'He's called Laelaps,' shouted Hephaestus.

'I can't imagine why,' said the almighty, leaning to the side of his lightly mauled pet. 'While you're here, I need a word about the mortals. My initial plan hasn't worked. It turns out that women are no punishment at all, and by and large, the male and female of the species are getting along much too well for my liking. In fact, they're getting on so well, Gaia, Demeter and her blessed daughter are constantly nagging me about earthlings outnumbering gods and taking over.' He wiped himself free of dog slobber and smiled indulgently at Laelaps. 'So, Pandora's second gift is seriously overdue and I want you to fashion a receptacle of sorts. Box, jar, whatever. I leave the details to you.'

'How big should it be?' asked the blacksmith wondering whether it was to be Pandora's prison or her burial jar.

'Not too big. She has to be able to lift it.' The king of heaven held his finger and thumb apart. 'About that size, but sturdy so it doesn't fall and shatter. Most importantly, it must have a lid that is difficult to open, but not impossible.'

'What will it contain?'

'Let me worry about that,' said Zeus, ruffling the mastiff's ears.

When Hephaestus left, he was greeted by his tripods, in phalanx formation, and they carried him to the earthly forge. There, he contemplated his latest commission. Soft silver should reduce the risk of shattering and would lend itself to an urn. He hummed and hawed for a while before deciding that a puzzle would make it hard to open, yet still possible. Pandora had a little skull, but it was packed with cerebral matter, and she had Athena's wisdom, so the puzzle had to be reasonably challenging, but what form should it take? Instead of casting the vessel, he decided to forge it, confident that the mechanism would occur to him while he hammered. As he shaped the urn on his anvil, he enjoyed the ringing sounds, which were due to the weight of the hammer relative to that of the argent metal, and he experimented with different notes. Apollo wasn't the only musician on Olympus! On and on he pounded, until the idea came to him like a whisper in a dream.

In the hall of the gods, the smith positioned his work beneath the sky dome so the sun's rays spangled the eight deities embossed on the pithos. The Olympians abandoned their goblets and platters to get a closer look, but those not featured soon resumed eating and drinking, making no attempt to hide their hostility. When Zeus tired of admiring his own image, he complained. 'Did you misunderstand my orders, Heph? This is the antithesis of difficult to open. It has no cover, so how will things stay in?'

'Trust me, things will stay in,' said the god of fire, enigmatically. 'Fill it up and find out. What's to go in it, anyway?'

'Why, everything evil that a godly mind can construe. The mother of mankind was endowed with all the gifts so her pithos must be similarly plenished with all the spites.' He called on the pantheon. 'Come, be generous. This is my legacy, so dig deep.'

Curiously, the god of foresight headed the queue, dropping in a bright entity that refracted rainbows around the hall. In the process of trying to see what it was, Hephaestus tilted the urn too far so his friend's donation nearly slithered over the lip. Quickly, Prometheus scooped a dab of honey from a nearby bowl, smeared it under the elusive trait and pressed it down firmly, watching as it struggled against its bounds, then reluctantly stood aside, moping as the other deities rummaged through pockets, pouches and purses, before making their deposits.

As every divine light cast a shadow, so every brilliant faculty given on Pandora's birth day was now matched with its opposite. Aphrodite offered lust, vanity, infidelity and indolence. She had no choice in passing on these vile qualities, but did she have to be so happy about it? Hermes conferred yet more gossip, lies and quarrels, along with confusion, misdirection and delay. Ares tossed in bloodshed, hatred, violence and war. Hestia tried to avoid giving anything, but after the almighty put his foot down, she handed over cold, sorrow and loneliness. Apollo donated dissent, disease, politics and plague. Demeter added the need to toil all day in order to eat. Hera slipped in jealousy, envy and resentment. The list went on and on… Hephaestus peered at the churning spites and wished he'd made the puzzle harder to solve. Zeus imparted cruelty, debauchery, excess, malice, oppression, pomposity, promiscuity and vengeance before inquiring whether everyone had contributed.

'Heph? On second thoughts, you've more than done your bit. Dion, I didn't see you drop anything in.'

Dionysus swore, ambled over, and with an apologetic nod at Prometheus, emptied his pouch before handing the pithos to his father, who examined the topmost elements.

'Murder, mayhem and madness? You do me proud, Dion, you do me proud.' He clamped a thumb over the mouth of the urn and returned it to its maker. 'Seal it.'

As the greatest god handed it over, his thumb slipped and madness burst out, flapping its horrible wings. Buzzing loudly, it made a beeline for Hera. Before it found its target, the messenger took to the air and swatted it. Artemis caught the runaway spite before it hit the floor and lobbed it to Athena, who thrust it safely back in its container. Hephaestus quickly slid his fingers over the metallic versions of Gaia, Selene, Hermes, Helios, Aphrodite, Ares, Zeus and Cronus. When he touched each heart in turn, a note rang out. Together, the benefics and the malefics harmonised and the divine assembly stood quite still, radiating joy.

'What is it?' asked the enthralled almighty. 'What is that mellifluous sound?'

'The music of the spheres,' replied the modest inventor.

'Not bad,' said the king of heaven, turning the pithos in his palm so his likeness was uppermost. 'But how does it work?'

'Providing the melody plays without interruption, the malevolence is contained, so men, women and children will remain content.' If content were an apt word to describe their current levels of massacre, onslaught and anarchy. 'Unfortunately, their clay ears are too coarse to hear the celestial chorus, just as they can't feel Gaia spinning beneath their feet.'

'So many of the finer points of creation are wasted on mortals,' said Zeus, inverting the urn over its maker to check it was airtight. The transparent cap was no more than hardened air, which revealed the swarming evils of the world while imprisoning them. In a final test, he shook the pithos as if readying to throw a fistful of knucklebones. 'Very clever, Heph, but how does it open?'

'Simply play the notes backwards, but I warn you, it's a truly terrible noise.'

A worried-looking Prometheus appealed to his patron.

'That seal is too weak. Since Pandora is blessed with intelligence, curiosity and music, she's bound to crack the code.' He gave his most winsome smile. 'Is there *any* way of persuading you from this course, O mightiest of mighties?'

'Even you, dearest Prom, cannot deter me from my path. I must balance the theft of fire. They've had it too easy down there for too long. Now, before I bequeath this receptacle, I have to be certain it opens. Apollo, as resident minstrel, you do it.'

The sun god set down his lyre and ran an experimental fingertip over the silver reliefs of the eight divinities.

'Athena, Artemis, Hermes,' said Hera, snapping her fingers. 'When the lid evaporates, be ready to prevent any spites from escaping. We have enough aggravation on the mountain as it is.'

The messenger hovered overhead while the goddesses of war and hunting flanked Apollo, each as fierce and beautiful as the other. When the musician had its measure, he played the urn as if playing a small but complicated flute. Once the greatest god had witnessed the container being opened under guard, and despite strenuous protests from his favourite, he pronounced himself pleased and instructed Hermes to deliver it to earth.

The messenger was accompanied on his errand by the god of fire and the god of foresight, who begged Pandora to bury the present and tell nobody of its whereabouts. Wisely, she followed his advice, insisting her husband turn his back while she hid her gift. This caused a fight with Epimetheus, who pointed out that whatever was hers was also his, but she touched him in the way he liked so much and whispered in his ear, until he embraced her and went indoors, all thoughts of the pithos forgotten. While he was gone, she scraped a hole in the loose soil and secreted her present, tamping earth over her buried treasure before plucking a plump and velvety pink bloom and tucking it into her white hair.

'Are we all so easily gulled?' asked Hephaestus.

'We are where your mother and wife are concerned,' sniggered the messenger.

Prometheus shushed them with a glare. 'Pandora has hidden her bequest and is helping my brother to forget about it. Hopefully, it should remain underground and mortals can go on as they are: imperfect, but not all bad.'

His fraught expression undermined his optimistic words and no wonder when he could foresee the harrowing events the future had in store. The first woman was doomed to fail and her brother-in-law knew it. This devious plot wasn't one of the king of heaven's usual outbursts, which led to raging storms that blew over as soon as his temper cooled. Instead, this bore the hallmark of the type of calculated revenge that expressed itself in punishments like having a liver torn out for eternity. The more Zeus loved someone, the more he wanted to punish them, especially when he felt slighted, and never more so than when slighted by a favourite.

Hephaestus was sure the almighty was bent on destroying mankind because it was the surest method of hurting the god of foresight. When his plan to inflict the 'beautiful evil' on men had backfired by enabling procreation, he'd armed Pandora with the means to devastate the populace. If that failed, he would come up with a new ploy. Assuming the mortals didn't destroy themselves first, Zeus *would* finish them. Nobody could play a longer game than the king of heaven. It might take months or it might take millennia, but one day, he would obliterate Prometheus' precious creations once and for all.

Lifting the Lid

Most of the Olympians were by the window on the world. The gods of fire and foresight stood either side of Zeus, who'd slung a comradely arm over each of their shoulders. Behind them lay the metal mastiff, good-naturedly chewing the thighbone from a carthorse. Baffled, Hephaestus watched the messenger tiptoe out of Epimetheus' home. What business had the mischievous god there, and why was he sneaking about in the middle of the night?

When Pandora stormed out to her rose garden and stomped about its perimeter, he had a hunch what poison had been dripped in her ear and hoped a walk in the garden might calm her. Prometheus caught his eye and they each made to move, only to find the almighty's comradely arms now imprisoning them while Laelaps put down his bone briefly to growl.

'Keep watching, you two,' said the king of heaven, 'and you may learn an overdue lesson.'

It soon became clear that Pandora hadn't been soothed by the fragrant roses and the anger hadn't leached from her bare feet into the soil. As feared, she flung herself down and dug frantically, unearthing her present. Selene's gentle beams illuminated the pithos, but even her lunar beauty failed to pacify the furious woman, who shook her fists.

'I don't want soothing, moon goddess,' she panted. 'I want revenge on my husband. How foolish does he think I am? Who goes hunting at this hour? No doubt you're watching him lie with his lover as I speak. And who can blame him for seeking out someone young and lovely instead of old and wretched? Keep your secrets if you must, Selene, but a superior deity has revealed everything to me.'

Insulted, the moon vanished, leaving no light, and arrived on Olympus, depressed and jaded. Sleepy Helios was ordered to cover for her and the grumbling god took up his station, waking the earthly inhabitants before their time.

'My sister-in-law is wrong,' said Prometheus. 'While Epi isn't without fault, he has been unswervingly faithful.'

'I know,' said Zeus. 'That's one of the many joys of the messenger. Your brother's infidelity, or lack of it, is immaterial. Gods and mortals suffer from the same tendency to believe whatever gossip they hear, the more scurrilous the better, rarely questioning whether Hermes could be mixed up or have an ulterior motive. Regardless, his victims gobble the nonsense down time and time again.'

'I'd prefer it if Epi *had* been unfaithful,' said Aphrodite, stretching extravagantly and drawing everyone's attention to her. But the pantheon had seen and heard it all before and returned to the action below.

'And where exactly is my brother?' asked Prometheus.

'Holed up in Tartarus, along with my interfering daughter, until this is over,' said Zeus. 'Don't want either of them having an attack of misplaced chivalry.'

With all his might, Hephaestus willed Pandora to give up and go to bed, but she sat down and placed her present in the nest formed by her crossed legs. It seemed she would exercise free will and follow her chosen path. The path set, of course, by the king of heaven.

'Watch me,' she shouted, 'as I empty out my dowry. My faithless husband will not have it, and he will not have me.'

As per the almighty's instructions, the silver urn was difficult to open but nowhere near difficult enough. Of all the Olympians, the smith was the god most like mankind, and while his inventions amused the other deities, his was not a lofty intellect. Too late, he realised that he'd let the greatest god's esteem go to his head, unaware he was being duped. He may as well descend to earth and lift the lid himself.

Pandora ran her hands over the pithos, looking heavenwards for inspiration. She didn't find it there, but from a more earthly source as the messenger materialised once more and mimed the secret code to her. The gods of fire and foresight squirmed under the dread weight of Zeus' arms as she pressed the heart of Gaia, whose refrain sang in the soul as much as the ears. The first woman had unlocked the first catch.

Lulled into a trance, she touched the lunar goddess, who whispered of madness. As the tides rose and swelled the seas, Pandora bled from the womb and wept copiously. Screaming, bleeding and drenched from the rains, she sought Hermes, and his voice rang out in a million chattering lies. Eyes swivelling as she tried to distinguish truth from falsehood, her fingertips brushed Aphrodite and an enchanting aria softened the air, disguising the undertones of lust, obsession and betrayal that were the shadow side of love.

Mesmerised, she found Helios, but his joyous notes were overwhelmed by flames that incinerated forest and field alike. Next, was the hated god of war. Here was a chance. Ares was the trickiest to undo as his heart was small and hard to locate, but locate it she did, and his bloodthirsty battle cries resonated with the screams of warriors and horses in their death throes. The penultimate catch was Zeus. Undeterred, she opened it. Lightning ruptured the sky and thunder elevated war into a discordant crescendo that clanged from heaven to hell.

As the cacophony peaked, Gaia heaved, knocking Pandora and her pithos to the ground, but she scrabbled in the mud, retrieved the slippery vessel and staggered to her feet, laughing, her mouth wet, red and open. Triumphant, bloody and drunk, she screamed into the void, and Hephaestus prayed to all the ancient gods. Oblivious to divine prayers, she found the heart of Cronus, and the universe reverberated with the echo of a lead door slamming shut. The sombre god's death knell annihilated all other sound, leaving something quieter than silence, as if the gods had suddenly stopped singing in order to draw breath.

Whatever bleakness had occupied the first woman's soul was nothing compared to the grim contents of the pithos, which pulsated as its seal dissolved, releasing a murmuration of evil that flocked against the sun, blocking out his light, and filling the hush with a high-pitched whine. On the wings of Pandora's revenge, the spites raced to the ends of the earth, permeating the spirit of every man, woman and child.

The white-haired mortal clasped the urn, replete with vengeance against her man, against all men. Goodness deserted her and no longer did she possess beauty, wisdom or grace, but only hate, which boiled in her veins so her skin erupted in welts, her eyes reddened with gore and her mouth filled with a never-ending lament. Locked in place by the almighty, the two gods were forced to watch as the mass of spites descended on Pandora, and she collapsed, still clutching her pithos.

Zeus liberated his prisoners and ordered the messenger to hasten them earthwards. As they left, Aphrodite lounged on a divan, flicking her hair and revealing her soft throat to Poseidon, as though the dreadful destruction had never happened.

~

On earth, all was silent. Led by Hermes, the gods of fire and foresight walked a landscape strewn with countless corpses.

Above the bodies floated their shades. By the time the celestial envoy reached Pandora, the Fates were already there and Atropos cut her life thread. The chief psychopomp gently placed his caduceus against the mother of mankind's brow before leading her shade to the underworld, legions of souls in his wake.

Prometheus gathered her dead body and Hephaestus eased the pithos from her death grip. He couldn't look at his friend, instead concentrating on working his way from Cronus to Gaia. As he sealed the urn, a symphony soared and spread across the world, and the few surviving mortals swayed to the sound, numb after being exposed to all the wickedness the pantheon could conceive.

Although some semblance of harmony had been restored, the horde of spites had escaped, never to return. Hephaestus looked at the dead woman. He had created her. If only he could have told Pandora that she was not to blame. That she and her daughters must not allow this incident to taint them in future. That she was destined to open the pithos. That Zeus had decreed it. That it was her fate.

Fate or no fate, he'd never forgive himself for the part he'd played. As creator of the urn, he bore responsibility. Without his invention, the king of heaven could never have exacted such a dire price. This ravage was because of the blacksmith's inability to say no to the greatest god, whose approval he craved. In exchange for his liver, or some such, he could easily have invented a vessel with an unbreakable seal. If only he were more like Prometheus, with the courage to defy the almighty.

In time, mankind would reproduce but they would inhabit a different world. No she-goats, no milk to suck, no trees, no honey to drip from them, and not a solitary acorn. Everything good had gone. From now onwards, men and women would have to work all day if they wanted to eat. Thanks to the blacksmith and his cowardice, the golden age of man was over and paradise forever lost.

He inverted the pithos. Inside, secured with no more than a dab of honey was the god of foresight's gift to mankind. Hope. To stop mortals ending their misery in the only way they knew how. Hope. Little more than a wish, a prayer, a thing both fragile and elusive. Hope. A reverie half-remembered when woken from a deep slumber. Hope. Running through fingers, fading and slipping off the edge of dreams. Hope. A scrap of bright silk wound tight around mortal eyes, blinding them to the darkness of the world. Hope. The bringer of much delusion. Some gift.

Part III

The Good Father

Gaia was fertile and the mortals were repopulating her, but Aphrodite's belly remained stubbornly flat. Every new moon, the god of fire pressed his hot face against her womb, which was devoid of life and ocean cold, much as she was towards him. What did he expect? Their marriage was scarcely consummated, and he'd been a fool to hope it was anything other than a punishment from Zeus. Still, he loved his wife, secure in the knowledge that she'd never reciprocate.

He arrived home one afternoon to find her prone on a couch, weeping and swigging nectar straight from the flagon. After navigating bowls smeared with ambrosia, he knelt down and embraced her. When she didn't attempt to push him off, he became seriously concerned.

'What's wrong, Aph?'

'Isn't it obvious?' she said. 'I'm ugly. That's what's wrong. This morning, Poseidon walked past without laying a single tentacle on me.'

A small mercy, but Poseidon's lechery seldom failed him, so her distress was understandable. Surreptitiously, he observed the crumbs in her cleavage and the stains on her chiton.

'Nobody could ever think you ugly.'

'As if your opinion matters.' The forlorn goddess slumped in her grubby garment, hand trailing in a bowl of succulent figs and sweet pumpkin seeds.

His eye followed the curve of her hip, the valley of her waist and the swell of her breast, noting that her belly was a shade more rounded than when he'd last touched her.

'You know how fickle the sea god is, Aph, and I bet a young princeling's taken his fancy.'

'Since you are evidently too blind to see.' She placed his hands on her. 'Perhaps you can feel what's brewing in me!'

His heart lurched. 'You're with child?' When a loud snort answered his question, it was all he could do not to punch the wall in a fit of joy.

'Ten out of ten. He realises, at last. Obviously, this won't be your firstborn, will it? You have that serpent-tailed monster already.'

'Erich? No more than a constellation these days.' After being so careful to raise him safely to adulthood, Athena had inadvertently dropped a mountain on him. 'But how can you be pregnant, when we haven't?' At least they hadn't since the day she'd kicked the boulder from the top of Aetna and slaughtered the mortals in the cornfield, which had put her in a strangely agreeable mood.

'What are you implying?' she demanded. 'That I've offered my rump to Boreas?'

'Of course not. The North Wind isn't responsible for half the pregnancies he's blamed for, but it *has* been a while since…'

'A while, my foot,' she said. 'It's not my fault if you've forgotten. You get so drunk with Dion, sometimes you have no clue what year it is.'

It was true. He was often the worse for wear and barely able to remember his own name. A dark thought about Poseidon crept into his mind, but he pushed it aside. While Aphrodite enjoyed flirting with the sea god, it was only for sport, and she found him repugnant.

'Then I'm definitely the father?' He bent to kiss her, only to find himself kissing air as she turned from him.

'Yes, more's the pity. Let's pray it doesn't turn out like your Erich.'

'This baby will be perfect,' he said, 'because he'll take after you.' He tried not to think about his wife being his grandmother's sister.

Poor Erichthonius, simultaneously son and great uncle. Imperfect, unloved and fatherless. The circumstances of the boy's conception weren't his fault, and neither was his appearance. Hephaestus should have visited, despite Athena's warning to steer clear, but it was too late. This was the problem with mortals. By the time you got around to visiting, they'd invariably died. But he wouldn't make the same mistake twice. There was no way to make amends to Erich, but he vowed to be a good father to his next child.

Silently, he prayed his second-born would not be repulsive. With every passing hour, his wife reminded him more and more of his mother, and there was nothing to suggest she wouldn't dispose of any flawed progeny as Hera had disposed of him, so he must keep watch *and* try to reassure her.

'Cheer up, Aph, your looks will return.' As soon as the words were out of his mouth, he regretted them.

'That's easy for you to say,' she snapped, 'but you're repellent to begin with, so you don't know what it means to lose your looks, as *I* apparently have. Clearly, I'm destined to be hideous until *it* decides to arrive.'

'Him, Aph, not it. And you'll always be lovely to me.'

Ignoring him, she went on. 'I'm so revolting, I'll have to hide myself until this is over. I hate being pregnant!'

These words chilled him and he resolved to fix his wife's unhappiness to help ensure this child saw the light of day.

'You needn't hide, I promise.' He kissed the tip of her nose and received a swipe from a slightly puffy hand for his trouble. 'I won't be long.' He eased the flagon from her other hand. 'How about some goat's milk?'

Hephaestus shared the necessary measurements with the Cyclopes. They goggled as they took in the information but swiftly recovered and pressed sand into troughs before tipping copper and tin into a cauldron and fanning the fire. When the mixture melted, the giants poured the blazing orange liquid into the mould, and once it had set, they broke the cast, revealing a curvaceous bronze. All three swallowed a lot and a sheen of sweat beaded their top lips.

The blacksmith decided to tell the gilded girls to melt the form once the job was done as the goddess of love might not take too kindly to the goliaths pawing at her, albeit in proxy. He shut them out while testing a variety of metals to gauge the best effect and these experiments revealed the solution in quicksilver.

After a successful mission, he emerged into a welcome sea breeze, soot-stained, sweaty and grateful to the tripods for a ride home.

Aphrodite hadn't moved from the couch, which was now surrounded by grape skeletons and cheese rinds. There was a trifle more of her than earlier, and he hoped the gift would fit. She struggled to lift her head from the cushion.

'Aph, do you want a clean robe?'

'There's no point bothering if I'm not the most beautiful being.' She scrubbed a grimy sleeve over red eyes. 'Even you can't bring yourself to look at me and that's why you're always at the forge.'

'I'm sorry,' he said. He cradled her in his arms but recoiled from her unwashed hair and whistled for his favourite tripod to go and fetch the gilded girls. 'How do you feel about a warm bath and a haircut, not too much, and then a surprise?'

'Is the surprise more nectar?'

'No.' He eyed the empty wineskins, pooled on the floor like wrinkled bladders, and didn't add that over-reliance on nectar wasn't helping her cause. 'So, about that bath?'

The tripods carried the divine couple to a travertine pool at the foot of some falls. The water was so blue against the dazzling white stone, it looked as though the pool held the sky. The metal mannequins busied themselves scattering rose petals until its surface was a lightly lapping tide of pink silk.

When the goddess shed her robe, the sun shone approvingly, and she lingered before slipping beneath the healing waters. While she reclined, smiling blissfully, the jealous husband tried to ignore the prospect of Poseidon making love to her as she bathed. When she sat up at long last, she consented to having her locks lathered with fragrant oils of orange and jasmine, and the gilded girls snipped a few coppery threads here and there.

Glowing once more, the goddess of love arose, droplets sparkling on her skin. Revelling in her nakedness, she stood beneath Helios, allowing him to kiss her body dry. This was galling, but Hephaestus kept quiet, knowing how badly she needed this attention. A rush of air rippled the pink petals – Zeus taking too close an interest. Quickly, the god of fire covered her in a white chiton and smoothed it across her softly swelling belly. He coiled his hands in her hair and drew her to him, nuzzling at her warm neck, and when she breathed in his ear, he squirmed with pleasure.

'I'm ready,' she said, 'for my surprise.'

'Not here,' he said, glaring at the big yellow ball, who feigned innocence and kept shining steadily.

'Ah, but I want it now,' she panted.

'And you shall have it, my beautiful wife.'

She reared back and he tugged his loincloth straight. This present was a bad idea when she had such power over men, but he hated seeing her dejected, and he feared for their child's safety, so there was no other choice.

Once home, he dismissed the tripods, who took their time shuffling away, dragging their third legs behind them. After they'd gone, he closed the shutters to keep Helios out and lit a candle. While his wife might prefer an audience, just this once, she would be for his eyes only. After that, he'd have to share her with the world. His mind strayed to the forge and he wondered whether the bronze had been melted down. When he imagined the Cyclopes and tripods taking turns mounting it, his fists clenched.

Aphrodite prodded him. 'The surprise?'

He positioned her in front of the mirror and passed her a parcel. She tore off its wrapping and revealed a length of slithery chainmail, which she poured from hand to hand. 'It's too big for my neck, even though it *is* abnormally thick at the moment, so what is this for?'

Standing close, he laced the chainmail around her middle. The links tightened, forcing her breasts to stand proud, skimming her widening waist and exaggerating the flare of her hips.

'A magic girdle!' With some effort, she peeled her gaze from the looking glass. Quickly, she tied on her sandals, tossed her favourite ruby necklace over her head and dragged a comb through her hair. 'I'll be out late, so don't wait up!'

Humming to himself, the god of fire left the smithy, carrying a sack. From learning of his second son's existence, he'd worshipped him and – much to the mother-to-be's annoyance – had stayed by her side in the final days of her confinement, ready to assist with delivery. Finally, she'd had enough and chased him out of the house and back to work.

The pregnancy continued to gnaw at him, both how it had come about and its relatively short term, but then divine pregnancies varied wildly when it came to conception and gestation. Consider Erichthonius, accidentally conceived – mercifully without physical congress between his parents – and born mere minutes after the unfortunate incident with Athena and the wool. And the poor lad's pitiful existence was over so quickly. Instead of dwelling on the past, he put aside his guilt and suspicions and hurried home.

There, he found the child lying on a rug, gurgling as he played with his perfect toes. Hephaestus scooped up the rosy cherub and inhaled his heavenly aroma before kissing him and pinching his chubby cheeks. When the infant squealed in delight, comets danced and stars aligned on high.

'You're making him fuss and he won't sleep.' Aphrodite gathered the newborn to her breast and nursed him while the smitten father emptied his sack, spreading out the contents. 'What on Mother Earth are those?' she asked, poking the metal artefacts with a cautious toe.

'A few playthings,' he said, crestfallen.

'A suit of armour and a shield? Battle dress is a ridiculous present for one so tender.' She frowned as the tot padded at her with dimpled hands and shifted him from her right breast to her left. 'And what about that sword and spear? They're as big as trees. Although,' she said, smiling dreamily, 'he might need them if he takes after his Uncle Ares.'

'Let's hope he doesn't.' Hephaestus wasn't entirely convinced their son was the reason for this smile. He could tolerate the fact that his wife – whose duty it was to love everyone – didn't love him, if only she would not love his brother. What could she possibly see in the god of war, who was easily the most-hated deity? 'I suppose these toys *are* on the rugged side, so let me try again.' He brushed a bronze curl from a flushed cheek. 'I'll take Eros along with me.'

'You think my sweetling wants to spend his days sweating in a hot smithy?'

'He'll never know unless he tries. I'll guard him with my life.'

'You'd better.' She thrust the burping baby at him. 'Get his wind up. Wait.' She dipped her fingertips in the hearth and smeared a band of soot across the child's eyelids.

Comforting the now-yowling infant, he asked what she was up to.

'Trying to stop the flames blinding him.'

'I've already made my new apprentice an eye-patch.'

He set off with the sack of unwanted armoury over one shoulder and little Eros riding daintily on the other, and wondered what toys would be more suitable for someone so soft and plump. As he walked, an ingenious idea suggested itself to him.

At the forge, the golden mannequins tickled the blindfolded boy while his father fashioned wings of halcyon and fastened them to his son's shoulders. Satisfied with the first part of his plan, the blacksmith returned to work, swatting away the aerial godling whenever he swooped too near the fire.

Eros fluttered through the door, as iridescent as a dragonfly, and Aphrodite exclaimed.

'Wings! How enchanting. And a golden bow and a quiver of matching arrows. Oh, my miniature god of war, you *do* take after your Uncle Ares.'

'No, he doesn't,' argued Hephaestus. 'For a start, nobody dies when our son shoots them. Instead, they'll fall forever in love with the next being they clap eyes on.'

Here, he signalled to Eros with a wink. On cue, the tiny god nocked an arrow, drew the bowstring towards him and fired at his mother's heart, but before it reached its target, her hand shot out and stopped the arrow in its tracks.

'Really, Husband, was that wise?'

Gently, he retrieved the arrow and turned his back, pretending to adjust its flight.

'Gods,' he muttered, 'when was love ever wise?'

The Secret

Helios lit up the Mount Aetna forge, aglow with news that the god of fire didn't want to hear. Aphrodite had lain with Ares. The blacksmith tried to harden his heart towards her but he was too deeply ensnared. With blood as inflamed as Gaia's molten core, he hammered and banged, generating infernal sparks the size of asteroids until his rage plumed from the mountain. The smoke defaced the sky and blocked out the gossipy sun. Rivers of red lava carved a path down the mountainside, turning beasts and mortals to stone as they ran. Hot rocks tumbled from the summit until the eastern flank collapsed, sending an immense wave roaring across the sea, wiping out hundreds more lives on distant shores, filling Hephaestus with further self-hate. Once he'd vented his wrath, he shook his fists at Helios.

'You're a damned liar! Why would you fabricate such a malicious tale?'

'You know me. I'm as honest as the day is long. Haven't we always been friends? Truly, what I told you is what I saw.'

He snorted. 'I'll cut the bastard into a thousand pieces for this and skewer them over the forge fire.'

'Nobody would blame you, but think of Eros.'

As he thought, his brow furrowed. 'He's *my* son.'

'If you choose to believe it.' Helios beamed a long ray onto the lame god's left ankle.

'My mangled leg was a gift from my loving mother *after* my birth and not before it.' No matter what the big yellow ball believed, the beautiful boy was his.

'However much you hate the idea, Heph, the little lad is your brother's love-child.'

'*Half*-brother,' he said. His detested sibling had probably deceived him, not once, but numberless times. From cuckoo to cuckold. Perhaps the brute was at his wife whenever his back was turned. Vivid images flowed through his mind until he was afraid the pain would break him. Marital betrayal was one thing, but for Eros to be fathered by another… He sank down until his head rested on his knees. How could he stand to lose his son, who he loved more than his own life? Eventually, the distraught god looked up to see Helios waiting patiently. 'Why haven't you told me about this before?'

'I'm telling you now, aren't I?' Helios shrugged, the resulting heat haze making the horizon shimmer. 'It was the first time I caught them, I swear on the Styx. They'd stayed in bed too long, otherwise I'd never have spotted them. It could be the *only* time they—'

'Stop. We both know how unlikely that is. I'll ask Selene tonight. She'll have seen them.'

'Worth a try, but she always takes the side of lovers. The moon goddess never tells. Hermes has been begging her for aeons to give up her secrets.'

Hephaestus got up and stormed to the forest, bent on retribution, tearing down trees as he went. Struggling to make sense of what he'd heard, he uprooted hundreds of trunks, piled them high, heaved them into the smithy and set them burning, his fury fanning the flames. When the fire was hot enough, he filled his largest vat with copper and tin, pacing while they melted. He would gladly tear his arch-enemy limb from limb but he could never harm Aphrodite. His child, though, Ares' whelp! The cauldron bubbled and spat as anger crashed against love in his heart.

It would please him till the end of days to murder his half-brother, if he could only kill an immortal. Although impossible to finish his adversary, he could certainly finish his gaming. He wondered about waking the Cyclopes, but their size meant they'd not get to grips with the intricate task he'd devised. Instead, he woke the gilded girls and instructed them to cast a million infinitesimally small moulds, and never mind asking why. As ever, they were happy to help, their deft hands soon obliging their master. Ignoring their puzzled looks, he poured fiery bronze into the moulds, his temper refined to a white-hot concentration. When he was surrounded by a mound of metal links, he asked his mannequins to knit them together while he cast another million links, and a million more, and a million more.

Selene shone down on the smith and the gilded girls working through the night, but said nothing, and Hephaestus refused to acknowledge her, knowing what she knew. Once the work was done, he tightened his leg support and braced himself. Grim as death, he slung the net over his shoulder before dragging it up Olympus on the long climb towards the source of his sorrow. The tripods would have taken him, but tonight of all nights, he needed to feed on his pain.

Outside the marital home, he crouched in a shady recess of the veranda to wait for dawn. As the sky lightened, the goddess of love opened the door and skipped into the garden with Eros. When he was certain she was out of sight, the jealous husband hefted his bronze web and entered their chamber. The sheets were rumpled and there was a small dent in one pillow while his own was smooth. Perhaps Helios was mistaken. He paused. Helios was not mistaken. Quickly, he fastened the net to each bedpost. The adamantine mesh was finer than air, but impossible to break, even by a god of Ares' strength and stature.

Satisfied with his thankless task, he found his wife strolling, with her son fluttering nearby. As she planted each foot, blades of grass and blue flowers sprouted, and around her head, sparrows serenaded each other. Something, or someone, had brought out the best in her, but it wasn't him. It hurt to watch, loving her so deeply, and not being loved in return. Love was surely the greatest punishment of all. The king of heaven had known this better than anyone when he'd forced them to marry. The boy darted high above a pink rose bush, selecting the plumpest specimen for his mother, who promptly placed the bloom behind her ear. He wished fervently, but futilely, that Helios would prove to be nothing more than a big, fat liar.

'Afternoon,' said Aphrodite, sarcastically, not a trace of guilt on her beautiful face. 'So, you've managed to drag yourself out of the smithy.'

'Only for a short while.' It took all the strength he possessed to force out the lie. 'I've left an important job undone that'll take tonight and most of tomorrow.'

'Oh, must you work, my sweet?'

He regarded her pout. Pure artifice. 'I must,' he fibbed, 'but I'll be home by nightfall. Try not to pine in my absence. Come on, Eros, you can visit the grotto and play with the seahorses while I'm busy.'

'Excellent idea,' she said. 'I need a decent night's sleep.'

The cherub hovered uncertainly, but fluttered after his father as he limped out of the garden, quietly closing the gate after him.

In that small gap in time when mortal men's hearts stop beating, just as Selene closed her eyes and Helios opened his, the adulterers approached their peak. From his vantage point at the foot of the bed, and hating himself far more than he hated his sibling, Hephaestus watched the violent deity rearing over his wife. Her honeyed limbs entwined the massive god, and she gazed at him as intently as if looking in a mirror.

Bracing himself against the bile brewing in his guts, the blacksmith snapped a catch, which sprung his net. At the sound, Aphrodite pushed off her rampant lover, who withered under his captor's furious glare. But in an instant, Ares' fear transformed to ire and he was all war again, baring his teeth, rending at his confines.

'Get me out of here, you shrivelled goat, and fight me fairly.' The big lump flung a hand at Aphrodite, still prone, a high flush on her skin. 'Observe how it takes a proper god to satisfy your wife.' He kicked at his prison but tangled his sandal in the mesh and lurched forwards, tumbling to the floor, head first.

'Is the *proper god* having a bit of trouble?' asked Hephaestus.

Ares cursed and thrashed. 'Set me free or I will cause you pain beyond measure. I'll slaughter your son, or should I say *my* son. The agony will be so great, you'll beg for your own death and I'll devour your entrails.'

Feet planted wide and arms folded, the blacksmith made himself shorter and squarer than usual, smirking at his rival's stream of increasingly preposterous invective. On and on Ares ranted until he ran out of words and attempted to rip his way to freedom, his face red and his knuckles white, limp penis slapping against his thigh as he laboured.

Aphrodite lay on her side, batting her lashes. 'Dearest, you're always at work and neglecting me. It gets so cold at night and lonely, too. Sweetest Heph, don't turn away from me. Please let us go. Let *me* go. You wouldn't want Eros to come home and find his mother like this.'

'You should have thought about him before.' He despised her more for using their child than for her infidelity. The boy might as well have fired an arrow of lead into his heart. 'He's safe with my foster-mothers. The pantheon can decide whether to release you.'

'At least allow me to dress,' she pleaded, paling at his announcement. 'I can't appear before them wearing nothing but sandals.'

'You will go as you are. Your humiliation has to equal mine.'

~

Ignoring both his wife's pleas and her lover's threats, Hephaestus hauled them to the palace and staggered into the great hall, trying to avoid a barking and prancing Laelaps. Paying no heed to the gasps that greeted him, he threw down his catch, disgracing them before the enthroned pantheon. It gave him no comfort to witness his beloved brought so low. Every goddess spared Aphrodite her gaze, except Athena, who mocked her. Every god except Prometheus surged forwards for a better view, with Hermes and Apollo elbowing their way to the front.

Apollo dug the messenger in the ribs. 'What would you give to be in Ares' sandals, net or none?'

'What *wouldn't* I give to be in Ares' sandals?' Hermes winked. 'Or in Aph's, come to that!' The lascivious friends clutched each other and laughed.

'Oh, not again.' Zeus grabbed Laelaps' collar, pushed through the jostling gods, and groaned. 'What is the meaning of this exhibition, Heph? You've made yourself appear more ridiculous than you already are.'

'I'm returning my wife,' he said, taking no notice of the insult. 'She's faulty.'

'I see no fault.' The greatest god ran a proprietorial eye over his naked aunt. 'Your steady influence was supposed to tame her passions. That was my other reason for giving her to you.'

'I doubt a hundred Olympians could do that, so you have to take her, and as I recall, there was no *giving* involved, so I'll have my bride price back while you're about it.' He pointed at the mastiff.

'Absolutely not.' The almighty rubbed Laelaps' ears with one hand and clutched his collar with the other. 'Apart from anything, we can't afford the wars, so you'll have to patch things up. Listen, a spot of adultery isn't the worst thing to happen in a marriage…'

Hephaestus was aware of his mother looking at him. There was a softness to her, perhaps because they'd both ended up with faithless spouses.

Hera spoke up. 'My son has a point. Permit him to swap Aph for a kinder partner. Homely Hestia would suit him and they could sit by the hearth together. Nobody should have to live the life I do.'

But the king of heaven hardened his stance. 'You will remain married, blacksmith. Feel free to banish the goddess of love to one of her islands, but I urge you to consider young Eros, and be quick about it because while you stand here arguing about trifles, Poseidon is eyeing the parts of your winking wife that only you should see.'

'Not true,' said the sea god. 'I fear the lad has been badly used. Don't forget, he lived in my domain and I feel bad for him. Heph, free your brother and I promise to ensure he repays you.'

Hephaestus had to preserve a shred of dignity before backing down. 'You have a deal, but if my *half*-brother defaults, you must take his place in the net.'

At this, Apollo cackled. 'With Aph for company? If you make an offer like that, expect a queue of gods dragging sacks of silver behind them.'

Poseidon silenced them with a thump of his trident.

'If Ares defaults, I'll repay the dowry and marry Aph myself,' he stated nobly. 'Thereby taking the problem off your hands.'

'It's a reasonable offer, Heph,' said Zeus. 'Accept, before I sweep you off my mountain. And get these two out of my palace. The sight of your naked bride has us as hard as marble.'

With a curt nod, Hephaestus released his captives. Ares squared up, ready to punch him, but when the blacksmith feinted at the god of war's unprotected testicles, he cupped them and scuttled out.

'As for you, Aph,' said the almighty, 'go straight to the sea at Paphos to restore your virginity. Although I suspect there's not enough water on earth for such a task.'

The goddess of love stood up with as much poise as she could muster, and her husband was shocked to realise he was glad to see the back of her. Unfortunately, he wasn't alone, and when she walked away, every god's eye was glued to her swaying backside.

The Morning After

Selene hung low over Dionysus and Hephaestus, who lay belly-down, peering over the edge of a cliff as nine women entered a pit. At its centre, roped to a stone pillar, was a muscular white bull pawing the soft sand. Swirling around him, draped in pearlescent robes and garlands of laurel, the priestesses' faces were masked so they resembled cows, sows and mares. Chanting in monotone, the moon worshippers spiralled closer to their captive, stealing forwards to adorn his thick neck with garlands.

Satisfied with their decorations, they chewed laurel leaves and green juice trickled down their chins. Faster and faster they danced, singing and shaking wands of myrtle. Moonlight washed their flowing mantles as they swept across the sand, voices soaring and feet stamping a rhythm through Gaia. As the frenzy grew, pebbles loosened from the cliff and rolled into the pit, further agitating the enraged creature, who snorted and rived at his immoveable stake. The whirling dancers held hands and flung their high priestess forwards. In her cow mask, she ran rings around the bull, reversing her direction. Eventually dizzied, he halted, drunk and panting, eyes rolling. In an instant, she mounted him, clutching the rope biting into his shoulders. He reared then threw out his hind legs, but she kept her seat, a sheen of sweat on her brow, robe riding up above her left thigh, to reveal a sheathed knife.

As the chant reached a crescendo, the beast redoubled his efforts until the priestess tore off her garment and pressed herself along the length of his back, whispering in his ear and stroking him with her right hand. In the pause between one heartbeat and the next, she unsheathed her blade and plunged it into the milky breast. Even though the gored animal bucked and bellowed, his rider clung on. When he finally stumbled, the eight wild women advanced on him. Chanting louder and louder, they set about him with their own blades.

When the skinning was complete, the disciples carried the bloodied pelt to their chief and cloaked her naked body, crowning her with the horned head. She reclaimed her myrtle wand, climbed the pillar, and stood resplendent, moonlight reflecting off the horns. Her sisters continued their butchery, carving the morass into sections: forequarters, mid-section and hindquarters, which were cut in three again. These nine pieces were set out and the priestesses circled them slowly, singing a dirge while the steaming blood soaked into Gaia, raining on the shades in the underworld, making them feel alive.

The moon blessed the sacrifice with her radiance, favouring the portion containing the liver, and with it, the bull's passions. The high priestess waved her wand at the rich organ and ordered it set over a pyre. A fragrant wisp tickled Hephaestus' nostrils and his belly rumbled at the scent of charred meat. He hoped it had gone unheard in case his greed offended Selene.

Once the offering was burnt in tribute, and its smoke ascended to the goddess, her followers shed their robes and dipped their fingers in ash to anoint each other's skin with the sacred crescent.

Lambent in soft shadows, their ashen bodies gradually merged with the night until only the whites of their eyes showed, and they descended on the remaining eight portions, tearing the flesh with their teeth. As the sky darkened, the stars joined Selene to watch over the sanguine feast until, sated, the worshippers fell asleep amongst the grisly remains.

'Poor bastard.' Dionysus let out a long breath. 'But sooner him than me.' He raised a wineskin to the moon. 'Do you know how often Selene's tried to have me torn to shreds in her honour? What kind of parent wants her son ritually slaughtered?' He winked. 'Bad mothers, eh? We have that in common.'

'I can't disagree,' said Hephaestus, privately considering that Hera came off slightly better in this contest. Being immortal, the vine god would live through such a sacrifice, as had Prometheus, but would endure unknown suffering in the process. 'If that's what she wants,' he said, gesturing unsteadily at the scene below them, 'then how do you stop her?'

'Unlike your mother, mine won't cross Zeus, and although she still gives me the horrors, I'm quite safe. A perk of being fathered by the almighty.'

Despite his stupor, Hephaestus was stung by this remark. Given the vast number of gods created by the king of heaven, how had *he* been born fatherless? But while Hera had denied him both a father and his divine birthright, *and* she'd thrown him off Olympus, Selene had far darker designs for her son, so the smith had escaped relatively lightly. Feeling more pity for his drinking partner than himself, he agreed to a final session. After that, he'd patch things up with Aphrodite, for Eros' sake, if not his own. Thankfully, the boy was staying with Thetis and Eurynome, unaware of his parents' separation.

'Stop brooding, Heph. Get some of this down you. Drink to forget!'

Forgetting his wife and mother was as good an excuse as any so he took a deep draught and settled down to enjoy the starry firmament reeling above him. But the god of the vine had other ideas, lurched to his feet, grabbed his hungover comrade by the hand and pulled him up.

'Enough of this lying-around lark. Adventure awaits. Hurry!'

Hephaestus didn't want to hurry and he didn't want adventure either. Although Dionysus was full of hilarity, there was always trouble in his wake, but he couldn't ditch his friend when he was in such a dark mood. To be on the safe side, he'd stick to wine and stay off the ivy ale. And the mushrooms. What could possibly go wrong in one night?

When Helios arrived to redden the sky, the lunar goddess took her leave, the stars fading with her. The sun leered at the naked priestesses, bloody and ashen, writhing in the remains of the bull. As the earth warmed up, the intensifying perfume of the corpse brought the carnivorous insects, the carrion birds and the four-legged scavengers to feast.

Awaking with a snort, Hephaestus gingerly separated his tongue from the arid roof of his mouth. In the distance, a debate was underway between lambs, rams and ewes, or was it donkeys? He could do with drinking some water, and spending some, but he dreaded moving. Although it was early, there wasn't a breath of air. He prised open an eye and squinted. Fortunately, a roll of cloud stretched over the sea, shielding him from the worst of the rising sun. It was a mercy when a gentle breeze stirred the morning, sending rose petals spiralling to earth, but the waft of honeysuckle sickened him and he remained lying down, too pathetic to stand up, brain pulsing.

'Ah, you're awake. Excellent timing!' His energetic companion waved a wineskin at some vulgar shapes formed by the clouds. 'Look, a phallus fit for Ouranus, a dog meddling with a horse, and here comes Hera, being tupped by a mortal!'

Pretending not to hear, the god of fire concentrated on not vomiting. Under the influence of Dionysus, he could dance like a partridge and brimmed over with so much joy, he could eat the universe in a single bite. His image in the reflecting pool was charming – handsome, even. He could see the goodness in everyone and his spirit soared until the fine chain holding it to him was in danger of snapping. But after the ecstasy came the agony, and he was filled with remorse. Why, oh why, was the world spinning so fast? And why did he smell so revolting? He was haunted by a memory of braying and a donkey's backside. Guts roiling, he sat up to behold several donkeys tied to a nearby tree. Dear gods, what had he done?

'Never fear,' said Dionysus. 'No animals were harmed, but we'd overstayed our welcome and you were too drunk to walk back, so I fastened that lot together and strapped you on. Careful, it's becoming a habit.'

Relieved, Hephaestus closed his eyes but in the dancing pink and gold behind his eyelids swam a further inkling of what had transpired. A minor scuffle after a mortal called Jason left his wife for a different woman but that had been early in the proceedings and didn't warrant a mention. There was something else, though, something spiralling. Rings? A ringlet? No. Coiling? Definitely coiling. A snake? He clouted his temples, worried what had come loose inside. Only someone with a badly cast brain would forsake the goddess of love for… what, a serpent?

Convinced his mind must be playing hide and seek with him, he opened his eyes to find Dionysus grinning impishly, fingers running through his tangling black locks, scrunching them so they reared from his scalp like cobras. Appalled, the smith remembered *exactly* what he'd done. How could he sink so low? He prayed Aphrodite wouldn't get wind of his transgression. Selene might wink occasionally, but she was discreet. With any luck, Helios had slept through the whole thing because *there* was a god who couldn't keep his trap shut.

What had he been thinking? He hadn't been thinking, of course, he'd been drinking. Never again. No more wine. No more ivy ale. No more mushrooms. No more… Medusa. As her name dawned on him, he saw her marching towards him. The Gorgon had been magnificent until Athena altered her, but she was all monster now. And here she was, large as life and twice as horrible, rubbing her swollen belly. He wanted to cry.

'I thought you should be the first to know,' she said, coming to a halt beside him.

'But it was only yesterday, wasn't it?' Time had a way of warping whenever Dionysus and his assorted beverages were involved.

The god of wine cackled. 'You've only lost a night, you old sot, but in any case, we have endless nights for carousing, so why worry?'

'I worry because my wife will have my nutsack.' Or worse, she'd refuse to return and he'd spend eternity alone.

'Don't despair, *lover*,' said Medusa. 'Aph won't mind, and I'm sure she's kept herself nice and busy during your absence.'

A flake of iron scored his heart at these words and he curled into a ball. How could he have been so stupid? He could no longer complain about his half-brother, when they were as bad as each other, and he'd effectively given Ares free rein.

'This… thing,' he said, flinging an arm sideways. 'It can't be mine.'

Medusa knelt by him, forcing him to face her. 'As you can see, I'm no looker, thanks to your good friend, Athena, so prospective lovers aren't exactly queuing up, are they? Fathoming out who the father is won't be *too* hard because it's a lottery of one. You may depend on it.'

Her slithery coiffure did little to settle his stomach as he found himself entranced and his eyes followed the swaying of the snakes. Hopefully, he'd soon awake from what was obviously a dream, but hearing a donkey farting and smelling its bowels opening destroyed that hope. Could this day get any worse?

The Gorgon's belly contorted in a hideous fashion, setting her serpents seething, and when it went rigid, she groaned and got onto all fours.

'Help me,' she panted.

Queasily, he positioned himself at her rear, flashing back to the conception. He was in no fit state to deliver a baby, but the other potential midwife had suddenly made himself scarce. Medusa was straining and her snakes stood out straight, straining with her. Like it or not, this baby was coming.

Following an awful tearing sound, a head emerged. It was ugly, with curling brown hair, but with no sign of any writhing. That was something, he supposed, supporting it in readiness to ease out the body. But instead of a shoulder, another head appeared. Twins. Just his luck. While pondering how to break this news to his wife, a third head popped out. Triplets? How many more could be in there? Was it an entire litter? He may as well lay his own nutsack on the chopping block and hand Aphrodite the axe.

Grappling with three heads, he was relieved when a shoulder surfaced and a fleshy mass slid out. Amidst the carnage, he counted two arms, two legs and one penis. So, not triplets, but a three-headed monster. He might have known.

Medusa pressed the infant to her breasts, where two mouths suckled ravenously, leaving the other to howl. She gave it her thumb to suck, which failed to pacify it, so she unlatched the first to let the third feed, only for the deprived mouth to begin yelling. As she was otherwise engaged in developing a suitable method of rotation to satiate the gruesome child – who was growing at a terrifying rate – the new father stretched out a foot, ready to skulk away, when he was caught in the act.

'Going somewhere? Leaving me and little Cacus to fend for ourselves?'

Cacus? What a name. There was no point in lying. 'I need to go home.' He stared at the ground. 'I'm truly sorry.'

'Not half as sorry as you will be when you learn how dear wifey has been keeping herself busy.'

'I can hardly castigate her when I don't have a leg to stand on.' Depressed, he decided they deserved each other.

When 'little Cacus' had finished suckling, he wiped his

mouths on his mother, belched loudly and breathed out flames.

'He takes after you,' crowed the Gorgon, patting out a small blaze and rearranging her serpentine tresses.

The boy may have inherited his father's fire but his looks and humour were unquestionably from Medusa. The newborn sniffed the air, stood up, marched towards the herd of donkeys and bit into the haunch of the nearest animal. Heedless of the anguished braying, he continued munching.

Hephaestus coughed. 'Well, seeing as the lad's weaned, I'd best be off.' He felt terrible for the harmless beasts, he really did, but there was nothing to be gained by staying. 'Bye, Son,' he said, waving tentatively, 'I'll come and see you soon, I promise.'

And he really intended to. As he'd intended to visit Erich. Dear gods, what was in him that created these monstrous sons, and how could he abandon them so easily? Not once did it occur to him that each foetus was imbued with the regrettable circumstances of its conception, thereby punishing the innocent children for their father's sins.

Deep down, he was as cruel as Hera. Doubly cruel, in fact, because he knew the pain of rejection and of being fatherless, and subjected his own sons to it anyway. Not long ago, he was remorseful about not visiting Erichthonius, but here he was, deserting Cacus. What made him so susceptible to beauty yet repelled by ugliness? Was it self-hatred of his own physical short-comings?

Regardless, it was shameful behaviour so he would try to be a halfway-decent father, but he dreaded telling Aphrodite about this new son and didn't know what he dreaded more, her wrath or her mirth. There was every chance she'd laugh in his face, delighted by his infidelity and its unfortunate outcome, which would hurt far more than her anger. And how would he look lovely Eros in the eye ever again?

The Marital Aid

The god of fire raised his eyepatch, wiped the sweat from his brow and admired the newly cast home entertainment system that was sure to save his marriage. No creature made from humble clay, this, but a vision in bronze. A substantial boy and none too steady on his wheeled feet, he wasn't as big as the god of war, but was undeniably on the large side. It had taken the blacksmith an age to pour bull's blood into the solitary vein, which spiralled from ankle to neck, via the groin, with a wooden peg at either end to prevent leaks. Satisfied, he set off, wheeling his latest invention along, still warm from the mould.

Recently, Aphrodite had reinstalled herself in the family home, and he hoped this gift would go down so well it would overshadow his infidelity, if she ever got wind of it. More importantly, she'd have no need for his half-brother again. A baby blacksmith might not be out of the question and then they could put the whole Ares episode behind them.

The unsuspecting goddess of love lay on the couch, eyes closed and mouth open, with Eros sprawled beside her. No longer a dimpled cherub, but a handsome youth with skin as smooth as marble, bar the odd bump and bruise from flying blindfold to amuse his mother by creating ill-matched couples and occasional throuples.

Hephaestus nudged his wife awake and she sat up, blinking in disbelief at her new household appliance. She twanged their son's mask, and he flew clumsily into the air, narrowly missing her temple with his trailing foot.

'What on Mother Earth is that?' she said, swatting Eros away.

'Not *what*,' the long-suffering inventor chided. '*Who*, who is that? Everyone, meet Thalos.'

Everyone stared at Thalos, who for his part, stared back.

'He doesn't say much, does he?' remarked the ungrateful recipient.

'No, he'll never be an orator, Aph, as I skimped on his brain to concentrate on his… other organ.'

She pressed her knuckles to her mouth to smother a laugh.

'So I see.'

'He'll never be an athlete, either,' said Eros, darting up to tweak an impervious bronze nose, 'so what's he in aid of?'

'Give him a chance, both of you. He's solid metal, including his brain, so he's not designed to be athletic or clever.' It was impossible to explain the indelicate intended purpose with their son awake, so he'd have to improvise. 'He's designed to help with babysitting and so on.'

Eros swooped down. 'I'm too old for babysitting, in case you'd not noticed.'

'Of course I'd noticed. I meant—'

'Oh, gods,' said his horrified wife, 'you meant for future children, didn't you? Sorry to disappoint, but no way am I putting myself through *that* again.'

'You'll change your mind once you witness him in action.' Hephaestus exchanged glances with the boy, who managed a watery smile. 'He'll do the chores you hate.'

'That would be *all* the chores, then,' said Eros, fluttering at his mother's head until she kissed him. Pleased, the youth sighed, snapped his blindfold in place and resumed his nap.

Although the lad was cheeky, he wasn't wrong. The goddess of love was keen on domestic elegance, comfort and luxury, but not on the labour necessary to bring about these qualities. Likewise, although she'd enjoyed petting and nursing her infant, she couldn't cope with the drudgery of mopping up various bodily fluids on an hourly basis.

After checking Eros was fast asleep, Hephaestus encouraged his wife to explore Thalos, who was preferable to Ares, he told himself firmly in an attempt to stifle his mounting jealousy. Bemused, she ran her fingers over the metal man's genitalia, which didn't raise so much as a smile. Frowning, she tapped his neck. In fairness, it was more of a chop than a tap. When there was no reaction, she gave up and poured herself a cup of watered wine. As she sipped, the metal head jerked, the red eyes flashed, and the phallus stiffened and grew to such an extent that Aphrodite was forced to step backwards. Clearly, a few modifications were in order.

'He takes a while to warm up,' she said, raising her cup in a toast, 'but he was certainly worth the wait!'

The blacksmith ignored her mirth but was concerned that the mighty member showed no signs of deflating. He'd definitely spent too long working on it to the detriment of other faculties because it was evident that Thalos was even stupider than Ares. It should be easy to rectify. More blood to the brain, less to the phallus. It was a pity the same remedy couldn't be applied to the god of war.

'Perhaps,' said Aphrodite, 'when his swelling subsides, your bronze man could run an errand for me.'

'He'll be glad to, providing you're not in a hurry as there won't be any running involved. What's the errand?'

'Hera's stolen my girdle. She sent that light-fingered messenger to lift it when I was away. Ouranos alone knows what she's up to, but I want it back.'

It was a huge relief that the magic girdle was gone, but the thought of his mother cavorting in it was too grotesque to countenance.

'Thalos is rather inexperienced for such a fraught operation so I'll retrieve it for you.'

'While you're about it, seeing as he's too unresponsive for my liking, why not send him somewhere he can be useful?' She studied the unwanted gift at length. 'You know who *would* appreciate him? Medea. Her three have been playing her up something terrible, lately. It must be hard being on her own with them. She'll be grateful. Also, I probably owe her a favour after the little mix-up with whatshisname? Jason.'

Little mix-up? That was one way of describing the fracas that had occurred when the alleged hero abandoned his family for a fresh bride. If only his wife would stop meddling in people's marriages, but she was trying to make amends now, he supposed, and the mortal woman could undoubtedly use all the help she could get.

Medea answered her door, each fist clenching a bawling twin by its scalp, with their unfortunate sibling strapped upside down to her chest in a homespun harness. Its face was worryingly red, purple really. By the looks of the poor mites, their mother enjoyed child-rearing less than Aphrodite did. Their skin was rough and reddened, they were thinner than air and the smallest was missing a hand.

'Yes?' she demanded. 'What do you want at this hour?'

It was the middle of the day but her brood likely kept her up at night so Hephaestus reserved judgement and waved a hand at the prospective babysitter standing behind him.

'From the goddess of love. An apology.'

'Huh! Not before time. But what good is it to me?'

'*He* can lend a hand with the—'

'What? Who's been gossiping?' Her fists tightened, pulling on the infants' hair, setting their bawling to a higher pitch. 'That wife of yours wagging her tongue, I dare say.'

'Not at all. The truth is,' he added in a confidential tone, 'I daren't leave the goddess alone with him.'

He stepped aside to reveal the manservant's most obvious charm and the youngest child squealed. Maybe it had been a mistake to turn up without adjusting the blood supply since most nurses weren't endowed with such an appendage and in bronze to boot.

'It looks neither use nor ornament to me,' she said, distinctly unimpressed.

'Appearances can be very deceiving,' he said. 'You'll see.'

'Hmm, I'll think about it, but it's not coming anywhere near the children in that state.'

'He's quite safe, I promise.' Providing the eyes didn't flash and the phallus remained flaccid, he was almost certain of it.

She released the twins, who landed on their backsides and rubbed their heads. Lightning fast, she whipped out the ankle peg, and Thalos haemorrhaged from his single vein, engulfing the toddlers in a burgundy tide.

'Don't worry,' said the dispirited blacksmith. 'I'll clean them up.'

Medea shrugged. 'Suit yourself.'

Once Hephaestus had washed the tots, calmed them down and fed them, he returned to the forge to top up Thalos. Carefully, he ensured the blood supply circumvented the phallus. So there would be no more accidents, he hammered the pegs in harder to be on the safe side.

He showed up at Medea's house not a moment too soon and caught her lunging with a long knife. On seeing him, she dropped her weapon,

'Here you are,' he said, keeping a cautious eye on the blade as he pushed the bronze man forwards. 'More child-friendly.'

'Fine. It can stay. You can go.'

He reached for the knife, which lay dangerously close to an infant who couldn't afford to lose another hand.

'Leave it,' she growled.

'I was just…'

'Well, just don't. Why are you still here?'

'I'm going.' He stole a final peek at the children. 'I'll pop by in the morning to check Thalos is earning his keep and not outstaying his welcome.'

Medea breathed deeply.

'Alright, alright,' he said, 'Till tomorrow, then?' He gave a cheery wave, but she ignored him, instead busily sizing up the nursemaid.

Hephaestus traipsed home, watching the sun sinking in the west and the sea glowing like a garnet, but the evening peace was suddenly shattered by loud shrieks coming from the house. As he retraced his steps, the screams got louder then stopped abruptly. He burst through the door to find three tiny corpses. The bronze man had a roseate glow, reflecting the bloodbath before him, but he was spotless, and although he hadn't moved from where he'd been left, his eyes were flashing.

Screeching, Medea clutched her head and dashed wildly across the room, bare feet slapping in the gore as she careened into the babysitter and started to beat him.

'Why, you monster, why?' Weeping, she threw herself down and rolled in her children's blood.

'Come on, Thalos,' he whispered. 'We'll find you a place to live on Olympus. Perhaps Hera will trade you for Aph's girdle.'

Silently, he considered the crazed woman and her children. The mortals had a saying for this sort of thing. *May as well blame the knife as blame the mother.* It would be more accurate to hold his own wife responsible. Someone would have to tell Jason about the day's dreadful events, and for the love of Ouranus, that someone had better not be Aphrodite.

Friendly Fire I

When Hephaestus entered his family home, he was struck on the temple by a mirror, which hit the floor and splintered. He collected the shards before there was an accident, pleased that the scallop-shell frame was intact. The compact was a favourite gift and Aphrodite had spent endless happy hours admiring herself. There was not much to admire today, though, as anger had eroded her loveliness and a snarl replaced her usual pout. He seized her hands to placate her, or failing that, to prevent her hurling any more missiles.

'So you know,' he said.

'Ugh!' she said, shrugging free. 'Medusa? I could have understood your minor indiscretion if you'd gone after her before Athena uglified her.'

He stared at his feet, face burning. 'I'm sorry, Aph.'

'Don't be. Your belated discovery of the delights of adultery is not what's upset me.'

She flounced from the house and he limped after her, wondering what *had* upset her, if not his betrayal and the resulting child. His wife could certainly walk fast when she was in a temper. He caught up with her in the hall of the gods, where she was poised at the window on the world, tapping her foot so the cymbals on her anklet jingled.

'Down there,' she said. '*That's* my problem!'

On earth, crowds bustled about a marketplace, conversing, bargaining and fanning themselves. There were a few goats and donkeys here and there and children chasing dogs.

'See that woman?' She pointed. 'Psyche. Her beauty is rumoured to surpass mine. *She's* my trouble, not your Gorgon and her horrid offspring. We have to rid ourselves of this usurper!'

We? It was hard to make out anything clearly at this distance but he'd often heard that Psyche was the most beguiling being in creation. He kept this to himself. Of late, silence was the wisest option when it came to Aphrodite and anyone she considered a rival. She placed no greater value on mortal lives than she had that dark day on the mountain, unless especially attractive male specimens were involved.

'Have you visited any of my temples recently?' she asked. 'Scarcely attended, the majority of them, and some are completely empty. The altars are covered in cold ashes and I couldn't tell you when a sculptor last bothered to honour me. They'll be worshipping *her* next, sculpting statues of *her*. Who does she think she is?'

It seemed no time at all since Pandora and her sisters had populated earth, and then repopulated it after the incident with the pithos. Countless new generations had been born, with each an improvement on its predecessor. Perhaps it was just as well they didn't live forever or they'd soon overtake the gods. Two particularly jealous Olympians already had cause to despise earthly competition. Hera because Zeus would not restrain himself. And Aphrodite, who dreaded being outshone. Even now, her face was scrunched up in hatred, her chest heaving. She was becoming increasingly prone to these fits of jealousy. Only a week ago, he'd witnessed her hacking the curls off a hitherto plain neophyte, who'd blossomed late and grown suddenly pretty. But never before had he seen her this vexed and he feared for the welfare of this unwitting mortal. The goddess' vanity had been piqued frequently following Pandora's creation, and numberless women had vanished in mysterious circumstances, but she'd never openly threatened a challenger. Still, his wife was nothing if not full of surprises.

'Why worry, Aph, when her looks are sure to fade? Within a decade or two, she'll be an underworld shade, and by the end of this century, her name will be forgotten.'

'I did consider murder,' said Aphrodite, taking no notice of him, 'but then she'd be frozen in men's minds as if she were an immortal, and I refuse to grant her that gift.'

So the woman would survive, at least for the present, but there were many fates worse than death and it would take the goddess of love no more than a minute to come up with a few.

The suggestion he was about to make appalled him, but it would allow Psyche to live out her life in relative safety.

'Instead of killing her,' he said, 'mar her in some way. Uglify her.'

'Like Medusa, you mean? Oh, you'd love that, wouldn't you? Fortunately, I have a better idea. A plot.'

When Eros was informed of the scheme, his forehead creased, but however anxious it made him, his mother had him wrapped around her little finger and he quickly acquiesced. It wasn't worth Hephaestus intervening, because in her subsequent wrath, Aphrodite would no doubt develop a harsher punishment. While her plan was unkind, it was less cruel than the potential alternatives. If only she'd leave the boy out of it. Freshly equipped with his bow and a fettered boar tucked under one arm, the god of love set off on his quest. He turned to look at his mother, a question on his lips, but she waved him off, a cunning smile coarsening her fair features.

'And you reckon this plot of yours will succeed, Aph?'

'Naturally,' she said. 'My darling child fires at the unconscious jezebel then releases the pig. She wakes up, sees his stinking majesty and falls in lust for as long as it draws breath, and with luck, after its demise, she'll grieve it with every beat of her widowed heart.' Her eyes sparkled so the gold flecks came alive. 'Isn't it a brilliant scheme?'

It was a far from brilliant scheme. Eros' aim left a lot to be desired at the best of times and he and his arrows had been responsible for many unlikely couplings, sometimes with animals and sometimes with inanimate objects. More than one tree had found itself the victim of sudden and inappropriate mortal adulation.

'Aren't you worried about our boy's aim?' he asked.

'Of course not. He'll be firing at close range, so what could go wrong?'

The god of fire was woken by a frantic flapping. Half asleep, he unfastened the shutters to find Eros silhouetted against the moon, wings tattered and struggling to stay airborne. As Hephaestus opened his arms to ease him through the window, he moaned dramatically and collapsed against him. Selene winked in sympathy and he spotted a makeshift bandage around his son's thigh. Gently, he lay the boy down to tend him, lit a torch and peeled off the sooty mask. On closer inspection, the binding looked suspiciously like the hem of a woman's nightrobe, and he wondered what calamity had taken place.

When he unwound the bandage, he saw a cut that was small but deep, and ichor dripped steadily, blooming into velvety red roses. His wife was still in the arms of Hypnos, so he nudged her, receiving a drowsy mumble in reply, and he left her in the god of sleep's embrace.

'You'll need a stitch. Where does your mother keep her sewing box?'

The youth scoffed lightly. 'Mother, sew?'

He should have realised she wasn't given to any of the household arts. Athena would have needles and silk, but it would be quicker to fetch some from the forge. He whistled and his favourite tripod shook itself awake and stood to attention, ready for instruction. While he waited for it to come back from the smithy, he nipped his son's flesh together. Unusual. A god's wound should mend itself, but before he could puzzle over it properly, the obedient tripod arrived with a selection of sewing equipment. When the needle pierced him, Eros shuddered and looked away until the stitching was completed.

'There,' said Hephaestus as he snipped the thread. 'It's bound to heal, but only a deep wound would drip so heavily.'

The second the drudgery was done, the sleeping beauty yawned and sat up. 'Good morning, Son. I trust your mission was accomplished?'

'Yes,' said the patient, 'and no.' He sighed, gloomier than Hades. 'But mainly no.'

'What's that supposed to mean,' she asked, 'and what happened to your lovely leg?'

'The pain in my thigh pales to insignificance compared to that in my heart.'

'Your heart? My gods!' She scanned her son's chest for signs of injury.

He smiled at her. 'Not that kind of pain, Mother.'

'Please tell me you aren't mooning over the pig. By Ouranus, anything but that.'

'Not the boar, you'll be relieved to hear, but sweet Psyche.'

'Oh no, anything but her! I retract my prayer. The swine would have been preferable. I might have known that little cock-shaker would take you from me. Not content with stealing my crown, she had to have you too.'

Ignoring her histrionics, Hephaestus asked the boy what had happened, and he relayed the unhappy tale of the tussle to get himself, his loaded bow and a furious pig through the chamber window.

'When my prisoner scented the maiden, he bucked so the arrow stuck in my leg. Then I took off my blindfold to sort myself out and you can figure out the rest for yourself.'

'I can't bear it,' said the distraught goddess. 'You, in love with that abhorrent creature for eternity!'

This was an overreaction because the mortal carried within her the seed of her own destruction and she would be dead soon enough.

The god of love clutched his belly. 'This yearning is unbearable.'

'Does she feel the same way about you?' asked Hephaestus. 'Did you shoot her, after all?'

'No, the boar was stampeding so I didn't dare risk it. Imagine my despair had Psyche fallen for that swine. Just thinking about it sickens me.'

'Once your cut is healed, return to her.' Aphrodite nestled beside her desolate son and smoothed his brow. 'This time, use a coarse old billy-goat.'

'Give up, Aph. If he loves this woman, he should marry her.'

'Marriage? You're as bad as Hera.'

'Go and make her yours, lad, but check nobody else is there. Sweep for spiders beforehand and remove the blindfold so you don't aggravate the situation.'

The boy was not blessed with the most accurate of aims, and while that was half the fun for his wife, Hephaestus was glad Eros had his eye on the beautiful mortal and not the tusked beast when he shot himself.

As he readied to depart, the young god filled his quiver and shouldered it, glancing backwards.

'Don't mind your mother,' said Hephaestus, clasping him. 'She'll get over it.' But not before Psyche's death.

Now that his second son was paired off, he should keep his promise and pay his third a visit. Cacus must be of marrying age, but who would want a lover with Gorgon blood, let alone one with three heads? Maybe a poorly aimed golden arrow could help.

The Bad Father

The god of fire was at the smithy, casting a commemorative statue of Psyche in an effort to comfort Eros, who was distraught following her recent death. That was the problem with gods and mortals mixing. Shortly after the wedding, the bride had withered faster than a ripe plum going to rot, and in his grief, the god of love had to be restrained from throwing himself on her pyre. Not all members of the household had taken it so badly, however, and despite her son's pain, Aphrodite hadn't attempted to disguise her delight at the passing of her rival.

So absorbed was he in his thoughts that Hephaestus failed to notice the goddess of war outside until she banged on the wall with her helmet. He looked up to see her in the doorway, grey eyes twinkling.

'Ah, there you are,' she said with a grin. 'I bear sad tidings.'

He would never have guessed it from her demeanour, but when she relayed her message, he almost dropped his mould.

'Are you certain about this?' he asked.

She stared at him, unblinking. 'Absolutely.'

'Then Cacus has to be put in the picture straight away. I don't want him finding out third-hand.'

'Agreed,' she said. 'I'll do it. A familiar face might soften the blow.'

It was painful to acknowledge that he was a stranger to his son but he had to break the news himself, ideally before the present company, gossipy Helios or mischievous Hermes beat him to it, and he pointed out that as he was the boy's sole surviving parent, the responsibility rested with him.

'Suit yourself,' she said, putting on her helmet and tightening her aegis.

He shuddered when he realised what was hanging from it. The goatskin mantle was embellished with the head and skin of Medusa, along with clinking phials of her lifeblood. It was bad enough that Perseus had slain her but flaying was a step too far.

Not content with destroying her beauty, the vindictive goddess was now flaunting the remains as a trophy, ostensibly because she'd caught Poseidon fucking the Gorgon in one of her temples. Raping, more like. It was hard to imagine her lying with the slimy sea god voluntarily and equally hard to understand why the goddess was so worked up. If anyone had cause to be aggrieved, it was surely Medusa, who had suffered twice, and if anyone deserved punishment then it was Poseidon.

Of course, Athena argued that her transformation of the formerly beautiful woman was to protect her from further assault, but her justification sounded suspiciously akin to that trotted out by jealous Hera after changing Zeus' victims into trees. Seemingly, the otherwise reasonable goddess had succumbed to the pantheon's twin vices of temper and jealousy, but irrespective of the motivation behind it, his child's mother was dead, and someone needed to have a word with him.

He'd seen neither hide nor hair of his youngest since the day he was born but knew he was alive because of the tales that reached his ears from passing sailors and merchants, and with luck, less than half of these would be true. If only he had learnt from his own experience of growing up fatherless and tried to be more present. After all, his son couldn't help inheriting the family temperament, or the Gorgon blood that flowed through his veins.

Hephaestus was rightly ashamed of betraying Aphrodite, but he shouldn't have allowed conception guilt to infect him to the extent that he showed more kindness to Eros, who was not his child, than to Cacus, who was. In all honesty, the god's treatment of his sons had everything to do with his feelings for their respective mothers, and nothing to do with his parental duty.

Fortunately, it was seldom too late to patch things up, but he wished it wasn't such a long voyage over land and sea to the west. Still, he could always use the opportunity to stop off at the forge on Aetna while he was in the vicinity.

Trust the lad to live in a cave halfway up a mountain. It was almost as if he didn't want to be visited. Hephaestus thanked the tripods and heaved himself up to the peak, clutching a sack of consolation gifts. In his haste to make amends to his estranged son, he'd over-compensated. With the benefit of hindsight, he should have slaughtered the beasts first as the cloven hooves and curved horns had done him no favours during the arduous ascent.

Above the cave's doorway, hundreds of mortal skulls had been arranged in crude stars and triangles. What would Prometheus say if he saw this gruesome artwork? As abodes went, it was far from welcoming, but that was hardly surprising when the lad had been deprived of family life. Perhaps this was a chance to forge a relationship of sorts and he could show his youngest how to create more pleasing designs from less-perturbing materials.

He knocked and took a few steps backwards. After a while, the door opened a crack and three flames coursed through it.

One fire-breathing head appeared, followed by a second and a third, neatly stacked, one above the other. Grimacing, each mouth spoke in turn.

'God of fire, is it?'

'The divine blacksmith?'

'To what do I owe the honour of receiving such an esteemed visitor?'

'Fair enough,' said the bemused father, 'I deserved that, but we have to talk.'

Bored with baiting his father, Cacus jabbed a thick finger at the writhing sack. 'For me?'

Hephaestus handed it over, ignored the subsequent savoury smoke and pretended to admire the distant valley as the fruit of his loins chomped his way through the selection of animals, showing no mercy, despite their pitiful bleats.

When the banquet of charred flesh was over, he followed his deplorable progeny down a twisting passageway that led deep into the mountain, feet crunching as he walked. His heart sank when he found himself in a vast cavern, with skeletal decorations to walls, ceiling and floor.

They ended up in a natural nook, furnished with two chairs and a low table, which he prayed were constructed from ivory. The table was dressed with a lead decanter and goblet, and the host filled the goblet and held it out, its contents glittering blackly.

'No thanks, Son. I gave up after a disastrous session with Dion.' He cast his mind back to that fateful night. It was a challenge keeping track of time when last week felt like a hundred years ago and a thousand years ago felt like yesterday. He shivered at the horrible memory of the conception. 'But it was kind of you to offer.'

'Well, that's the niceties concluded.' The boy threw the troubling beverage down the neck of his middle head and belched, the flames surging. 'So, if you're here to talk, then let's talk.'

How to explain what had happened without the mountain burning down?

'It's about Medusa. She… that is, you see, she's… passed.'

Cacus breathed steadily then snatched up a hairless leg, complete with foot, and gnawed on it before wiping each set of lips on his sleeve and proffering the scorched limb.

'Where are my manners, Father? After you.'

'I'd better not. Thanks all the same.'

'Your loss.' Cacus shrugged and continued chewing.

'Did you hear me, Son? Medusa is dead.'

'Ridiculous,' said one of the mouths not engaged in eating. 'Death is impossible for her. You must be mistaken.' He yawned and tossed the stripped bones into the void behind him.

Gods, this was going to be harder than expected. 'I'm not mistaken. A mortal killed her.'

All three heads swivelled towards him at once, jaws dropping and fires abating for the moment.

'A mortal? No mortal can kill a Gorgon. Which mortal?'

'Perseus. Do you—'

'The same Perseus conceived when Zeus came on his mother in a shower of gold?' The boy sneered. 'If he dared face up to Mother, I imagine he was instantly turned to stone, as it is her speciality.'

'Ah.' Hephaestus scratched his ear, playing for time. 'He calculated a way to look her in the eye and live to tell the tale.'

'That little piece of piss? Somehow, I doubt it.' A frown crossed his brows. 'Assuming such a deed were feasible, how would he do it?'

'With a mirror. More of a shield.' The blacksmith coughed to clear his throat. 'Which he used to reflect the glare and so….'

'And so my mother turned herself to stone.' Cacus was panting, and his flames grew hotter and brighter with every short breath. 'You created the mirror for him, didn't you?'

'No,' he replied truthfully. 'It was obvious Perseus was up to something, demanding a shiny shield, and I chased him.'

'So he stole Hades' shield, which you did make.'

'Sorry, lad.' He decided it would be unwise to mention the theft of Hermes' winged sandals.

'Because of you and your friend, I have a rock as a parent.' Finally, as acceptance dawned, he wept, teardrops flowing from all six eyes, extinguishing his own fires. Steam rose around him as his meaty shoulders shook. When it cleared, he dried his tears, sniffed prodigiously, and the flames gradually rekindled one by one. 'This can't be right. I know Perseus and he's not that clever so he must have had help from Hermes, or Athena. She's always hated Mother so I bet it was her.'

Hephaestus did his best to appear non-committal. The boy wouldn't fare well in an encounter with any Olympian, let alone a war deity, so he'd try to distract him.

'Wait, I forgot,' he said. 'There's also some good news.'

The response to this was three arched eyebrows. 'My mother is dead and you're telling me there's good news?'

'Granted, her death isn't anything to celebrate,' he ventured, knowing this was an opinion not widely shared.

'Quite the understatement.' His son's voice rose and heat surged from him. 'I suggest you get to the good bit. And quickly.'

'Sorry. Anyway, as your mother died, she gave birth, so you have twin brothers.'

The boy's complexions darkened. 'What part of you, Father, can conceivably consider *that* good news?'

'Pegasus and Chrysaor,' he said, stumbling on. 'A flying horse and a golden giant.' It was difficult to reconcile these graceful newborns with their half-brother, or with either of their parents. Chrysaor was a handsome youth and Pegasus a winged miracle. 'You can meet them at the funeral.' Assuming Athena could be persuaded to relinquish the Gorgon's remains so the appropriate rites could take place.

'You have no idea, do you? First you announce my

mother's death, and now you ask me to share her with this pair of interlopers. I suppose Poseidon raped her again?'

When Hephaestus inclined his head slightly, Cacus glowered and burnt so brightly that even the god of fire came over all hot. He surveyed the carpet of bones stretching into the belly of the mountain. Undoubtedly, these younger brothers would be viewed by their elder purely in terms of their potential for flavour and sustenance.

'Speaking of unwanted siblings,' said Cacus, 'how is that fey creature you pretend is your real son, and who you love more than me?'

'Eros? Recently widowed and in mourning for his wife.'

'Nice to have a wife to mourn.'

'Er, yes.' His homely child had every right to be bitter so he adopted a conciliatory tone. 'How about attending your mother's funeral together. Just the two of us. How would that be?'

'You've not once darkened my door in the past, so you needn't trouble yourself in the future. I'm fully capable of grieving alone, without any interference from you or these new brothers.'

The bad father remained silent and concentrated on concealing his relief.

The All Seeing Eye

Heaven was in yet another uproar after Zeus had been, in his words, putting himself about a bit, or in his wife's words, fucking anything with a pulse. After losing all hope of a monogamous marriage, she'd cut her ambitions to a more realistic size: that her husband shouldn't lie with mortal women. When this failed, she cut them further: that he mustn't impregnate mortal women. But whenever she loosened the bounds, her faithless spouse delighted in overstepping them, and despite the marital ruling, a recent indiscretion had resulted in more progeny. A boy named Heracles. This namesake, supposedly in Hera's glory, was an insult too far and instead of spending the morning basking in goat's milk, she spent it plotting how to hurt her current rival.

Before the newborn had drawn a thousand breaths, the jealous queen sent a pair of serpents slithering into his cradle and within the hour had taken delivery of a covered basket from the apologetic mother. Whipping off the cloth, expecting to find an infant corpse in tribute, she'd found her snakes, strangled. Nervously, the woman explained that her son had seized a serpent in each chubby fist and throttled the life out of them. The almighty pronounced himself delighted at siring such a robust child, who was no doubt destined to become a legendary hero, but his wife's murderous expression changed his tune, and he tried to justify his latest lapse.

'It's unfair to expect monogamy,' he whinged, 'and impossible too. Aphrodite can corroborate. Where is she?'

Eros glided over, carefully avoiding his father and his grandmother. 'She's visiting her islands. Bathing.'

'Of course she is,' said the greatest god, with a wink, before resuming his excuse-making. 'Not once did I promise fidelity so don't blame me.'

At this pathetic sop, the greatest goddess stamped her foot. The mountain heaved and a sizeable chunk calved itself from Olympus and flattened a village. When she raised her foot for a second attempt, Prometheus hastened to his patron's side, teardrops sparkling on his dark lashes.

Immediately, Zeus' expression softened and he groaned. 'Oh, very well. From this day forwards, I vow chastity. No more women, whether mortal, divine or bovine. For all my days. That is my solemn oath.'

The blacksmith would bet his favourite anvil the almighty's fingers were crossed behind his back.

'That leaves you the male half of the universe,' Hera conceded, 'but don't imagine this is over.' Her eyes were no more than slits, yet still she noticed her husband mouthing to his lover. 'You must have no more to do with that by-blow and his mother, and if I catch you up to your old tricks, your child will be very sorry.'

Hephaestus beckoned the mortal woman and escorted her to the gate.

'If you have an ounce of sense,' he told her, 'admit Heracles to a monastery until he's of age. Can you do that?'

'If I must,' she said tearfully.

'And give up lover-boy, or nothing will save your son, monastery or no monastery.'

~

After Heracles' birth, Hera diligently enforced her spouse's oath and was determined not to let him out of her sight, while he was frequently heard declaring that he would prefer death to marriage. The insult was water off a duck's back to the queen of heaven, who lay on her couch, feet in her husband's lap, ensuring his genitals didn't sneak off of their own accord.

So far, the promised abstinence from adultery had lasted a few days. The celestial sovereigns lived in harmony and the world wallowed in warm weather and gentle rain, without disturbance by heatwave, storm or earthquake.

In the beginning, Zeus occupied himself by taking Laelaps hunting, but the hound instantly caught any prey he was sicced on and his master grumbled that it defeated the object as he lugged home hundreds of carcasses after each outing. Eventually bored with this diversion, he delegated the task of exercising the dog to Thalos. Thereafter, the bronze man and the golden mastiff were often seen roaming Olympus, red eyes flashing in sync. Free to resume his former pursuits, the errant husband wasted not a minute in returning to earth, where he seduced a beautiful maiden by the name of Io.

When news of this seduction reached Hera, she took swift remedial action, followed by a visit to the smithy, where she shoulder-barged Eros, who narrowly avoided landing in the fire.

Ignoring her grandson, she issued a peremptory command to her son. 'Stop what you're doing. Zeus is omniscient and I'm not so I need you to balance the scales. I want an invention to keep an eye on him. And don't be all day about it.'

This high-handedness did not endear her to Hephaestus, who was about to suggest she apply her powers of prophecy, but quickly dismissed that notion because her prophetic ability was about as reliable as her other half's omniscience. Instead, he suggested spying through the window on the world. But his mother rejected his idea as it only displayed the outdoors and not in nearly enough detail. What she hankered after was the means to see inside buildings as if she were standing in them. He envisioned the king of heaven's wrath if he obeyed his mother.

'My request appears to trouble you,' she said. 'Remind me how many children you have.'

'Three. Two since Erich passed on. Eros and Cacus.'

'So you continue to labour under the illusion that the absurd archer belongs to you and not your brother?'

The youth quailed and the blacksmith patted his shoulder.

'Half-brother. The boy is mine in heart, if not in blood.' An unwise claim. He should have denied paternity and saved at least one son from his grandmother's machinations. That decided him. He would surrender to her demand and risk punishment in order to protect his sons. Both of them.

The god of fire looked up at the Cyclopes, and the trio shrugged in unison, rocking their heads from shoulder to shoulder, their tattoos making him giddy. But their solitary eyes inspired him. If his mother wanted to keep an eye on her spouse, then that was exactly what she would do.

After an afternoon of forging prototypes, and a few test flights with Eros, the blacksmith was ready to share his gift. He returned to the great hall just as the king of heaven was on his way out.

'Dear heart,' called the almighty, hurrying past, 'one of yours, for you.'

With unusual alacrity, Hera showed up. 'Stay where you are,' she said. 'I insist you see what my son has made for me.'

Hephaestus fumbled with his apron, reluctant to unveil his creation in the presence of Zeus, who wouldn't take kindly to being spied on.

'It can wait until I return,' replied the greatest god. 'I have an urgent appointment.'

'With that Io, I'll wager,' said Hera. 'Good luck finding her without Laelaps to help you. The greedy creature is sleeping off a rather large and soporific breakfast.'

Glowering at the drugged hound, Zeus flung quicksilver onto the fire and Hermes materialised, napkin tucked into his chiton, wielding a lamb shank.

'About time. I have a job for you.'

'I live to do your bidding, mighty of mighties,' said the herald with his mouth full. 'And please, no need to apologise for interrupting my repast.'

The messenger tossed the mutton aside and so deep was the canine's coma, that he didn't turn a hair at the juicy bone. The two gods dissolved, but before anyone could speak, they reappeared.

'Where is she?' shouted the thwarted suitor, waving his fist 'What have you done with her?'

'Io?' said his wife. 'Comely, isn't she? I expect a passing robber has taken her, but don't worry because she's been replaced with my best milk-yielding cow.' She jabbed him in the chest. 'Did you think I'd not notice your plaything disguised as a heifer? She's quite safe and I've chosen a special bull for her first covering. Assuming that it *is* her first.'

'If any harm comes to her, you will pay,' said Zeus, rubbing his sternum. He signalled to Hermes and they vanished again.

No sooner had they left, than Hera's hand shot into her son's pocket, and while he recovered from the sudden friction, she examined her present.

'What's this? What use do I have for a ring? I belong to nobody. Is that how you view me? Under sentence to my husband, like his prisoner?'

'Not at all,' replied Hephaestus, hating how his voice squeaked and lowering it to a more suitable register. 'The ring is merely a convenient setting for an all-seeing eye.'

She held it out as if it might bite. 'How does it work?'

'Wear it on your thumb and simply direct it to your

preferred destination to capture images. On its return, it'll replay everything it's witnessed.'

With each word, he was sealing his own fate. If the king of heaven knew his wife could scrutinise his every move, it could only end with the blacksmith chained to a rock and waiting for a brace of eagles to dine on his liver.

She tried on the ring and deemed it adequate. No son could wish for higher maternal praise. Despite knowing the furore his handiwork would cause, he flushed, but the moment passed when she began shaking her wrist violently.

'It doesn't work,' she complained.

'It works,' said Hephaestus. His sons' safety depended on it.

'Then tell me what to do.'

'Flex your thumb.' He stayed her hand with his own and mimed the required motion. 'A shade less vigour should do it.'

With exaggerated gentleness, his mother did as instructed and the eyelids parted to reveal a swivelling crystal ball. In a stage whisper, she gave directions and released it. Together, they watched it fly to the window, where the orb plummeted to earth, a lot faster than its maker had fallen after being thrown from the mountain. Six fathoms short of smashing itself into oblivion, it stopped spinning, righted itself, sped across a field and entered a distant barn.

The queen of heaven drummed her fingers. 'How long—?'

Before she could finish her question, the all-seeing eye arrived with such speed and force, it all but knocked her off her feet.

'It's running fast,' said the blacksmith. 'I'll adjust it.'

'I'll adjust you if you're not careful.' She smoothed her robe, gathered her dignity and flexed her thumb.

The eye filled with moving pictures and the goddess eagerly absorbed the unfolding scene. Inside the barn, a herd of cattle were being tended by her hundred-eyed pet giant, Panoptes. In their midst was a lovely white heifer, with limpid eyes and long black lashes. As she daintily tiptoed in search of clover, the cowherd's gaze never left her.

'So, you remain undiscovered, my pretty Io,' said the triumphant Hera. 'And with Panoptes guarding you, even if my faithless husband does locate you, he'll be forced to leave you intact.'

Her smile slipped when Hermes manifested in a corner of the barn, pulled out a small set of pipes and began to play them.

'What's that messenger up to?' she asked. 'Summon Zephyr and I will soon put paid to this… this, whatever it is!'

One Hundred Eyes

Patiently, the god of fire explained to his mother that the all-seeing eye could only display what had previously occurred.

'How useless are you?' she barked. 'Fix it so it shows events before they happen so I can undo them!'

Despite her temper, the greatest goddess remained glued to the scene in the barn. Although Hermes was not as accomplished a musician as Apollo, he played the pipes sweetly enough and the cattle lay down, breathing steadily, including lovely Io. Soon, Panoptes was struggling to stay awake and slumped against the wall, lulled by the music. As each of his hundred eyes twitched and closed, his huge chin rested on his chest, and he slid to the floor in a crumpled heap.

'Excellent plan, Zeus,' said the queen, pale with anger. 'Having my sentry put to sleep so you can rescue your heifer!'

The piper nudged his victim with a winged foot, and satisfied he was unconscious, pulled a dagger from his chiton and slit the loyal cowherd's throat. Hera collapsed as his lifeblood soaked the hay, not even bothering to watch as the messenger woke Io and led the sleepy calf to her beaming lover.

'My blameless servant dies so my swine of a husband can

lie with that heifer of his! If only he were smaller, I could resurrect him,' she said, a solitary tear rolling down her cheek.

Hephaestus had never seen his mother cry and always assumed she either couldn't or didn't want to. While he knew her sharp words were only an echo of her inner pain, he still struggled to approach her. Instead, he called to Thalos and the bronze man wheeled himself over, offered his hand and hauled the queen of heaven upright, dusting her down and patting her until she shoved him away.

'What harm did that kindly soul ever do anyone?' she sniffed. 'Nothing will make up for his murder. Nothing.'

Not blessed with looks, so too unattractive to grace the palace proper, the giant had been unwavering in his guard duties and not once had he failed his mistress until outwitted by Hermes and his lullaby. Now, Hera was in mourning and it was impossible to avoid wondering why she favoured the ugly Panoptes when she couldn't tolerate her child. Perhaps her son's ugliness reminded her of a flaw of her own that was difficult to admit, and wasn't he guilty of the very same offence with Erich and Cacus?

But there was no time for reflection. What could he do to honour the deceased and comfort the bereaved? Having a bad mother didn't mean he had to be a bad son, and it was hard not to sympathise, especially when her wandering spouse was the cause of so much misery. Plus, the giant was a placid sort, unless crossed, and it was wrong to have him slain so casually.

Hephaestus returned from the barn with the gruesome remains loaded across the tripods. The body was quite a weight and his knees buckled when he lifted it, trying not to push his thumb through any eyes as he heaved it into the smithy. Afterwards, he sat in the doorway to catch his breath and allow his aching leg to recover. While he rested, a peacock sashayed past. It was something to behold, yet there was some room for embellishment he realised, as he looked from the bird to the corpse. It would be a horrible task, but what could be better than creating an eternal tribute to his mother's faithful servant?

His feathered friend was none too keen on being imprisoned in the forge, where it screeched in protest, flew up to the roof and roosted on a beam, tail spread beneath it. Content on its new perch, it started to sing, forcing the blacksmith to stuff wool in his ears. Give him a dowdy song-thrush any day. He stared at its scaly toes, wondering how to detach it without injury to it or himself. Brute force was no good. This needed a gentle touch. He tossed some quicksilver into the flames and the messenger turned up, hip and lip thrust out.

'Yes?' he asked in a bored voice. 'Who granted you permission to summon me?'

'I need you to run an errand, which is the very least you can do in the circumstances.' He tipped his chin at the carnage.

'Only obeying orders,' said Hermes. 'What was I supposed to do?'

'You could have left the cowherd slumbering and let the cattle loose. Once Zeus had Io in his clutches, he wouldn't have cared about anything else. You know he's mostly hot air.'

'Agreed, but there's no point bellyaching after the fact. What's this errand?'

'Fetch Artemis. Tell her it's for Hera and she'll come. Besides, she owes me for her hunting gear. This is what she must do…'

In the heat of the forge, the stench from his quiet guest was sickening and the racket from his noisy guest was getting on the blacksmith's nerves. While waiting, he gouged out the hundred eyeballs, setting them aside for cleaning and polishing, but it was grisly work prising each orb free of its socket.

After a cleansing dip, he caught a few sharks to roast while he waited. As he disposed of the final fin, the huntress came towards him, her forest-green chiton girdled and hitched over her knee, auburn hair tied up neatly, a lean dog springing lightly at her side. Over one bronzed shoulder was slung her bow and arrows, and over the other, a bloody bundle, which she emptied out at her sandalled feet.

'What were you thinking?' he asked, quickly stuffing the pile of dead peahens back into the sack. 'Do you want to get us both strung up in Tartarus?'

'You never said you wanted them alive.' She shrugged. 'I'm a hunter, not a shepherd.'

'Shepherds don't round up peacocks,' he said.

'Then, what does?' she asked.

'A peaherd? Oh, never mind, I'll do it myself.'

Luckily, peafowl were as loud as they were conceited, so it was easy to find their gathering place, and he snuck up on a muster of females surrounding their lustrous male. Within minutes, he'd trapped a half-dozen dull-brown specimens and held his quarrelling cargo at arm's length to evade the pecking and scratching. Meanwhile, the arrogant paramour went on strutting, blissfully unaware that its adoring audience was suddenly absent.

At the smithy, Hephaestus released the frumpy females and the wary cock overcame its high dudgeon and descended. Just as well it hadn't seen the contents of Artemis' sack. When it began to parade, the hens affected ignorance of its presence, each discovering some remarkably interesting substance that required immediate investigation. Undeterred, it performed for its small but tough crowd, raising its feathers and rattling them. So absorbed was the haughty creature in its courtship dance that the god of fire was able to walk behind it, carefully positioning the beautiful eyes.

Wiping his hands on his apron, he stepped backwards to admire the results of his labour. Perfect. Now Panoptes could keep watch for eternity. It was a worthy way of honouring the dead and proof that it was possible to gild the lily by making the bird twice as handsome and no doubt twice as vain. Once his ministrations were over, the peacock regarded him beadily.

'We're finished, sir, and you'll thank me for it, I promise.'

At the sight of the newly resplendent fan, the formerly coy handmaidens became coquettish, clamouring for attention, and the blacksmith feared that the object of their lust would not survive their affections. He closed the door, leaving the groom to the mercy of its brides while he built a pyre for the giant and for Artemis' quarry. It was a dreadful waste of flesh but no amount of fine fare was worth his mother's wrath if she learnt he'd dined on a bird sacrosanct to her.

For weeks, Hephaestus tripped over broody peahens, a cantankerous cock and dozens of hatchlings. His son found the youngsters so amusing, he was eager to take the entire harem and their offspring home. Of course, Aphrodite had refused them houseroom, so the rowdy family had stayed at the earthly forge. Once the chicks were sufficiently mature, he grabbed a handful of squawking fluff, fastened their sire to his shoulder and roused the tripods to carry them to Olympus. When they arrived in the hall of the gods, he removed his hat with a flourish and set it before the king and queen of heaven.

'You're too late,' deadpanned Zeus. 'We've already eaten.'

The greatest goddess scowled. 'Why are you wearing one of my sacred birds?' She snapped her fingers and the cock leapt down, leaving him rubbing his clawed skin.

The god of fire placed a finger against his lips. Unaccustomed to being shushed, his mother opened her mouth, ready to rant, but paused as a chick hopped out of the hat, followed by another and another until thirteen peachicks huddled together. On his command, they ruffled the baby fluff that passed for a tail and strutted in an innocent parody of their father, who swaggered forwards to show its brood how it was done.

When she saw the majestic fan, speckled with the giant's turquoise eyes, Hera applauded. 'My dearest servant, memorialised so cleverly! This is more than adequate. Come here, Hephaestus.'

Blushing, he allowed himself to be clasped to her bosom. It was two heartbeats, three at most, but a feeling suffused him like none he'd ever known, and when he felt her lips close to his ear, he fought the urge to weep.

'These watchful beauties will be on the constant lookout for my straying husband,' she hissed, 'but first, he must pay for the slaughter of my humble Panoptes.'

One Hundred Knots

The queen of heaven's head rolled across the floor and came to rest against a heap of peacock corpses. Although the marble nose was chipped, her features were otherwise intact. So many columns and walls had collapsed, it was a wonder the palace was still standing. With this final act of vandalism, the almighty had finally worn himself out and he fell asleep as quickly and sweetly as all belligerent infants eventually do. Beside him was Laelaps, paws up and dead to the world. The great hall lay in ruins and the god of fire silently calculated the number of decades it would take to rebuild.

This wave of destruction had come about because, in revenge for the murder of Panoptes, his bereft mistress had sent a gadfly in eternal pursuit of Io. Consequently, the lovely heifer was never stationary, chased endlessly from land to land by the biting insect, with her frustrated lover helpless in the face of such a formidable hex.

Hera studied her broken statue and appealed to the divine assembly. 'My husband needs to listen to reason. He can't be allowed to simply kill anyone standing between him and the current object of his lust, and I'm not sure we can afford another of these tantrums.' She clapped her hands and a doleful Thalos arrived, carrying a substantial spool of rawhide. 'Together, we must fetter Zeus, and when he awakes, he'll have to see sense.' She paused to suck a pomegranate dry. 'Are you all with me?'

There was some foot-shuffling but her glare made it plain that any deity not with her was against her. Surprisingly, apart from Hestia, there was broad assent. Hera seemed to have garnered some sympathy, especially amongst the other goddesses, but if they hoped she'd be more benevolent than their current ruler, they were in for a shock.

On her command, Hades and Poseidon seized their unconscious brother's feet, and Apollo his head, while the rest of the pantheon busied themselves with binding the king of heaven. Hephaestus was surreptitiously undoing the knots, but as fast as he untied them, his fellow Olympians retied them. Aphrodite, though not supposed to lift a finger except in love's labours, was unexpectedly dextrous. Centuries of practice, the jealous blacksmith concluded as she toiled over her nephew's groin. Thalos wheeled to and fro, eyes flashing, desperate to wake up Laelaps and his master. Overhead, Eros fluttered, giddy at the excitement in the air, aiming an arrow at what passed for Hades' heart.

'Have a day off, lad,' said Hephaestus, swatting at the boy until he pouted and swanned off to watch the proceedings from a safe distance. Let him sulk. The king of heaven's predicament was more pressing, and he would not forget today in a hurry. To a certain extent, it was easy to sympathise with his mother, mainly because butchering Panoptes was so obviously cruel. But this plot of hers spelt disaster and he wasn't sure her motives were as honourable as she'd made out. Did she really want only to negotiate, or had she a more sinister plan in mind? Regardless, the second her husband had been bound with a hundred knots and transformed into a hulking cocoon of rawhide, Hera called a halt and the Olympians downed tools.

Immobilising the greatest god was a terrible tactic, but the tranquillity was a welcome change and it was a shame when the brief respite ended. Awake, but unable to move, Zeus lambasted the pantheon and vowed a punishment worse than death for everyone who did not go to his aid. This was a significant threat to those encumbered by eternal life, and more than a few nervous glances were exchanged.

'Oh, smite me!' said the queen, ignoring this bluster. 'My darling, your thunderbolt is missing, and your hound is in the arms of Morpheus, so pray tell *how* you propose to punish us.'

Teeth gnashing, the almighty flailed, succeeding only in falling off the couch. Hera stepped backwards to avoid him, only to find Poseidon blocking her path, and he took the opportunity to run a wet thumb down her breastbone.

'As Zeus has been rendered impotent, lissom goddess, it is my duty to reign over heaven, earth and the seas. Furthermore, I proclaim that you will marry *me*.'

On hearing this accusation of impotence and witnessing his brother's latest attempt at a wife-grab, the captive gave a bone-shattering roar, but the sea god silenced him by thumping the floor with his trident.

Not perturbed in the slightest by her spouse's protest or his rival's proposal, Hera simply skirted her smarmy suitor. 'Proclaim nothing, you fish-faced fiend. *I'm* easily the most suited to the post.'

Sole rulership. So that was her aim. Not to be outdone, Hades stormed out of the shadows.

'Stand aside,' he snarled. 'As the eldest, it is *my* place to govern the realms.'

The three would-be rulers stood braced for combat while the almighty continued to wrestle with his bonds. Did they hope to keep him trussed for eternity? Hephaestus tried to catch his mother's eye, but her gaze was fixed inwards, on ambitious visions of glittering cities and vast kingdoms, and no doubt also on some horribly drawn-out humiliation for her husband. Not relishing the outcome of a skirmish between the powerful siblings, he decided to visit the undersea grotto in search of some sound advice. But first, he had to remove his immediate family from danger. Hefting a surprised love deity under each arm, he left, hoping the tripods would arrive before his leg gave out.

~

The blacksmith deposited his furious wife and son at the earthly forge and instructed the Cyclopes to hold them there until his return. When he arrived beneath the sea, it was night and Eurynome was out wandering. Thetis listened to his news, arranged her finest seaweed stole around her shoulders and settled into her throne.

'This is very bad, Heph. It'll lead to civil war, which is in nobody's interest. A hundred knots, you say?'

'Yes,' he replied. 'My mother is hellbent on becoming the ultimate ruler, no matter the cost to peace.'

'The queen of heaven is foolish, and if I release him, Zeus is honour-bound to discipline her. But Hades, Poseidon and Hera look set to tear the three realms to shreds if left unchecked.' She clicked her talons together while she thought. 'Come with me. We're going to the land of giants.'

He followed her to the forbidden grate at the rear of the grotto and pressed his face between the bars, gazing at the murky void beyond. 'But without Hermes or Zephyr, the fighting's likely to be over before we get there, never mind back,' he said. 'I wonder if Pegasus would give us a ride?'

'No need. This is an ancient wayfare where neither Selene nor Helios dare show their faces, so no time passes. Fetch your net.'

He rummaged in his old chamber before returning with the trap he'd used for Aphrodite and Ares.

'My net is strong, but I suspect it's too small to capture anything bigger than my half-brother.'

'You worry too much, Heph. There's more than one way to snare a giant. If you're ready, we'd better go. This passage can be painful for you sky-dwellers, so nip your nose when crossing the threshold, or you'll know about it.'

She tapped the grate with her sceptre to open it and enveloped them in a cloud of sepia. Blindly, he groped until gripped by a force so overwhelming it was like being sucked rapidly through a whale's intestine.

Almost instantly, they were spat out on a beach where dawning Helios highlighted a peak encircled by distant clouds. Reeling from his strange journey, the god of fire stared at the surf brushing the shore, foaming brightly and receding. Eddies of mist rose as the sun burnt down, drying the sands from dark gold to bone white.

The seawitch peered at the mountain. 'In the belly of that barren rock, dwells Briareus. He is the solution to this problem, but there is a blood price.'

'Surely,' he said, 'there has to be another answer?'

'If we don't pay, the coming conflict will have an immeasurably higher price, so we have no choice. A hundred virgins is the fee.'

'But—'

His foster-mother held up her hand to silence him and went on. 'There's a dwelling nearby with plenty of innocents ripe for the plucking because they're preparing for the new year rites.' She looked at him steadily. 'Don't feel guilty, Heph, you were always too tender-hearted. It's their fate to die. That's why they were born, just as goats are bred for eating.'

Thetis was not wrong. Since the death of Pandora and the end of the golden age, thousands of young mortals were chosen for ritual slaughter every year. It was their birthright. Once selected, they'd be flayed alive, their entrails dragged out and their organs devoured by cannibal priestesses at the height of their ecstasy. It was the tradition nowadays and free will meant even Prometheus was powerless to prevent it.

One Hundred Virgins

Before them was a white-domed monastery. From it, raced a glut of laughing boys who scampered over the rocks and dived into the water, their bronzed bodies as sleek as a shoal of fish. How could anyone send them for slaughter?

A chubby child drew the god of fire's attention. Clad in no more than a halo of dark curls, he was engaged in the solemn task of filling the sea with the shore. Fully absorbed, he crouched on his hunkers, dimples winking on his knuckles as he grabbed fistfuls of sand, sprang up and flung it into the surf. The strenuous effort of his labours overbalanced him so he toppled onto his backside and sat chortling at the gulls above. Determined, he scrambled to his feet and jumped up and down, stocky legs splayed, as if hoping to join the birds. Behind him, his companions chased each other, teasing as they ran, none of them taller than a ewe.

How were they so exuberant when they lived so close to death, and what were their parents thinking, entrusting them to such a place? Perhaps the same as he'd been thinking when he advised Heracles' mother to put him in a monastery to preserve the infant from Hera's wrath.

'Try not to dwell on it,' said Thetis. 'They'll meet a

glorious end that prevents the war of all wars. Think of it. We forfeit a few minors, and the three realms are saved, along with mortalkind.'

A few? 'It's still a horrific sacrifice, though.' Perhaps it was easier for his foster-mother, who had never given birth and saw life as expendable.

'Their families will remember them with pride,' she said. 'And they'll be reunited in the underworld, so they won't be truly lost.'

This logic was unconvincing, yet no suitable alternative presented itself. Even if sacrificing a hundred lives prevented thousands from dying in a great war, he doubted Prometheus would ever forgive him for his part in this.

'The arithmetic makes sense,' he said, 'but when I look at them, all I see is Eros, and I want to protect them.'

'Then try to see them as Erich or Cacus,' she said. 'Their welfare seems to weigh on you less heavily.'

He cringed at her bluntness, but she wasn't wrong. On the rare occasions he considered his monstrous progeny and their vile conceptions, he was overcome with revulsion and shame, the same revulsion and shame he felt about himself and that Hera no doubt felt about him.

The seawitch scowled at his dawdling and propelled him towards the frolicking crowd. Seeing the deities approach, the children prostrated themselves on the white sand. This was the last day on earth for these little mites, but his foster-mother was right. Sparing them would mean a worse death in the new year, whereas serving the almighty today would only curtail their fleeting lives by a few months.

Swiftly, he cast his bronze net over the prone children and pulled it tight before they knew what was happening. With one voice, the captives screamed, their red throats open to the sky as if they were fledgelings demanding sustenance, while their more fortunate colleagues fled. He counted his noisy catch, a dozen or so too many, so he started to unfasten his net, until a cold hand thwarted him.

'Keep them. They won't all survive the climb and we don't want to be short.'

Before he could argue, the elder priests came running, tripping over long robes, shaking their fists and waving staffs, alerted by their charges' shrieks. The elders had a good mind to protest. Come the new year rites, they'd be over a hundred devotees shy of the required number and would have to offer themselves to sate the ravenous priestesses. Athena had a lot to answer for. Once the older mortals saw the visiting deities, they immediately lay face down on the beach.

'Can't I take out some of the younger ones,' he asked, 'and swap them for their guardians?'

'No,' she said, 'because it's highly unlikely that the elders *are* virgins, oath of celibacy or not. The hypocrites do as they please and then spare their own hides by sending the youths in their stead.'

Hephaestus shut his ears and shouldered his scratching, biting and kicking haul and trailed up the mountain after his foster-mother. He wished they'd stop squalling and enjoy their final minutes, because if Ares couldn't escape this snare, these poor lambs stood no chance.

As the day wore on and the sun rose higher, the exhausted sacrificial offerings stopped fighting and started sobbing, their salt tears stinging the burning skin on their porter's nape. The ascent was hard going, and he regretted not bringing his staff, but the arid rock was hot beneath his feet, and the warmth radiated up his leg, providing blessed relief from his endless pain.

~

After a long trudge, they arrived at a vast cave, its entrance sealed with a boulder, and the seawitch cried out her petition.

'Briareus the Strong, I seek your aid, in the name of the triple goddess. In return, I will pay the blood price.'

At this, the children set up a high keening that was painful to hear and they clawed anew, so the blacksmith tightened his grip, but they stilled at the terrible grating sound made by the makeshift door as it was dragged aside.

From the shadows came a loud sniff, followed by a rumbling voice. 'Pure. Good. Hearts beating. Perfect.'

With this pronouncement, the huge householder emerged and planted his mighty feet. Like the Cyclopes, his solitary eye was tattooed with concentric rings. Unlike the Cyclopes, his torso was covered with a forest of waving arms. At the sight of the hundred-hander, the boys shuddered. Soon, the smell of excrement filled the air. It wasn't a demise the blacksmith would wish on any mortal, let alone on these tenderlings.

His foster-mother had no such compunction. 'Pay the price. Now.'

Guilt-ridden, he put down the net and loosened it. The ogre bent double, casting the visitors into cooling shadow before straightening up so Helios' rays scorched them once more. Each enormous fist clenched a boy, which left fourteen, thirteen of them crushed corpses that Thetis flicked off the edge of the ridge, and one miraculously unharmed survivor, he of the curly hair. On noticing him, the giant held up his hands and carried out a headcount.

The quivering tot promptly wet himself and Hephaestus picked him up. 'Your price was a hundred virgins,' he said over the screaming, 'and that's exactly what you have, so this lad goes free.' The elders would assume he was dead and wouldn't miss him. 'Run as fast as you can, Son. But not to the priests. Do you understand?'

The infant nodded, tear-stained and snotty.

'If you ever find my forge, I promise to help you, but for now, flee. Pray to your father to save you.' Futile, of course, since Zeus was currently incapacitated and in any case too self-involved to care about his mortal children. He knelt to release the silent child. 'Go,' he whispered, tapping the boy gently, setting him toddling downhill, yowling as he grazed his baby flesh on the thorny shrubs.

The drooling giant stared after the escapee with some regret before addressing his petitioner. 'What is your demand, Daughter of the Nereids?'

'A minor chore,' she replied innocently. 'I need you to untie a few knots.'

'Is that all?' When Briareus shrugged his massive shoulders, the children vomited at the rippling motion.

'Yes,' she said. 'That's all.'

'Then I agree to do your bidding, but if you'll excuse me.'

He raised his uppermost arm, tossed the nearest boy into the air and caught him in his powerful jaws. When he chomped, a thin trickle of blood ran down his chin as a pitifully small shade flew overhead. The ninety-nine who were next in the queue panicked, and no wonder. This wasn't the hushed sacrifice Hephaestus was used to. Where were the sombre prayers he'd so often witnessed? For pity's sake, why could the masticating monster not flick a wrist and snap his prey's neck before lobbing it into his cavernous maw?

'We should have drugged them,' said the god to his foster-mother as they watched the pathetic shades rising. 'That's the usual way, isn't it?'

'Mm, with poppies and toadstools,' she said. 'but we don't have the luxury of time and our friend prefers his game alive and wriggling. Stop fretting. The martyrs will be remembered, in mortal times at least.'

Cold comfort, thought the god of fire as the hundred-hander's middle arms arced to his mouth. With any luck, the boys would swoon. The chewing was slowing, so each death was taking longer than those before it, and he pitied the wailing souls trapped in the lowest hands. How much worse their terror for knowing what fate had befallen their playmates. Guts churning, he turned away from the mangled mass. If only giants would close their mouths while they ate. When the ritual feast ended, the gourmet's heavy-lidded eye closed and he stretched himself out for a lie down but rapidly reconsidered after receiving a quick whack on the sole from a sceptre.

'Ow!' He clutched his sore foot. 'What was that for?'

'Indolence,' came the reply. 'Get up, unless you really want to feel my wrath.'

Grumbling, Briareus obeyed and lumbered down the mountain, rocks tumbling around him. With every step, his bulging belly sloshed. They should have let him sleep off his gluttony. Not wanting to risk being doused in the contents of that particular stomach, Hephaestus kept his distance. Halfway down, the gods spotted the tiny fugitive underneath a shrub, pudgy knees knocking. Hiding proved pointless as the giant smelt the mortal and rubbed his paunch greedily, but after a sharp glance from the seawitch, decided he was sated and left the child unmolested.

When they reached the gateway to the grotto, their hefty accomplice half drowned as his shoulders wedged in the grate, and Thetis almost shattered her sceptre, to say nothing of her patience, trying to lever the big lump through.

'If I'd realised we needed a midwife, I'd have called for Artemis,' she said. 'Can't you make yourself any smaller?'

Out of his element, Briareus tried to hunch himself up, to no avail, so the seawitch cast a spell to reduce him to a more manageable size and forced him through. After the odd trio surfaced from the sea, ready to trek up Olympus, the enchantment faded and the giant returned to his former dimensions, complaining that the whole process had made him dizzy. They were barely out of the foothills when he tapped Thetis on the shoulder, nearly flooring her.

'Er, this job had better not involve any gods.'

'Too late to complain, when you've already digested the fee,' she retorted. 'You know what happens if you break your bargain…'

'You're very underhanded,' said the giant, ugly face falling and tattoos crinkling as if about to cry. 'You never mentioned anything about gods.'

'And you never asked,' she said. 'So move it.'

'The pantheon might be cross for a few decades,' said Hephaestus, 'but they'll get over it eventually and the king of heaven will be in your debt forever.'

'Are you telling me that it's *Zeus* who's tied up?' Briareus gaped, revealing tombstone teeth encrusted with entrails. 'Well, why didn't you say so in the first place? *I'd* have paid *you* to see that.'

One Hundred Hands

It was dark when the trio arrived at the Olympian summit and entered the ruined palace. The king of heaven was still cocooned in rawhide, and the pantheon had divided into three clear camps beside their champions, who were engaged in a heated debate. Flanked by Ares and Eris, Hera was busy declaiming from the pedestal that had, until the recent mêlée, held her statue. Poseidon lazed on his throne, the prongs of his trident wedged into a wall, pinioning an apoplectic Hades, whose obsidian eyes burnt with hatred. On seeing the hundred-hander, the Olympians clamoured for their weapons and their deposed ruler struggled under his restraints as the bloody-jawed giant approached, each footstep making the surviving marble statues shiver on their plinths. Thalos lay on his front, wheels whirring helplessly, and a hungover Laelaps circled the visitors, growling. Thetis silenced the mastiff with a withering look and attempted to calm his master.

'Briareus means no harm. He's here to free you from your shackles.'

At this news, the almighty flopped on his couch and allowed the giant to carry out the necessary ministrations. For a being so massive, he was adept and it was quite a spectacle, watching his five-hundred digits unravelling the knots. As a result, the prisoner was liberated before the sea god could reclaim his weapon. Zeus rubbed his stiff limbs, stretched and beckoned Laelaps. Hephaestus was mildly surprised to see Aphrodite teetering forwards, bearing a thunderbolt across her outstretched arms. With a pretty curtsy, she returned it to its rightful owner. Briefly, he wondered how she'd persuaded the Cyclopes to set her loose, then decided not to pull that particular thread. Unsurprisingly, his wife had realised which way the wind was blowing in time to join the winning side. Eros was nowhere to be seen and hopefully stuck in the forge. With any luck, the boy's involvement in this escapade might be overlooked. The gods of the sea and the underworld were less fortunate and backed away from their former captive.

'Halt!' bellowed the greatest god, bolts of lightning shattering one of the few intact columns, bringing down a portion of ceiling so the two collaborators were trapped amongst the ruins. 'Stay there while I give thanks to my saviours. First, Briareus the Strong, I award you the gift of prophecy.'

The astonished giant genuflected as he was anointed with a thunderbolt. When he straightened up, his eye swivelled, and he staggered slightly, clutching his head while the unexpected gift made itself at home inside his skull.

'Heph and Thetis, the pair of you prevented a terrible war, so I am in your debt. I promise on the Styx to repay that debt. Anything. Anytime. Anywhere. No questions asked.' The king of heaven then dealt with his brothers. 'I can't blame either of you for being ambitious, but you must return to your own domains. Next time, I will not be so merciful.' He eyed his male siblings until they paid obeisance. 'Consider yourselves banished.'

Poseidon shook off the rubble and gave the object of his lust a last lingering look, grasped his trident and swept out of the great hall, leaving a trail of putrid matter behind him.

Hades grumbled, 'As the eldest brother, this realm should

have been mine.'

'Not that it needs repeating,' said the almighty, 'but I won the sky and earth by lots, fair and square, so be on your way. For back-answering, you will be exiled for a thousand years, but you need not be lonesome. I'm not a monster, so you may help yourself to a bride.' Zeus followed his brother's gaze. 'But hands off my wife.'

At this, the god of the underworld grunted, shoved on his helmet of invisibility and vanished. Hephaestus wondered which poor soul he'd pick. Aphrodite, maybe?

'It takes ages to get to Hades,' moaned a disembodied voice from the smithy. 'Even with an anvil, it'll take nine whole days and nine whole nights to reach earth and the same again to reach home. Is it any wonder I'd risk everything to escape such a distant and depressing place?'

The blacksmith watched in dismay as his favourite anvil floated to the window on the world and jumped through it.

'Bad luck, Heph, but at least he's gone.' Zeus pointed to the lesser traitors. 'It's tempting to drop you lot on a mountainside to graze for the rest of your lives, and it would serve you right since you've behaved like sheep!'

One by one, the gods bowed their heads, including Athena, which left Ares and Eris, their red stare fixed on their father.

'Twins, lower your eyes. You would have relished the war brought by this mutiny. Your bloodlust does you no credit. Submit, unless you want to spend your lives wearing itchy wool and chewing grass.' The king of heaven glowered until they complied. 'That leaves a single transgressor to deal with,' he said, turning at last to his wife, who remained on her pedestal. 'As for you, my precious, I should be able to trust you above all.' He smiled up at her, showing all his teeth. 'What shall be your punishment, dear heart?'

Hera peered down, hip cocked and arms folded. 'Some might argue that marriage to you is punishment enough, *dear heart.*'

Briareus guffawed but was cut short when the sky dome started to open, its quadrants creaking slowly apart, before jamming with an awful grinding sound. The god of fire groaned inwardly. How had the pantheon managed to wreck that? It would take an age to fix. Finally, it juddered open to reveal the black welkin twinkling with stars, and Zeus called down his owls. Dark-winged and gigantic, they swooped and pounced on the greatest goddess, catching in their claws the serpentine armlets snaking around her biceps. They escorted their shrieking cargo to the high heavens, where two hooks had appeared, and dangled the rebel queen by her bangles, leaving her kicking against the constellations and throwing down curses on her husband.

'You know,' said the almighty, stroking his beard and considering his spouse. 'It's not nearly enough.' He recalled his night birds, and they flew into the forge, returning with an anvil apiece, which they secured to Hera's ankle bracelets. The Cyclopes had created her jewellery, which would never break, but her joints would, and while they'd heal afterwards, she'd be in agony during her suspension. The blacksmith's aching ankle reminded him of the legacy bequeathed him at birth, but he wasn't callous and could stop this suffering. He righted Thalos, and asked him to respool the rawhide thong before making his approach.

'Mightiest of mighties, you promised me a reward for saving you.' He listened to Hera's arms and legs cracking as they grew ever longer, so the anvils gradually neared the sky dome.

'You're redeeming it already, Heph?'

'Yes. I want you to release my mother.'

'And if I refuse,' said Zeus, keeping a wary eye on Briareus 'you'll have your pet giant retie me?'

'He is beholden to me under the blood price and must do my bidding.'

'You'd waste your wish on your mother, after her mistreatment of you?'

'Yes.' He shifted his weight.

'Despite my alleged faults,' said the almighty, 'I am just, and she won't be up there forever, even if three-hundred nights does seem like a lot.'

'Hah!' shouted the greatest goddess from on high, wincing as every joint in her body ruptured. 'This is nothing, and it will feel a good deal shorter and more pleasurable than our wedding night!'

'Do not try my patience, Hera, or I'll increase the torture by letting you watch me couple with the nymphs. All of them. Now, Heph, the sentence isn't too long, so you could choose something personally beneficial instead, and nobody would think any the worse of you.' He wagged a finger at the blacksmith's lame leg. 'You could spare yourself from a lifetime of pain. It's no small thing, a wish granted by me, and you will never have another.'

So much for no questions asked. 'My mother's liberty is what I want. Let her go.'

'My wife loves only herself. She would not do the same for you.' Zeus looked at Hephaestus, who did not disagree. 'Oh, suit yourself.'

He whistled at his owls, who soared up to free the queen from the sky hooks before lowering her to the floor, where her stretched limbs pooled around her, temptingly close to the seawitch's feet.

'But anyone who wastes a divine wish is a fool, Heph, and there is no room in my realm for fools, so I have no choice but to cast you out as well. Begone.'

With that, the king of heaven defenestrated the god of fire, who fell once more from the mountain, watching the stars tumble as night turned into day. Finally, he hit the sea head first, his skull shattered on impact and he sank to the seabed. Best to lie there until it knitted together, always assuming it did knit together. And if he ever got back to the palace, he'd fit a big lock to the forge door.

The Herald of Winter

Under the long rays of Helios, the grain ripened and the god of fire inhaled the tranquil day, redolent with the sweetness promised by the coming harvest. His son fluttered overhead, chasing butterflies and bees. The lad was sulking after missing the excitement with the hundred-hander, but he'd soon come around as he wasn't like Aphrodite, who was slow to forgive.

A pleasant breeze rippled across the field, transforming it into a golden sea, with waves rolling to the horizon. Within earshot, mortals revelled and everywhere hummed with happiness and abundance. This enjoyable wool-gathering was interrupted when Eros stopped flying, hovered, drew back his bow and fired at someone, or something, hidden by the tall crops. Carefully, Hephaestus investigated, staying out of sight to avoid risking the unfortunate victim falling for him against their wishes.

Nestled amidst the yellow corn lay his cousin in thrall to Morpheus. Why did she do it? Her lips were the same hue as the poppies springing up from her ichor. Sure enough, she had a gold arrow stuck in her heart. He should seek help but decided to keep watch in case she woke up and saw a passing mortal or beast, and he sent the boy to search instead.

Eventually, a figure hurried towards him, russet gown hitched up. Wisely, Eros had made himself scarce. Thank gods the girl would be safe, although there was a risk she might wake up and fall in love with her mother, but they could fret about that if it happened.

Before the goddess of plenty reached her daughter, the warm ground roiled, and she stumbled. The hillside ruptured and from the opening burst a clatter of galloping hooves chased by hundreds of hoofprints and wheel ruts from an unseen car.

Only one deity could cloak himself with invisibility and it was obvious what he was after. The exiled groom was here to claim his bride, and who could be more perfect than someone who was often unconscious, or dismal as death when she *was* conscious?

Demeter was quickly up on her feet and running, mane flowing behind her. The smith picked up the sleeping maiden and stumbled towards his aunt as fast as his old injury and the churning soil would permit, knowing he couldn't cover the distance, but trying anyway. He sped up, foot dragging and lungs burning with the effort, praying Persephone wouldn't wake and see him, but she slumbered on, despite the thundering hoofbeats.

As the hellish horses gained on him, he felt their hot breath on his neck and suddenly his cousin was plucked from his arms. His despairing aunt readied to throw herself in front of the unseen steeds and Hephaestus only just restrained her. A whip cracked, the hoofprints obediently curved in a tight crescent and the maiden followed them, soaring towards the hill.

As she neared the breach, there was a deathly war cry and the kidnapper appeared, revealing his ebony armour and a chariot drawn by four jet stallions, their bridles glittering darkly with diamonds and graphite. In one hand, Hades held the scarlet-plumed helmet that conferred invisibility, and in the other, his hostage, whose eyes were finally open and fixed on her captor.

'Persephone! Get back here now, my girl! Do not eat so much as a single seed from his hand, or there'll be trouble. Do you hear me?' Demeter's orders were futile as her daughter vanished into the fissure. When the passage to the underworld closed itself, she shook her fist at heaven. 'Are you happy, Zeus? My child is about to be raped! Come down here and save her.' But her plea went unheard and the distraught goddess turned on Hephaestus. 'Why did you hinder me? Why? I could have rescued her.'

'Because Hades wouldn't have stopped for you. The three brothers have that in common. Refusing to allow any obstacle to come between them and an object of their lust.'

'So? You should have let him drive over me. What's the point of continuing by myself?'

'You're immortal,' he said, 'so you have no choice but to live, and you'd have hurt yourself for no gain. Besides, it's too early to lose faith as the god of hell may tire of her.'

'But Seph won't tire of *him*, will she?' She poked him in the chest with two fingers. 'You made the infernal bow and arrow so you can undo the enchantment, surely?'

'No, because erotic love is all-powerful.'

It was beyond him to reverse such a spell, but the goddess wasn't listening anymore. Instead, she was scanning the horizons, fists clenched.

'Where is Ares' bastard?'

Under the circumstances, he allowed the insult to pass without comment. 'I've no idea where my son is.' His aunt's intentions were clearly far from benevolent, so he tried to deflect the blame. 'It's my fault, though, not his. As you say, I forged his weapons, so take out your anger on me, not Eros.'

'You would put yourself in harm's way to save a child not of your own blood? You *are* a fool and Zeus was right to shove you out of heaven. I'll deal with the pair of you later. For the time being, help me dig.'

She clawed at the hill. It was a fruitless endeavour, but he joined her in the hope of softening her up. Quietly, he worked at her side, retracing events in his mind. It was only a bit of mischief, and Eros couldn't have known the outcome, or could he? Gods, was it possible he was in on it? This misadventure had Aphrodite's name written all over it. Had she inveigled the boy into a new scheme to rid herself of beautiful women, divine as well as mortal?

So busy was he contemplating his wife's potential for plotting, it was a while before he realised that for every handful of soil removed, another immediately replaced it.

'The doorway is sealed,' he said, straightening up. 'I'm sorry.'

'Not nearly sorry enough, Heph.' Raising her eyes to the heavens, she shouted. 'Zeus, you'd better get yourself down here, if you know what's good for you. Do not dare to ignore me again.'

This call was heeded and the king and queen both arrived, courtesy of Zephyr. In a rare act of affection, the greatest goddess took her sister's hands.

'Tell me all, my dear.'

'Hades has taken Seph.' Face folded in anger, she jabbed a finger at the almighty. 'As *you* knew he would. You gave him licence to snatch a wife. So this is entirely your doing and if you refuse to fix it, I'll go into mourning and the whole lot of you will pay!'

'Steady on,' said Zeus. 'Everything on earth will perish, and we'll have nothing decent to eat. How long do you intend to mourn?'

'Until my daughter is restored to me.'

'But what are we to fill up on in the meantime?'

'I don't much care,' she said.

'Well, start to care!' The greatest god shook Demeter, but she hung limp in his hands.

Casting furious glances at her husband, Hera drew her sister to her bosom. This was distressing. If the harvest goddess withered, it would be the finish of the world and all the mortals, and Prometheus would be devastated.

'We need to retrieve the blessed girl,' whispered the queen, 'to prevent her mother entering mourning. And she's quite right, Zeus, you *are* responsible for this mess. Sort it out. Speak to Hades. Reduce the length of his exile or some such.'

'He's not the easiest deity to negotiate with,' he moaned. 'Or the easiest sibling, come to that, so let me think.'

'What is there to think about?' his wife prodded him, ignoring the fizzing thunderbolts. 'What are you going to do?'

'I'm not going to do anything because he can't keep a divine being down there against her wishes. Trust me, she'll get fed up of his melancholic ways in next to no time.'

This was doubtful since the subterranean couple were cast from the same mould. Even so, Hephaestus had to speak up. 'There's a complicating factor,' he pointed out, tapping his chest. 'An arrow.'

On hearing this news, a platinum eyebrow was arched. 'And the first person she saw after being shot by the pesky archer was my brother? That puts an entirely different complexion on matters.' He turned to Demeter. 'She'll want to remain in his realm, I imagine.' He shuddered. 'Vile place that it is, but if your daughter desires Hades, then I can't change that. Of course, there is no more powerful feeling than erotic love.'

'I disagree as maternal love eclipses all,' she said, eyeing her sister. 'With the occasional exception that proves the rule. Unseal the door,' she insisted, 'and I'll fetch Seph myself.'

'You might recall that my brother and I aren't exactly on speaking terms since I exiled him and he won't permit me to unlock the entrance to his domain.' In an unusually gentle tone, Zeus explained. 'As things stand, only the psychopomp may enter the netherworld uninvited.'

'Don't worry,' added Hera. 'We'll ask Hermes to go down there.'

'Ask?' came the retort. 'Surely you mean tell.'

'We *could* force him,' replied the queen, 'but we want him to be at his most persuasive.'

'Hera makes a fair point,' said the almighty, bundling his protesting wife into the West Wind's chariot. 'Unless the messenger persuades your girl to return of her own volition, or Hades becomes bored with her, then she's gone for ever and you won't see her again.' He shrugged. 'It can't be helped.'

'Then I'm sure you will understand,' said the harvest goddess, 'that if Seph *has* gone for ever, you won't see spring again.' She shrugged. 'It can't be helped.'

Demeter's eyes blazed and she exhaled plumes of vapour, as if her insides were on fire, but crystals coated her lashes and brows, and she was shaking violently. Hephaestus feared for her. Gods weren't meant to die but they weren't meant to be lame either and he'd managed that. Her umber tresses bleached from root to tip and the rich red faded from her robe. Still trembling, she raised her arms, sleeves trailing, and began turning, newly ashen locks and hems whirling around her. As she span, she rose above the cornfields and the air filled with her dreadful wail.

Unable to bear it, Helios retreated, and the birds deserted their trees, darkening the sky as they took wing in search of the sun. Furred beasts went to ground while men, women and children raced to and fro, reaping the withering crops, and dragging grain and goats alike indoors. Once everything was under cover, they reappeared, wrapped in rugs, to kneel on the hard soil and send up offerings they could ill afford.

Mankind wasn't alone in feeling the cold. The hairs on the god of fire's body sprang to attention and his hide pebbled and shrank against his bones, until it felt too small for him. He shivered and rubbed his hands together, hunching against this unfamiliar sensation. His feet were blue, the knuckles of his toes throbbed, his recently repaired skull ached and the pain in his ankle worsened until he was more miserable than he could remember.

The lamenting goddess continued to wail and her frigid breath snaked through valleys and along rivers so they sparkled with frost. Here and there, black spikes penetrated the overhanging mist – trees stripped of their foliage and fruit – but their bark was soon shrouded in feathery rime.

Dense clouds pressed down to merge with the fog drifting across the former fields and as the sun moved further and further away, Demeter's tears started to fall. Unlike rain, which fell hard and straight, they drifted as if they were swan down, blanketing the lands.

This was a new and terrible world. No more was the earth green. No more was the sea blue. Where there had been forests was now snow. Where there had been water was now ice. When Helios was no longer visible, Selene rose, reflecting the sinister orb. Never had Gaia been more beautiful. Never had Gaia been more ominous.

Part IV

The Monstrous Flock

The harvest goddess was still punishing everyone for the loss of her daughter so winter showed no sign of diminishing. Now and then, the never-ending nights were lit by the scarce light from the overworked moon, sole luminary since the sun's departure. The residents of heaven were famished and none more so than the king.

Demeter was yet to wreak revenge on Eros for the rogue arrow, but his father kept him close, not least because the Olympians were a vengeful lot to begin with, and that was before discovering the compound delights of hunger and cold.

Home was no haven either as Aphrodite, never the most motherly of mothers, was distinctly frosty towards her son lately. Hephaestus was down to his final few tree trunks because wood had to be conserved for fuel. With careful husbanding, he would manage to finish the sword he was forging and maybe a few gewgaws, but no more.

Despite crops withering and animals perishing, the privations had failed to destroy the mortals. Unable to bury their dead, they had burnt them, mourned them, picked themselves up and carried on, adjusting to the new world. This resilience must stem from their creator. If any being could prevail amidst desperation and suffering, it was Prometheus.

As the fruits of the earth had withered on the vine, the adaptable species increasingly relied on the fruits of the sea, and the coastal dwellers were proficient at fishing. Inland, their cousins salted meat, while others dried their meagre stores of grains, pulses and vegetables. From their paltry winter larders, they ensured the pantheon received their portion, often at the cost of their own bellies.

Although the almighty had predicted that women would desert men in times of poverty, it drew them closer, with woman after woman standing back, urging her husband and children to eat first, and many had faded and died, sacrificing themselves to save their families. Pandora had received Prometheus' divine breath, as had her sisters, and so they'd also inherited his noble principles. Shivering and starving, the clans knitted together more tightly and cared for each other, apart from a few murderous types, but these were restricted to the religious orders in the main.

Mankind's survival hardly improved the almighty's temper, and he paced continually, heavy footed, triggering avalanches and further tormenting those down below. In the face of his wrath, Demeter remained steadfast. No Persephone meant no spring. Even mighty Zeus was powerless to countermand her curse and Prometheus despaired at the plight of the dwindling population.

When a knock interrupted the blacksmith, he set down the sword, waited for his son to slink into the shadows and unbolted the smithy door. On the threshold stood a scrawny youth in an outsized lion skin, which slid off his shoulders. No longer the curly-haired tot who'd escaped the jaws of the hundred-hander, but a young man who fancied himself a hero.

The runt didn't wait to be invited and barged in, dragging a club behind him.

'I want a suit of armour and a blindfold before Selene sets.'

The deity stared down his presumptuous guest. 'Come in, why don't you?'

'Sorry, mighty smith,' he added with a peremptory bow. 'But you promised to help me if I ever found my way here.'

'I did. Brush that snow off you and keep back from the flames until you've thawed. So, it seems Hera has not been a friend to you.'

'With the greatest of respect, she is a friend to nobody but herself. You heard what she did?'

'I did.'

'But *I* didn't,' announced Eros, slipping into the light.' What has my grandmother done to you?'

'She cast the demons of jealousy into my mind, and I killed my wife and children in a rage because of her.'

'By Ouranus!' exclaimed the god of love.

'And that isn't the worst of it,' Heracles went on.

'What could be worse than slaughtering your family?' The widowed deity frowned and stared into the fire.

His father squeezed his arm in sympathy while their uninvited visitor prattled on. Separated by several centuries, the youths appeared similar in age, but how they differed in temperament. Eros was still mourning the death of Psyche, whereas it was difficult to believe this self-centred pup had shed so much as a tear over his butchered loved ones.

It required quite a leap to reconcile this annoying adolescent with the charming child he'd once been. Life must have been unkind to him after leaving the monastery and it was no surprise that Hera had inflicted such horror. A mother who could hurl her baby from a mountain was capable of anything, and she'd never stopped being jealous of her husband's conquests and the resulting offspring.

After a nod granting him permission, the mortal shuffled nearer to the flames.

'Anyway,' he continued, 'I've been sentenced to twelve labours to cleanse myself of the blood guilt but whenever I complete a labour, another is added, invariably more dangerous. Hence my request for armour.'

'Never mind that,' said Eros. 'Worry more about fiddling with your garment like a nymph on heat. Father can forge you something to prevent it gaping, can't you?'

'Indeed.' He held a lump of iron to the flame. 'Within the hour, that robe of yours will gape no more.'

'It's not—' Heracles coughed. 'It's not a robe, begging your pardon.'

'Does it cover your arse?' enquired the blacksmith as he hammered.

'I suppose it does.'

'Then a robe it is.' Ignoring the peevish mortal's pet lip, the smith dunked the hot metal in a hogshead. A loud shush presaged a cloud of steam, which hid the lad from sight until he emerged a few moments later, damp and red-faced. 'While it cools, regale us with the story of how you got your ro… lionskin.'

The big-game hunter sat on his dignity and began.

'It's the pelt of the Nemean lion. I throttled it and decided to wear its hide as a trophy.'

'You have quite the knack for throttling, as I recall.' A serpent in each fist was no mean feat for a newborn.

'Lucky for me, or I'd be in Hades already!' The mortal pushed out his puny chest, proving he had the almighty's pomposity, if not his stature. 'For my second task, I conquered the nine-headed hydra and dipped my arrows in the venom running through its veins.'

At this, the archer perked up. 'Don't tell me,' he said, 'You used the arrows to shoot the golden-hooved hind that belonged to Artemis.'

The huntress had relayed this tale to the pantheon, but in her version, the mortal had played a less-than valiant role.

'Yes, I did.' Heracles looked fed up at losing an opportunity to boast. 'Then, there was a terrifying mountain boar with a vile disposition, and… here I am.'

'Here you are, said Eros. 'Haven't you missed a bit out?'

The lad's neck flushed and his voice rose. 'No, that's the lot, as far as I can remember.'

'What about cleaning up after the largest herd of cattle known to mankind?' asked the mischievous god of love.

'Oh, yes. I *had* forgotten that,' he confessed. 'A case of rerouting two rivers to flush out the… royal stables, only to be lumbered with a more horrible chore.' He paused to wipe away angry tears. 'These labours are progressively harder and they're all insurmountable. Hermes, Artemis and Athena have helped me up to now, but they've finally admitted defeat, so will you help me, Heph? Please?'

It took an effort to warm to this sniveller, especially when he seemed more upset about the punishment than the crime, but it was impossible to avoid feeling some kinship with anyone who'd suffered at the hands of Hera.

'Since you asked so nicely, I will keep my promise, but what you want may not be what you need. Describe your problem to me and let me work out how to solve it.'

'No time for that,' Heracles replied, waving an arm no thicker than a broom-shank. 'Look, the moon has started her descent so I'll make do with a shield. I'm tasked with protecting the grain stores by ridding the bogs of thousands of nightmarish birds.'

Of course, everybody knew Ares had created them, and as with anything from his hand, they were nasty, dangerous and slapdash. The flock had been chased by wolves into Stymphalos, where they'd proliferated and ravaged the surrounding farms. The mortals built a giant scarecrow from rags, which his spiteful brother set ablaze in the vain hope of triggering hostilities between neighbours. Instead, the farmers had scattered the ashes and tightened their belts. He sized up the prospective pest controller. Talk about sending a boy to do a man's job.

'Scaring off a few dicky birds doesn't sound *too* problematic to me,' said Eros.

'Imagine cranes,' retorted the visitor, 'except black and monstrous. One on its own could carry me off.'

'In fairness,' said the god of love, 'a sparrow could do that without breaking a sweat. Hmm,' he wondered aloud, 'do sparrows sweat?'

'No,' stated the god of fire. 'Son, aren't you missing your mother?'

'I'm not going out there alone.'

'Well, if you wish to stay, hold your tongue.'

The godling sighed, fluttered to a high shelf and perched, elbows on knees, chin resting on his knuckles. Mollified, the storyteller was persuaded to go on.

'Anyway, these *monsters* travel in hordes that block out the light, what there is of it these days. They have bronze beaks that can peck through iron as if it were skin.' He pulled his fingers from his nose to outline a yard-long proboscis. 'And their razor-sharp feathers moult everywhere. Did I mention their shit's poisonous? Pegasus is grounded because of it.'

It was a shame for the graceful horse, but it was hard not to laugh at the image of toxic bird shit raining down on Heracles.

The petulant boy peered at the lunar goddess before turning to appeal once more. 'Please, just give me what I came for.'

'These birds can pierce iron as easily as your hide, you say?'

'Yes, which is why I need two skins. My own and one forged by you. The mask is because their purple gaze transfixes men.' His shoulders slumped. 'I've got no chance, have I? What with the piercing beaks, the cut-throat feathers, the hypnotic stare and the deadly droppings.'

How easily downtrodden he was, but there was a simple-enough solution. 'I'll sort you out, but not with armour.' Hephaestus clamped a shoulder. Bones like a fish. Wouldn't last a minute against Ares' fiendish inventions supposing he was plated with a dozen layers of steel. 'Trust me on this.'

Allegedly conserving his energy for the coming onslaught, the would-be hero lounged on a bench as if in a lady's chamber. Meanwhile, the blacksmith made good on his pledge, limping between flame and anvil, hammering at speed, remembering the heavenly mandate to be a considerate host and resisting the urge to shower the guest in sparks whenever he glanced at Selene. Grumbling to himself, he plunged the second object into water and fished out the clasp he'd forged earlier.

'Here, fasten yourself properly with this.'

Gingerly, Heracles accepted the gift and scowled.

'Isn't this patterned on the aegis worn by Athena?'

'It certainly is,' he said, briefly picturing the unfortunate Medusa and her equally unfortunate child. 'You're welcome, by the way.'

'But Athena's a… a…'

'Choose your next words very carefully.'

'A war deity is what I was about to say.' Reluctant to wear something he considered feminine, he fixed his pelt, which should stay put. When the second item was removed from the hogshead, he glowered at it.

'A huge rattle? I have to see off demonic birds, not pacify a giant's baby.'

Hephaestus was sorely tempted to evict the ingrate but satisfied himself with giving the bird-scarer a gentle shake. Inside it, eight spheres clanged, their chimes reverberating off every piece of metal in the forge, forcing the lad to his knees, hands over ears, complaining they were bleeding and refusing to uncover them until the noise stopped.

'Show me the infant who'll be pacified by that,' remarked the blacksmith, handing over an old blindfold belonging to Eros. 'Make haste because Selene is dipping her toes in the sea as we speak.'

The guest raced to the door in a fit of panic. Inwardly cursing the requirement for xenia, the god tossed some quicksilver onto the flames. Hermes arrived and haggled long enough to secure a fancier winged helmet in return for a lift to the bogs. The mortal was duly deposited on top of a spur, and without thanking the deities, he donned his mask and grappled with the rattle, straining to get it off the ground.

As the moon sank into the water, thousands of bronze birds flew over the snow-bound fields, wings clanking and eyes blazing as they started landing, waiting for absolute darkness so they could demolish the stores in peace. Heracles fortuitously dodged a hail of deadly feathers and shouted in entirely the wrong direction.

'I told you I needed a suit of armour.'

'Athena's aegis on the clasp is protecting you,' said the god of fire, arms folded and feet planted apart. 'Try again. Follow my voice.'

Encouraged, the youth seized the rattle with renewed vigour, and amazed at his own strength, he swung it, or so he thought. In reality, it swung him, the momentum carrying it onwards. The carillon of spheres rang across the skies, startling the vast shadow, and the brutish birds took flight, painting the endless night purple. When the sky cleared of the hideous creatures, the victorious scarecrow ripped off his mask, threw down the weapon and cheered, whirling and half mad with glee.

It was a good job he'd fixed that pelt, mused the smith, or else it would be round the mortal's skinny ankles by now, leaving his soft parts exposed as tempting bait.

The Staff of Life

Snowflakes continued to fall, drifting to earth where they piled up, layer upon layer, and the Olympians shivered around fires, sharing measly piles of mutton, complaining bitterly at the lack of grain. In a world of plenty, the divines had never stored anything so they would soon be forced to plunder the mortals' provisions and that would be the finish of mankind.

Prometheus wore a perpetually anxious expression while he patrolled the window, keeping an eye on his increasingly desperate people. On an alarmingly regular basis, priests carried terrified boys to the top of high hills and burnt them to ash in enormous cauldrons. The children's screams spiralled heavenwards in the smoke but while Demeter shuddered she did no more than stare into the heart of the palace flames, her tears hissing as she grieved for her own child. The god of foresight frequently explained to the religious orders that this practice of saining was wasted on her, but they were a curiously stubborn lot.

Hephaestus had been sent on a mission of mercy by his wife but was struggling to ascend Olympus in its icy state. Despite their newly fitted grips, the tripods couldn't carry him up the mountain either, so kindly Pegasus gathered him from the ground and deposited the shaken god on the summit.

After recovering from his impromptu flight, he hobbled into the great hall, where the spikes on his leg support squeaked against the marble floor, earning him glares from the swaddled gods. He edged towards the restorative flames but kept his distance from the almighty, who currently resembled an extremely large and irate polar bear, pacing about in his hooded fur cloak, Laelaps beside him, insulated in a matching coat. Even Thalos had been given a furry hat, a pair of mittens and a phallus warmer.

Zeus had shown scant concern about Persephone's kidnap until he was personally affected and now he was furious. His temper had not improved when one of his many earthly sons stole some ambrosia from the rapidly declining heavenly supply, an act of pure hubris as the mortal king was renowned for his deep stores. The greatest god was busy plotting a fitting punishment, in between berating the harvest goddess. She sat quietly, head lowered, tendrils of snowy hair trailing on the floor, ignoring his threats until, in exasperation, he blew out his cheeks, inadvertently creating a blizzard across the eastern islands.

'Listen here, Demeter. This has to stop. There have been no crops since I don't know when and we have nothing tucked away. The mortals are starving and they're running out of women so mankind won't stand a chance. Look at poor Prom. He's worried sick.'

The pale goddess raised her eyes, but gazed beyond him.

'Spring will not come back while my daughter remains underground. Return her to me or endure eternal winter. The choice is yours.'

Hera prowled past. 'I am tired of dressing like a bear. Sort it out, Husband,' she demanded, gesturing at her outfit.

The queen of heaven was wearing the skins of what appeared to be the entire population of silver foxes sewn together, with a fine hood framing her face. She didn't remind Hephaestus of any bear he'd ever seen.

Zeus snapped his fingers and pointed at the glimmer of gold that had materialised briefly and was doing its best to dematerialise.

'Hermes, stop that. Where have you been?'

'Take a wild guess.' The messenger reappeared and gazed at the fire. 'I'm frozen solid and sick to the back teeth of the underworld. You have no idea how many shades I've escorted there lately.'

'Forget about all of that. I want you to fetch Persephone.'

'What? At least let me thaw out first.'

Zeus regarded him gravely. 'Chief psychopomp, as collector of souls, you're the only god permitted to come and go in the nether regions so it has to be you. Get going.'

Hermes shivered theatrically in his elegant deerskin and vanished.

The goddess of love twirled in her magic girdle, which Hephaestus had successfully retrieved from Hera. Eternity wasn't nearly long enough to erase the image of his mother trying to tantalise the almighty, who had lost all interest in flesh, whether mortal, animal or divine.

'Are you ready, Heph?'

'Ready?' he asked with a wolfish grin. 'Ready for what?'

'Certainly not *that*. A visit to some palace or other. We're all going. Orders from above.'

He groaned. 'I could do without it, to be honest. I want to forge a shield before my woodpile's confiscated. Can't you take Eros instead?'

'He went on ahead with Dion. Anyway, attendance is mandatory, apart from Hermes, who's still on his errand, and Prom because he's too upset. Obviously, you-know-who and his cheerful bride won't be there. As for me, I'm looking forward to the feast. They're laying on a never-to-be-had-again delicacy.'

This aroused his interest. 'Whose palace?'

'Tan-something-or-other.'

'Tantalus?'

'Maybe. Oh, wait,' she hooted, 'Is he the idiot who tupped the cloud version of your mother?'

'No,' he said in a measured tone. Aphrodite knew perfectly well it was Ixion who had committed that particular crime, but she enjoyed tormenting him. 'Tantalus is the idiot who stole ambrosia.'

'Ah. How very foolish.'

'This titbit of his needs to be good if he hopes to avoid a terrible death. Do you think Zeus intends to reprieve him?'

'Unlikely,' she said. 'The almighty's just famished like the rest of us and this is an excuse to fill his belly at someone else's expense.'

Hephaestus wondered what would be dished up. Would this king slaughter the last of a kind to appease the greatest god, who seldom acquitted anyone? Usually, the punishment for hubris was Nemesis, so the mortal was getting off lightly entertaining the pantheon, although it would cost him dear as the gods ate prodigiously at the best of times and were insatiable now that famine dogged the earth.

He threw on his finest brown bearskin and watched his wife in front of the looking glass, shivering amidst a dozen discarded gowns, all identical as far as he could tell. It was futile pointing this out or there would be a lengthy discussion on the topic and she'd try on a dozen more to spite him. Resigned to waiting, he perched on the couch and tried not to tap his foot while she smoothed an emerald silk chiton over her hips.

Aphrodite's lovely form curved as pleasingly as ever but was much thinner. Although there was a paucity of grains, the blacksmith's clever ice drills meant they always had plenty of seafood, but she was fed up with it, so what could he do other than watch her fade away?

'Ugh, all my clothes are hanging off me. I can't wait for tonight. I'm dying for a decent meal.'

He glanced at the platter on her bedside table, neatly stacked with fish skeletons, but held his tongue or they'd never leave the house.

'They don't count,' she said. 'You know what I mean. From the day that blessed girl eloped, we've had no corn, no grapes, no olives and not a drop of honey. Dion is fretting about his wine supplies, and this cold is unbearable, to say nothing of suffocating under bulky furs. I couldn't tell you when Helios last kissed my skin.'

His blood flared at the thought of the big lecher kissing his wife. Still, while it was chilly, she was nicely covered up. This, he kept to himself, otherwise he'd have to endure a lecture on polyandry or whatever it was Aphrodite favoured. The merest hint of free love for all made him deeply unhappy, so he pushed the notion from his mind. When she anointed her pulses with rose oil, he inhaled, dreaming of warm summer days seemingly gone forever and recalled his cousin wending her way through cornfields, absently picking scarlet poppies and alternating between eating their seeds and weaving the flowers of resurrection into her hair.

'Aph, what are the chances of Hades allowing Seph to come home?' he asked.

'Zero, I imagine. Assuming she even wants to leave him. Where's that necklace you made for our hundredth wedding anniversary?'

He scrabbled on her dressing table until he found the chain hung with a hundred ruby hearts and placed it around her neck. Eventually satisfied with her appearance, she nodded at a cape of blond wolf pelts and he wrapped her in it.

'Artemis reckoned these poor souls were as thin as poverty when they were put out of their misery,' she said, not bothering to thank him. 'When wolves go hungry, it has to be a bad omen for everyone.'

'But not for us, Aph. We have a delicious treat in store,' he said, in the vain hope of hurrying her up.

'True. It's supposed to be the banquet to end all banquets. Originally, it was a bring-your-own-wine party. Can you imagine? That's not much of a night out, is it? Thankfully, your mother put him right. No wine. No guests.'

Hephaestus shrugged. 'Can't blame Tantalus for trying it on when Zeus and Dion could drain a vineyard's worth in an evening. What do you reckon this delicacy is?'

'Bread, I hope,' said Aphrodite. 'Gods, I'd die for a loaf. And cherries. Ripe, red cherries, running with sour juice. Olives, bitter and salty. Nuts. Almonds and pistachios. Or maybe some cashews.' She sank onto the couch in a swoon. 'All this gnawing on bones and wearing furs makes me feel quite primitive.'

He slipped his hands beneath her cape. 'Mm, primitive, you say?'

'Oh, my little hobbling partridge.' She shoved him off. 'You're wasting your time. When the famine is on me, I'm too hungry to think of love.'

He wondered if she was seeing Ares again. Conceivably, she might be telling the truth. None of them were themselves. Feasting solely on the fat of the land and the fruits of the sea had left their breath as foul as their tempers, and all of them craving the fruits of the earth. If the goddess of plenty didn't recover soon, there'd be no birds or beasts to speak of, forcing everyone to eat fish until the oceans froze solid. Hopefully, this evening's invitation was an augur of happier days ahead.

~

The earthly palace wasn't half-bad and the king's extravagant tastes put some of the more frugal deities to shame. A sandstone citadel reared from a rocky outcrop overhanging what was ordinarily the Aegean Sea, but was now a thick sheet of ice. It was built on such a vast scale that Zeus cleared the doorway with room to spare. Inside, minstrels strummed harps and lyres so passably that the music impressed Apollo, who leant on a wall, humming. Many fires burnt with lumps of a black substance Hephaestus didn't recognise. He plucked out a burning cube and examined it. Denser than charwood, oilier and more pungent. It smelt old. Ancient. He smiled when he realised what it was. How clever to mine Gaia for trees long dead, though he was surprised she hadn't erupted in response. When the few remaining living trees had been chopped down, he would commandeer their subterranean ancestors for fuel.

Turning pink in the warmth, the arriving Olympians shed their cloaks, which diminutive servants hauled away to heave onto their master's bed. Once the pantheon was assembled, their host appeared with his seven sons. Tantalus, his muscular torso oiled and braced in supple leather straps, was careful not to overstep and listened intently to the list of divine requirements. Several swarms of serving girls staggered under the weight of trays, each holding a single goblet brimming with retsina. Others proffered platters of pastries bejewelled with dried berries and honey-glazed nuts. If the householder was perturbed by the guzzling gods, he restricted himself to briefly widening his sapphire eyes and gesticulating wildly at his staff to fetch more of everything. The palace had deep pantries and its owner seemed happy to empty them to regain the almighty's favour. Faced with the probable alternative, it was a small price to pay.

Hephaestus watched the oiled king working the room. Waving politely to Ares and Eris while giving the unpleasant pair a suitably wide berth. Examining Athena's aegis without shuddering. Admiring the goddess of love's robe as if it were new. Demonstrating his fuel to Hestia. Consoling Demeter and wishing her daughter a safe return. Asking Thetis how she'd made it through the ice and enquiring after Eurynome. Finally, he showed off his knowledge of history by commiserating with

Eros on the loss of Psyche. Once he'd greeted each god, Tantalus struck a gong. Aphrodite flinched at the harsh sound and neatly avoided a surreptitious pawing from Poseidon, who adopted an innocent expression and announced to nobody in particular that this feast had better be a damned good one.

Two massive arched doors opened to admit the deities to the dining hall and a waft of savoury air greeted them. What was cooking? Tomatoes, garlic, marjoram, olive oil and a meat that Hephaestus couldn't place. Reminiscent of lamb. Above all, came the warm aroma of bread, which would sweeten his wife, and the night filled with promise. But what was that mysterious smell?

The Return of Spring

Determined to regain favour, Tantalus had thought of everything. The dining table was a ring of marble surrounding a pyre, and above it hung a bubbling tureen, sending up spirals of enticing steam. The king and queen of heaven were initially put out by the round table, which meant everyone would have equal status, but softened once they were shown to a pair of suitably majestic thrones. When the divine guests were seated, their host climbed a ladder to an ostentatiously humble wooden stool, careful not to sit level with the pantheon. His sons followed and knelt, three at each side.

All the place settings were gold, reflecting the firelight so the room glowed. It was vulgar, but silver was expensive, and the ambience did mimic Helios nicely, providing longed-for warmth and cheer. Men and women shinned up ladders and onto the tabletop, wheeling round barrows of figs, nuts and cheese, while others played lyres and pipes. Dancers in glittering veils clicked castanets and undulated their way around the diners, navigating sharp cutlery and taking care not to get trapped beneath goblets being drunkenly replaced.

Once the mezedes had been devoured, the host clapped and the hall fell silent as his staff heaved on mighty chains to lower the tureen onto a waiting trivet. The royal family strolled forwards to oversee the mouth-watering stew being ladled into bowls while scores of servants stacked olive-studded loaves on platters. The smith's belly rumbled at the sight and smell of the food, but his enjoyment was somewhat ruined by the princes sobbing their hearts out, perhaps overwhelmed by the honour of serving the divines.

Fortunately, their misery was soon drowned out by excited chatter as the gods sampled the bread. Aphrodite looked faint with delight, her lips sweetened by wine. Hephaestus pocketed his own loaves to give his wife later. Living on meat didn't worry him, especially when it was part of such an aromatic dish, but as he prepared to take his first mouthful, a blue speck stared up at him. Stealing a glance at the crying brothers, sapphire-eyed to a boy, he lowered his spoon and ate a loaf from his pocket instead.

It seemed his fellow gods had reached the same conclusion. His mother peered at a nose, while his wife hid what was either a penis or a pinkie with her napkin. Like Dionysus, Eros had enjoyed a liquid supper and dozed, food untouched. Opposite, distracted Demeter chewed on a morsel until Thetis leant over and explained what she was eating. The harvest goddess dropped her spoon with a splash and ran from the hall, followed by her sister. The almighty examined a hairless leg, frowned and summoned the earthly king.

'Tantalus, you have caused offence by stealing ambrosia and compounded the sin by slaughtering your youngest – my grandson, no less – and feeding him to us. What did you hope to gain from such madness?'

'Gracious Father,' pleaded the king. 'I served up my youngest to honour you. It was the greatest sacrifice I could think of. Was Pelops not enough?' He gestured at his six remaining princes, who looked shiftily at each other. 'I apologise for the offence,' he gabbled. 'Of course, my heir is a more fitting tribute.' He snapped his fingers at the kitchen staff. 'Have him prepared, immediately.'

On hearing this, the eldest backed towards the ladder but was blocked by his sensible siblings who'd swiftly closed ranks, having no desire to enjoy their younger brother's fate. Zeus thumped the table, slopping drinks, toppling pyramids of loaves and terrifying suddenly airborne dancers and musicians.

'We don't wish to eat any of your children! Whatever gave you such an idea? I give you a chance to make good after you insulted me and this is how you repay me?'

Tantalus threw himself on the heavenly ruler's mercy and kissed his fingers, but the greatest god recoiled in disgust.

'This is a truly vile crime, which requires an imaginative punishment. Ares, seize him and hold him until inspiration strikes me.'

As the bawling captive was arrested, the queen of heaven settled her distraught sister in a chair, then approached her husband and whispered in his ear. At length, he inclined his head in assent.

Thetis gathered all the bowls and emptied them into the tureen. Hera passed her sceptre over the stew and stood aside as the revenant prince rose in the steam above the boiling liquid, minus a shoulder, so his arm dangled oddly. Regardless, the deities raised their chalices in tribute, relieved the Fates hadn't been here to witness this illicit resurrection.

But instead of joining in the celebration, Demeter was aghast.

'Look! I've eaten his whole shoulder! I'm a monster.'

She sobbed and banged her head against the marble, though it was strange behaviour, fussing over an individual prince when she'd killed millions by bringing winter.

Hera rolled her eyes. 'Can you fix it, Hephaestus?'

'More than likely,' he said, reaching for a flagon until he felt his mother's icy glare. 'Oh, you mean now?'

'What do you think? Have you seen your aunt? She's the last person we want to upset.'

'Come on, Pelops,' said the smith. He nudged Eros awake. 'You too, Son.' Best to keep him away from the unhinged goddess. He tucked the youth into his bearskin and set off, trying to ignore Ares putting his prisoner in Eris' charge and stalking towards his wife.

~

At the forge, the god of love amused himself by exploring the top shelves while his father examined the patient, who was fortunate the queen of heaven had restored him. Far from being a sign that she was growing a heart though, her actions were purely self-serving. By sparing the boy, she hoped to soothe her sister and improve the prospect of ending this abominable season so she could swan about in her flimsy robe once more.

But none of this was the youth's fault. Gods, he was pale, whiter than milk, and like veal raised in the dark, this mortal was a stranger to Helios. Surely to Ouranus, no parent would do that to a child to save his own skin.

No matter how this pallor had been achieved, he was too insipid to carry off gold, which would have been the first choice. Only one material would suit this youth. Morse. Fortunately, Hephaestus had a pair of walrus tusks somewhere, a gift from Thetis and Eurynome a few dozen birthdays ago, and he knew they'd approve of his intended use.

Working with such a miniscule piece of sea ivory was subtler work than he was used to, but after some careful chiselling and sanding, he sculpted a replacement shoulder that blended perfectly. He laid a finger each side of the lad's neck to check his handiwork. It was colder than the original, but not by much.

'Father, remember these?' Eros descended from the shelves and opened his hand to display the sword and shield made for him when he was an infant. 'These are a perfect fit for the tiny fellow and should cheer him up after his night of terror.'

Pelops seized the gifts, and on seeing his reflection in a

sheet of steel propped against the wall, he primped, vainer than Aphrodite, which was saying something.

~

When they arrived at the earthly palace, Hephaestus placed the naked prince on the table, where he cavorted, showing off his new prosthetic and arsenal. Round and round he pranced, until he veered too near Poseidon, who stopped him in his tracks by coiling a tentacle around his elegant ankle.

'Is that sea ivory gracing your shoulder, young man?' he bellowed.

'Why, yes, it is,' squeaked the cowering mortal.

'You know what that means?'

'N…no, mighty one,' he stammered. 'What does it mean?'

'All things of the ocean belong to me.' Poseidon confiscated the miniature weapons and closed his fist. 'So that makes you my possession.'

'Not true!' protested Demeter. 'He belongs to his father.'

'What's it got to do with you, Shoulder Eater? Your concern is too little, too late. He'll abide with me, won't you, my pet?' He ran a talon down the boy's pallid chest so a ribbon of scarlet trickled down it. Thankfully, the mortal fainted and wasn't conscious as Poseidon unfurled his tongue and lapped his blood. 'Mmm, a delicate vintage, and all the sweeter when the heart is beating.'

The boy came round in time to hear this and wailed for his father, who ignored him and continued smiling.

'Fear not,' said the sea god, 'I've no intention of eating you. Just fancied a taste. You're quite safe with me.'

'That's cold comfort,' said Aphrodite. 'So, what *do* you have planned for your hysterical princeling?' she enquired sweetly.

'I plan to employ him as my chariot driver,' replied Poseidon, dabbing his lips with the tablecloth.

Her eyes danced. 'Is that what you call it nowadays?' She

laughed raucously and drained her chalice. 'Pelops, you were better off in the soup.'

Apparently, the mellowing effect of the bread had worn off already, so it would be a cold bed for Hephaestus tonight. No change there then. He sighed and ate another loaf. From the tail of his eye, he caught Eros nocking his smallest arrow. The archer waited until he had a clear shot and then fired. His victim squawked as the barb found its target. When the boy recovered, he'd still be a prisoner but would serve a happier sentence.

While the newly smitten mortal was busy worshipping his idol, Zeus barked at Eris, instructing her to free the earthly king so he could feed his guests.

'Tantalus, we can't eat this ghastly concoction, but we *are* hungry, so fetch everything you have, including more wine, and bring back those dancing girls.'

The captive hesitated. If he'd hoped to avoid providing a feast simply because he was under arrest, he was sadly mistaken.

'Jump to it, man. We'll stay here until Hermes returns and then he can take you to your punishment, which I must say is rather novel.'

'But he'll be gone for ages,' complained the king, failing to fully understand his real predicament.

'That's right. So your stores had better be plentiful.' The almighty eyed the six princes. 'Chop chop!'

After several nights of feasting on hastily assembled delicacies and drinking the royal cellars dry, the revellers were in high spirits, apart from the harvest goddess who huddled over the fire. Their merrymaking was interrupted when a draught blew through the palace and the flames fluctuated, revealing a vision of the messenger, beckoning to someone in the shadows.

After some coaxing, Persephone appeared beside him, still

wearing the poppies from the cornfield in her hair, except they were now leaden and matched the grimly sparkling scales of her granite gown. In her left hand, she held a split pomegranate, spilling its ruby seeds. Her lips were redder than usual and her mother covered her face in anguish.

'Hermes, why are you not here in person?' asked Zeus.

'There's been a spot of bother, I'm afraid.'

'Isn't there always *a spot of bother* when you're involved? Go on, let's hear it.'

'I bargained with your brother and made him the offer you said he couldn't refuse, and well…'

'How dare he refuse me!' Thunderbolts scorched a few divine tresses and frightened the household, who scuttled for shelter.

'In fairness, your brother's not entirely to blame. He was ready to agree to the deal, but…'

Demeter shut her eyes briefly before picking up his thread. 'Visitors can leave, providing they don't eat anything while they're down there.'

Hermes held up the girl's hand. 'You see my problem?'

'My girl has eaten the red fruit of hell,' she said, 'and so belongs to Lord Hades.'

'Wait, all is not lost.' Zeus tapped his jaw.

The ruler's thinking was not accompanied by the usual thunderbolts. Underneath the thin veneer of bombast, there was something else. Fear. The almighty couldn't threaten the harvest goddess as he threatened the other gods. The world had been reduced to a parlous state by her sorrow, so who knew what she might do in rage. If this stand-off could not be resolved, there was no choice but to wait out winter, however long it took. While the pantheon would not perish, they would starve and freeze, suffering without their creature comforts.

At last, the greatest god spoke again. 'Inform my brother that if Seph is not released by the time Selene sets tonight, his banishment will extend from a thousand years to eternity.' At this, Demeter lowered herself and grasped the king of heaven's knees but he prised her free, stood up and stepped over her prone form. 'Tell Hades that I'll seal the earth, seas and heavens against him until the end of days, so he will *never* leave his realm.'

Another draught interrupted this diatribe and the underworld god appeared in the flames, Hermes to his right and Persephone to his left, gazing up at him.

'Little brother,' he said. 'Always a bad sport. It was tempting to call your bluff, but just the *thought* of infinity in this hellhole is too much to bear. You win and I submit, to a degree.' He exhaled, and the fire surged. 'Seph may live above ground for two seasons, but she must return to me for the third, as my wife.' He gazed upon his doting bride. 'Indeed, this is what she wants.'

The grieving mother sprang to her feet. 'What have you done to my child, you sickening bastard?'

'Nothing she didn't want me to do,' he laughed. 'Isn't that right, my dear?'

Without taking her eyes off her lover, Persephone nodded. She tilted her face up for a farewell kiss before slipping her hand into her mother's. Demeter pulled her daughter from the flames and into her arms. The messenger shrugged and skipped out behind her. Only the smith witnessed Hades' tears as he faded to black.

'Oh, Seph!' The ashen goddess flushed, russet flowed into her robes and pigment tinted her hair. Around her, the palace warmed and became so stifling that hosts, guests and servants rushed outside.

As the exhausted moon sank, the sun soared earthwards, lighting the sky. Cheers rang out and Helios glowed with pleasure, his warming rays melting the snow, which soaked the earth. Crops sprouted, trees budded and flowers blossomed until the lands sang with colour and the air filled with laughter.

Pegasus took flight, circling overhead. Beneath him, birds chased chittering insects, bees buzzed and butterflies danced. In the fields, animals lowed and mated. Children cheered and climbed trees in search of fruit. Men and women sent up burnt offerings and embraced. Everywhere, Gaia was springing to life.

'I'm sorry,' said Persephone, 'but I love him. Hades has certain… qualities.' She swallowed and kissed her mother's knuckles. 'And I'll return to him each year, as promised. Not because I must but because I want to.'

'I'm sorry too,' said Demeter, 'and I'll mourn you whenever you go to him. Not because I want to but because I must.'

A Test

Under the shade of a weeping myrtle, the god of fire breathed in its cleansing perfume and enjoyed listening to the waves lapping the shore. Overhead flew Eros, wings glittering in the sunshine. Winter was over, life was good again, and would remain so until Persephone returned to Hades at the end of summer. Demeter would forever have ice in her heart but had resigned herself to her daughter's fate, so the blacksmith no longer feared for his son's safety.

Life was not so good for Tantalus. For punishment, Zeus had planted the earthly king up to his neck in a lake. Above him was a tree bearing every fruit known to mankind, but whenever the hungry prisoner tried to eat, the Four Winds whisked the branches out of reach. And although the water was level with the hapless king's chin, whenever he lowered his mouth to drink, the nymphs fled, taking the lake with them. A slow execution, and a shame really, as Pelops was better off with Poseidon than he had ever been at home.

In the distance, something crested the surf, casting a beautiful prism. Iris? Whatever the cause of the colourful display, it was getting nearer and the god of love tore off to investigate. Helios was showing a close interest too and his rays glinted on the sea so it sparkled. As the rainbow drew closer, the sun shone more intensely so it was possible to see that it came, not from Iris, but from a woman astride a harnessed dolphin.

Her blue-green locks flowed in her wake, and her hair was all she wore. Eros skimmed low and exchanged a few words with her, but instead of returning to his father, he glided in the direction of Mount Pelion. What was going on?

Hephaestus' eyes widened as he recognised the rider. Despite having the wisdom of the ancients, she seemed in the first flush of youth. But why the nudity? Thetis hadn't appeared bare-breasted since he was a suckling infant, and she'd always kept *some* clothes on, even if only a few strategically placed shells. She laughed as she rode. Never had he seen her this happy. And where was Eurynome? Generally, his foster-mothers were inseparable during daylight so this was a bad sign.

He swallowed and focused on the harness. Plaited seaweed, encrusted with hundreds of sparkling gems, while the rein was stringed with pink and white coral that glowed against the sleek grey vellum of the dolphin.

While he was busy puzzling over the clever illusion, the seawitch reined hard and steered inland, sending a crescent of foam washing against the coastline. Oh, why did she have to be naked?

Intent on hiding, he crept behind the myrtle and scurried towards a tunnel in the rock, which opened into a high-ceilinged cavern with an indigo pool at the bottom. There was a handy ledge halfway down that he could doze on until it was dark so his foster-mother would never be any the wiser.

His nap was interrupted by the sound of swimming. Emerging from the water, the goddess rose on her tiptoes, laced her fingers and arched her arms. With a yawn, she curled up, cradling herself. How had she descended so quickly and quietly? Witchcraft, he supposed. Hopefully, she'd not noticed him and he could sneak out, but that plan was ruined when he heard running footsteps.

The runner hung in the air briefly then plunged from a great height into the pool, where he coughed and flailed his way to where Thetis was asleep. What was his game? Rape? Most prospective rapists would have waited for Eurynome to go wandering before making a move, so this one must be either very stupid or have a death wish.

Cursing, the man hauled himself upright. In the centre of his chest was an arrow. Belatedly, realisation dawned. Had Eros been instructed to lure someone here and shoot him? It was fortunate the smith had not revealed himself. That could have led to an awkward situation, which would have amused Aphrodite for months, if not years.

Without blinking, the archer's victim yanked the arrow free and tossed it aside. His last act of grooming was to squeeze his golden braid dry. So, not a rapist or a stalker, but a suitor, who had no choice in the matter by the looks of things. Wasting no time, he clasped the sleeping deity, who awoke instantly, lips curving as she turned in his embrace.

Finally understanding that this assignation had been preordained, Hephaestus blushed at what was coming and made to leave, but his lame leg meant he was not fast enough.

An orange light flickered under the seawitch's skin as she flared into a column of fire and the smell of charred flesh filled the cave. Just as the burning man began to faint from pain, his flames were quenched by a torrent of water that forced him so far upwards, his nose pressed against the roof and he struggled for breath. The flood subsided and he crashed to the floor, only to find himself nose to nose with a roaring lioness.

The big cat circled, slashing lazily with her paw, opening bloody stripes on his scorched hide. No flowers bloomed from the crimson drops, yet he was undeterred and leapt onto the cat's back. With a hiss, the lion became a coiling serpent, crushing the mortal, his complexion turning blue, until he found himself tangled in the tentacles of a giant cuttlefish, steadfast when squirted with ink and stung by suckers.

In the face of such determination, Thetis shifted once more and the would-be lover writhed in the arms of a laughing goddess.

She could definitely look after herself, so Hephaestus eased himself off the ledge. Unfortunately, he missed his footing, and his heart and stomach fought each other to get out of his mouth. A drop like this held no fear for him. It was a mere splash in a puddle compared to some of his previous falls, but it would be an unfortunate entrance and he'd rather not create a disturbance. He scrabbled at the smooth wall for a fingerhold and climbed out with no further mishaps.

As he walked along the passage, the sand underfoot grew warmer and the sunbeams brighter, and then he stood once more on the hot beach, squinting against the blinding glare. His mind's eye was crowded, not with serpents, cephalopods or felines, but lovers. He didn't want Helios to know and shook his head to clear the images. What did it all mean? It was his fault that his foster-mother wasn't allowed a divine husband, but she had Eurynome. What could this man offer that the creatrix could not?

The answer was obvious, of course. A child of her own. If Thetis had a new consort, she would dispense with her old one. And once she gave birth, Hephaestus would be superfluous to requirements as well. Judging by the tests she'd inflicted on her future spouse, the seawitch was ensuring she got the very best specimen, who was bound to produce a son both handsome and heroic.

It was ridiculous for the blacksmith to feel this jealous when he was a grown-up with a wife and children of his own but he couldn't help it. He stared angrily at his feet. The sun should have gone west long ago. If only Helios would lose patience and sink, but the yellow ball stayed aloft, keeping a sympathetic watch over the lonely god of fire.

The Dry Patch

Once Eurynome learnt of the pregnancy, there had been some intense sighing, and everyone had walked on eggshells for weeks. The seawitch hadn't helped her case by explaining she was desperate for an infant and the creatrix of the universe could give her everything but that. This went down very badly and Eurynome stormed off.

After such a tense period, it had been a relief to begin with, but she'd been wandering for months now. There had also been a difficult conversation with Zeus, accompanied by terrible lightning storms, and the almighty had only simmered down when Thetis swore a stygian oath that the mortal, King Peleus, had fathered her child, promising she'd not lain with any male deity.

The god of fire kept out of it and busied himself decorating a cradle with sea urchin finials. As he made the finishing touches, he wished fervently that the crib was to hold a baby blacksmith, but knew at heart there was no chance of that when his wife was more prone to roaming than the wide wanderer herself.

He'd scarcely seen her since spring had returned and the dry patch looked set to extend to winter. Fortunately, his cousin was due to return to Hades, so the second cold season was imminent. Hopefully, it would bring cosy days spent at home, with Aphrodite wrapped in furs.

His brooding was interrupted when Hermes appeared.

'Grab your birthing tools, Heph. It's the big day.'

'What am I?' he grumbled. 'The goddess of midwifery?'

'Hardly. You're not as pretty as Artemis or her hound for that matter.'

He laid down his hammer and hoisted a waiting sack.

'Where is Artemis, anyway?'

'Hunting, so forget about her. Come on or Peleus will end up with a broken arm, or worse.'

Squeamish to a fault, the messenger vanished from the grotto the instant he arrived. Chiron was administering to the expectant mother, who sat upright on her throne, belly thrust out, talons gripping her lover's forearm. Gently, the smith extricated the expectant father and substituted a walrus tusk.

'Go for a walk, Peleus. You don't need to witness this, believe me.'

When he hesitated, the Centaur grasped his friend by the shoulders and steered him out. Hephaestus couldn't blame the man for not trusting him.

When they were alone, Thetis fixed him with her night-black eyes. 'All is not well. Save him, as I saved you.'

'I'll have to cut you,' he said.

'Do it.'

He slit her with his sharpest blade and she clenched the tusk so hard it snapped. Quickly, he thrust a hand into her womb. When he touched the small being that would steal his place in the seawitch's affections, Hera's prophecy echoed in his mind, and he pressed an experimental finger on the cord that ran from mother to infant. If the babe never saw the light of day, nobody would ever be any the wiser.

'Problem, Heph?'

'No. I'm going to pull him out. Ready yourself.'

Carefully, he withdrew the slippery lump and tucked it into

the crook of his elbow. But as he raised the blade to separate his foster-brother so he could breathe for himself, the temperature plummeted. From the forbidden grate, a trio of deities emerged. The Moirai.

Before anyone could speak, Lachesis whipped out her measuring rod, Atropos cut the umbilical cord in three places and Clotho spun the two resulting lengths of navel string in the air. Hephaestus pressed the newly squalling bundle into the waiting mother's arms and she put the boy to her breast, but he turned his little face away as if sulking.

'Daughter of the Nereids,' said the Fates, raising their voices above the rumpus, 'we congratulate you on the birth of your son. Your *mortal* son.'

'You're wrong,' Thetis argued. 'He has a divine parent and that confers eternal life.'

'We are never wrong,' they intoned. 'You know us. Why would we issue a judgement if it were untrue? But your child *does* have divine blood coursing through his veins, so we bring him a gift to celebrate his first breath.'

The goddess regarded her visitors warily. 'What is it?'

'The gift of choice. He gets to choose.' Clotho held up the shortest piece of navel string. 'Either a short but glorious life.' She waggled the longest piece. 'Or a long but dull existence.'

Atropos swished her shears and consulted her siblings. Following a brief discussion, the trio cleared their throats.

'To clarify, when we say *long*, we mean in mortal terms.'

'And if he chooses glory?' The seawitch's voice was no more than a croak.

Clotho nudged Lachesis, who measured the shortest string and gesticulated to Atropos, who snipped it in half. 'A couple of decades,' they conceded. 'He will fall in battle, which is the most noble end for any man.'

No mother should have to learn this, let alone so soon after delivery, and she sat quietly, trying again and again to persuade her son to latch on.

'You can't suck, can you?' she said, running a thumb across

her sullen infant's mouth. 'And you'll perish without milk, never mind falling in battle, so I must name you.' She whispered the secret word in his delicate ear, but the dreadful sisters overheard it and spoke his name aloud.

'Achilles,' they said. 'No lips.'

Thetis said nothing but opened the wooden chest that stored the lovely cloaks and blankets she'd knitted all those centuries ago. Unable to watch the coming investiture, the blacksmith said he would invent something to help the boy live long enough to choose his own destiny. It was easy to be altruistic as his rival would be dead and forgotten in next to no time.

He set off for his earthly forge, leaving behind a caterwauling newborn, a silent seawitch and three of the worst well-wishers any new parent could hope to have present at the birth of their child.

It took only a few minutes to fashion a pair of lips from soft rose gold but the god of fire was waylaid as he left the smithy.

'Have you seen Peleus,' asked Hermes. 'Hera's looking for him because he's keen to marry by all accounts and she's organising the wedding.'

'The king wants to marry my foster-mother?' Good luck with that. 'And I've seen neither hide nor hair of him since he went walking, but he won't go far, thanks to Eros and his arrow. Holed up with Chiron most likely.'

'I expect he'll stay there until the nipper's older and less irritating. But he'd better get a move on as this young prince isn't destined to survive much beyond boyhood.' He winked. 'Good news certainly travels fast, eh?'

Ignoring him, Hephaestus went on to the grotto, where the goddess was pacing, desperately blowing at some copper wind chimes in an effort to create a distraction. Where had *they* come from? With a pang of jealousy, he realised the Cyclopes had created them for the recent arrival. Ashamed of his pettiness, he fitted the lips to the famished baby.

Achilles snuffled until he found his mother's teat, and as he suckled, his cheeks rounded and he batted blindly with his miniature fists until he fell asleep. Thetis looked at the god of fire so gratefully, he almost cried.

'This decree from the Fates,' she said. 'It *is* true. I feel it in my bones, but I can't just give in. Here, take him for a minute. Scrying will show us the answer.'

She rummaged in a large trunk, pulling out various crystals and goblets before selecting a stone chalice. Instructing him to follow her, she led him out of the cave, still cradling his foster-brother. When they emerged from the sea, she scooped up some water and walked to the smithy, sloshing with every step. After standing the half-empty vessel on a cold anvil, she took Achilles and asked for some fast-melting metal.

Obediently, the blacksmith placed an ingot of lead in the bowl of an iron ladle and heated it. The grey bullion melted into a shining pool that reflected the hammers hanging from the roof. With a turn of the wrist, he dripped the gleaming liquid into the chalice, sending up a small cloud of steam, then picked out the curious artefact and handed it to her. The blunt wedge had transformed into a jagged crescent, embellished with intricate shards and blossoms.

She rotated the distorted metal in the firelight so it cast shadows on the wall, her avid face flickering as images appeared. A funeral pyre. Apollo armed with a bow and arrow. A one-breasted warrior on a wild horse. A thousand ships. A flush of princesses. A beautiful queen and an equally beautiful boy. A golden apple. A baby being dipped in a river.

Evidently, Thetis understood these auspices and ordered him to summon the psychopomp. He tore his eyes away from the dancing silhouettes and threw some quicksilver onto the flames. Within seconds, a partially dressed messenger arrived.

'Carry us to the Styx,' said the seawitch in a tone that brooked no argument.

'You want to cross over? Charon can ferry the departed across but not the living.'

'It wasn't a question,' she said flatly.

'Because you asked so nicely, I'll drop you at the near shore but it's not a pleasant trip and it takes a while.'

'Do you have elsewhere to be?' she demanded.

'*Fine*,' he groaned. 'But whatever you're up to, you'd best be sharp because the ferryman will not be pleased.'

In less than a blink, Hephaestus found himself on the seabed at such depths that he worried his skull would implode. With a flick of his caduceus, Hermes prised up a trapdoor to reveal a dark whorl that repelled any attempt by the water to enter it. He embraced his passengers, pulsed his wings and forced the family downwards, where they were swallowed by the mouth of hell.

Exhausted and hungry, they landed on a beach of ash. So this was the underworld. It had been a protracted journey, even by a god's standards, and Achilles only stopped howling when either asleep or feeding. In the dim light, ghastly cataracts crashed from jet cliffs, creating whirlpools wider than Zeus.

On the far side of the river, a cadaverous old man waited in a boat while legions of shades jostled, endlessly keening for their loved ones. A triple-headed dog raced up and down the bank, barking noiselessly, alerting the ferryman to their presence. Watching the strange hound, the blacksmith idly wondered whether Cacus might like such a pet, maybe in bronze.

With an eye on the rapidly approaching Charon, the seawitch plucked off her son's tiny robe and nipped him on the back of his dainty ankle. Solemnly, she dunked the shuddering infant in the river and he came up wide-eyed and open-mouthed. Possibly, he was screaming, but it was impossible to tell over the thunderous torrents and the wailing shades.

What was she planning? To drown her child and deprive Ares of another war trophy? The god of fire watched as she anointed her progeny nine times, protective slime clinging to his baby flesh and coating him more thickly with each dipping. Except for the dry patch where her fingers pinched him.

Switch hands, Thetis, switch hands, Hephaestus thought but did not say, his guilt washing away in the violence of the water.

Sibling Rivalry III

That dry patch of skin on his foster-brother's heel worried the god of fire at night. A grain of sand in the tender oyster of his heart. But as the years passed, the pearl hardened and fleshed over until it was all but forgotten...

Looking at him today, it was easy to believe that Prince Achilles *was* invincible. No longer an infant, he was astonishing to watch as he dashed along the coastline and bounded from rock to rock. To compensate for being born with no lips, he seemed to have springs on his heels. Of course, the pantheon loved him, and he was a special favourite of Eros and Aphrodite, who adored him for his beauty. Fleet of foot, he regularly raced Prometheus, with the archer flying overhead, acting as pacemaker. Artemis was so impressed by his hunting prowess that she allowed him to accompany her to the forest. The young athlete ran down stags and killed the surprised creatures, dragging their carcasses home, cervine blood smeared across his face, yellow hair tinged red. Apollo taught him to play the lyre and even Athena was fond of him. Whenever Pegasus saw Poseidon showing too close an interest, he would swoop down, rescue the lad and take him for glorious sky rides. Most importantly, as Peleus had not put in an appearance since his son's birth day, Eurynome had stopped wandering and returned to the grotto. She doted on her step-son and he doted on her. *Light-hearted*, Thetis called him, but this was only a maternal kindness because he was equally light of mind. On and on the marvellous child skipped, light as the air his head was filled with.

'Catch me if you can,' sang out the insolent pup as he danced by, kicking up half the beach and showering the god with sand.

Cursing himself for taking the bait, Hephaestus set off in pursuit, struggling to keep up, leaving behind him a curious trail: a heavy footprint with a thick mark etched alongside. It was beneath an Olympian to be so jealous of a boy, and a mortal one at that, especially when all memory of him would fade within a century. Nonetheless, there was no harm in bringing him down a peg or two in the meantime.

The next morning, the blacksmith appeared, clutching a pair of staffs and shod in matching leg guards, each of which had a long, narrow blade fixed to the bottom. Thus attired, and ignoring Eurynome's smirks, he glided across the shore, easily outdoing his obnoxious sibling and enjoying the overdue honour of finally winning a footrace. But his triumph was short-lived because Achilles was huffish when beaten and scampered onto the crags instead.

'Hah,' said the boy. 'You can't catch me up here!'

Unfortunately, he was right and Hephaestus couldn't invent anything adaptable enough to cross such uneven terrain. Inspired by the notion of springs, he'd tried forging a set and bonding them to his leg supports, but it was both painful and mortifying to crash repeatedly onto unforgiving stone before an equally unforgiving audience.

'Hurry up, crabfoot,' called the gloating prince, 'and I'll give you a head start.'

Ashamed of such pettiness in front of his son and his foster-mothers, but unable to prevent himself, the blacksmith picked up the largest boulder he could find and heaved it into the surf, pleased with the resulting surge that swept his young rival off his feet and left him floundering. The spluttering lad had not inherited any affinity for the sea and was as cumbersome in water as he was agile on land, but he was rescued by Eros, who threw his father a judgemental look while depositing his precious cargo safely. Once recovered, the brat did a final lap of the rocks, pausing only to impersonate the god of fire's clumsy gait. The mocking imp needed a lesson in humility, otherwise he would be sure to meet an awful end. Hephaestus ignored a small voice protesting that, courtesy of his dry patch, the child was due to meet an awful end, regardless.

That night, the smith scratched a makeshift mould in the sand and filled the shallow outline with molten metal, recreating the cheeky mortal in two dimensions, from the tip of his flawless nose down to his flawless toes. When the flatwork was cool, he propped it against a tree and considered it under Selene's radiant eye. Deciding something was missing, he held the iron manikin's left foot over a flame until it glowed red and he pierced its heel. A message for the recipient, should he wish to read it. Before dawn, he took his creation to the grotto, placing it so Achilles would see it on waking and perhaps learn that he would not be perfect forever.

'Be still,' he said to the shadow brother. 'For now.'

A heartbeat after Helios rose, the child leapt screaming from his bed, hair in disarray, fleeing from his own shadow, which chased him around his chamber. The practical joker doubled over until his laughter broke the spell, and the graven image clattered to the floor, cold and unmoving. Achilles blinked and rubbed the sleep from his eyes.

'Heph! You'd better not steal my shadow again.' He stamped his lovely little bare feet. 'Stick it back on me, now.' Pale-faced, he pushed at the fabricated likeness with a toe. His smooth brow furrowed when he found the imperfection and he heaved up his iron twin to examine it. 'Why have you put a stupid hole in its heel when I haven't got a hole in my heel? My mother dipped me in the River Styx so nothing and nobody can hurt me.'

The oyster of bitterness shifted in the god of fire's heart but he pressed a hand to his breastbone to quiet it.

'She certainly did dip you. Nine times. I was there.'

'Well, you have to make me a new shadow because the Fates said I can pick my own destiny so I'm going to be a warrior when I grow up and warriors don't wear rotten holey old shadows.'

So, his foster-brother had made his choice, which meant the insufferable mortal would be out of his hair sooner rather than later. The boy marched off, towing the unwanted gift by its damaged heel. He was closely followed by the remarkably cheerful god of fire, the recently woken seawitch and the creatrix, who had just returned from her nightly wander.

When the prince emerged on the shore, he hurled the effigy against the crags, smashing it to smithereens, spearing his ankle with a rogue shard in the process. Incensed, he yanked out the offending piece of metal and threw it at the smith, ranting that this was all his fault. All the while, ichor gushed from a deep gash, blooming into masses of yellow flowerheads, proving he did have golden blood coursing through his veins. But the Fates, unsurprisingly, were right. He wasn't immortal since the wound showed no signs of knitting itself together. Taking no notice of his tantrum, the seawitch laid the injured party out, raised his leg and applied some of the yarrow blossoms to staunch the bleeding. Concerned, Eurynome watched over them, offering silent support. In spite of Thetis tending to her son, the flowers continued budding. It was the first time she had ever looked her soul age. Oblivious both to his mother's sorrow and the cause of it, the lad freed himself the second he was permitted to move. He sprang up, kicked a boulder in temper, clutched his toes and yowled as he hopped about.

'It's no laughing matter, Heph.' The exhausted goddess wiped her hands clean of ichor and sighed. 'That boy of mine is far too vincible for my liking.'

'Does he need a few more dips in the Styx?' Hephaestus asked this in the full knowledge that they were barred from the underworld after all the unpleasantness with the ferryman and his horrible dog.

'Impossible,' she said. 'As you well know. Sometimes, I think your character is as warped as your ankle. But I have a plan. My lad may be the fastest mortal on earth, but he's not the brightest, is he? Don't answer that. A warrior must be as sharp as he is swift, and he needs more experience than I can give him. So, as much as it grieves me, I'm sending him to live with Chiron for a few years.'

'To study the art of healing?' That was one way of protecting a vulnerable ankle, he supposed.

'Amongst other things,' she said. 'The Centaur will school Achilles in the art of war, just as he taught Peleus.'

'How kind of Chiron to offer his services.'

'Who said he offered?' The seawitch winced as the prince limped towards the crags and aimed a kick at another boulder with his good foot before falling flat on his back. 'There'll be a price to pay,' she said, glancing at the creatrix. 'Isn't there always?'

Poor Thetis, giving up her son now in a futile attempt to save his life later. Resisting the urge to ask exactly what this training would cost her, he asked instead how the boy would react to the news of being sent away from the grotto.

'Without a fuss, I expect, as he's bent on becoming a hero.' She cleared her throat and smiled weakly. 'Besides, his cousin is already at the Centaur's cave so he'll have someone his own age to play with.'

'His cousin?'

'Yes. Do you know him? Patroclus.'

Surely not Patroclus the Child Killer, he thought but did not say.

A Marriage of Convenience

Thanks to Eros and his arrow, Peleus remained besotted with Thetis. Although having no further interest in her child's father, she'd not reckoned on the depth of his feeling. As suspected, there was indeed a price for her son's martial training and that price was a promise of marriage. For weeks, there had been spectacular sea storms until the reluctant goddess relented. On hearing about the betrothal, Eurynome simply blinked and went wandering.

According to hearsay, since leaving home, Achilles was already on his way to becoming a fine warrior. He'd made a fast friend in Patroclus the Child Killer, and they got along famously, by virtue of a well-aimed arrow from Eros. So far, the young man was wisely watching his step and hadn't repeated his earlier misdemeanour of splitting a playmate's head open on a rock. Trouble only developed when the prince tired of his infatuated companion and dallied instead with the Spartan queen, who was caught displaying herself naked on the city walls for his pleasure.

Horrified, the seawitch had averted a minor war by asking the Spartan king to pardon her son as a wedding gift to his parents. In return, she swore to keep the lad out of mischief and kept her word by sending the queen to him in dream form so he could continue to amuse himself without incurring any further royal wrath. When the novelty wore off, he switched his attentions back to Patroclus and everyone was happy again, apart from the bride, her jilted consort and the almighty.

After some initial grumbling, Zeus had contented himself with a few electrical storms that sent forest fires sweeping over the mainland. In time, he came around, letting it be known that the match was his idea from the outset, that he'd awarded Thetis the most noble king on earth, and that he had instructed her suitor in the art of winning her over without dying in the process.

The god of fire was sorry for depriving his foster-mother of a divine husband to save Prometheus. Yet, he was also sorry for Peleus, doomed to yearn for a deity who had no desire for him beyond his ability to father her child.

Outside Chiron's cave was a crescent of new thrones, each designed to order by the celestial blacksmith. Aphrodite had arrived first, courtesy of Zephyr, as she wanted to be in place so every guest could admire her diamond chiton. Hephaestus had pointed out the etiquette of not upstaging the bride, but as usual, his wife ignored him. Eros was sulking under a bush because Briareus had confiscated his bow and arrows.

Gowned in dove grey, Eurynome was taking comfort in an alarming quantity of ivy ale. Certain he could hear her heart breaking, Hephaestus gave her his throne and patted her softly.

Astonishingly, Cacus had been invited and came to say hello, tarrying long enough to scorch his step-mother's shin before clumping off in search of something containing bones.

'He has Medusa's charm,' said the goddess of love, rubbing her blister, 'and your looks. I hope your firstborn turns up, too. Perhaps he could injure my other leg. Always supposing he's capable of wriggling this far.'

'He died, Aph. Remember?' It was going to be a very long day.

When the rest of the pantheon were seated, the almighty made quite an entrance, bearing his biggest thunderbolt, accompanied by Hera. As a mark of respect to Thetis for her loyalty in refusing Zeus across the ages, and as a reward for agreeing to the sacred institution of marriage – albeit late and under duress – the greatest goddess brandished the bridal torch overhead so it would be visible in every kingdom. Next, she raised a trumpet to muster the nymphs, who arrived in droves, and the mountain was soon alive with the susurration of leafy trees, surging waterfalls and babbling brooks. Hundreds of Centaurs cantered up, smart in their grass chaplets and armed with fir branches.

Restored to his pre-Pandora dimensions, Epimetheus rushed up at the last minute, which was excellent timekeeping for him, and received a pained look from Prometheus for his troubles. Straight behind him were the bride and groom, flown to the summit by Pegasus, who landed with a soft whicker, kneeling to allow the betrothed couple and their boy to dismount. As if the tagalong couldn't have stayed in Chiron's cave and let his parents have their moment. In fairness, Achilles was no longer a boy and was taller than his father, muscular and handsome, with shining golden hair. Fortunately, Hephaestus rarely saw him now he'd started training.

To welcome them, Apollo played a beautiful composition but even his sweet lyre music did little to cheer Thetis, who was clad in a flowing skirt of sparkling fish scales and two abalone shells, strung together with ribbon eels. The nine-eyed crown nestled amongst her braided tresses, and each of the jewels swivelled to glare at the groom, who wore magnificent gold armour, which Helios bathed in crimson as he dipped down to offer his congratulations.

Darkness reigned as the guests searched for the moon, and

tearful Eurynome used the opportunity to slip out, almost unnoticed. Hopefully, the creatrix would take some consolation from the fact that this marriage would last only as long as the groom. Following some encouragement from Hera, who held her flaming torch very close to his ear, Zeus gave the seawitch away.

The blacksmith carried out the ceremony in a perfunctory manner. Forced to use his second-favourite anvil, he worried belatedly that it might upset Athena, given its unfortunate history. His actual favourite was still trapped in the underworld, despite his best efforts.

In retrospect, it had been a terrible mistake to ask the ferryman for a lift to the other side of the Styx to retrieve the anvil from Hades. And he certainly hadn't expected Charon to react so badly when he'd set foot in his boat. Gods, he was both strong and vicious for all he looked so frail, and who knew his ferocious three-headed dog could swim, let alone so quickly.

Not for the first time, Hephaestus was grateful for his leg-guard, and thank Ouranus that Thetis had already reswaddled her infant before the hound reached them. Hermes managed to extract them with seconds to spare, costing him no more than a winged sandal and a ravaged caduceus. While his foster-mother had started speaking to him again within a few years, the messenger was yet to forgive him, even after receiving replacement sandals and staff.

Once the nuptials were complete, the sky gradually silvered and Selene revealed herself in all her fat glory, beaming down benevolent blessings. The joyous husband clasped his wife at waist and shoulder, swooped her backwards and kissed her, to the cheers of the congregation.

Zeus insisted on making a speech, which was rambling and rather too familiar. Evidently, gossipy Helios *had* seen everything that day in the cave because the almighty regaled the guests with the tale. It was lucky for all concerned that Eurynome had left.

'… and the mortal was so determined to make his suit, he can count amongst his courting injuries flesh burns, a near drowning and a thorough clawing.' He broke off to wink at the livid bride. 'To a sweet married life, however short.' He lifted his chalice and drank deeply before continuing. 'Anyway, that reminds me of the—'

At an impatient signal from Hera, the Muses struck up a melody while the Fates harmonised. Creatures with wings chirruped and creatures with feet stamped. The air thrummed with song and the volume was so loud, the mountain moved beneath them as if it wished to join in. Adding to the honour of the occasion, fifty Nereids performed a complicated spiral dance, their seaweed skirts and marine locks floating in the warm breeze. While still able to stand unaided, the Centaurs lined up with their boughs, forming a shady colonnade for the couple to promenade through, but once the newlyweds had passed, they dropped their branches, jostling to show off their aptitude for divination.

'It's a boy,' they nickered. 'It's a boy!'

The Fates' lips twitched at this hubris, and no wonder. The three Moirai were the ultimate deciders, so this inebriated mob had no business prophesying. Hephaestus felt like he'd eaten cold clay. Was the seawitch to have another baby? What if it was divine? He caught his foster-brother's expression and realised they held this fear in common.

'Amateurs.' Thetis shooed away the false prophets. 'It shows how potent your powers of prophecy are. My womb is completely empty and I plan to make sure it stays that way. One bout of childbirth will do me for this life.'

The foster-brothers shared a look of guilty relief and grinned at the Centaurs, who were up on their hind legs, whinnying.

'Chiron,' barked the groom. 'Keep your charges under control. Clear off, you drunken lot!'

With a final neigh for good measure, they galloped off,

sending up a cloud of dust as they raced towards the gilded girls, who were carrying fresh pitchers of ivy ale.

After the singing and dancing came the gift giving. Most of the Olympians had clubbed together to pay for the new husband's armour. The frugal pantheon had refused to cough up for silver though, seeing as it was only for an earthly king. The sea god, who always had to be different, gave a brace of stallions. Immortal, both of them.

'Typical,' said Aphrodite in a stage whisper. 'Trust Poseidon to give a man two horses that will outlive him.'

And trust the goddess of love to point it out.

A Sting in the Tail

Hephaestus had outdone himself with presents. For the groom, golden armour and a shining spear with a shaft hewn from Pelion ash and hand-polished by Athena. For the bride, a looking glass instilled with a special power. He handed it to her and she gazed into it, smiling at the moving images of her son, ranging from his first wobbling steps through to his most recent swordfight and ending with him dancing with his mother at her wedding. There was no need to mention that the present would survive into the future, long after her child was dead.

With tears glazing her eyes, the seawitch drew him into her arms. 'Blessed boy, how clever you are.' She kissed his cheek and he blushed with pleasure.

Soon, a cluster of deities had formed, demanding miracle mirrors of their own. The blacksmith promised them only to those with mortal spouses or children, on the basis that the divines never changed or aged and therefore didn't need them. He did make an exception for his cousin and aunt, in light of their extenuating circumstances. What he'd failed to realise was that the gods loved nothing more than admiring themselves. This invention opened up a whole world of possible entertainment and he'd just deprived them of it. To appease the angst caused by his refusal, he had to agree they could be in a group portrait. Assuming he could herd them all into position before winter.

'Members of the pantheon, gather behind the newlyweds. Achilles, stand between your parents. Alright, you too, Patroclus. Aph, could you step back a bit? No? Well, maybe to the side of Thetis then.'

He nudged his foster-mother forwards and held his wife in place while he reordered the congregation, encouraging the giants to shift to the rear and the daintier nymphs to the fore. He snapped his fingers to hurry Epimetheus up, then positioned his three-headed son next to the hundred-handed Briareus in the hope that he might appear less ugly by comparison. He patted out a sudden blaze and apologised to the singed Dryads.

'Hold your breath for a couple of seconds, Cacus. Right, everybody. Smile. That means you too, Seph.' Taken aback by the selection of fixed rictuses, he tried again. 'Say cheeeeeeeeeese. That's it. Lovely. Stay still. Keep smiling. Nearly there… Done!'

In the ensuing surge of those keen to view the picture, Narcissus was at the front of the queue. Aphrodite, no stranger to the looking glass herself, paced furiously, muttering about certain individuals and their overweening vanity, until impatience got the better of her and she wrested the mirror from the shocked boy. That was her next birthday taken care of, supposed the god of fire.

Despite Dionysus being in charge of refreshments, the party wore on with hardly any fighting, only a smattering of injuries and very few deaths, which were mainly due to drunken Maenads on the rampage. Zeus had drained a river's worth of nectar and was in a magnanimous mood, twirling the nymphs, showing off his thunderbolt and making them giggle. As the greatest god's wandering hands were occupied elsewhere, his piqued cupbearer searched for alternative empty vessels to fill. Thalos wheeled himself around, gathering dirty platters, red eyes flashing in delayed appreciation when the occasional nymph rubbed his phallus to get a rise out of him.

Somewhat overdue and somewhat pale, a queasy Helios rose, revealing the pantheon dozing on couches after perusing over a thousand entries in the traditional wedding contest to find the most appetising cuisine on earth. Really, the competition was no more than a cunning ruse to have the celebratory supper provisioned without the Olympians having to lift a finger or spend their silver.

Stuffed with a final meze comprising raisins, almonds, dolmades, kebabs and various cheeses, the chief judge sat up and groaned, pointing to a delicate Dryad, festooned in fragrant pink blossoms.

'It was almost a dead heat with charred lamb,' he announced, 'but meat isn't quite as easy on the eye. So, in conclusion, it is my absolute pleasure to award the highest of accolades to the almond—'

But before the almighty could garland the victress in laurel leaves, a faint noise interrupted him and he slapped at his temple, narrowly avoiding killing Melissa.

'Mightiest of mighties,' she hummed, 'I haven't had my turn in the tournament.'

'You're too late, five eyes, so buzz off!'

Several of the more ambitious nymphs tittered, but undeterred, the plucky bee fought her corner.

'I wasn't late. I was here all along, but you were so busy feeding your face that you didn't notice me.'

Exasperated, the king of heaven sighed. 'Fortunately for you, querulous queen, I'm in a whimsical frame of mind today and am willing to consider your food, but I doubt you'll beat the almond tree.' He waved at Hermes. 'Rouse yourself and take note that I've authorised this entry at the eleventh-hour.'

Not bothering to sit up, the drowsy messenger lazily scratched a mark on the ground with his caduceus.

'Done,' he yawned.

Melissa presented a pitcher, prised it open and measured out thirteen amber drops, which she dripped onto each judge's tongue. The honey was sweeter than all the fruits of the earth and more fragrant than all the flowers.

'Amazing!' The almighty smacked his lips. 'Easily the best I've ever tasted. Is there any more?'

'Plenty more, O wise and mighty ruler,' she said, 'if you bestow the laurels on me, but if not…' Smugly, she popped a miniscule piece of beeswax into the neck of the pitcher, sealing her treasure.

This bargaining was nothing short of brazen, but the queen got her way, and the judge shrugged at the disgruntled Dryad in lieu of apology.

'You win, Mel.' He raised the trophy. 'But this garland is too big for you to wear, so instead, I will fulfil your heart's desire. Take a minute and then tell me what it is.'

While she made up her mind, the exultant winner whooped and flew a lap of honour around the irate loser's head, teasing her mercilessly.

'Hmm,' she said at length. 'Mortals and beasts steal my stores day in, day out so I want a bow and arrow or a spear to prevent them.'

'While I suspect you're exaggerating the extent of the problem,' said Zeus, 'if that's what you want, then that's what you will get. Heph, create some sort of defence system. I have a suggestion.'

No surprises there. The blacksmith listened intently, troubled by what turned out to be less suggestion and more outright demand.

'Come on, flower lover,' said Hephaestus, lurching slightly, 'no time like the present for your, er, present.'

'Someone's had too much mead,' said the disparaging bee. 'How steady are your hands? This is delicate work.'

'Steady enough. Here, let's have a proper look at you.' He examined the diminutive creature. As there was scarcely any room for manoeuvre, there were only a few methods that would achieve the required result. 'Wait here.'

He whistled for the tripods, who were busily carrying plates of delicacies, stalked by the bottomless pit that was Laelaps. Once the tripods had delegated their duties to Thalos, they carried their master from Mount Pelion to his Olympian forge.

On the blacksmith's return, Melissa waggled towards him.

'Heph! At last. You've been gone ages. Where's my prize?'

'Patience, my teeny friend,' he said. 'I've created two options.' He held up both fists. 'Let's start with the prettiest version.' Which was also his preferred version. Carefully, he secured his favoured prototype to her head. It spiralled like a pig's tail and ended in a spike. 'There. Whenever you spot a robber, simply dive at them and spin as fast as you can until it burrows into their flesh. That'll teach them.'

Under the weight of the spiralling spike, she collapsed onto her knees. In a frenzy of flapping wings, she tried to stand up but eventually conceded defeat, fell forwards and lay still, dazed with exhaustion 'This won't do, Heph,' the miserable bee whined. 'Even if I could fly with this thing attached to me, I'd be dizzy from all that whizzing round and round.'

'Suit yourself, drumble-dore,' he said, removing the spiral and setting her back on her feet. 'You might prefer my second attempt, although it's less visually pleasing.' It resembled a thorn but was modelled on a snake's fang. 'See, it has a hollow sheath so when you pierce the raider's skin with the dagger, the venom sac empties into them.'

Her five eyes lit up. 'Perfect! I choose this one. That poison should make the villains think twice. Hurry up and fit it so I'm ready to attack.'

'Are you sure you want it?' asked Hephaestus. 'A god's gift, once given, can never be retracted.'

Confused by the question, she frowned at him. 'Who wouldn't want a gift from the gods?'

'You're positive you want this one?'

'Of course I'm positive,' she insisted. 'Put it on me now! *Please*.'

'Then, on your head be it.' He pointed at her backside. 'You know what I mean.'

After he'd done the dreadful deed, the gleeful winner twitched her fat fuzzy body in an effort to inspect her new accessory, which was regrettably outside her field of vision. Seeing her disappointment, the god of fire borrowed his wife's compact so the queen could admire herself. Exhilarated, she whirred over to the king of heaven.

'Thank you for recognising the quality of my honey, Zeus.' She wiggled her dinky bumblebee bottom near the greatest god's nose, her minute dagger quivering. 'May I test out my prize on you?' In her excitement, she broke wind, and forgetting themselves, the nymphs sniggered at the sound of the tiny parp.

'You may *not*,' he thundered. Far from amused, he swatted at her with both hands. 'And get away from me!'

'Apologies!' Chastened, she zigzagged out of harm's way. 'I meant no offence, greatest of greats.'

'Very well,' he said. Apology accepted, but listen carefully. Before utilising your weapon, there is something you must understand. While you foolishly imagine it's there to protect you, it has in fact, been designed to end your existence.'

Her brow furrowed and she scowled. 'How's that exactly?'

'It is intended as a deterrent only,' said the almighty. 'If you use it on someone, you'll leave behind the sting and venom sac when you fly off, along with your entrails.'

At this news, the little queen wept. 'How could you, Zeus? How could you?'

'Pipe down, insolent insect, and compose yourself. You

asked for help to defend your hive and you got it,' stated the king of heaven. 'You were given a choice and you made it. Next time, be careful what you wish for and be less bombastic while you're about it. Learn peace in your heart, Mel, and you'll be quite safe. Just keep your temper,' he concluded self-righteously.

'If you gods struggle to keep your temper,' she sobbed, 'what chance does a humble bee like me have against acquisitive mortals, who possess not a single vestige of restraint?'

'Oh, do stop droning on,' snapped the greatest god. 'Once mankind learns of your sting they'll behave themselves and you won't be forced to unleash it. That is the very nature of the deterrent. Besides, your quandary is temporary since the sweetness of honey will outlive both the bees who produce it and the earthlings who crave it. Now, be off with you and let me enjoy the rest of the festivities.'

The Golden Apple

Once the dust had settled over Melissa's prize, the wedding celebrations continued, but Hephaestus found himself at a loose end. After searching for his wife, he was nonplussed to discover her locked between Ares and Poseidon, both leering in a sickening fashion. Achilles was dancing so closely with Patroclus that it was only possible to tell them apart by their hair, the one flaxen and the other sable.

To his astonishment, Cacus was showing off to the Naiads, breathing flames on their watery bellies and sending up billows of steam, much to their giggling delight. There was hope for the lad yet. The Cyclopes were nowhere to be seen. Doubtless sleeping it off in the shade. At this rate, the god of fire would have to make do with Thalos for company, but even he was busy, wheeling around, Laelaps at his heels, both of them enjoying the revels.

He was almost pleased to notice Briareus involved in an altercation and went to his aid. The source of the disruption was Ares' twin sister, whose shrill tones cut through the Muses' singing. The flustered gatekeeper was scrolling through the guest list, lips moving as he skimmed thousands of names.

Meanwhile, Eris scowled at him, hands on hips, tapping her toe.

'Sorry,' said the hundred-hander as he rewound the papyrus and tied it neatly. 'You're not on the list so you can't come in.'

'What?' She stamped her foot and a rockfall ran down the mountain, flattening the unsuspecting valley dwellers. 'I *insist* on knowing why I'm not on the list.'

The giant sighed, bending a few fir trees on a neighbouring hill. 'I expect you weren't invited, because you always create mayhem.' His massive eye swivelled. A sure sign he was using his god-given gift of prophecy. He definitely couldn't do any worse than the Centaurs. 'I know you plan to wreck the celebration,' he said, 'but if I allow you in, you'll ruin far more than just a party.'

The blacksmith eyed his half-sister, remembering her vindictiveness that time on the beach. He'd avoided her ever since, but they were adults now. 'Oh, let her in,' he said. 'The feast is about done.' How much trouble could one minor deity cause?

'Can I at least search her bag first?'

The affronted goddess of strife clutched the small pouch to her chest.

'Probably best not,' said the blacksmith, flashing back to his wife's fury when he'd once opened a bag of hers, hoping to find a comb.

Briareus shrugged and allowed the visitor to enter.

'Shift, cuckoo,' she snapped, shoving past her half-brother.

Before Hephaestus could change his mind, she twirled into the party, seized a horn of nectar from a passing tripod and drank deeply, taking in everything that had been withheld from her. She scanned the crowd until she spotted her mother sitting with Aphrodite and Athena in a rare display of harmony. The sides of her mouth turned up and her nose twitched as she made a beeline for the goddesses, who were reclining on silk chaises.

'Upsadaisy,' she sang out, emptying her pouch. 'Please do mind your lovely toes, ladies.'

The trio looked up as a golden sphere rolled towards them. All three snatched at the treasure, but the queen of heaven caught it easily, waved it in the air and summoned her spouse, who came quickly once he saw the uninvited guest.

'What are you up to, girl?' Hera demanded. 'And this had better not be scrumped from one of my trees.'

'You might like to read it, Mother. I've engraved it with a special message.'

'Hmm. What does it say? Your writing has hardly improved with age, has it?' Holding the golden apple at arm's length, she squinted. '*To the Fairest.* She showed it to her husband. 'Due to some misplaced doubt about who *is* the fairest, there should be a beauty contest, with you as judge.'

The almighty's eyes widened for a fraction of a second before he confiscated the fruit. 'No need for that, my darling wife,' he said. 'Left to its own devices, this apple should eventually end up with its rightful owner.' With that, he hurled it from the mountain.

'It was already *with* its rightful owner. Who could be fairer than me?' said the greatest goddess.

'Me.' Still reclining, Aphrodite twirled a russet ringlet around her finger. 'No question.'

'Rubbish!' The war deity sprang to her feet. 'Hera, being queen does not get you a bye. You have to compete like the rest of us. Aph, good looks alone are not enough. They must be coupled with wisdom.'

In an unprecedented move, Aphrodite also got up. 'Doing the odd bit of weaving doesn't count as wisdom, Athena, and as for your temper—'

'Quiet!' exploded the king of heaven, fixing his eye on the troublemaker. 'Eris, look what you've started. Ouranus only knows where it will end. You might be my daughter, but you weren't invited for a reason. Now, begone while I attempt to undo this mess.'

But the damage was done, and the goddesses kept arguing, with each determined to be deemed the fairest. Muttering that there would be no peace until the matter was resolved, Zeus capitulated and agreed to hold a contest, but refused to adjudicate, citing a conflict of interest as he was husband, father and nephew to the respective contenders.

In the ruler's sandals, Hephaestus would declare his own wife the winner, without hesitation, and live with the wrath of the losers. This competition was futile in any event. Aphrodite would win hands down as her beauty drove gods and mortals alike to madness. He hoped the greatest god knew what he was doing.

'I'll ask the most beautiful male mortal to do the judging,' said the almighty, 'but first we have to work out who *he* is…'

'It's Paris of Troy,' said the god of love, fluttering overhead.

'Are you certain, Eros? There are millions of men down there.'

'Absolutely certain.'

'Then this Trojan is our judge. Hermes, be a lamb. Nip down and fetch him. Laelaps, go and bring back that wretched apple.' Zeus smiled placatingly at the three opponents, withering slightly under his wife's fierce glare. 'Of course, *you're* the fairest, O light of my life, but you wouldn't want me to simply give you the title when I'm so biased, would you?'

Hera's expression made it abundantly clear that this was *exactly* what she wanted, but her husband turned away from her, whistling nervously, to await his emissary's return.

~

Laelaps and Hermes reappeared, along with the Trojan, who carried the golden apple. Eros was obviously smitten and it warmed the blacksmith's cockles to see his son in love again. Zeus welcomed the young mortal and looked him up and down with an approving eye. Undeniably pleasing, with tumbling locks and honeyed skin, he was oiled and taut in all the right places. More than a few guests sat up to admire him and the sea god's eyes glittered darkly. The lad would be lucky to make it home with his arse intact. Hephaestus would ask Briareus to relinquish his son's bow and arrows so the youth could fall for the archer instead of finishing up in Poseidon's harem.

'Paris,' said the almighty. 'I have a simple task for you.'

As the nature of the allegedly simple task was outlined to him, the boy shivered, and with good cause, as the two losers would treat him with great disfavour. The young judge gave the contestants a cursory once-over and swallowed hard.

'All three are equally fair,' he said, 'so it's a draw.'

He bowed ostentatiously, before being floored by several improvised missiles: a pomegranate, a scallop shell and a wooden shuttle.

'Don't be so pathetic, boy. I sent for you because I wanted your opinion, so let's have it. Who is the fairest goddess?'

The terrified boy's lips moved but no sound emerged.

'I can't hear you.'

'Is… is it… your wife, Hera?'

'Are you asking me or telling me?'

The Trojan glanced to either side of him. 'Asking?'

'Utterly useless,' groaned the king of heaven. 'You have eyes in your head, craven child, so how difficult can it be? Get a closer look. Go and inspect them at close quarters.'

The now pallid youth took each goddess aside to examine her, jealously observed by the other two, for fear of him spending a heartbeat too long with their adversary. Each entrant whispered to him throughout her examination and Hephaestus wondered what threats and promises the mortal's ears were being subjected to. When the shaking boy nodded, Zeus raised the golden apple.

'Excellent. Give me your decision, lad, and we'll—'

'Aphrodite,' said Paris, grinning.

The radiant winner plucked the trophy from under the noses of the raging runners-up.

'Correct verdict,' confided the greatest god as he put out a hand to protect the young man from the coming onslaught. 'May Ouranus have mercy on us both.'

Friendly Fire II

Repercussions from the wedding day were still rumbling on. Shortly after awarding the golden apple, Paris of Troy had wisely made himself scarce. That the Trojan had declared Aphrodite the fairest could hardly have surprised anyone, let alone the two runners-up, but hostilities had hung over heaven and earth ever since.

Once they'd finished laying waste to Mount Pelion, the combatants had resumed their battle on Mount Olympus. The god of fire had resigned himself to a few years of rebuilding, but if the sky dome got broken again, he'd refuse to fix it.

Unsurprisingly, the winner of the celestial beauty contest had been delighted with the outcome. Blissfully aware of her rivals' rage, she'd tripped blithely through the piles of rubble littering the palace as statue after statue was torn down and used as a projectile by one goddess against the other.

Hephaestus had encouraged his wife to stay at the smithy for a while. This was for her own safety and to prevent her from adding fuel to the fire. For further security, he'd fetched Thalos to stand guard while she paced the confines of the forge.

'Naturally, the boy had no choice,' she trilled. 'Zeus

showed infinite wisdom in delegating the task to a mortal.' She paused to admire her reflection in a sheet of metal and blew herself a kiss. 'Imagine what would have happened had he adjudicated the contest himself. Hera would have had his testes for earrings.'

Castration in the name of jewellery would be getting off lightly. The night of the hundred knots had been bad enough. That had almost ended in civil war and involved nothing nearly as combustible as the vanity of three goddesses.

'So,' she continued, 'I might offer Paris a knick-knack to say thank you.'

'You might offer?' He hesitated. 'Or you have already offered?'

'*Offer*. *Offered*. You make it sound as if there's a difference.' She laughed, though the dulcet peal failed to disguise her scheming nature.

'That's because there *is* a difference, Aph. Offering a gift to a judge is blatant bribery, and there was no need because you'd have won anyway.' It was beyond him why she cared so much about the opinions of others. 'So, what did you offer him?'

'I let him choose for himself. Nobody likes a surprise.' She glanced at Thalos. 'You never receive anything you want.'

'What did he choose?' Hephaestus patted the bronze guard, certain the answer to this question would be far from reassuring.

'Surely you can guess what the most beautiful man would want.'

Unfortunately, he *could* guess. 'Presumably the most beautiful woman. Who is that these days?' He dreaded the prospect of a mortal beauty contest if the goddesses' behaviour was anything to go by.

'Helen, obviously.'

'Helen? You can't mean Helen of Sparta?'

'Of course, Helen of Sparta.'

'There's the somewhat unfortunate matter of her being married to Menelaus of Sparta. You know, the king.'

'Oh, him.' She flapped a manicured hand. 'He won't mind. This is hardly the first time it's happened. She's been taken dozens of times in recent years, including by Achilles. Remember how he had her splayed against the city walls? Where is he, by the way? He seems to have vanished from the face of the earth.' Seeing his grim expression, she hurried on. 'Trust me, it's nothing. Less than nothing.'

'The king of Sparta is *not* nothing.' How could Aphrodite fail to see the trouble she was brewing?

'Achilles lived to tell the tale, didn't he?'

'Only because Thetis intervened,' he said, 'and no mortal would dare to cross her.'

'I was forgetting your seawitch. I seem to remember she then sent Helen to your foster-brother in dream form? Honestly, talk about spoilt!'

She had a point, but he ignored her attempt to change the subject. 'You can't procure a queen without expecting consequences.'

She twirled and dropped a kiss on top of his head, as if he were Eros.

'Always such a worrywart,' she said. 'Menelaus is most likely sick to death of his wife and he'll jump at the chance of a new one.'

'Not everyone shares your revulsion of monogamy, Aph. Many prefer to be with one person for life.'

'Gods!' She recoiled at this horrifying notion. 'Life is a long time to be monogamous for deities, for mortals too, and they only last a minute. There's really no cause for concern. This is my domain and it'll all be fine.' A slight crease appeared on her flawless forehead. 'I'm quite sure it'll probably all be fine.'

'You've already handed Helen over, haven't you?'

'Sort of.'

'What do you mean, *sort of*?'

Suddenly finding something of interest under her nails, Aphrodite refused to meet his eye, and when she spoke again, her voice was noticeably higher. 'I mean, yes.'

'And what else?'

'Nothing else,' she squeaked.

He had a very bad feeling about this. 'Aph, please promise me you didn't.'

She winced. 'I did.'

It transpired that Eros had shot the ill-fated queen so she'd fall desperately in love with Paris. When would their son learn to say no? Hephaestus loved the lad dearly, but he was as irresponsible as his mother when it came to thinking about consequences, or rather not thinking about them. And these consequences would no doubt include bloodshed on a dreadful scale.

Once Hera learnt of this outrage to a royal marriage, she stopped fighting with Athena and summoned the pantheon. The messenger was despatched to advise Menelaus of his eloped wife's whereabouts so he could return the queen to the marital bed. The Olympians were now enthroned in what remained of the palace, awaiting news. When Hermes materialised, he barely shimmered and had to lean on a wall for support, miming his urgent need for a cup of nectar.

The greatest goddess clicked her fingers at Briareus. 'I take it Helen of Sparta is back *in* Sparta and all's well that ends well?' she asked.

'Ah,' said the messenger, accepting the proffered chalice and taking a gulp. 'Not exactly…'

'See,' said Aphrodite, 'the man's happy to be rid of her. I tell you, monogamy's for the swans.'

'Not another word from you, Aph,' thundered the greatest god, peering around Laelaps, who was sitting on his knee, panting. 'You've caused enough trouble as it is. So, I hereby banish you to your islands until this chaos is sorted out.'

Indifferent, she crooked a finger at Eros, who flew to her

side. The blacksmith took a step towards his family, but the king of heaven stopped him.

'Not you, Heph. I need you here. Say your goodbyes but be quick.'

It was no surprise when his wife turned away without a word, but it *was* a surprise when Hephaestus realised he wouldn't miss her. What he'd felt for her wasn't love, but a desire to possess what he lacked himself. Beauty, grace and physical perfection. He embraced the lad and confiscated his bow and arrows. With war coming, there was no room for mischief. Blinking, he watched Eros usher his mother out of the door and into exile, wondering when he would next see him.

In the great hall, Zeus was still trying to extract the latest news. 'Hermes, stop quaffing my best nectar and tell me what happened.'

The messenger shrugged. 'Menelaus is a tad unhappy with the situation.'

'What situation?' asked Hera. 'I told him the exact location of his queen and her lover. How hard can it be to snatch her from this Trojan child?'

'I'm not sure she wants to be snatched. Besides, I'm not altogether sure her husband wants her back. His male pride's been injured, or Sparta's male pride's been injured. You know what these kings are like, always over-identifying with their kingdoms. Anyway, the king's been wronged. Sparta's been wronged. Either way, it's not looking good.'

Between mouthfuls of nectar, the messenger explained how the royal cuckold had sought help from his brother, Agamemnon, who, after exhausting diplomatic routes to right this grievous injustice, had mustered a thousand-strong fleet. The ships were ready to sail on Troy, but at the last minute, a priest of Apollo had predicted that the war was unwinnable without Achilles, who was suddenly nowhere to be found.

'Heph,' asked Zeus, 'where's your foster-brother? Have you seen him since his parents' wedding? He's needed for battle.'

Sensing which way the wind was blowing, Thetis had forced her son into hiding. So much for the almighty's alleged omniscience and his wife's powers of prophecy.

'*I'll* find him,' said Hera, flexing her thumb so the all-seeing eye fell through the window on the world.

When it returned, the crystal sphere showed a palace chamber where half a dozen pretty princesses clustered around a tall girl clad in cinnamon silk. She was certainly handsome, if a little angular, and as for those feet! This secret had kept the blacksmith warm at night ever since the wedding. It had to come out eventually, he supposed, but for the seawitch's sake, he held his tongue.

'Hmm, yes. Very nice. Especially that blonde in the middle.' The greatest god ogled freely, ignoring his wife's obvious vexation. 'Remind me to pay her a visit once we've located blessed Achilles. Oh, who's that sneaking in? Is it Odysseus? Apollo, isn't Odysseus mad or something nowadays?'

'Or something,' replied Apollo, tuning his lyre. 'In truth, he's saner than you.' He smiled and strummed a chord. 'Pretending to be insane was only a ruse to get out of fighting.'

'There's a lot of it about,' muttered Hephaestus.

'So if he's not mad, what's his game?' asked the almighty. 'Planning to deflower a few maidens before going off to fight, perhaps?'

Athena snorted. 'I suppose by *deflowering a few maidens* you mean *serially raping a few maidens*?' She stared down her parent until he lowered his gaze. 'I thought as much, Father. You've a good right to look sheepish!'

Red-faced, he harrumphed and returned his attention to the earthly chamber. There, the crafty Odysseus drew two swords. One, he threw on the bed, and the other he kept in his hand. Odd behaviour for anyone plotting serial rape. At the sight of a man bearing arms, the daintier girls squealed and fled, but their hefty sister seized the spare weapon and used it to disarm the intruder, backing him against a wall, with the point of the blade pressed to his throat.

'That big blonde is nifty with a sword, no?' The greatest god adjusted his chiton.

On the crystal, Odysseus burst into laughter. Joining in, the bellatrix clasped the hilt of the sword to her heart and went down on one knee.

'What on Mother Earth is going on?' asked Zeus.

The pantheon huddled around to watch the blonde opening her bodice, but instead of plump curves, she revealed rippling muscles, and Odysseus laughed even louder.

'Father, are you blushing?' asked Athena.

'Hah! No, I'm just a bit too warm. I knew it was Achilles all along. An excellent joke. Daughter, go down there and get that boy out of his mother's frock and into his father's armour. He's got a war to win.'

Hera poked her husband. 'Can't you do something to end this wrangle before it escalates?'

'Like what?'

'Like intervene. Send the queen back to Menelaus – they are married, after all – then redirect the wind to blow those ships home.'

'Sorry, m'dear. I have to remain neutral.' Zeus popped a roasted carcass into his mouth and chewed thoughtfully. 'Although the sooner this skirmish is over, the better. The mortals are too distracted to make proper sacrifice lately. This goat is tougher than Achilles and Odysseus put together.'

'Well, *I'm* not neutral and am firmly on the side of the Spartan marriage,' said the queen of heaven. 'And if you're so determined to be non-partisan, you can sleep by yourself until this is finished.' With that, she stormed to her quarters, ordering Briareus to slam the door behind her.

Troy

Men, women and horses massed along the shore, waiting. Above them, the pantheon stood at the window on the world, also waiting. The seawitch gripped Hephaestus hard enough to shatter bone and he wished for a walrus tusk to take the place of his arm. Something had shifted in Thetis after her son's whereabouts were revealed by Odysseus, and she was prepared to sacrifice however many virgins were necessary to save his life – hundreds, thousands – but the young prince would hear none of it. His immortality lay in the coming conflict, so there would be no stopping this war. In spite of his mother's best efforts to protect him, the lad had chosen to tread the short path to glory.

The thousand ships were slow in sailing to Troy, for the winds had not favoured them. Desperate, Agamemnon had sacrificed his youngest daughter to Artemis. Suitably appeased, the huntress raised the wind so it filled the sails. This willingness of the mortal to kill his little girl in order to bring back his brother's bride puzzled the blacksmith. A virgin for a jade. It seemed a high price to pay. Another innocent casualty that could be laid at the feet of Aphrodite and her boundless vanity, to say nothing of the thousands who would lose their lives during the fighting.

When the fleet hoved into view, Achilles graced the prow of the foremost vessel, attired in his father's golden helmet and breastplate. In a belated fit of guilt, the blacksmith had forged an impenetrable shield, greaves and heel guards, but as he made land, the fledgeling hero – labouring under the false apprehension of his own invincibility – divested himself of these gifts and tossed them overboard.

Unshielded, and with naked shins and heels, the irksome youth leapt off the ship and onto the shore. Screaming supplications into the wind, he charged at the fleeing foe, hurled his spear and spilt the first blood.

Supposing baptism in the Styx *could* confer immunity to injury, there was still the small matter of the dry patch, following the dip in the hellish river. Mother and son had both witnessed ichor flowing from an ankle wound the day the iron shadow was destroyed. The gash caused by the shard had not healed itself and only the seawitch's intervention had prevented her child from bleeding to death.

So why had it never occurred to either of them that he was not immortal? The Fates had been unequivocal when they set out his destiny. Why would neither of them accept what had been laid down? Why deny kismet? This would be a good time to warn his foster-family of the need to guard the boy's vulnerable heel, but would they listen when they'd ignored their own eyes in the past?

Despite an extended stand-off due to the contagion sweeping through the invading army's camps, Olympus was on a war footing. Although avowedly non-partisan, Zeus was an enthusiastic spectator and clomped through the hall in full armour, a caparisoned Laelaps at his heel. Thalos followed, bearing a tray containing a selection of savoury comestibles and sweet libations. Apollo lolled on his throne, twanging his lyre to amuse his dancing mouse, while Athena and Ares dozed like docile infants.

At an immense plotting table, Briareus used a hundred rakes to push wooden mortals and their mounts into a corner where he set fire to them. Hephaestus had made the intricate models during the hiatus so Prometheus could keep watch over mankind without having to witness the real-life carnage.

'How goes it on earth, Apollo?' asked the king of heaven, frowning at the encampments proliferating outside the city walls.

'The invaders continue to be plagued by, er, plague,' replied the golden god, strumming a suitably dark chord.

'Still? After all these years? Leave that confounded instrument alone and come here.'

The musician eyed the mastiff, scooped up his mouse and plopped it onto his shoulder before obeying. 'Yes, O mighty one?'

'Never mind, *Yes, O mighty one*. Cut the innocent act and put an end to this plague of yours. First it was the rats and cats, then it was the dogs and horses, and now it's the mortals. There'll be nobody left to execute an invasion at this rate.'

'That's the general idea.'

'Well, it's a terrible idea and it makes for dull viewing. I know you're trying to preserve your boy, and who can blame you when Hector's such a fine youth, but this deadlock can't go on forever. Look at the state of my war gods. They're comatose with boredom and won't do their job, so stop this epidemic immediately. That is an order. Meanwhile, I will rouse Ares and Athena.'

If the almighty was so impatient to instigate bloodshed, mused the blacksmith, he'd do better to recall the goddess of love from exile than to wake the sleeping warmongers.

~

The plague had lifted and the survivors were ready to fight, but the combat was held in abeyance as Achilles had taken to his bed and hadn't been seen for weeks. Sulking because of an altercation to do with a woman by all accounts. In deference to the prediction by Apollo's priest, his men were reluctant to attack unless they had their talismanic leader with them.

Zeus pounded round the perimeter of the window, squinting. 'Any sign of that blasted boy yet? I can't believe he's pulled this vanishing act a second time. What's he up to? Frolicking in a frock again, or *playing dice* with that toothsome cousin of his, I'll warrant. Thetis, tell your lad to stop cowering under canvas, or else – oh, forget it, here he comes. Excellent. We might see some action at long last!'

Achilles tramped out of his tent, helmet crest askew and armour hanging from him in a slovenly fashion. Without ceremony, he mounted his chariot, brandished his sword to muster his men and hurtled towards the city to engage the enemy.

Throwing spears haphazardly, he maimed several members of the forward defence, seemingly more by accident than design. As he approached the great wall, Troy's most celebrated hero towered before him. Hector, son of Apollo and foster-son of the king of Troy.

Undeterred, Achilles leant back and lifted his spear overhead to take aim. Taking full advantage of this slip, the Trojan lanced him beneath his ill-fitting cuirass and his lifeblood washed the floor of the car, painting it scarlet. Choking, he collapsed and lay quiet, shade fluttering above.

The air rushed out of the seawitch and she slumped against Hephaestus. Shocked that his sibling had succumbed so soon, a strange lump clogged his throat and would not clear no matter how much he coughed. Thetis was colder than winter and he put an arm around her for support, edging her out of the door and towards the dreadful prospect of claiming the body so she could hold a funeral.

But they were stopped in their tracks when the victor

clambered into the chariot, grabbed his victim's helmet by its crest and yanked it free to reveal, not flaxen locks, but sable tresses.

'Look,' said Zeus, 'Patroclus the Child Killer. He was just in disguise. Though Ouranus only knows what the pair of them were playing at.'

'Thank gods,' she whispered. 'I'd better find my boy. The loss of his cousin will unhinge his mind—'

'Too late,' said the almighty. 'Here comes the lad now. No armour. Rather a novel attack strategy, I must say, but at least we can be certain that it *is* him.'

Sure enough, it was her son who went roaring into battle. Driving a plain wooden tumbril and wearing no more than a chiton and sandals, he careened towards the city, and the second he was within range, he hurled a spear at the triumphal Hector. It lacerated his throat and he crumpled, clutching a gushing neck wound.

Before the shade had even risen, Achilles whipped his horses into a frenzy, swept past, gathered up Patroclus, noosed the Trojan and lashed him behind the cart. Howling, and smeared in the blood of both his lover and his enemy, he tore off, circling the city wall, dragging his adversary through the dust, thereby abasing the dead, offending Apollo and insulting the king of Troy.

Prometheus approached Thetis. 'Please, try to talk some sense into him.' He clasped her hands and appealed to her on bended knee. 'Ask him to relinquish Hector's remains so his people can give him a proper funeral. The mortals have their rituals and we must respect them.'

Only the god of fire noticed the bereaved father leaving the palace.

~

It took a considerable amount of persuasion, but eventually, the degraded corpse was ransomed to the Trojan king. This contemptuous behaviour had not improved relations between the warring factions, and after a brief respite for funeral games, the armies resumed their respective positions.

The seawitch continued her vigil at the window and stared intently at the earth, avoiding eye contact with Apollo, who slumped on his throne, lyre and mouse untouched. Now that Achilles had returned to the fray, Hephaestus felt his foster-mother stiffen as she watched her child cutting a swathe through the enemy ranks. Always the fleetest mortal, no other could touch him for speed or accuracy, and the bodies piled up in his wake.

Most of the pantheon perched or leant on the windowsill while Zeus sprawled on a cushioned divan. Legs spread wide, he golloped fistfuls of fried whitebait and chased them with nectar. Never once did the greatest god take an eye off the scene unfolding below, but occasionally, he would sit up and groan or curse at a particularly noteworthy catastrophe.

The impartial almighty cheered on both sides, with Ares inciting general savagery and Athena disseminating clever battle strategies. To Hermes' chagrin, he was kept busy transporting shades to the underworld and providing regular updates to Briareus, who replayed the action by moving the replicas on the tabletop battlefield. Nearby sat Prometheus, shedding silent tears at every mortal fatality, irrespective of side.

Down below, the warrior prince was founding his own legend. Shadowed by a lengthening trail of butchered enemies, he impaled three Trojans, one after the other, barely pausing to draw breath or wipe the gore from his face.

War-drunk and dazzled by dreams of his future glory, Achilles failed to notice a thirteen-strong cavalry of single-breasted Amazons encroaching on him from the rear. There was not so much as a creak from their supple saddlery to give away their presence. Perfectly still and silent, their queen threw her javelin, which found its target and skewered his kidney.

Immediately her child fell, Thetis began keening. Hephaestus held her tightly and some of the other gods gathered behind the stricken mother.

The cavalry encircled the fallen hero and the regal Penthesilea slid from her horse and stood over her kill. Gloating, she retrieved her weapon, kicked her victim onto his back and placed a foot on his chest, pinning him while he groaned and twitched.

Golden ichor bled out of the boy and soaked into the thirsty earth. Around him, yarrow flowered in abundance. Slowly, his eyes closed and his ravaged shade rose above him. The ensign of death. So, the prophecy ordained at his birth had finally come to pass. Achilles was dead.

Resurrection

The seawitch quivered in silent grief but when the king of heaven lobbed a crab down his gullet, she thumped him with her sceptre, and he coughed up the offending crustacean, which was promptly gulped down by an opportunist Laelaps.

'How dare you eat when my son lies dead?' demanded Thetis. 'Remember, you are in my debt. When I freed you from the hundred knots, you swore on the Styx. Whatever I want, you said, no questions asked. What I want is to have my child resurrected.'

Grey-faced, Apollo fiddled with a broken lyre string.

'And he deserves this, does he, after his grave insult to my Hector?'

Ignoring him, she continued. 'Do as I ask, O mightiest of mighties, and I'll give you anything.' She knelt and grasped his knees.

'Anything?' Zeus licked his lips and took a last look at some oysters as Hera swept them out of his reach.

'Husband of mine,' she said, closing his gaping jaw with a finger, 'you did swear a stygian oath, so if you are able to revive a mortal from this distance, then you will do it at once, and you are to take nothing in return. Do you hear me?

Nothing.' With unusual tenderness, she raised the kneeling mother to her feet.

'If I must,' he sighed, 'but first we should consider the...' He mouthed a word. 'Upsetting as all this business may be, it is what *they* laid down and they're never very easy to deal with.'

At the mere mention of their name, however surreptitious, the Fates materialised, armed with distaff, ruler and shears, looking none too pleased at being disturbed during their busy time.

'Ah, there you are,' said Zeus. 'Atropos, I imagine you've already cut the life thread?'

The most dreaded Fate nodded and scissored the air, narrowly missing the almighty's testicles. In sympathy with his master, Laelaps yelped and scuttled away with his tail between his legs.

Hand covering his groin, the greatest god pleaded with his wife. 'So you see, my darl—'

'Just do it!'

'Yes, dear.' He bowed to the terrible sisters, taking care to avoid Atropos and her swishing shears. Gently, he blew through the window so his breath streamed down to earth. The divine breeze rustled the slain youth's hair until his nose twitched and he sat up, blinking.

'There, it is done,' said Zeus, somewhat redundantly. 'Is it alright with everyone if I finish my dinner now?'

'Thank you.' Thetis spoke without taking an eye off her son.

Hera touched her husband in the way he liked so much. Taken by surprise, the startled almighty grasped her hand and accidentally knocked the all-seeing eye out of its setting before escorting his wife to her chamber.

Down below, to the wonderment of almost everyone on the battlefield, the fallen hero had risen. Oblivious to the resurrection, the victorious Amazon mounted her horse, ready to ride away until she was stopped by a spear skewering *her* kidney. With an impressive vault, Achilles grabbed her by the braid, dragged her from the saddle and let her fall in the dirt.

'Hah!' The god of war leapt up in an uncharacteristic display of approval. 'Serves the virago right for getting above her station. Women have no place on the battlefield. She's fit for no more than dog meat.'

'Typical. Just what I'd expect from an ugly brute with a small penis,' retorted Athena. 'And she will *not* be thrown to the dogs. Penthesilea deserves a decent funeral, supposing I see to it myself.'

As soon as the queen's shade rose, her killer withdrew his spear. Bewildered, the pantheon watched as he turned the Amazon on her back, knelt at her side, cupped her solitary breast and lowered his lips.

'Really,' remarked Apollo, 'will that boy never get over his infantile inability to suck a teat?

Hephaestus drew his foster-mother to him and pressed her face against his chest to save her witnessing what was no doubt coming next. Without further ado, the lad clambered onto the body and penetrated the queen's flesh for a second time, with this action, violating both Penthesilea herself and the age-old sanctity of the dead.

Thankfully, the deed didn't last long. Sated, he got to his feet while one of his men, an especially repugnant specimen, gouged out the corpse's eyes with the tip of his spear. Oddly, this crime infuriated Achilles and he remonstrated with the ugly assailant, who responded with some filthy mimes of his leader's recent debauchery.

Whether driven by shame or bloodlust, it was impossible to tell, but the necrophile punched the soldier so hard that he smashed every tooth out of his head, mindlessly slaughtering his own ally.

'Unbelievable,' said Apollo. 'That my gracious Hector remains in the underworld while *he* lives on, only to perform such atrocities.'

Achilles had barely dusted off his knuckles, when the all-seeing eye sped past Hephaestus like a hungry falcon, grazing his temple as it flew to Hera's chamber, eliciting a loud squawk. After a silence as strained as it was short, the king of heaven marched into the hall, chiton tied carelessly, holding out the errant missile. As he advanced, anvil-shaped clouds clustered at his temples.

'Is this how your son repays me? I slight the Fates and his first act following resurrection is to outrage a corpse? While I'm as broad-minded as the next deity, even I have to draw the line somewhere.'

Before Thetis could cobble together a defence, Athena went on the attack. 'That's rich for someone who has never knowingly passed up an opportunity for sex,' she remarked, 'consenting or otherwise.'

'Enough, Daughter!' Purple-faced, the greatest god shoved the crystal orb at its creator. 'Fettle this accursed object, Heph. It caught me in the unmentionables at rather a tender moment. As for you, seawitch, what am I to do with your boy?'

She clasped his hands. 'Show him mercy, please. Perhaps dwelling amongst the deceased has confused him and he thinks he's still one of them. My child would never wittingly commit such sacrilege.'

'You have a point.' Zeus cast an uneasy glance at the Fates. 'It's not the lad's fault he was brought back from the underworld, but this sets a dangerous precedent and can't go unpunished, or else how will the dead ever enjoy their eternal rest? We simply cannot tolerate warriors corrupting corpses, murdering their own men and breaking the sacred rules of battle. If Achilles wants lenience, then for a start, he'll have to make sacrifice to Artemis.'

The god of music plucked two strings on his lyre and sang, 'Hec-tor.'

The almighty's brow puckered. 'Yes, as I was saying, he'll have to start by making sacrifice to Artemis *and* Apollo, and he needs to be cleansed of blood guilt for murdering his own soldier – Odysseus will do the honours – then I want your boy straight back in his armour. He has an important task ahead of him.'

'Can't you stop this war today?' asked Thetis. 'Call it a draw and send the ships home.'

'There has to be a winner,' replied the king of heaven. 'Deadlock is no good or the mortals will be up in arms again by winter. They have to determine whether the woman ends up as Helen of Troy or returns to being Helen of Sparta. So, we need a plan.'

'I've been thinking,' said Athena, 'about how to end this conflict without too much further carnage.'

'Ignore her, Father,' said Ares. 'Women know next to nothing about war, and carnage is the whole point.'

The goddess scowled and continued. 'Achilles is the finest Greek fighter so we should set him against his Trojan counterpart. Greece versus Troy. One more death, instead of many thousands.' She was careful not to look at either Apollo or Thetis while outlining her plan.

'Very wise, Daughter,' said Zeus. 'Perhaps your fellow war deity can identify the best soldier for the job, now that…'

Apollo snorted. 'Now that my poor Hector is dead? You can't bring yourself to say his name, can you?'

'I am sorry for your loss,' said the almighty, with a conciliatory nod, 'and I will have your son's likeness carved on my throne.'

'What a great tribute,' remarked Apollo, bitterly.

'Well, Ares?' asked Zeus, ignoring this comment. 'Who do you recommend?'

'Wait,' said the war god, holding up a meaty hand, 'I'm still thinking.'

While her brother mulled over past glories, Athena jabbed her father in the chest. 'Why ask that ignoramus when I know the perfect candidate? An earthly king, Memnon the Resolute.'

'I was just about to suggest him,' said her petulant sibling.

'Of course you were,' she said. 'Briareus, find his replica

and hold it up. He wears ebony armour and a red plume on his helmet.'

Straight away, the giant plucked the appropriate figure from the battle board.

'Very well.' The greatest god addressed the seawitch. 'Once your lad's been cleansed, he'll face King Memnon and that should be that. Daughter, go down and inform both armies about my strategy then find this other combatant and prepare him.' He tilted his head towards the Fates and lowered his voice. 'And take that lot with you. Why are they still hanging around when earth is a veritable bloodbath? Tell them to get a move on because after this final slaying, the war will be done with, so they'd better make the most of it.'

'As you wish, Father, but only if you promise to honour the Amazon. She fought bravely. And do a proper job of it to compensate for her dreadful humiliation.'

'Fine. Leave it with me. Heph, come here.' He watched Athena and the three Moirai depart. 'Do me a favour and carve Hector and Penthesilea on my throne by way of reparation. Place Achilles near to her but not abusing her corpse. Try to portray a more noble version of events and show him supporting the queen in her death throes or something.' He glanced shiftily towards his wife's quarters. 'She was an imperious beauty, so position the carving where Hera's not likely to see it. Frankly, I can do without the shouting.'

As Hephaestus went to collect some tools from the smithy, Thetis stopped him and whispered in his ear. 'My boy's life is not over yet, Heph, so don't add him to that throne. Give him a fighting chance and forge another shield. Do it for me.'

~

During the seawitch's absence to supervise her son's purification and sacrifices, the god of fire completed his memorial carvings and got to work on the shield, along with some new greaves and heel guards. He decided to deliver them in person, hoping to impress on the young warrior the importance of defence as well as offence.

The tripods carried him to earth, where he found his foster-brother alone in his tent, pacing. Even under the dark canvas, he had a golden aura, but there was no longer a spring in his step and the joy had drained from him. Hephaestus commiserated on the loss of Patroclus and the lad raised his chin a fraction in acknowledgement. While he had his attention, the blacksmith thrust the gifts into his hands.

'Impervious to any spear,' he said. Sensing reluctance, he pointed to the guards. 'At least protect your left heel. Look, when your mother dipped you in the Styx, she gripped you like this.' He pincered his finger and thumb to demonstrate. 'So she missed a bit. I should have mentioned it sooner.'

'Better late than never.' Achilles scoffed and allowed the armour to fall to the floor. 'But you're sadly mistaken if you think I want to be saved. This life can't end soon enough for me.'

Friendly Fire III

The two opponents faced each other, one wearing gold and the other ebony, ringed by their cheering supporters – soldiers whose hearts must be gladdened by the prospect of a comrade willing to lay down his life to spare theirs. Thetis stared up at the heavens. She was shadowed by the Fates, and the three sisters wore grimmer expressions than usual. A bad omen, but for which warrior?

Above, the pantheon crowded the window on the world. At the fore was Apollo, grief and rage doing battle on his formerly sunny features. Achilles had made the appropriate sacrifice, but whether this act had appeased Hector's father remained to be seen. And of course, there was the small matter of the prophecy.

The greatest god propped himself up on his divan.

'Heph, you fashioned Memnon's helmet, cuirass and so on, did you not?'

'Yes,' he replied, 'but that was a decade or so ago.'

'It's fine-looking armour. You know, I could see myself in ebony.'

Hera scrutinised the buckles straining to hold her

husband's breastplate in place above his midriff. 'The mortal looks so good,' she said drily, 'because *his* armour still fits him.'

Hephaestus scratched his beard to cover his grin. Outfitting an earthly king was a minor task, but when it came to someone of the heavenly king's proportions, he doubted Gaia contained enough metal to produce a second set of armour. Ouranus only knew how the Cyclopes had managed to mine the material to create the original.

His mother was right and the almighty's armour *was* on the snug side, but before he could broach the subject, the fickle ruler had grown bored and dropped a roast ox into his mouth. While he chewed, he loosened his buckles then delicately spat out the skeleton and threw it to Laelaps. Zeus considered the combatants for a moment then addressed the blacksmith.

'As both warriors are equipped by you, this encounter between Greece and Troy could go either way, could it not?'

'It could,' he agreed. Not least because Achilles had refused to shield his ankles.

'Then let's attempt to foresee the outcome of the scrap. You there, bronze fellow, fetch my scales.' He gestured at Thalos, who obediently fetched a balance with weighing pans. 'You there, with all the fingers. Yes, you. Who else? Pass me the wooden fighters.' Briareus substituted silver discs and passed two exact replicas to the almighty, who positioned one in each pan and winked. 'How about a wager, Heph? Can you guess what my prize will be when I win?'

Hephaestus could guess all too easily and wondered what he could melt down to make it. He caught the eye of his bronze servant, who wheeled himself off as fast as was possible for a man cast from solid metal.

While her husband was otherwise engaged, the greatest goddess summoned Thalos to fetch her some water. Eager to prove his usefulness, the manservant was soon back, spilling most of the liquid in his haste. She frowned, accepted the half-full pitcher from him and leaned idly on the sill. How unlike her to drink anything so humble, thought the god of fire, until she tipped the water through the window. His mother could be very tiresome.

'Oops,' she said. 'How clumsy of me.'

As a torrent engulfed the earthly spectators, Briareus updated the battle board accordingly. Hermes materialised briefly, glanced at the latest situation report, tutted loudly and left.

'Hera,' said Prometheus, appalled. 'Don't you think my mortals have suffered enough?'

'I'm bored,' she said, unconcerned at the mayhem below. 'They'll be mere memories in a few years, so why worry? Besides, this proxy war is meant to save thousands of lives, so it all balances out in the end.'

Feeling sorry for his friend, the blacksmith whistled for his favourite tripod, who took instructions and hurried off. The dutiful appliance quickly returned, accompanied by its nineteen colleagues, carrying the forge's largest pair of bellows. Hephaestus seized them, positioned himself next to the palace fire and aimed a stream of hot air at earth so the warm breeze dried the land, without scorching the survivors.

When steam rose and formed dense mist, Zeus protested he couldn't see anything, and the armies certainly needed no further precipitation, so the smith harvested the clouds and scattered them over the arid lands, where the dwellers would be glad of some unseasonal rain, if a little surprised.

A beringed hand squeezed his shoulder. Prometheus, grateful for his help. 'If only the other gods were less impervious to injury,' he confided, 'then perhaps they'd feel the mortals' pain and treat them better. Although it might not seem so at times, Heph, your wound is a blessing. It makes you less divine and more earthly.'

Coming from any other deity, this platitude would have infuriated the lame god, but his friend had endured untold agonies on behalf of mankind, so he accepted it in the spirit it was intended.

Zeus was concentrating on the scale and the great hall was

unusually hushed. 'Come here, Heph,' called the almighty. 'Fix this. It's broken. The pans haven't moved.'

'That's because the warriors are busy sizing each other up,' he pointed out, 'so the balance is in perfect working order.'

'Hmm, you said that about the all-seeing eye. Oh, something *is* happening!'

The left pan started to descend while the right ascended. As the ebony replica reached its nadir, Achilles lunged with his sword and in a single magnificent stroke, decapitated Memnon. Scarlet blood pulsed from his neck and his headless shade emerged as his body toppled over.

Behind him, his servants were building a pyre. Prometheus shuddered as the victor flaunted the plumed head of the Trojan proxy before stripping the king of his helmet and armour and hurling his severed remains onto the flames. Soon, the king's weeping mother approached, knelt beside the funeral fire and lifted her face to heaven, pleading for her son to be resurrected.

'Word was bound to get out,' moaned the greatest god. 'You do it for one, you're expected to do it for all, and I dare not upset the Moirai any more than I already have. Yet, the mortal was a worthy opponent and died a hero, sacrificing himself to protect his comrades, so I'll meet his mother halfway.'

With that, he snatched some embers from the palace fire and tossed them into the air. The glowing pieces of charwood sprouted wings, flew to earth and circled the pyre three times before turning on each other, biting and clawing until they fell into the flames, sacrificing themselves to the honour of the dead king.'

'It's not much of a memorial, is it,' remarked Athena, 'as these things go?'

'At the very least, Memnon has been treated with respect,' retorted Apollo.

So, it seemed Achilles' atonement had failed to assuage either the god's wrath or his sorrow.

'Is that it, Father?' said the goddess of war.

'But what else can I do?' He frowned, static and white clouds fizzing around his temples. 'Wait, I have another idea. The Fates have no interest in creatures and won't mind. Every year, when Helios completes a round of the zodiac, the birds will resurrect and fight to the death at Memnon's tomb. Will that do, Daughter?'

'Not really,' said Athena. 'Try harder.'

He sighed deeply. 'The flock will, um, sprinkle water like a mother's tears…' His shoulders sagged. 'I'm done. That's it,' he said, dismissing any further discussion with a flap of his hand.

Below, Thetis was consulting her son, checking his armour, tightening the laces, pointing to his unprotected heels and wagging a talon at him. In response, the boy threw back his head and groaned, shooing her away. Reluctantly, the seawitch set off for the shore, pausing every now and again to turn and look at the stubborn prince.

Her fretting was understandable, but the war was finished, Helen would return to Sparta and Achilles was alive to tell the tale. So was that it, then? Had the mortal cheated the prophecy, after all? Just as well. Zeus had resurrected him once, but the almighty had made it abundantly clear that he wouldn't disobey the Moirai twice.

Unseen, the god of music put aside his lyre, lifted his bow from his throne, veiled himself in a cloud generated from his father's temples and descended to earth.

Outside the mighty gate to the city of Troy, Achilles stood atop his chariot, regaling the men with the finer points of his triumph. As he orated, a wisp of cloud came to rest nearby and someone emerged from the mist, except it wasn't Apollo, but Paris, who strolled towards the massed ranks, holding his weapon with the nonchalant bearing of a man who believed the war to be truly over.

As the young Trojan approached the Greeks, the armed men shifted, readying their swords and spears, but their leader waved them down and nodded a greeting to the beautiful youth. Once the army had settled and the vainglorious sermon was underway again, Paris ranged to the side and gazed at the hero, a curious smile on his face.

Still smiling, he nocked an arrow, raised his bow, took aim and fired. As he let go, smiling Paris became laughing Apollo, and the arrow found its target and sank – as it always had to – into the vulnerable bare patch on the boy's heel. Ichor gushed from him, soaked his feet and flowed to the ground.

The Fates appeared, humming and creating a warning ripple in the air. Clotho passed the life thread to Lachesis, who swiftly measured it against her stick, and Atropos cut it. The hero's eyes widened as he fell from the chariot, his landing softened by a bed of golden yarrow.

When his shade rose, the hole in its ankle was plain to see and Hephaestus pushed from his mind the memory of the iron twin cast for his foster-brother in childhood. Hermes arrived, bowed respectfully and touched his caduceus to the dead boy's brow. For the second and final time, the chief psychopomp led his shade to the underworld.

Apollo spat on the corpse and walked off. Not only had he avenged himself for the insult to Hector, he'd done it disguised as Paris, who'd instigated the bloody war by stealing Helen of Sparta. It had a certain element of poetic justice, Hephaestus supposed, if you ignored the part played by Aphrodite in all of this.

A Period of Mourning

The seawitch used a sharp rock to hack off her blue-green tresses and laid them across her son's body, which rested on an unlit pyre. Peleus stood next to his newly shorn wife and Hephaestus stepped aside to allow them their privacy.

Nothing could have prepared him for the chill of death on Achilles, and telling Thetis about Apollo's arrow was the worst thing he'd ever had to do. She'd sat in silence, dry-eyed, this goddess who'd saved him as an abandoned infant and put him to her own breast all those years ago. He was guilty of taking his foster-mother for granted while throwing himself at Hera and Aphrodite, doing their bidding and making trinkets according to their every whim. No matter how hard he'd tried to milk love from them, there had been none to give, and while briefly diverted by baubles, they'd never wanted him and never would.

Peleus drew his wife away from the pyre but she paused to kiss their son's left heel, blessing him in death where she'd failed him in life. She shouldn't reproach herself. Nobody – not god, not man – could outwit the Fates. Men, women and children got whatever Clotho spun, Lachesis measured and Atropos cut. Like it or not. Mortals struggled to understand that death was always coming for them. How much harder for a deity with a mortal child.

Courtesy of his divine blood, Achilles had been given the choice between a long, dull existence or a short, glorious one. Now, the warrior prince was wreathed in glory, but what comfort was that to him, or to his parents as they mourned during the drawn-out days ahead?

So many of mankind's meagre minutes were squandered on vain attempts to defeat the three sisters and achieve immortality, whether by flexing puny muscles, fighting futile wars or spouting embarrassing poetry. Their names might survive them but it was meaningless when their shades were trapped in the underworld.

In the time of gods, mortal lives were but a blink of light in the chasm of eternal darkness. Better by far for them to bow to the limits imposed by the Moirai and enjoy their few hours in the sun while they lasted.

The god of fire groaned at his own high-handedness. Easy for him to judge when the passing of aeons was of no significance to immortals, who had the luxury of infinity, which made them lazy. Why hurry when there was always another day, another century, another millennium? Hadn't he just wasted two decades burning with petty sibling rivalry? And although it was the whole of his foster-brother's short existence, it was barely a beat of the heart for the blacksmith.

Her face half-hidden behind clouds, Selene cast shadows over the white sands. Under the sombre moonlight, Thetis inclined her head a fraction. It was time. Hephaestus walked towards the grieving couple. Their boy was about to make his final journey, clad only in his mother's hair. At the slightest touch from the torch, the pyre wood crackled and flames licked the corpse, searing the beautiful skin. Achilles would leave earth in a furious blaze that mirrored his life. He had appeared as bright, brilliant and fast as a comet, yet his name would still be consigned to history and soon forgotten by all but his parents.

After Peleus departed, the seawitch spoke without turning.

'You knew, Heph. Right there at the River Styx. Why didn't you tell me? Did you hate him that much?'

Lost in shame, it was tempting to remain silent. 'You saved me,' he said at length. 'But I did not save Achilles, and for that, I am sorry.'

When she spoke again, she kept her back to him.

'It's pointless blaming you. The Fates decreed it. Nothing could save him. I know that. Not magic. Not prayer. Not love. Deep down, I understood the inevitability of the prophecy. Just the same, you should have told me…' She trailed off and her shoulders trembled. At last, she was weeping.

Words were not enough so he placed a hand on her shoulder and the two deities stayed like that as night wore on around them. It was a relief to avoid her gaze, because there was a second charge, as yet unspoken. Long before the Moirai issued their proclamation of mortality, Hephaestus had destroyed any chance of Thetis bearing immortal children. When he'd tricked Zeus into pardoning Prometheus, the price had seemed worth paying, and he'd assumed the seawitch would be overjoyed at giving birth to multitudes.

Not even the celestial blacksmith could invent a scale to weigh the torment of the body against that of the heart, but now he understood that sparing his friend from physical punishment had come at an immeasurable emotional cost to his foster-mother, and there could be no reprieve from her lifelong sentence. As if a new infant could replace a dead sibling. The loss of one child was breaking her, so how might she endure the loss of hundreds, or thousands?

In a dark corner of his mind, a thought was concealed. Had he really deprived Thetis of an immortal husband to spare Prometheus from eternal agony? Or, had he done it so he could keep his foster-mother to himself? Mortal children would come and go but the god of fire would abide. Whatever his motive, he could not turn back time. Instead, he would create a funeral gift for the seawitch. First, it would help her to remember. Then, it would help her to forget.

Helios slid quietly into the sea, staining it carmine. Selene rose and absorbed the colour. A blood moon, to watch over the grief-stricken goddess. Hephaestus set down his present. A gold cinerary urn. It already contained the remains of Patroclus and was intagliated with moving images taken from the wedding mirror. He'd fashioned these pictures into all the days of the boy's life, etching them so they flowed across the shining surface with every turn. Everything that had made the god jealous in the past would gladden his foster-mother in the future.

When the fire had burnt down, he gathered together the bones, arranged them on a flat rock and hefted his mallet.

'Stop.' The seawitch approached him. 'I can't stand you putting the hammer to him. I brought him into the world and I will see him out.'

Stalwart, she pulverised the bones with her hands and poured her son's silvery remains onto those of his lover, raising the urn to the moon for a final blessing before giving it to the blacksmith.

'Once sealed, it can't be opened again,' he said. 'Are you ready?'

'How can I ever be ready?' She looked out to sea and drew in a juddering breath. 'Do it.'

With his thumb, he traced the poppy engraved inside the lid, then capped the urn and slipped the catch to seal it. Nevermore would these ashes see the light of day. Just like the boy's shade, which was doomed to walk beneath the leaden sky of the underworld, shoulder to shoulder with all the shades of the dead. It would be worse there for Achilles than for most mortals. Since neither mother nor son could cross the Styx, they would not meet again.

Thetis knelt at the shore, staring at the horizon, oblivious to Helios and Selene passing in their endless dance. Skies darkening and lightening. Tides ebbing and flowing. Stars birthing and dying. Planets whirling through the heavens. Clouds weaving intricate patterns, forming and reforming, merging and parting, dreaming the islands in white. Gaia, perpetually trying to mend her fractured self, paying her respects.

Alone in her grief, the seawitch clutched the gold sepulchre. Deeply carved, the pictures would last down the ages, but not for always, and with each touch – a hundred, a thousand, a million – they would grow fainter and disappear, and with them, finally, her memories. One day, the urn would be rubbed smooth until it was no more than a plain metal pot that would not open.

The goddess caressed the etchings, fingertips remembering the days and nights of her son. Watching her, Hephaestus realised what a fool he'd been. While the engravings would eventually fade, the memories of a bereft mother could never fade. The death of a child was too much for even a god to forget. Thetis would mourn for longer than the boy had lived. Thetis would mourn for as long as *she* lived. Forever. Forever was a long time for a mother to mourn.

Also by Helen Steadman

Widdershins (Book 1 of The Widdershins Series)

England, 1649. A sadistic witch hunter. An apprentice healer accused of witchcraft. Can she escape the hangman's noose?

When John's parents die at the hands of a witch, he faces a choice. An easy life with a woman who serves Satan, or a hard life with a preacher who serves God. The cursed orphan chooses the church. Raised on raging sermons, he discovers his true purpose: to become a witchfinder and save virtuous souls from the jaws of hell.

In a town mesmerised by superstition and fear, two destinies collide. As John rounds up the local witches, Jane gets more than she bargained for when bartering with the apothecary. Instead of trading herbal remedies, she finds herself on trial for consorting with the devil. Can she prove her innocence, or will she be condemned to death?

If you like historical novels based on real witch trials, you'll love Helen Steadman's *Widdershins* and its sequel, *Sunwise*.

Spellbinding historical fiction recommended for fans of *The Familiars*, *Tidelands* and *The Witchfinder's Sister*.

Sunwise (Book 2 of The Widdershins Series)

Filled with vengeance, John will stop at nothing in his sworn mission to free the world from the scourge of witchcraft. When his quest to vanquish evil is thwarted by Jane, he decrees that she must die.

After defeating the witchfinder, Jane must continue her dangerous healing work. Alone in a hostile and superstitious village, she struggles to keep her little girl alive.

Determined to keep his vow, the witchfinder must put mother and daughter to death. When John brings the witch hunt to Jane's home, can she save herself and her child from certain slaughter?

If you like historical novels based on real witch trials, you'll love Helen Steadman's *Sunwise*, the sequel to *Widdershins*.

Spellbinding historical fiction ideal for fans of *The Familiars*, *Tidelands* and *The Witchfinder's Sister*.

The Running Wolf

England, 1703. A German swordmaker is jailed for smuggling Jacobite blades. Queen Anne will hang him for treason. Can the wily bladesmith escape a death sentence?

Hermann Mohll is a German swordmaker who risks his life by defecting to England. Trying to save his family from poverty, he is caught smuggling swords for the Jacobite rebels.

When Queen Anne takes a close interest, the smuggler is suspected of high treason. Mohll finds himself facing the ultimate punishment. Will he be hanged, drawn and quartered?

In this tangled web of secrets and lies, just who is telling the truth? Can Mohll hold his tongue and escape the death sentence?

If you like historical fiction inspired by actual events, you'll love *The Running Wolf* by Helen Steadman. Based on the real-life adventures of the Shotley Bridge swordmakers, who defected from Solingen, Germany in 1687.

The Running Wolf is a standalone historical novel, ideal for fans of *Pillars of the Earth, World Without End* and *Column of Fire* by Ken Follett.

Acknowledgements

God of Fire started life during my MA in Creative Writing at Manchester Metropolitan University (MMU) from 2013 to 2016. Amongst many other things, the MA required a portfolio and an elective project. The portfolio requirement was a full-length novel, and for this, I researched and wrote the novel that became *Widdershins*. For my elective, I chose a historical research project, which required a shorter piece of writing in a different genre. (My main lesson from this experience was that it is harder for me to write something shorter.) Because of the need to work in another genre, I opted for poetry and wrote Hephaestus as fifteen sonnets, but I always felt that he wanted the space afforded by a novel, rather than being squeezed into two-thousand or so syllables. Hephaestus remained squeezed into the confines of the sonnets while I wrote *Sunwise* and *The Running Wolf* during my PhD in English at the University of Aberdeen (UoA). I submitted my thesis on 29 February 2020 (and was very glad of that extra day due to it being a leap year). My plan was to continue researching a novel about Grace Darling that I'd started at MMU. But March 2020 had different ideas. Confined to barracks and unable to visit archives, islands, lighthouses, etc, I decided it was time to dust down Hephaestus and give him the space he so clearly needed. A mere seven-and-a-bit years after my initial research, here is *God of Fire*. While this book has benefited greatly from my research and learning at UoA, supervised by the marvellous Dr Helen Lynch, it is very much a product of my time at MMU, so I will thank everyone there again. Tutors, Sherry Ashworth, Helen Marshall, Livi Michael and Nicholas Royle; classmates, Susana Aikin, Cynnamon Conway, Anj Karakus, Eleanor Moore, Marita Karin Over, Julie Taylor, Chris Thomas and Cate West; and the DIY group, Jodie Baptie, Dot Devey Smith, Zoë Feeney, Fin Gray, Nicola Ní Leannáin, Bee Lewis, Jane Masumy, Christopher Price, Sue Smith, Kate Woodward. And an honourable mention to Wyl Menmuir for his prescient remark about the Muse. In particular, extra thanks are due to Dr Livi Michael, writer and senior lecturer, whose 'From Historical Fact to Contemporary Fiction' course led to my work on Hephaestus. Heartfelt thanks must go to those who did the heavy lifting and provided specialist advice. I am grateful to Cat Blacksphere who critiqued several chapters, to Marita Karin Over who critiqued the majority of the novel, to Finn Over, who shared his vast knowledge of mythology and kept me on the right track, to Julian Webb, developmental editor, who not only did a sterling job of identifying a large number of areas for improvement, but also gave me the benefit of his classical education, and to Michael Murray for advice on the anatomy of a bull. (Any mistakes are of course entirely my own, and I apologise heartily for them in advance.) *God of Fire* is a beautifully dressed book with outstanding cover art and that is due to the immense talents of Heike Schüssler of Judge By My Covers. The audiobook is a very entertaining listen, thanks to Christopher Swift and his phenomenal storytelling abilities, which brought my characters to life so humorously. Final thanks to all those ancient poets, writers and historians, and to those less ancient, for recording and translating the Greek myths, which I have borrowed from to create this new retelling.